Sophia Michelle Delanner

about
anna...

A Novel

INFINITY HOUSE
New York

All of the characters in this book are fictional. Any similarity to persons living, pretending to be living, or dead is almost, but not entirely, accidental. In an effort to maintain anonymity and avoid distressing any of the above, though also to ensure simplicity of identification, all of the characters have kept their real names. All events are based on an almost true story. Any references to historical events, real people, or real places are used fictitiously. All translations from the original Russian, German, French, Spanish, and Quechua into English were done in attempt to speed up the reading a little, and for no other reason than this.

Published by Infinity House

Copyright © 2015 by Sophia Michelle Delanner

First Infinity House edition January 2015

Interior design by Sophia Michelle Delanner
Cover design by Sophia Michelle Delanner

Library of Congress Control Number: 2014921786
Infinity House, New York

ISBN-13: 978-0-9909281-0-2 ISBN-10: 0990928101
ISBN: 978-0-9909281-1-9 (ebook) ISBN: 978-0-9909281-2-6 (ebook)

Printed in the United States of America

For my daughter

Reality is merely an illusion, albeit a very persistent one.
—Albert Einstein

While there is life, there is hope.
—Marcus Tullius Cicero

Man is a wolf to [his fellow] man.
—Mother

prologue

t he Russian proverb "one battered person is worth two unbattered ones" merits consideration. Are not those unpummeled by fate on the foolish side, lacking wisdom gained through the miracle of enlightenment that only a good thrashing can offer? At this point in life, when I have been clobbered so many times that it is borderline indecent, this statement makes me prized beyond rubies—a luxury item. Ah, just you wait. To undermine my ironclad logic, there is another old saying that states that less-dilapidated people bought in bulk are bargains—a penny a dozen on market day. How to reconcile the two? But this rude statement, with its faulty rationality and scandalous, camouflaged stinginess, is a fact unproven by science. Let us disregard it, since the research methodology utilized is questionable at best. In all fairness, the trouble of proving this hypothesis is rivaled only by the hassle of disproving it. I could be a sensible woman, though it would be nice to feel a little bit priceless.

Allow me to share a few highlights to justify my outrageous claim. The mighty former Union of Soviet Socialist Republics was the place where I was given birth to by my mother, unwillingly on her part, but that could hardly be considered my fault. I did not begin my life alone—Mother was there for the birthing, but that is as far as she would go. It was only a matter of time till I realized how doomed I was. So far, four developed countries on two densely populated continents have been listed as all-too-impermanent permanent places of residence on my lifetime résumé. I am still pretty young, you know; a big chunk of life is ahead of me, and who knows where the all-powerful winds of fate might blow me next, and what new adventures, exciting and hazardous, may be churning in their bellies? More strange cities. More strange faces. The predictable familiarity of the places I have been to, the allure of the places I have not. I intend to focus neither on the number of cities nor on the number of habitation units here, skimming over any applicable particulars as inconsequential.

Streaking through the abridged version of my life story would include a few life-altering situations, a handful chosen at random—conclusive evidence of my existence—such as two marriages (not bragging), and consequently, two divorces, one confirmed rape, several unceremonious attempted rapes (still not bragging), and one official death, which turned out to be a minor misdiagnosis and a temporary setback. Not my fondest memories. I would be happy to forget all these experiences, but no, no such relief yet. As Mother says, clucking her tongue, hands on her hips, "It's your rotten luck that bad things cling to you! Ay-yay-yay!"

And ex-boyfriends and more ex-boyfriends traipsing through my life. I have run into all manner of relationship troubles—nothing to brag about, even if I was in the mood to brag a little. The root of the trouble? The gentlemen callers who charmed me and shared my bed were but salt in the wound, obstacles in my noble quest for my sole soulmate. Each one carried away a generous sliver of my heart, carved a hollow space into my soul, and only gave me fibroids, as they say. No, there is no end to how naïve a person can be. Nobody said living is logical.

Being a single working mother with all that it entails and keeping body and soul together on days and nights when the stars themselves were too tired to shine might add weight to my claim. By comparison, life and adventures in Middle-earth seem like a walk in a park. Though in the aftermath, I have a wonderful daughter, the best daughter a mother could ask for. If it is all the same to you, allow me to throw into the mosaic of minor nuisances my being homeless for a while and other stuff I cannot be bothered to remember anymore. What is done is done. And that is not the story I wanted to tell you. I mention all of this for the sole purpose of illustrating that I am one tough cookie and not for the dubious pleasure of getting it off my chest.

Long ago I noticed how much easier it is to go through whatever life imposed on me if I kept my ability to laugh at things—all sort of things, including myself. It is also true that I am terrified (like you cannot imagine) that if for some reason I did stop laughing for one moment, a terrible silence would commence, and in this silence I would have no choice but to glean how unbearable my life has been with its thousands of small and large disappointments, and then I might just hang myself.

There were days when in pulling myself from the edge of hell, it was tough to keep my head above the surface and not get sucked into the whirlpools of madness (not whining), when I was so stressed out that I would forget my name and home address. Ah, but in sleepwalking through those stretches of time, I would also forget why I should care about remembering such things. Perhaps not a bad thing, if only for the purpose of variety, when they were followed by a cavalcade of days to be endured through their monotonous tediousness—the endless, endless yesterdays. And then, interspersed among periods of utter loneliness, as a localized, pulsating vortex of energy within the universal field of consciousness, were—O glory!—intervals of a magnificent union with the same nurturing field, cozy and snug, when I felt the ebb and flow of life inside me.

If you ever thought this "universe" thing had been created for the sole purpose of giving you the finger at the worst possible moment, wait—it gets worse.
Its plot is contrived to get you killed at the end. You will lose everything. All of
it. One might get the impression that the gods (wherever they are), in pursuit of
their own therapeutic relief, look for ways to toy with and complicate humans'
miserable lives to the point at which the business of living becomes an unending
torment, ruining everyone's nerves in the process. Me, I never found it amusing.
Such a thing can push one into refusing to believe the reality of these horrible
gods, thus repudiating the pleasure of their existence and, in this very act of denial, driving them to madness. How about *that!*

Gods or no gods, I thought it a good idea to forge ahead and enjoy life,
adapting a frame of mind appropriate to such a journey, the bits of it that lay
before me, all while ignoring two of Mother's favorite sayings—"Man is a wolf
to [his fellow] man" and "Prepare yourself for failure since it's the only thing *you*
can expect"—lest those words end up engraved on my headstone.

From the outset, there was an absurd consistency in my never being in the
right place at the right time doing the right thing, an endless string of chronic
near misses. I have long since ceased to ask why. Let it be placed alongside the
other mysteries of the world. Alas, *Homo sapiens* is a resilient animal. I have met
more than my fair share of incomparable goblins, things that crawled out of the
woodwork on moonless nights with a thousand eyes, and several angels.

I am fortunate to have been granted a number of days drenched in sunshine,
smelling of cinnamon-baked apples, sweetened by ethereal joy. My life has zigged
and zagged this way and that, yet I heard my call to freedom—I will be eternally
grateful for that. Oh but what it took to escape the dark and narrow prison of a
mind…Sing praise to God that this elegant universe with its infinite possibilities
will always be full of wonders, the world ordained and just (true, though it may
sound like the opening pitch to an irritating infomercial).

My fellow adventurers, my wrinkles—an inevitable development—have been
earned with honor. Though I was showered with the shrapnel of heebie-jeebies
along the way, I have learned to look life squarely in the eye, and in either one.
As I journeyed through time and space, experiencing the wonder of life to the
utmost of my human abilities, it seems as if reason were away on extended vacation, odds are, in Hawaii. Ah, those beaches of fine, white sand—so dreamy,
so inviting! A permanent move to a galaxy far, far away—too far away—is also a
probable event, a possibility I had not even considered, but it might explain things.

I feel obliged to add that I suffered some bruises, scratches, and dents along the way, navigating the minefields of my lot while life smacked me in the face, and—as if to relieve the boredom brought on by the monotony of repetition and to experience some diversity—in the belly and somewhere else. I will not say where. The whole experience was deflating. And yet…and yet, in general, so far the signs of wear are still invisible to the eye—what a mercy—and my complexion is not grayish yet. Ah, but nothing lasts forever. Looking back, the background for those unquestionably educational events was predominantly blurred. What started as a speck of double-stringed DNA proved durable enough, and now look at me fly…unless you talk to my mother. The heart *is* big enough to love, lose, and love another time to lose again. What a unique vehicle, through which the cosmos can experience itself, I am! What a marvel.

Despite the fact that I was brought up a convinced atheist in the overpowering shadow of Karl Marx's famous statement that religion is an opiate for the masses, I came to believe in spirits. To begin with, this nonbeliever stance was something I had been persuaded into rather than adopted out of real faith. Besides, theological beliefs can be dangerous too, and have been known to start a few wars, far more than those initiated in pursuit of all-engulfing, everlasting love, though not as many as for opportunistic conquests of someone else's land; but, you know…a few. How many lives were sacrificed on altars of implausible ideas that had to be abandoned later on! So being an agnostic is not without its advantages.

Like everyone else heading for the inescapable grave to rot and disappear forever, blissfully unaware that such satanic things as Abaddon could exist (with its vaporous shades of tar pits and boiling mud, and ghostly epicene shadows of human black mold), I never worried about the whole concept of being burned in the scorching fires of Hell. Ah, the sweetness of ignorance. As it is said in Ecclesiastes 1:18, "For in much wisdom is much grief: and he that increaseth knowledge increaseth sorrow"—so true.

On the other hand, there is nothing to avert the looming disaster should it be discovered that yes, there is indeed a place where alleged sinners are burned for the duration of eternity. No redemption, none. Something tells me that a written note from my current therapist would not do me much good, even if it states I should be excused from such unhealthy activities, justifying it with the simple fact that none of my actions are ill intended, but that my being subjected to a case of bad parenting propelled me onto such an unfortunate path, and that I am really, really sorry.

It is a damn shame that neither the existence nor categorical absence of such a place of damnation can be confirmed at this point in time. I should look on the bright side—there is nothing I could do to rewrite my past or change anything within it. It is what it is, so I should take a liberating lesson or two from a clever bunch of Zen Buddhists and, after exerting a considerable effort, erase the bits driven by worry from my mind.

While being transported forward in the winged chariot of time, I have learned that life is not about the past or the future—it is about the ride. One thing is certain in life, and that is death with its icy tooth—the unopposable inevitability of it—followed by decay, like it or not. Yes, everything turns to ash. Death. Decomposition. You might have heard it before, but I think some things are worth repeating. The statement, which declares impermanence with its slippery hold to be the only permanent and reliable thing in this creation, is the sort of statement that might generate enough of an invigorating shock to make anyone stop and contemplate it for a second or two, before the frail echo of this utterance itself will die and quickly be forgotten. Oh, you know...

With this acknowledged so that it will not curdle into another brown lump on my conscience, consider yourself adequately warned. If I were to risk being annoying by sharing what I have learned so far, it would be this: Blind to the future as we all are, be true to your sense of self. Is not the unsolicited advice the best or what? Ah, the sacred journey that is life, to be measured in memories squirreled away. One day I will embroider "Bloom where you are planted" on some lucky pillow, in a satin stitch in cheerful colors. It came to me in one of those fleeting moments of absolute clarity that comes within the few short intervals between prolonged periods of insanity and confusion—is not lucidity marvelous!—articulated in an intimate way in a velvety baritone. If you had heard this persuasive, oddly disquieting voice, you too would have believed anything it whispered in your ear. *To whom, to what did it belong?* I wondered.

I try to keep my eyes and ears open. Look what crossed my path the other day—a quote from Pierre Teilhard de Chardin written on my daughter's Yogi tea bag: "We are not human beings having a spiritual experience. We are spiritual beings having a human experience." Says it all, yes? So for what it is worth, here is my story. As a former free-roaming spirit who is earthbound for the moment, undergoing the hustle and bustle of being enclosed in the denseness of a physical body, forced to deal with the frustrating limitations of an ego, and who can also glimpse at will the vast spaciousness of the spirit within and thus looks forward to unfathomable escapades in the future, let me welcome you into my world. Welcome! And, by the way, I am delighted our paths have crossed.

Shall we dive in?

one

On this particular Sunday, the last Sunday in August, at the sweltering end of a summer of endless rain, the sky was shamelessly cloudless. There was nothing to stop the scorching sun from cooking the city asphalt into a stinky, sticky mess, and the earnest luminary did its ruthless job well. As if smuggled in, one lonesome spider's web of a cloud began to gather itself into a nebulous formation in the middle of the weightless dome, received no encouragement and dissolved at once. For us mere mortals who happened to be in the habit of inhabiting a pale blue spot of a planet (atop its northern hemisphere) suspended in the golden rays of a smallish yellow sun, adrift on the outskirts of an ordinary galaxy, the eighth month was the muggiest of all.

Heading for a lake to escape the tired and dusty city had been Karl's idea. If you will allow it, shall we pause here for a second? My story, technically speaking, began not here—*ahem*…far from it—but for our purposes, this moment might be a great place to start. So with no further delays, and your permission, ladies and gentlemen, I would like you to meet my current boyfriend, Karl—a six-foot-four, blue-eyed, yellow-haired, wide-shouldered, poster-worthy German with a soft spot for whole-wheat blueberry pancakes. Less than an hour ago, he had been preoccupied with driving his BMW motorbike, of a solid build, on a Bavarian road, also of solid build, not taking his eyes from the road for an instant. (In fact, the way this road of envious sturdiness had been constructed was the way roads everywhere ought to be built.) On his monument of a bike, Karl evoked silent respect in whoever encountered him, and on his bike or off it, he was not someone to mess with. He dealt with things in a thorough, unhurried manner, and true to his character, his even-paced speech was often irksome.

At the moment, he was slathering a suntan lotion all over his pasty body, splashing the spicy aroma of tropical oils around him; maximum strength, with the utmost thoroughness. Five wasps, crying with joy, rushed to investigate. They parked themselves in irregular orbits around Karl, but being unable to use this aromatic bacchanalia to their advantage, decided against pursuing it any further and took off, buzzing in a businesslike manner, carrying their promise of trouble elsewhere. Focused on the task at hand, and too busy to attend to uninvited annoyances, Karl ignored these intruders. Perhaps because of this thoroughness of his, I felt safe around him, safer than I had felt in a long time. As far as unshakeable rocks go—Karl was mine. Who knows why I thought no harm could come to me when I was in his presence, but I did.

And over there, on the moss-green, double-folded cotton blanket near Karl, can you see that woman?

Please, call me Anna.

No, no, not the blonde babe. *On* the blanket. To his left...*there.* The petite, slim, and tanned short-haired brunette with intelligent hazel eyes, which had been busy for the moment admiring Karl with unfathomable delight. And admiring. Several happy minutes passed by, and there I was, still admiring. Nothing exciting seemed to be happening, though. His movements had fallen into monotonous, sleep-inducing routine, and to cheat the embrace of oncoming drowsiness, and also for lack of better things to do, my eyes wandered from him and onto the forest surrounding the lake.

The whole picturesque landscape gave the impression that the position of every tree and bush and rock had been well thought out, as if here, nature, not unlike a model housewife, felt an incredible pressure to leave nothing to chance and had been driven halfway to insanity by the uncontrollable urge to keep things in perfect order. Well, one never knew when Monsieur Monet might be passing by, now did one? He might be enchanted by the presentation, and, deciding on the spur of the moment to immortalize all of this, this whole magnificence thingy, might even place his easel over there near that moss-choked stump.

Clear as day, the unleashed sun was on a mission to blaze up everything beneath it. Half-blinded both by the life-giving orb and its bright reflection in the lake, I shielded my eyes by placing my hand at my forehead, instantly gaining a better perspective on things. Yes, this would be the ideal patch for the easel. Now, what could Karl have possibly done with my sunglasses?

I gazed at him. His ritual of self-anointing completed, he stretched his impressive frame out on the ground and conked out. Poor man; he deserved the rest. Another inquisitive wasp checked out Karl's checkered shorts, carefully folded over his backpack, and headed toward Karl's belly. I brushed it away.

"You don't look German," said a baritone with a Bavarian lilt behind me.

I turned around to find a solidly built redheaded man with meaty cheeks and a thick neck, a declaration of friendliness blooming on his face. The sun lit a million tiny starched tongues of flame on his manly, hairy torso, arms, and legs, singing a hymn to the color orange. I smiled back and whispered, so not to disturb Karl, "I'm from Moscow."

He got excited. "*Mein Gott!* I've heard polar bears roam the streets of that city!"

"*Ja, ja.* Dangerous creatures too. Once, I've seen with my own eyes—and it happens often!—two hungry bears maul a freckle-faced child in the Red Square. A big crowd gathered to watch. Bi-iig! What a spectacle! The largest beast bit off the child's head—the blood spurted everywhere. Fountains of blood! The mother screamed and—Where are you going?"

Too late. Whoever he had been, he had run for the nearest trees.

"Who was that?" Karl sounded groggy, his sonorous rumble of a voice breaking up.

"Nobody," I said.

"What did he want?"

"Nothing. Go back to sleep."

Not a single leaf stirred on the trees of a mature dark-green, now late in August. The sea of greens with its transitory richness, flecked with yellows and reds, flooded the distant woody hills. One adventurous cloud assembled itself for a moment—a perfect white puff—and a lazy, deep-blue shadow swam across the faces of fat, complacent, sleeping-the-sleep-of-the-innocent hills.

The canopy of nearby trees, while fulfilling their obligation to provide the comfort of a cool shade, also harbored an ear-piercing, uncoordinated choir of a flock of small and gray, whatever-they-are-called birds, skittish little darlings, if a bit chaotic. Each bird kept lifting in the air for an instant and settling back on the branch, hobnobbing, singing the afternoon away, and disrupting the otherwise flawless order of things without giving it a thought. There seemed to be some sort of insignificant misunderstanding of local regulations on the part of birds. Ah well..."birdbrained" was not just an expression.

A chipmunk, conducting himself like a neat shopkeeper, attended to his hot-summer-afternoon chipmunk business and discreetly chirped between the roots of the spreading old oak, where a few rays of amber sunlight filtered through the leaves. By quite a coincidence, it happened to be the same old oak that a dog passing by had pissed on ten minutes earlier—a warm and sluggish stream—before the canine crashed through the tangled underbrush like a wild boar and disappeared forever. An adorable calico mutt with a curled-up tail of course had certain needs, but this fact had no significance whatsoever.

Farther to the left, my venture-prone eyes stumbled upon an enormous and hairy—um, make that "furry"—bottom positioned at a coquettish angle on a plaid blanket and well lit by the sun. The golden sphere itself had clambered high into the polished sky—gloriously mindless, stretched-to-infinity solid azure. Good

God, how could have I forgotten? For future reference, it is not all that difficult to distract me, providing the object responsible for the distraction was worthy enough.

Now, I feel obliged to mention that Karl and I were not just on any beach—we were on a nudist beach, common here in Germany (and in my mind's eye, I saw Mother shaking her finger at me, her other hand on her hip, hearing her shout, "You have no shame!"). Not an attractive crowd. I thought I would never get used to it, but as with everything else in life, there are no guarantees. Who knew what might happen after twenty years of intensive exposure? And besides, it had been noted on previous occasions by several independent observers that I was capable of making judgment calls that were not entirely correct (please read: "I could not have been more wrong") and behaving in general with an insane amount of optimism. But in my defense, this was not every day.

Perhaps instead of just goggling at the world, being as absentminded as I was, I should get up and wander around a bit, yes? I gave it a try. One, two, three…and nothing. Again, one, two, three…

I got up, arched my back, and stretched my arms over my head, ignoring the open stares coming from several directions at once. Men ogle me. As it so happened, the one guy I was interested in was sprawled at my feet basking in the sun, flat on his back with one arm thrown out on an odd angle, legs splayed, mouth open, snuffling and grumbling in his slumber. I looked at him. Alfresco, the whey-colored skin on his torso and limbs reddened as bright as that of a boiled crustacean's, his face sheltered by a carefully folded T-shirt. Karl grunted in his sleep, mumbled something, growled, then turned his pale side up.

Ah, at last, there they were, hiding from me under his thigh—my sunglasses. They looked intact from up here. I bent down, picked them up, checked for damage, found none, and slid them up on my nose where they belonged. With my vision less restricted by the stupefying glare, I was pleased that I could stop squinting, and I turned around only to discover the guy on the neighboring blanket winking at me with brazen assurance.

"Hey, cupcake," he murmured.

"Ah, kerfuffle." I looked away from him in the other direction for a few long minutes, then tentatively squatted down, reached into my beach bag for the tattered volume of *Great Expectations,* and hugged it to my chest with both hands. Good prose had always been my reliable place of escape, my lone place of comfort where, giddy with anticipation, I could lose or find myself.

. . .

Was life not wonderful at the sweet beginning of a promising relationship? When everything one ever dreamed of seemed to be but a teensy-weensy step ahead? The boundless happiness of being a part of a couple now showed definite signs of being within one's reach. One could almost smell it. Oh, this delicious, elusive union…Oh, the mystifying allure of destiny's workings in its miraculous unfolding…Oh, the unspeakable majesty of a world without time…Those magical times when the first delicate blooms of romance, not yet wilted and still generous, give off enchanting, life-affirming scents and colors…The thrilling times when the relationship is about to flow over the rim with puppy-like infatuation. Grab it.

Alas, more often than not, it is destined for failure and will end up in tatters as soon as these infatuation levels plummet, leaving nothing in its wake, as though the magic were gone forever, to be replaced with day-to-day power struggles and annoyances. Gone. Forever.

Non, non, mes amis. C'est impossible! Only till the next sweet beginning, of course.

■ ■ ■

The ever-changing wind, as if feeling a little neglected, whistled in from nowhere like an angered Norse god, turning the mirrored surface of the lake into the wrinkled skin of a grotesque animal from an alien world. It ran over the grass, skimmed the tops of the surrounding trees, bending them sideways in the process, twisted and turned several leaves that had already managed to fall— the harbingers of the rustling showers of gold that would hit the ground before long—and at its own caprice, threw them back up into the brilliant air. A few pirouettes later, accompanied by a wave of rustling commotion in the trees' crowns, the playful breeze brought me an offering—a puff of fresh, slightly cooler air, and with it, a small green leaf that showed a smidgen of autumn's dazzling ochre around the edges.

The wind could not help it—it had been born gusty. The master manipulator just had to curl and spin around the small leaf—the first casualty of the season—which had fallen from its mother tree for the first time in its short life, so flustered and alone, riding the turmoil and shaking from head to toe. The mighty wind took the grass-colored trooper on a roller coaster ride before letting the poor thing lose altitude and rest, out of all places, on Karl's new beer belly—a smallish protuberance on its way to pride.

I reached for this victim of violent kidnapping, picked it up by the stem, vigilant not to interrupt the peaceful rhythm of rising and falling, the up and down, up and down movement of Karl's warm flesh. He was, as usual, overworked and sleep deprived. Waking up the gentle giant from his rest was not a part of the plan. Softie as I was, intrigued by the intricate symmetry of thin veins, I let the delicate splash of emerald lie for a moment in the ephemeral safety of my palm. Such a tiny piece of the puzzle, but so indispensable in playing its part in the endless circle of life, this little marvel carried as a special gift to me the fullness of the vibrant, live smell of a tree in its prime, bursting with foliage.

Though it spoke of things eternal, the wind spoke in ancient tongues, long dead, that no one comprehended nowadays. Swift to spring up, the wind died down with no less haste, recovering from its last fleeting bout of madness with no ill effects. One swooping movement, and it erased from the lake the myriad of identical ripples with matching shadows it had created a moment ago, letting the lake be for now. What an accurate illustration of that old adage that looks can be deceiving. How very true. Again a lazy breeze, enchanting and unhurried, it delivered rationed portions of the forest's fragrances and freshness to anyone who needed it.

The spirit of peace descended from above, and lapped in it, the lake reflected whatever it felt like reflecting—the melted white sun below, no less blinding than the one high up in impossible blueness, the comfy hills and the lacy trees flocked by the water's edge, and the boats with oars freed, suspended in nothingness. Greedy me, I soaked it all in. The fairy-haunted world around me had come to a lull, filled with intention. Under the eerie grip of this powerful spell, I headed toward the lake in a desultory stroll.

The bluish-green water was as warm as milk freshly squirted out of a cow. I stepped into it, submerged my feet into the divine delights of slippery silt, summoning swirly clouds and tendrils of muck from the bottom. The unceremonious silt, with its innate sliminess tinged with naïveté, in its eagerness to make a meaningful connection with just about anyone or anything was not so selective in its choice of close acquaintances. It took this opportunity as an open invitation and proceeded to ooze between my toes. A string of air bubbles rose to the surface.

A flushing-red dragonfly charged headlong with a dry rattle for a closer look at the commotion, hovered over the water for an instant, then flitted away over the brocade of water lilies and algae to vanish between the reeds. A spitting distance off, a spotted trout jumped, twisted in midair, and fell back into the water with a soft slap, leaving circles on the mirror-like stillness. And another one leaped and fell, the circles overlapped, messing things up. A small school of silvery, whatever-they-are-called fish darted by in a brush against my legs, chasing one another near the murky bottom. On this hot, but otherwise an unremarkable afternoon on one of those equally unremarkable days at the end of August, I was deliciously, shamelessly, utterly happy.

That was six years ago. Had it been so long?

the Russian Easter masquerade party in a Fifth Avenue loft in trendy downtown Manhattan was an event to be awaited with anticipation. What I was not looking forward to was my boyfriend's costume, and for that matter, my costume too. No matter the occasion or the season or the phase of the moon, Alex dressed up as a Gestapo officer in full regalia. One had better make a lot, and I mean *a lot* of hoopla, heaping praises on him—how masculine he looked in it and how sophisticated the whole affair was, when in reality I hated, hated, hated the whole thing.

Things might necessitate a persnickety consideration if I ever found myself in need of filling the vacancy to father my future children. The way things were at the moment, I figured I could afford to take my time, keeping it simple and not pondering too long over the implications of such a decision. Change the way you see the world and your reality will change too, or so I have heard. I should point out—and was not it ironic?—that no matter what changes took place in my outlook on the world, the reality refused to comply. This stubbornness gave no indication of going away, but swelled like a river in flood instead. *Why didn't it work?* I would wonder. *What was I doing wrong?*

As one might expect, the other parties we had attended over the past few years were hardly ever costume affairs, though such an insignificant fact never deterred Alex. The part of his brain responsible for the dressing-up bit had short-circuited a long time ago. Things were never any different. To him going to parties meant an excellent chance to show off his Nazi uniform in its hard-to-forget glory, even if one tried and tried. The idea of putting on a regular shirt and pants (and appearing *ordinary*, God forbid), to shine in some other way aside from showcasing his tendency for absurd apparel, seemed too much for him to handle. Ah well…Nowadays everyone seems to be dealing with their self-esteem issues on one level or another, and I am almost certain you yourself have heard of such incidents, though Alex's flaunting it was a very different matter and nothing short of alarming. But I have long since stopped dwelling over others' absurdities; let him struggle with it on his own terms while I will pray for a happy end.

Alex rummaged through the flea markets of New York and Europe for uniforms and trinkets, his every find celebrated with a pomp as a personal victory, only by him. Not to mention that humanity at large found those Nazi dudes neither glamorous nor charming (and I was in perfect agreement with those who said so); this fact did nothing for Alex. The nuance that he was not exactly the Aryan archetype affected his determination not one bit. Short, stocky, and balding with short arms and no chin to speak of, he overcompensated by pumping iron at the gym for two hours every day. Though still paunchy, he ended up with a mountain of muscles and looked like a lumpy, overstuffed sofa.

We had been arguing about this too-passionate hobby of his forever, and—I do share your skepticism—it looked more and more unrealistic that such an issue would go away on its own. I want to take this opportunity to inform everyone that this had been just one of the thorns in our relationship, and a big one at that. Alex had no clue what the whole fuss was about while I failed miserably to explain it to him many times over. Many. Though even today I do not fully understand the chain of events that had brought us to this point in time, what seemed to be at the root of the underlying issue was nothing more sinister than blocked communication passageways between us in general—the absence of a dialogue that ought to be the cornerstone of any decent relationship, but seldom was.

I was not surprised when, against my feeble protests, Alex dressed up yet again as—you have guessed it!—a Gestapo officer. Fed up with the whole concept, I had no plausible explanation as to why I went along dressed up like a provocative lady of ill repute ("*ooh là là!*" or, if one preferred, "*hubba hubba*"), hanging on to the officer's arm. In Alex's thinking, my dressing up like a harlot, even if lacking in social refinement, looked irresistible, so he suggested I wear the outfit. Um...let me rephrase that last statement, please. He did not suggest it so much as he demanded it, so I have little to say about that. It occurred to me then, this time with full clarity, that the chasm between us was growing deeper by the minute, although Alex, giddy with happiness and with a smirk on his face, seemed to think we made a charming couple. Disillusioning him required more energy than I could spare at the moment. I had no heart for it either.

. . .

Alex, as sarcastic fate would have it, was fourth in a row of boyfriends, none serious, who had come and gone in the last four years since I had moved back to New York; an indecently long trail of people I would rather not remember, added to the disturbing procession of predecessors who must be forgotten if the last sliver of my self-respect is to be kept alive. Their voices and faces were an untidy, chaotic jumble, the sort of jumble that upon my looking back and pondering with regret, made me wish I could forget entire chunks of my life. Let me make it clear right away that all those predecessors, without exception, had been good neither for my ego nor for myself. Some were pleasant and kind, some not exceptionally so; some were attractive, some not so much; some were smart and others not at all. At all. One was brilliant, a real rocket scientist, who also had an extreme case of advanced-stage manic egotism beyond redemption. I am sad to report that one hand, one meager hand was all that was needed to count the re-lationships that had made any sense for me to have been entangled in. And yet…

At some points in time, in moments of inexplicable, prolonged weakness, I managed to fool myself over and over again into believing that indeed, it was somehow all worth it—it would work itself out in the end. It never did. What one might find downright puzzling was the simple fact that in my preoccupation with these very matters, the matters so close to my heart, I chose to ignore in its entire-ty the teeny-weeny distress *ping* that went off in the back of my mind every time I happened to stumble—not unlike a tumbleweed—upon what seemed to be an eligible suitor, or, as in the alarming majority of cases, he stumbled upon me. You know, that feeling that something is not quite right, but it is hard to pinpoint what is wrong? That is the one. *As long as some human warmth is in the offing,* I thought to myself, like a starving dog. Interesting. Who was I trying to fool? Even so I would feel a distinct bewilderment and all-too-familiar frustration—I should have known!—such was the feeling at that moment, the end result…well, I had ex-pected this to happen. This last fact would make me wonder how I had managed to live so long and stay so despicably dumb. I have nothing to say about that one.

New York boyfriend number one was interesting beyond belief: a bit of a recluse, in no sense an unkind person, though not an especially caring one, a walking, talking encyclopedia who knew everything there was to know about anything—when he was sober. He drank himself unconscious from morning till night for weeks at a time, an uninteresting phase when he had trouble recalling his name. Then, what is in a name? "That which we call a rose by any other name would smell as sweet," it is said. At times like this, he had not the slightest idea who or where he was, nor whom I might be. He addressed me as his mother, and there was no charm hidden in it anywhere. Then he would bashfully snap out of it, and with a guilty smile and a conciliatory manner be interesting beyond belief again…until the next drinking spree. Always drowning in misery when sober, while serene and sentimental when drunk.

I assume it will come as no shocker that boyfriend number one was soon replaced by boyfriend number two. Boyfriend number two, a horse of a different color, drank not as much as boyfriend number one did, which was an improvement in itself, but then again, he earned nothing. He refused to get entangled in anything remotely material because as a sculptor, his higher destiny was to dwell nowhere else but in the abode of spiritual realms, or so he adamantly declared to anyone who cared to listen. Ah, the creative type. The thought of wasting his God-given genius on the mundane and earthly carried no appeal for him. How noble of him. This motto in no way prevented the man from living under my roof and putting away food I brought to the table, the same roof and food that, in my humble opinion, no matter how one might want to look at it, belonged in the category of material objects in the material world.

It was to be commended (despite the fact that he stopped in front of any mirror-like surface he walked past to admire himself), that at forty-six he had managed to stay young at heart, a free spirit. And this is indeed important—to keep one's spirit young. Neither fame nor riches had found him thus far, but in case he was discovered, he was prepared, already on a pedestal. He had erected this sky-high pillar by himself, a colossal edifice to enable everyone to reflect upon his special value, and then, with no assistance, he had climbed onto the top. He was ready for fame, riches even more so. My place was at the foot of this glorious contraption; my job was to adore him. From morning till night. For weeks at a time. In this ritual of exalted adoration, with barely suppressed eagerness, I was to clap my flippers like a trained seal with a snub nose while barking, half-expecting him to toss a small mackerel, preferably unspoiled, into my wide-open mouth.

Boyfriend number three was a tall, dark, and handsome fellow. I went gaga. In that period of my life, I was in a state of despair and needed someone, anyone, to go gaga about. No one had to be dashing. The sex god was British, in episodes even funny, and always sober. He worked, owned his apartment, and was also, while almost generous and somewhat interesting, a nag and a pessimist in full bloom. As for his belonging to a breed notorious for their superb emotional restraint, he was an atypical Englishman. Each morning he added measured portions of psyllium fiber into a glass of green smoothie to cleanse his bowels and aura, nibbled on homemade granola, and went on to predict doom from morning till night. He nagged and nagged, which was less fun than it promised to be and was hardly inspiring...well, for anything. Guess how that relationship ended and how soon.

The next, the Interloper, did not last long. Not sure if this classified as a relationship per se, but I feel obliged to mention him for statistical purposes. On our third date (we had progressed from drinks to the meal—yay!), while I contemplated dispensing with the goodbye handshake and getting to more intimate stuff—say, a kiss—his cell rang. And what do you know—his lawful spouse ordered him home for dinner. An interesting development, no? That is, interesting only to a point. Preoccupied with other matters, it had slipped his mind to bring up he was a little bit married. What I got out of it, while recollecting the lost expression on his face, was a wholehearted laugh all the way back home and then some. I laughed as I have seldom laughed in my life, a guffaw that brought me to tears. I had to blow my nose, and then I laughed and laughed. I did not crack up on his account—well, perhaps I did a little—but for the most part I laughed at myself for volunteering to walk into yet another predicament, not entirely unlike the million others I had found myself in before. On second thought, I had had as much fun as I could handle. *I'm done with dating*, I thought. *Finito*, I thought. Then, soon after, Alex showed up. Please contain your surprise. As wise Yoda once said, "Impossible to see the future is."

Alex drank socially in pleasant moderation. Not amazing or interesting, he was an inarticulate man but with air of dependability and homeyness. He worked, swore he was unmarried, and his nagging was bearable. Even if some things were mildly annoying, by default these were overall excellent qualities to have in a man—perhaps not the exciting sort to sweep one off one's feet and curl one's toes, but solid basics, dependable, that were essential to have if the relationship was to go somewhere. Something was not quite right with him, though…hmm.

But Alex had a major, major point of attraction—he made me laugh. A killer sense of humor, his most fantastic feature, got him out of a jam on many an occasion. Allow me to reiterate—it hurt less when I laughed. Alas, his funny side was not all. Wait till you hear this—Alex loved me *just the way I was* without changing anything about me, or at least that was how things were at the beginning. I was unaccustomed to such treatment. It was a novel sensation, a huge plus, a wonderful triumph of the soul, an amazing experience for me to relish, which took an ever-increasing hold on my heart and mind. The universe can be so accommodating at times.

Except—and why did it always have to be this "except" thing?—he would blow up like Krakatoa with huge plumes of smoke and dust, killing everything in its path with pyroclastic flow, unleashing tsunamis while it blew itself out of existence; he was almost as loud. Thank heavens the repercussions were less devastating than in the case of the volcano itself. No volcanic winter followed. These fits happened on occasion at first, once in a blue moon, but increased in frequency as Alex relaxed into the relationship. Gradually, bit by bit, they had progressed to daily occurrences over the last few weeks. No physical violence accompanied them, not yet, but there was a lot of thunderous yelling. His rages became the norm, which by itself was not enough to set me running half-breathless to the nearest police station to file a complaint.

All this fighting was no foreplay—Alex vented his frustrations with the world's imperfections. Not counting that the wrongs with society in general became more and more my fault, the list of my flaws, nonexistent at first, were soon blown to mind-boggling proportions. With each new day, his narcissistic side thirsted for additional verification that he was the cream of the crop, but why bother proving his worth to anyone when being domineering toward me required less effort on his part? And while he nurtured his delusions of entitlement, this domineering bit was easier to execute by isolating me from other people.

I silently watched my friends dissolve out of my life one by one, into the swirling black nothingness that devoured my world whole, all while Alex's chances of feeling like my master skyrocketed. To his genuine surprise, I wanted no master, not for all the tea in China. His drinking picked up momentum too. More nights when I stayed in his place, he would have quite a bit to drink, stumble across the rug, then pass out on the floor. The relationship deteriorated faster than you can say "restraining order." What was *wrong* with me? Why could not I have the sort of problems that normal people had? You know, like do not leave the toilet seat up, put the cap back on the toothpaste tube.

■ ■ ■

Enough of that. So here we were at the Russian Easter masquerade party. At the entrance to the loft, Alex bumped into his fervent "I will forego the food if you let me talk about the Great Patriotic War" * buddy, who was in his late sixties and garbed as a Soviet army general with the polished Order of Lenin and two Gold Stars of the Hero of the Soviet Union modestly pinned to his jacket. Both uniform junkies had made a strict pact concerning who would wear what—wandering into one another's territory was verboten.

The general's neat, thick mass of silver hair gave off a restrained luster, yet this noble image was tainted by the shifty eyes on his oily face and his hippopotamus of a belly peeking out of the rank jacket; the lowest three buttons had to be left undone, and his stained undershirt made a public appearance. The general's cap was pushed back so that it sat on the crown of his head at a jaunty angle. He sweated stale alcohol (sublime proof of him being an inveterate drinker) and sent any freshly germinated sprouts of respect awakened by those highest-distinction awards on his chest down the drain, considering he had earned none of them.

---

* The term "The Great Patriotic War" is used in former republics of USSR to describe the period from June 22, 1941, to May 9, 1945, in the many fronts of the eastern campaign of World War II between the Soviet Union and Nazi Germany with its allies.

"Hey, *Obergruppenführer!*" ** Alex cried darkly, extended his right arm in a bombastic "*Heil Hitler!*" salute, and clicked his heels, eyeing his competitor's medals with open envy. Only one tarnished Iron Cross shone among the assemblage of metal on his chest.

"*Parteigenosse!*" *** The general swayed and produced a gurgling sound, scratching his stomach. "*Sieg heil.*"

I knew exactly where this was headed, and within the next ten seconds I was proven right. With all due respect, the fascination of Russian males belonging to a certain age group and older with the subject of rise and fall of the Third Reich has never failed to amuse me. I was in no mood to stomach yet another war debate tonight. About five minutes into it, as any polite person would, especially those with innate good manners, I got away without a peep, pasting on a beaming, almost angelic smile to compensate for the too-obvious deficiencies of my wardrobe. A little nervous at first, I drifted from group to group. As a lady of ill repute, I was greeted with ovations—*ooh là là, très bien!*—by the prevailing majority of partygoers, who were for the most part male. The room buzzed as a giant beehive, the costumes dazzled, the background music was pleasing.

"…was supposed to separate my laundry," an Imperial Stormtrooper explained to the finest of Robin Hood's gang. "My girlfriend moved in with me. Now we have white…what do you call them, 'linens'? Oh man, I'm telling you, the thread count is everything!"

"…can't say I admire his latest piece," were the words exiting the semistitched slit of a scarecrow's mouth. "His art is too controversial. His colors are offensive and depressing…"

"…the latest model of BMW? That thing can make a grown man cry." Toulouse-Lautrec was on the verge of tears.

"…We showed him! Hitler better think the next time he decides to attack Mother Russia." Mad Hatter twisted in his fingers a button attached to the vest of Hot-Pink Rabbit, whose pants were missing entirely.

"…done with control-top pantyhose," the moonfaced Catwoman said to two almost-identical witches (one was a head taller and a strawberry blonde), a puff of smoke curling out from the corner of her generous mouth. "I'll try a panty girdle…"

"…what Putin had told them?" a barrel-chested executioner leaning on his ax asked a prince. "If it were up to me, I'd waste no time with all this yada yada. I—"

"Where the hell have you been all night, pumpkin? I've been looking for you!"

** Senior group leader (German).
*** Party member (German).

Combined with a slight push, this last question was addressed to me. His fleshy neck bent forward, my angry boyfriend, the benevolent Gestapo officer, was breathing noisily through his nose and looking at me with disparagement. Unnoticed, several hours had elapsed.

"In this room," I said.

Based on the speed at which his stunned expression morphed into the familiar one of fury, my calm tone had come as a shock to him. Believe me, it had surprised me too, though not unpleasantly. This was not a polite expectation forming on his physiognomy. No, no, not the facial expression of a happy person. I could tell rage was building inside him, the explosive outcome inevitable—though I did not want to be the alarmist here. He was getting ready to blow, but I was unstoppable. I had crossed a line that I never suspected to be there in the first place, and was gaining momentum.

"How *exactly* were you looking for me?" I said.

"What?" Alex managed with a grimace of impatience. He cracked his fingers, blinked a few times, cleared his throat, and repeated louder, "What?"

Fed up with being fed up, I had had it. This time I was standing my ground, though I did not quite know how this was to develop, nor exactly what I would be forced to face later on. But it was a bad time and place to indulge in speculations. My backbone itched for a while, trying to come out. The sensation of itching intensified.

"Why do you think I'm willing to participate in your Hitler mania?" I heard myself vocalize. I cannot say I disliked the sound of it, regardless of whether or not it might be considered a perfectly irrational behavior in some circles.

Ill at ease, Alex was visibly having problems finding the right words. Alex visibly had problems finding words, period. His face was strained, his mobile brows forming an inverted *V.* His voice burst with boiling anger. "What?" he began. "But he was—"

"I don't care what you think of your precious Hitler." I dared to interrupt him, a cardinal mistake, and then, oh dear, I just kept on pushing, at the boiling point myself. "Mulling it over and over. Why does it have to be a monster? Get fascinated with Leonardo da Vinci."

I was not sure what had come over me, but I had done it. He puffed up his chest and attempted two impossibles at once—sucking in his stomach while towering over me, despite the too-obvious fact that in my pumps, I was the taller one. Alex, so far relatively speechless, foamed at the mouth. Even if I wanted to have second thoughts, it was too late, him being the bullheaded man he was. Nothing to prevent him from blowing now.

He half-squatted and tensed, as if getting ready to jump over a fence. His face paled, reddened, then paled again with a bit of a greenish hue. He moistened his lips with his tongue and swallowed, his mobile Adam's apple twitching. Then he stopped imitating a frozen-in-space chameleon, came to life, and blow he did.

"You think this all sounds cute coming from a whore," Alex retorted in a loud whisper that could be heard at the other end of a huge room, as with an evil grin, he snapped the garter on my left thigh. He caught his breath, wrinkled his small forehead, and rubbed it with his beefy fist in jerky movements. After mulling things over for a second, then spitting and whirling like a dervish, he screamed, all but spelling out the words for me: "Why are you parading yourself in this whore outfit? To show your true nature? A whore—that's what you are!"

This spectacle caught the attention of the people standing nearby. Step by step they moved away from us, making a circle to witness a rapidly rising calamity from a distance. The murmur of conversations in the room dissolved, swept away in a rolling, quick wave, as withering silence swelled in its place. A single "Yay!" was smothered in its infancy and died on the spot.

I tugged at the hem of my skirt to pull it down a little. Nothing changed—the skirt stayed short. Alex watched me with contempt.

"A whore! You're lucky I picked you up," he shrilled, articulating each syllable. "You're nothing without me, nothing! What do you mean you don't find the subject interesting?"

Alex was right about my devotion to his interests. All of a sudden I saw everything with new eyes. The rift had been widening for some time, as often occurs in these situations, and it is all too easy to become blind to the obvious until, prompted by some external event, it surfaces, in some cases at the speed of light. As for me, the lowly whore, so lucky to be picked up by him…I realized I was on the verge of blowing myself.

Distrusting myself to move or speak, I made no move. I kept my silence. My knees were doing something resembling melting away, with wispy swirls dissolving in the surrounding air. But true to myself, again I thought I should give the guy a break—and that, *that*, my last thought, made me very, very angry. Such a disturbing development, though it opened my eyes to the simple truth: how about several breaks, as if it made any difference!

"A whore!" A triumphant note crept into his falsetto.

Though I was under the influence of too many *National Geographic* specials, and some cultures had indeed proven the method successful, a quiet voice in my head urged, "No, no, no, the 'let's kill him and eat his liver' approach isn't the wisest one to follow here." And as Aristotle said, "Intuition is the source of scientific knowledge."

"A whore! A whore!" Alex half-squatted, waving his hands and spitting. There was no love shining through, coming at me from his slitted eyes—Rasputin's had looked kinder. He lifted a little on his toes, slapped his thigh, squatted deeper, clapped his hands, tapped his foot. From a certain vantage point it looked like he was attempting a modest version of a Russian kick dance.

Bloody hell. A swift kick to the groin, however tempting, was out of the question, once I reflected upon the precarious nature of the stiletto pumps I was wearing, the more of an absence than a presence of a skirt, and a prevailing minority of sympathetic glances from spectators nearby, impatiently awaiting scandal. It would also involve the act of touching him, and I was in no mood for close encounters with maggots. A little disoriented, I got an image of a wild rhesus macaque swinging off a tree limb, throwing feces at things it did not like. Go, Banana Butt, go!

I tapped my foot. I am a coward, I am. I do not like confrontations. Regardless of the common approach to similar situations, I suppressed my natural response. In a vain attempt to shake off the idea of such undertakings creating an even bigger spectacle, I avoided the fact that it was already too late for that. Not a thing will prevent all sorts of rumors from buzzing, multiplying in the circles of our mutual acquaintances and others made of complete strangers. With a few seconds to decide on a plan of action, I racked my brain for an infinite array of possible ways to deal with this mess. There was no array. I had nothing. I shrugged.

"And nothing to say for yourself, I see," Alex gloated.

According to my best judgment—and believing it to be sound on the matter, even if I often proved to be prone to episodes of inconsistency—I thought the whole relationship too unilateral. Dealing with the Master of the Universe on an everyday basis happened not to be my thing. Go figure. It was my new personal low too—this was beyond demoralizing—down to the fireworks display ending, and, to top it all off, having such a spectacular display occur under the full gaze of the public. I had to do something radical. Pull it out like a rotten tooth.

I bid Alex no customary farewell—no crying, no screaming, no slapping his face—but turned around and walked out into the crisp New York night. Everything that had to be said had already been said. No matter how much Alex wanted to be revered for his greatness, in my eyes he would always remain a small man.

Fifth Avenue was empty and quiet at three in the morning. No pedestrians. A few impatient cars swooshed by, and again I was wrapped in silence—how strange such a lack of sound was in the Big Apple, even in the dead of night. I breathed in the cold, fragrant air and my newly acquired freedom. Freedom!

And relief…immense, overwhelming relief. Life of lies—it was over. No more pretending, no innuendos, no more unfinished statements. I felt shaken and exhausted, yet wonderful. I felt elated. Weightless. I was a little apprehensive about getting arrested for my skimpy outfit, and I hoped there would be no need to explain, in my own words, what it was I did or did not do for a living.

Still, with all sorts of stimulating hormones overflooding my bloodstream, I had to walk for a bit to cool off and absorb what had just happened, and I was in no hurry to grab a cab. The subway was out of the question, as was hitching a ride. Did I have money for a cab? I opened my clutch, relieved to see a twenty snug in there, next to a modest collection of cosmetic items and keys.

Keys! I had my apartment keys. For a moment I contemplated retrieving my coat from Alex's car, but no force in the world could make me go back and look at that face again. I breathed in a lungful of air. It smelled fresh and a little sweet—a good omen for the beginning of things new and wonderful. The chill of the April night had not registered with me yet. Off with my coquettish black half veil! Freedom! Spring was back!

An alien silhouette, too long-necked for the average New Yorker, was coming along the dimly lit street and heading in my direction, followed by another unfamiliar shape, just as strange, but shorter.

I was at a loss for what to make of them. They did not look particularly menacing. Would waiting for their approach be considered a good strategy? This was New York, you know. I had heard rumors. The word on the street had it that some strangers were less harmless than others. Setting all common sense aside, I stood still and waited. The distance between me and the shapes quickly diminished, such closeness becoming disturbing, yet still I was unable to determine what the hell they were. A bit closer yet. Closer. Closer…

My eyes recognized the creature now, but my bewildered brain refused to accept the reality of it in the middle of Manhattan. An inquisitive snout, soft and silky, parked itself on my naked shoulder with a loud snort. A warm breath caressed my cheek, and a big, dark eye looked at me from under long eyelashes.

I outstretched my arms and hugged the odd, yet magnificent, woolly creature. A good omen, indeed. I was hugging a llama.

In the crypt of the night, the overhead source of illumination swung and squeaked and creaked in a strengthening breeze. From shaggy shadows and into this unsteady cone of light stepped the wrinkle-faced animal's guardian, wearing a rainbow-colored poncho and a hard-brimmed hat. He smiled at me with a broad, partially toothless smile.

"Good evening, madam," he said. "Nice weather we're having."

Or that is what I thought he said. Or had it been, "Can you direct me to a number five train?" Or had he just inquired whether or not I wanted to buy his hat?

You will have to forgive me—my Quechua was rusty that night.

three

i must lose my virginity. Tonight." Hannah's radiant blue eyes looked serious and a bit worried. She held up her hand. "Mama, before you say anything—"

The universe tilted a little, and the soapy sponge—*bool'k!*—tumbled from my hands into the greasy skillet full of hot, scummy water soaking in the sink. *This isn't good,* I thought.

"I know what you'll say. 'Why rush things? Wait for the right man, fall in love, then have sex.'"

"That's right," I said. "Sex isn't a purely mechanical problem of how to fit thing A into thing B—"

"Oh God, no. God. Don't even start, Mama. This negativity of yours is driving me nuts."

"Negativity?"

"You're so old-fashioned."

"Try 'protective.' I don't want you to get hurt."

She leaned against the fridge, delicate and fine-boned and a little pale. Her shiny dark hair had fallen across her eyes. "You worry too much," she said with the confidence of youth, completely unfazed.

The alchemy of being responsible for creating a remarkable human being— what an education this had proved for me. "Wait a bit. Think about it more," I said. "The freedom of sex promises liberation, but creates a lot of other issues instead."

Her eyes moved about as she considered this, the fingers of one hand, with its Midnight Blue nail polish, tugging on the tiny silver dove on the chain around her neck. "I don't want to wait," she said. "I'm *seventeen*. God knows when the right person will come along. I want it to be done and over with so I'm like any other girl in my class. It's not a big thing. I'm not just another teenager with raging hormones. I'm capable of making rational decisions. And I don't need you to be judgmental and all." She tucked a strand of hair behind her ear.

"Not judging." I held up both hands. Soapy water ran down my arms, dripped from my elbows to the floor. I knew to tread carefully. The information window could snap shut any second. *Seventeen,* I mouthed. All eyes and limbs. I could not be more thrilled. I understood that eventually the subject would come up, but did it have to be tonight? What was wrong with twenty years from now?

"You're overreacting," she said.

"Am I?"

"I thought about it. Nothing you say will stop me." She was typing on her phone now, her thumbs flying, her hair veiling her face. "You don't want me getting too serious too young, do you?"

"No," I said. "But—"

"Then be grateful I have no plans to settle down yet. I mean, there's no point in getting involved now when I'm about to leave for college. This way is better— we'll be fuck buddies."

"Uh...what?" I tried to be tolerant and understanding. High school is hard. She was under a lot of pressure, my sweetheart. They were all under a lot of pressure.

"You know. No strings attached." Her face was innocent, her eyes luminous.

"Oh, well then," I said. "That sounds far better. I guess I should be glad you're making friends."

"Really, Mom? Really? Not funny. I picked Daniel to be my first."

Daniel? With sad, pink, patchy skin and sad, brown, poodle hair and sad brown eyes—that kid carried bottomless sadness with him. No less embittered than a typical seventeen-year-old, but perhaps more. He was a punk with a real talent for tasteless remarks, but not a bad person—gawky and confused and unspoiled with attention, he showed off how tough he could be and called his father Walt and his mother Wilma. He could not seem to catch a break ever since the day his unmarried mother, a respectable investment banker, had run off with her new boyfriend, an ambitious proctologist, when Daniel was four, and his relieved biological father, an accountant, had moved to Cleveland, Ohio, with his lawful wife and two kids.

His always-annoyed aunt, Jossie, Wilma's unmarried older sister...well, Daniel had to stay with her, this woman who never felt particularly maternal, had no interest in raising children, and never neglected to show it. She was a screamer too. The boy never engaged in a conversation, shooting down my attempts with a flat "Fine"—a cover-up for all the other words he could not say, and questions got stuck in my throat like a fish bone.

I felt sort of protective tenderness for him, more than what I would feel for a homeless kitten, but not enough to serve my openhearted daughter to him on a platter. And though Hannah pretended to be a little less smart than she was around Daniel, I was grateful it was not the one before him, Steve, a self-proclaimed five-star chef—the result of one summer job in a mobile burger joint when he was not getting tattooed.

"First what?" I asked.

"Come off it. Don't behave like you don't understand. Look at Angelina in *1G*. She's sixteen and pregnant with her second child." She smiled, lifting a shoulder.

"Oh, Hannah...It has crossed my mind. But what an interesting argument. Yes, I'm sure her mother, Rosamaria the alcoholic, is overwhelmed with her good fortune. And so is her father, in prison. And things wouldn't be so bad if Angelina's last boyfriend hadn't given her gonorrhea. He also gave gonorrhea to Rosamaria, and now they are both getting treatments from Dr. Gonzales in *6F*. All right. As you wish. I believe in us. We can do it. You go get pregnant, and I'll start drinking right away. But first let's call your father and talk him into turning himself in."

"Why is everything funny with you?"

A fire truck's siren loudened, followed by a second truck, and a third. I yanked out the stick holding the narrow windowpane up, and it slammed shut with the sound of a shotgun going off, followed by the angry flapping of pigeons' wings. The honking of horns on the street below muted a little. The sirens faded in a distance.

"I don't find this funny at all," I said. *Damn right.*

She flipped her bangs out of her eyes. "I'm seventeen and I'm still a virgin."

The perils of the modern age. I understand. I do. "Let it be our worst tragedy ever."

"Mama, my God! That's not fair."

Her eyes and cheeks glowed, framed by a mass of dark-brown curls. Bright blue eyes and dimples—my angel. Will I love her any less? No.

"Well," I said.

"Well, indeed." Hannah read something on her phone, raised her eyes to meet mine.

"I respect your decisions. It's your body. It's your life. Use protection."

"Mother! Stop treating me like a little girl!" She went out the door with a backward wave of her hand, her limbs graceful and long. The door clicked shut.

The young and the restless! No dread of falling. They know everything! I wanted to feel enlightened and progressive about sex. I also wanted to cry. I would be happier crying in the kitchen.

My cubbyhole kitchen was my kingdom. I reigned there—during the day, at least. Nights belonged to roaches. Orangey-brown and plump, they held soccer tournaments on discolored Formica countertops and frolicked when I brought in the newest version of a roach motel, scientifically proven to kill them, when the previous model had been discontinued as too toxic for humans. Like a new drug that would elicit a round of cheers from underage partygoers, they scuttled after me, happy for the opportunity to try it. They congregated near the entrance, holding counsel, and the most adventurous ventured in only to come out shortly and drop down dead...in theory. For a few hours, brown bodies lay on their backs on the countertop and the floor, their extremities churning the air with increasing velocity, only to flip over and scurry off to go about their business as usual some time later.

I jammed paper towels into crevasses in the walls and base moldings with a screwdriver, but new hordes kept trekking in. It was a lost war. And one day they were gone. All of them. It puzzled me until I discovered a strange object hanging from a ceiling beam in the basement. It looked like a ball of dung collected by a pitbull-sized beetle to feed its progeny, spreading around an odor too rich to be described.

I asked our superintendent Pedro what it was. He told me: "Friday," he said, and nodded. "Friday, Friday."

That sounds about right, I thought.

The idiot bulgy-eyed dachshund next door yapped. The eight-year-old Russian girl from the fifth floor, tone-deaf but stubborn, was still practicing scales, missing the notes, her thin voice breaking up. The couple upstairs bickered. The squares of sunlight slanted over the floor like a net. Back in Moscow, when I had a problem, I would get a bottle of vodka and invite a few friends over. By the end of the bottle, we would find a working solution, although some problems required multiple sittings. My expectations back then had been lower too; my biggest dream had been sewing a new dress. In New York I have been going to psychologists for years and none of my problems were resolvable. I was as confused as ever. "All right," my therapist would say. "Something to think about. We'll continue with this the next time." Did anyone ever get well? In some ways I miss Russia.

Nothing is what you imagine, I told myself, and opened the fridge. A few stalks of celery, two apples, a jar of mustard, and a half-empty jar of strawberry jam. I traced my finger along the edge of the wire shelf. *We are out of milk,* I thought, but was in no mood to see happy families herding their children through the aisles, loading shopping carts with jumbo packages of potato chips and chocolate chip cookies.

I took things out of the fridge, began cleaning the inside and the racks with a soapy sponge. Then I put everything back in. My hands still trembled. *Well, it was inevitable,* I thought. If only her father were alive, but since he had died so tragically...

T'foo! I spat and tossed the sponge into the sink. Where had that come from? Sergey was very much alive and well and uninterested in what was happening with Hannah. He often forgot she existed. The mistakes I had made. One thing was for sure—I would not be like Mother. I would not constrain my daughter. She would have the freedom I never had. She would have a good life. I knew she would.

Memories came uninvited. A flood of glimpses of my "gosling," like a flip-book in no order, took me back, rushing through the corridors of time. She had been a beautiful little one, born with long, dark fuzz extending every which way. Her intense, cornflower-blue eyes took up half her face, her thin stalk of a neck poked out of the faded-beige blanket like a baby Galapagos turtle's. The tiny body, the little face—so vulnerable and sweet and perfect that tears filled my eyes in surge of love and tenderness as I placed her at my breast. She arched her back, but did not let out any requisite cry. Her mouth moved in a sucking motion in search of a nipple, tiny fingers splayed like starfish. She took up all the space in my life—the sun in my solar system. From then on my life revolved around hers, ruled by the simple needs of this small and loud and demanding lump of love, and my happiness was simple and complete.

In the beginning handling babies made me nervous. I had no one to ask for advice—books contradicted one another, and Mother was of no help. I made mistake after mistake. The horror of my own unavoidable inadequacy was constant, but somehow Hannah made it out of infancy alive. A toddler with a partial set of teeth in bib overalls, who had just begun to talk in sentences, legs bowed on either side of a bulging diaper, would smile and clap and say in a small voice, "Take an umbrella. It'll rain." Hannah had this thing for umbrellas.

Still small, her hair cropped boyish short, she would ride in the shopping cart, her little feet dangling from the wire seat. Strangers would stop and say, "Look at those eyes! What a cute little boy!" and pinch her firm cheek. Hannah hated that. And one day, when an old woman stretched out her arm, ready to pinch, my baby yelled, "Oh shit!"

The skinniest one in her class, her thin shoulder blades jutted out like two wings of a warbler. I could count each vertebra. She was also the smallest, always the last one in the lineup among other plankton. Her pink book bag, covered with glittery stickers, was as big as she was, her little thumbs hooked under the wide straps.

She had grown up. A delicately thin girl with scraped knees and elbows and a contemplative streak had budded into a sexy young woman, leaving adolescence to enter adulthood. She would always be at the center of my existence, but I was no longer at the center of hers. It pained my heart, but I had to let her go to live her life. I could not shield her from everything. On the road to independence, bumps and blows will show the way. And like countless others, some things she would have to learn herself.

From the first punch of a baby not yet born, floating in the darkness of a womb, moving a hand or a foot (doing somersaults with a swift kick to your ribs with an elbow or a heel)—the whole miracle-of-life thing—you never stop worrying, and life becomes waiting, full of unnamed fears and hopes. Waiting for the first fever to subside (and all the others too), waiting to pick her up from her first day in kindergarten, then school, the first bra, the first party, then the first date, waiting to hear of her first boyfriend, the first kiss, waiting for them to grow strong, sprout wings, and fly away (feeling as if you have been exiled), waiting out their moodiness and stages, waiting to hear they are safe, lying in bed waiting for sleep—a labyrinth of worrying, worrying, waiting, worrying—countless sleepless nights. I learned to take nothing for granted. I felt powerless to stop her but privileged she came to me, announcing it at seventeen instead of getting pregnant at twelve. Hannah is a great kid.

To save myself a lot of grief, New York today cannot be compared with Moscow twenty years ago. Take Vadim and Irene, both intellectuals, both lawyers. He made partner. They have a beautiful house, a housekeeper, and all three kids have police records. Three hateful, foulmouthed children. The monosyllabic twelve-year-old leaves rehab for a youth facility and back again and does only what he wants to do. They are happy their daughter comes home at all. The purple-haired fourteen-year-old is on a cocktail of meds for her hyperactive-impulsive disorder, was detained for possession of drugs and shoplifting, and is a walking learning prop for the art of piercing after quite a few artists used her body to express their vision of true beauty—a series of bad decisions. She has more piercings than teeth. Zombie-like, always reading comic books and sneaking a smoke out in their courtyard, cupping her palm around a cigarette or a joint, her eyes and her pimply forehead hidden behind her bangs. Cries too, a lot.

The oldest, twenty-three, is a good-looking boy and a perfect student. He seemed the nicest one of three, but was suspected in running dope, got off on "not enough evidence," and is now serving time for raping a minor. None of them speak to the parents. All three loathe both parents equally. No matter where one turns nowadays, it is the same story: drugs, drugs, drugs. Vadim used to say, "Children are our future." He does not say it anymore. Irene just cries on the phone, "Where did we go wrong?"

I felt a tug as the seedling of loneliness stirred, the future ache of hollow longing, the unwelcome guest. In a few short months it would catch me by the throat. The streetlights came on, making the gray of the buildings grayer against the gray sky. The moon was bright, and the night cold. Some windows were lit, and I could peek at the pantomimes of other people's lives and loves trapped in yellowish rectangles. A faint blue glow flickered in quite a few. A Viennese waltz flew in from somewhere. The stop-and-go traffic was heavy, but the crowds had thinned, the sidewalk was almost deserted, a few figures hurried along. In the twilight I saw a man striding along Broadway, a little boy straggling a few steps behind him. Father and son. The man stopped near a fire hydrant and faced the boy, opening his arms in a pleading gesture. The boy stopped too, maintaining the distance, and shook his head. The father made a step toward his son, the boy retreated a pace. The man waved one arm and stomped along the street. The boy trotted behind.

I ensconced myself on a living room couch, switched on the Discovery Channel to take my mind off Hannah and to curb the multiplying negative thoughts. Glowing Adam (my Siamese cat in a brother-sister set—one Adam, one Eve) jumped on my lap, curled up, pushed his cold nose into my arm. *How do people get through life without a cat?* I wondered, hugging him tighter, and concentrated on the screen, where the world brimmed with sounds: things croaked, barked, whistled, howled, shrieked, squawked, guffawed, yelped, and God-knows-what-else to enact the great symphony of life.

The multicolored birds flitted and darted and fluttered about. Howler monkeys chased one another on branches of a gigantic tree. A chaser caught up with the chased, and they began mating, screeching as fighting cats, growling and biting. "As you can see, their manner is casual and very relaxed," the narrator said. The lush foliage of the rainforest faded away to be replaced by African savanna. Giraffes ran on stilts, their long necks swinging forward and back. The antelopes grazed, jaws moving from side to side. They raised their heads, stopped chewing, ears flicking back and forth. One or two stepped sideways—the lionesses hid in the grass, about to pounce. A hippo boy mounted a hippo girl, bellowing low.

I switched the channel. A partially naked couple kissed. I switched the channel again and to my delight, saw a mutilated body being put into a drawer in a morgue. *Perfect. I'll be too scared to think of anything else.* I fidgeted a little to get more comfortable, as Eve—Adam's biological sister as well as his sister in arms—as superior as a cat can be, joined Adam on my lap. The scene flicked to a couple having sex. I switched the TV off and picked up a book from the coffee table. *Anna Karenina.* I let it open at a random place and began to read.

That which for Vronsky had been almost a whole year the one absorbing desire of his life, replacing all his old desires; that which for Anna had been an impossible, terrible, and even for that reason more entrancing dream of bliss, that desire had been fulfilled. He stood before her, pale, his lower jaw quivering, and besought her to be calm, not knowing how or why.

'Anna! Anna!' he said with a choking voice, 'Anna, for pity's sake...!...'

But the louder he spoke, the lower she dropped her once proud and gay, now shame-stricken head, and she bowed down and sank from the sofa where she was sitting, down on the floor, at his feet; she would have fallen on the carpet if he had not held her.

'My God! Forgive me!' she said, sobbing, pressing his hands to her bosom.

She felt so sinful, so guilty, that nothing was left her but to humiliate herself and beg forgiveness; and as now there was no one in her life but him, to him she addressed her prayer for forgiveness. Looking at him, she had a physical sense of her humiliation, and she could say nothing more. He felt what a murderer must feel, when he sees the body he has robbed of life. That body, robbed by him of life, was their love, the first stage of their love. There was something awful and revolting in the memory of what had been bought at this fearful price of shame. Shame at their spiritual nakedness crushed her and infected him. But in spite of all the murderer's horror before the body of his victim, he must hack it to pieces, hide the body, must use what he has gained by his murder...

I closed the book and dialed Rita.

"It was bound to happen sooner or later," she said. "Aw, this is so sweet. She looks to you for everything, letting you in on intimate stuff. I wonder if what's-his-name is a good lover."

"Thanks. Now I'll be picturing that."

"Welcome. Do you have a good losing-my-virginity story? Mine was lousy."

"So was mine," I said. "Chaotic. The limited theoretical knowledge hadn't done much good. He had done it all wrong, though he had boasted about taking life lessons from his swearing drunkard neighbor nicknamed Horse."

"Did your mother ever talk to you about sex?"

"Mother? Sure. I was active in track and field, and when I got my first period I had no idea what it was. I thought I'd damaged something and that if I didn't die on my own, she'd kill me for going against her wishes and participating in sports."

"Why are you so upset?" Rita asked.

"Sex is bonding. Especially the first time. It's like an enduring dividing line—before and after. In her most vulnerable moment, Hannah will bond to a schmuck and suffer it for the rest of her life. Daniel is a troubled kid. Whenever they're together, I'm worried something bad will happen. No love. No magic. It'll be messy and horrible. A trauma instead of a celebration."

"Maybe the romance isn't so important anymore." Rita did not sound too convinced.

"It's in our DNA. It'll always be important."

"Sex is a wonderful thing."

"Yes, with the right person. With the wrong one, it could put you off for years. It's—" I paused. "Hold please. I have another caller. Could be Hannah." I switched the line.

"This is the Police Precinct Thirty-Three," a man's voice said. "We got a situation here. Daniel Nigorsky was brought in on count of driving a stolen vehicle under the influence and for assaulting a police officer. He may have to face charges. Your daughter was in the vehicle with him. She has no ID. We can't release her without verifying her identity."

Ah. One of those things. I switched back to Rita. "Rita, I have to go."

"Whatever it is she did—don't kill her. Could be worse. Could be anorexia or something."

. . .

I sat down on one of the molded plastic chairs connected together by metal rods, two seats away from a petite, angular woman in shapeless dark clothes, who had a small face and large, dark circles under her tiny, deep-set eyes. The narrow, windowless room smelled of old building and French fries. The speckled, brownish-gray linoleum floor, streaked with mud, had a forked, lighter trail where traffic had been the heaviest. The billboard on the opposite wall overflowed with wanted posters and pictures of missing children pinned to it. The pebble-textured panels of the ceiling hung so low it seemed I could reach it sitting down. Plain fluorescent tube lights buzzed like a swarm of angry flies. Hannah, my elfin Hannah, sweet and rebellious and bright, who was about to finish high school, had been arrested on a municipal charge of disorderly conduct when she refused to stay in the car while Daniel was given a field sobriety test. She was told to return to the car, but stated she was a US citizen and that she was allowed to stand on American ground.

"She's a firecracker, this one," the cop behind the desk had said.

What's taking so long? I dropped my head and closed my eyes. I heard a stifled cough and glanced in the direction of the sound. A woman near me clutched something in her nervous hands. Her body seemed rigid with tension, stretched as a guitar string to the limits. Her gaze was fixed on the floor, her lips moved as if she were praying, her thin dirty-blond hair quivering from the eager diligence. She raised her eyes, regarded me in silence, and with urgency slid into the seat next to me. She clasped my hand and pushed an object into my palm. A plastic crucifix.

"Praise Jesus! Praise the Lord, the man who died for your sins," she said in a honking voice, her cheeks turning pink. "I was a sinner like you before I found Jesus. Let him into your heart. He'll forgive all your sins, past and future. Repent! The devil is after you."

I shuddered in surprise and slid across to the next seat, away from her.

"You're a devil!" Her voice rose to a screech, her intense eyes drilling me.

The cop behind the desk looked up from his paperwork.

"Rose!" he said. "Rose, let her be. Your brother is on his way to pick you up. Sit tight."

A metal door opened, slammed shut. A policeman, a little short for a cop, with a sprinkle of dark moles on his young face walked into the lobby. I saw Hannah—pale cheeks and red, swollen eyelids—behind his shoulder and approached the reception counter. My eyes began to water halfway there.

The source of the sour odor of sweat and vomit and stale beer—a thin, middle-aged man with a long, bruised face—was cuffed and held by the arm by a policeman in mirror shades. The detainee seemed in a trance, but came alive when I neared him. He emitted a battery of nasty-sounding rasps and bent toward me, and I almost choked from the stench.

"Your girly here needs a man's firm hand to guide her in life." He nodded toward Hannah. The top two buttons on his bloodied shirt were torn off, and the tuft of black fur that grew in the hollow of his neck moved along with the rhythm of his nods. "And you, sweet buns"—he checked me up and down—"come to Daddy. Daddy will show you a good time."

"Is that why you beat up your wife?" the policeman holding him asked. "To show her a good time? Is that why she's in the hospital?"

"Eat me."

"Thank your neighbors for calling an ambulance," the rosy-cheeked cop behind the desk said. "You won't be charged with murder this time."

The man tightened his jaw, spat on the floor, his eyes glazed over.

"Ma'am, sign here," the cop behind the desk said, and pointed with a pen at Hannah. "You're free to go. You're lucky nobody got hurt. We'll keep your friend overnight. His parents can pick him up tomorrow."

"His aunt," Hannah said. "She won't come, and she won't drop the charges."

"Would she post a five-grand bond?"

"No."

"Too bad for him."

The street was empty and dark. A hunched man with a disconnected expression, wearing a shirt short in the sleeves and frayed at the cuffs, played an accordion on a windy corner. A sliver of a moon pierced through the dirty-gray clouds for a moment and was swallowed again. It began to drizzle. Rain fell quietly. The potholes in the wet asphalt quickly filled with puddles.

"You look cold," I said.

Hannah wrapped her arms around my neck. "Oh, Mama… Mama." Tears came from her eyes. We stood still for a moment. She separated from me, shook her head, blew her nose.

"Mama, I feel bad about what happened," she said. "I'll never do it again."

"Don't make promises you don't intend to keep."

She blushed, lowered her eyes, but then looked up and cocked her head to one side. "We didn't steal a car, we borrowed it. It belongs to Jossie. She just reported it as stolen. Why does she hate him so much? That's so unfair."

I tilted my head to mimic the angle of hers. "Life is unfair. And cruel. Messy too. In fact, it's a total catastrophe. Get used to it. But then, isn't life interesting?"

four

every time I was sick—it did not matter what the problem was—Mother had the ultimate panacea for it. Everything from a head cold to an ingrown toenail was prescribed the same cure and treated with equal enthusiasm. Mother would show up equipped with a package of carrots and a piece of gauze to make freshly squeezed carrot juice to relieve me of my multiple ills on the spot and restore full health. The woman had a definite purpose in life, which had something to do with the periodic grating of a certain amount of carrots.

By unlucky coincidence, I had been down with a bad flu for an entire week, but the sneezing, coughing, feverish achiness had eased up a little. At that point in time, it occurred to Mother to interrupt the little break she had taken from her routine of dropping in daily—that she ought to be heroic, overcome her fear of catching whatever it was I had, and rush to my rescue, though to her I was always an inconvenience, as she could not stand children even when they were children no longer.

Mother's constant physical presence in my physical space was—how can I put it gently?—overwhelming. It contributed to the tense atmosphere that prevailed between us and added endless fresh portions of ultracharged stuff I would have to forgive her for later on onto the enormous emotional baggage I was fortunate enough to be carrying already, thus solidifying and cementing things that would be best off dissolving forever.

Far from being downright miserable, I was at home in a state of blissful unawareness that the massive chunk of happiness was about to be brought down upon my head. Mother plugged in as soon as she crossed the threshold, speaking in her usual tone of perpetual annoyance.

"What's the matter? Flu? You have flu? See what happens to people who don't listen to their mothers? I can't understand what's wrong with you. You're the main source of all my grief. How do you always manage to get yourself in such a plight? Don't you dare to come near me. I'm warning you. I don't want to catch your contagion."

To emphasize her point and to protect her face, she averted her physiognomy from me while she raised her hand in a Shaolin kung fu blocking gesture, executed to perfection, though never in her life had Mother heard of Shaolin or kung fu and would furiously deny any association with it.

"Don't," she said again. To prevent me from getting any funny ideas and avoid any possibility of confusion, she swooped into our kitchen straight as unwavering arrow, keen on her target. As a real stoic, she endured the discomfort of the posture and kept her hand raised, not looking at me, not even a glance. One might think she was but feigning indifference, but that was not the case: her bona fide obsession with having the world revolve around her had ever dominated both our lives.

Ah, well…The main purpose of a family is to surround one with love through the trials that a bitch life threw one's way, its jaws snapping. That is what any psychiatrist might say if one took the trouble to ask the good doctor (please keep in mind that psychotherapy does not belong to a jolly group of exact sciences). This profound insight could also be learned from a bumper sticker on a passing vehicle, right below "Legalize it," but above the one that states, "A woman needs a man like a fish needs a bicycle," and to the left of "Jesus saves." How much easier it would be to breathe in the world with its fundamental chaos and uncertainty if the quality of parenting were to improve everywhere!

Love. Support. My natal family unit wanted nothing to do with this ridiculous notion. Love? For the child? For that pitiful half-mensch? I tried hard not to take it personally. For unfathomable reasons I thought I was adopted. Half the time I had a stronger suspicion I was an adopted Martian. Those could also be the beginning stages of paranoia.

As with every other time before, Mother installed herself in our small kitchen, redecorating the room along the way. How I wished that at least for once, she would resist this urge of hers to reorganize! Chills ran down my spine while my hectic stomach searched for ways to tie itself into another intricate knot, as yet again I faced the dreadful possibility that today might be the accursed day when she decided to stay for good! *Kum ba ya, my Lord, kum ba ya*…My song was a silent song in a physical cosmos overcrowded with Mother's presence, but how it thundered through my mind! *Kum ba ya*…

In her loud voice, Mother demanded a bowl, a grater, a pair of scissors, a teaspoon, a glass, and a plastic shopping bag. Her requests satisfied at once, without a second to spare, she chopped off both handles of the supermarket bag, butterflied the rest with one swift move of the scissors, and smoothing out the wrinkles, spread the resulting masterpiece on our kitchen table to define the working area. After seeing so many similar procedures for so many years, I had no clue why she had to do it like this, as the entire kitchen, including the walls and—ah, the mystery!—ceiling too ended up covered with tiny bits of carrot.

The next step—to precision-cut a piece of gauze. My participation was obligatory, not up for discussion, but limited to inconsequential for the final outcome bits. The gauze was stretched tight between her fists as if a small ball were to be bounced off it by a strict army sergeant.

Mother watched me with a critical eye—always with a critical eye. One might be compelled to think she lived to criticize. Snipping things was a procedure she cared to delegate to no one. With a theatrical sigh, guaranteed to be heard from the last row, she pointed the precise spot for the cut and grimaced.

"Here. Watch it!" she said, obviously enjoying the sound of her own voice and unaware that I might kill her accidentally.

My childhood revisited, I stood there, again a frightened, speechless girl, filled with expectations that would remain unfulfilled. Another lesson in tolerance for cruelties and obedience. Revenge aside, changing *my* attitude made no difference. She had ways of getting deep under my skin and throwing my defenses down, to no end. I can swear I have seen a mighty lightning bolt on the bottom of her left eye, well formed, ready to strike at a moment's notice—this observation refueled the fire of my already agitated state. I expected her to demand I do this act of cutting facing away from the door, in just one move (it never varied), holding the scissors in a vertical position with pointy ends facing down...but no, we had none of that today.

With shaking scissors in my shaking hands—the entire moment absurdly dramatic—I held my breath and made a cut. Right away, nothing terrible befell me. I dared to take in a small breath, in an assumption that perhaps I had done a satisfactory job this time. But I could never be sure—her lips were pressed together, forming a tight line, straight and impenetrable, and thus till the end of days, it will remain a mystery to us all. What a barracuda. So for the next hour, she methodically washed, peeled, and grated the carrots.

Since the world had presented itself to her only in a black light, life's hardships had put a permanent stamp on Mother's once-beautiful face—no sign of that beauty now. Her thin-lipped mouth formed a perpetual, world-weary frown, a jewel in the crown of her despotic countenance. Two deep vertical wrinkles crossed her forehead, having crept in there at one time in the past, as if by mistake, and wasting no time, they had deepened further and froze for eternity, emblazoned like her private coat of arms.

Once, a wispy cloud had passed in front of her face. Then another, still of the wispy sort. Over time, more and more undulating masses kept appearing, thickening, until a dark pall of worries hung over Mother. Ominous and everlasting, it obscured her soul, giving her a constant expression of displeasure that was replaced by calm indifference on occasions. Her mouth—ah, her mouth!—as a gratis, it did not close for a second. Clairvoyant and more than willing to share with anyone (me in particular) the yieldings that the miracle of such a visionary gift bestowed upon us, she would never waste an opportunity to tell me exactly how I should live my life in step-by-step, no-nonsense instructions—the most minute details of what I might, must, or should never do. Her—missionaries. Cannibals—that would be me. Nonnegotiable. As it was, cannibals had never *asked* for the missionaries to come, had they?

Increasingly petulant Mother glared at me in annoyance. "The thermometer, show it to me! A hundred and three? It's broken. Throw it away. You have no fever. You only imagine it…"

I sighed and tuned out.

"Are you still eating eggs?" she asked a second later, looking at me as if she could not quite place me. "I've told you so many times, the cholesterol…"

"I'm glad you broke up with that Alex character," she said after a brief moment of silence, reinforcing her own thousand-year curse on my soul. She had never made her low opinions of my choice in mates a secret. "Your life belongs to Hannah. Enough of this amorous nonsense. Don't put your neck into a noose. I'm doing you a favor here. Accept that you're damaged merchandise! Nobody wants a woman with a child…"

A lock of hair swirled away from the precisely coiffed mass on her head, fell over her forehead, touched her brow, softening Mother's Jack-the-Ripper features a little. She tucked back the unruly curl and attempted to paint a smile on her face, but the expression was too foreign to Mother. More of a distortion than a sign of endearment, it incubated nothing and did not linger long. She scowled.

"When was the last time you washed the floors in here?"

Oh just kill me, please. As any other opportunistic undead, she sucked away my soul, devouring life, which made her almost content with the world. I knew I would be sorry for putting up with her, as I soon was, but what could I do—she was my mother. We were family, lives intertwined forever, the inexplicable pull of blood. Goddamn loyalty!

And no one could claim I was not loyal. I wanted to surrender, as I saw no sense in struggling. Even if her entire existence were dedicated to one and only one purpose, which was to upset me, I was left with no choice but to put up with it all, because…ah well, one simply does. I could unfussily lie down right in the middle of the kitchen floor and play dead, or indeed die for real, but it would not stop her, so I must advise myself against this. It would not even slow her down, and in the end would make little difference. In my delirium, I could be tempted again into making another tempest in a teapot in connection to it—to call it an issue and push and shove to bring it into the open, hoping against hope that no fear of facing reality would show up this time around.

To avoid overstraining their critical minds when they approached rising problems, my mother, Galina, and her older sister, Bella, employed the empirically sound technique of closing their eyes—spoken as a metaphor—and keeping them shut, ignoring the topic and giving it ample time to go away, or, as a form of compromise, to resolve itself of its own accord; in any way, moving it into the realm of comfortable invisibility, whichever method happened first, as if when no one talked about what transpired, not a thing had taken place.

Nothing could be further from the truth, yet it was one way of reacting to fear. Ah, the undeniable beauty of denial—the most primitive of psychological defenses, but what a power it packed! As current titleholders for the Master of the Universe in the Art of Denial, those two shared the crown, having refined, refined, refined this art for decades, all while enclosed in the indestructible bubble of self-imposed fear.

Listen, I am all for denial as long as it makes the participants happy. A generous-sized herd of pink suede elephants had set up a permanent home in our little house. Or was it a generous-sized herd of pink suede demons that swirled around? I was trained not to notice either one or pretend not to notice. But once the matter in question occurred, it stayed around forever. It never got resolved since no one ever talked about it. Isolating it with silence isolated not the issue—to be frank, the issue itself could not care less—but rather the descending silence would isolate the people, giving rise to resentment.

It came to be not an altogether infrequent occurrence, when Mother and Auntie were not too busy arguing, each one with her hands on her hips—one almost a head taller and angular with an air of a divinity in our midst, the other short and round as an aged Flemish angel with a diabolical twist—who was right and who was wrong, who would get her way and who would not. The icy silence would be allowed to come in and reign after they were done arguing for the moment, and never a second too soon.

I sneezed and was jerked back into the present and mundane. Ah yes, the mundane. According to ancient Hindus, and modern quantum physicists too, this objective reality thing in truth did not exist—it was a clever, elaborate deception. As Albert Einstein said, "Reality is merely an illusion, albeit a very persistent one." Such a bright, bright idea, but it brought no relief. Following close in Mother's footsteps, as this was the simplest means to avoid dealing with the unpleasantness that was growing by the moment, I stood there clenching my teeth, in the hope that Mother would go away. Be gone, *be gone. Sayonara.*

However strong a telepathic suggestion I was able to conjure up and direct at her within my existing abilities, it elicited no desired response. Mother remained sitting and talking, doing everything in her power to annoy me without a flinch. Nothing in her face suggested she had been the least bit inconvenienced. To quote Friedrich Nietzsche, "*Was mich nicht umbringt, macht mich stärker.*" *

"The wind is so forceful today." Her mind had veered again. "I thought it would blow my beret off and I'd never be able to catch it. What would I do without my beret? I'll contract a cold, for sure…"

I looked at the caged tree outside. Not a single leaf stirred. From time to time, Mother paused and stared at me with unsettling stillness—a fixed, chilling stare, like a spider lying in wait—as if to ascertain she had been in some way successful in driving her point across, so with a sense of accomplishment and free of guilt, she could demand the highest level of respect.

"I don't understand how you walk around with this backpack of yours," she said, her brow expressing pity. "It's foolish. Anybody can steal your wallet…"

Not a shocking surprise that she was secretly convinced—for reasons I did not quite understand—she was a priceless jewel with the unsullied reputation of an expert. (Ah, the divine retribution, but *what* had I done to deserve this?) Mother ensured that everyone in her immediate surroundings knew it and knew it well. Her surroundings—that would be me again. I imagine it would cause quite a pleasant commotion in the world of scholars when she, such a knowledgeable treasure, was discovered at last. But the way things were at present, her being in our dark, cramped kitchen, hidden from the rest of the world, the discovery bit seemed indefinitely delayed. Pity no one but I knew about her unparalleled talents, and no one seemed to want to know.

The biggest fly in the ointment was that I, not being overly saturated with proper filial respect, contrary to what was required of me on an unconditional basis, had failed to consider it my sacred duty to uphold her image and reputation as the navel of creation. And I, so far unapologetically, had been the one who had also neglected to erect a shrine to her with my deepest admiration. Instead I attempted to get her dethroned. Mother, force of nature as she was (make it "force of nature specializing in destruction," and like the weather, impossible to control), may have had a rough time overriding my stubborn reservations on

---

* "That which does not kill me, makes me stronger." (German)

the subject of her omniscience, but had no intention of climbing down from Olympus or giving up the fight, and spared no effort to reach her goal. Mother give up her narcissism? Never. This jewel would *never* skimp on her effort and would continue to make life as such difficult for me. Like one of those marvelous, marvelous gifts that just keep on giving.

"Are you trying to kill me?" the jewel asked. "Because you're killing me…"

The vertical furrows between her eyebrows deepened when she, exasperated, narrowed her eyes and studied me, as if to check that my vexation with her was sufficient by now—or had her efforts been wasted?

"…nothing good will come of it." And with a small, knowing smile, she sighed a sigh, which told me she had no illusions about me and very little hope.

"A brick or a tree could fall on your head…" she said.

"The way you dress, any man could rape you. It's only a matter of time…" she said.

"Tell me the truth—all these men, are you having sex for money?" she said.

"*Blahbety-blah-blah-blahhhh,*" she said.

Merde! I felt a headache coming.

Mother interrupted her training session to give her undivided attention to banging a metal grater on the hard surface closest to her (which happened to be the edge of the metal kitchen sink), muttering under her breath and scaring half of the neighborhood inhabitants to death, all with the iron determination of getting every last carrot bit out. This action of hers evened the layer of carrot dust on all inanimate or somewhat animate objects in the room, me included.

And now, the last step: she meticulously measured with a teaspoon the amount of mush to deposit into a piece of gauze, then twisted the clump with her surprisingly strong fingers to squeeze the pulp and obtain the final product. Her movements were choreographed with precision, she had spent years perfecting them.

"Come and drink it. *In tiny gulps!*" Mother called out to me, choosing to ignore that I had been still as a stump, standing at attention with little enthusiasm but hardwired to obey, right there for duration of the entire process. One might make the honest mistake of thinking that I, a tiger caged, had been awaiting orders like a donkey—patient, if a little docile. But I awaited being swatted away at any moment, trained to expect an attack at all times from any conceivable direction, and was always surprised when it did not come, which was seldom, but did happen. How was one to turn this automatic response off?

On the bottom of the glass were about two precious tablespoons' worth of liquid substance, which possessed miraculous curative properties and misguidedly looked like ordinary carrot juice, but were in fact the black waters of death.

Such was the dosage to cure me of whatever made me ill, and it was pushed upon me as one fact among all other irrefutable facts of life. Resistance was futile. So, with resistance off, I drank my medicine. In tiny gulps. According to Mother, a bigger dosage would do irreparable damage to my liver, and to claim otherwise paraded a complete ignorance of the matter.

The trusted and reliable source of her vast medical knowledge was a Russian daily newspaper or Aunt Bella, yet another gift of fate, who in turn got her medical knowledge from the same paper, always managing to catch a different angle on crucial information, too often a diametrical opposition. For weeks after the article came out, they would hold heated symposia on the subject. That health-directed advice, a solitary paragraph long, came out daily, and both women were pleased to have several medically oriented subjects to discuss in one sitting. And again. When they had arrived at a satisfying consensus, Tweedledum and Tweedledee, as a unified pushy obstacle, rushed to pass their expertise onto me, smiling menacingly at one another, delighted in their own judgment and ignoring my resistance to the tide of their enthusiasm. I would rather be kept in the dark. It was like trying to stop the wind—impossible. Believe me, I had tried.

"Anna?" Mother patted my hand. "You're unreliable."

Her touch jerked me back into reality once again.

With a feeling of a job well done and some last-minute directions, which included the long list of things for me to avoid altogether—and it covered everything possible in the expanding visible universe—Mother was off, albeit reluctant to trust in my ability to take care of myself. Listen, I had managed to get myself into such a mess, which was to be expected from the flawed child that I was—I had managed to catch flu.

I looked around. It was hard to believe it had been solely a little old woman who was responsible for this vandalism and not an entire horde of horse-mounted marauders. As an aftermath of the invasion, I was left with a ringing in my ears, an irregular twitching in my left eye, a modest pile of dirty dishes, and the entire kitchen to scrub.

A thoroughly washed piece of gauze and little scraps of wet paper towel— she did not believe in wasting things—hung everywhere to dry out. This piece of gauze, left behind, was a dead giveaway she would be back tomorrow, and even if it was hardly worthwhile to speculate to a great extent on this particular matter, such a thought continued to torment me for several hours afterward. Hell no. The rare occasions when Mother took care of me: sweet—twisted, but sweet. I had learned to cherish these moments, those tender endearments of hers. At least she showed up and did something. A hollow comfort mixed with a certain sense of discouragement. This was not to suggest the existing situation was by any means hopeless, but it proved too true that becoming unduly preoccupied with finding satisfactory solutions was doomed to lead to further discouragement, and it was wiser to guard against such a bleak situation.

The front door screeched. *I have to grease it,* I thought, but made no move. I heard a familiar thud—the backpack met the floor—and felt revived, like a caught fish released back to a stream.

Hannah walked into the kitchen, put a large Styrofoam cup on the table, kissed my forehead.

"I brought you chicken soup," she said.

"How was school?" I got up.

"Fine." She stretched, grabbed a glass from the dish-drying rack, pointed at the piece of gauze. "Was Grandma here again? Why do you let her in? Sit down. You still have a fever. Let me reheat the soup for you." And she gave me a reassuring pat on the back.

five

my flu progressed nicely. It felt like I was coughing up my lungs nonstop: "*Hack, hack.*" Adam's near-twin Eve, who looked like a tiny, very minor demon, decided to participate in the conversation. She had something important to say, and said it in reverberating basso: "*Ve-eeh.*" It sounded more like "*Gesundheit*, please get better soon," than "Keep it down, will you? Geez," and a warm, fuzzy feeling glowed in my chest. Though one could never guess with any sense of certainty what was on a cat's mind.

"*Hack, hack.*"

"*Ve-eeh.*" For hours. Even in her sleep.

In two days' time I had lost my voice to a sibilation level, the sounds emerging from me were perfectly inhuman. When my best friends, Rita and Patrick, came for a visit, I was brave enough (please read: "stubborn and obnoxious") to handle the conversation, with my end of it carried out in a half-whisper, half-rasp.

"Isn't my voice sexy?" I, a true coquette, wheezed without conviction while I sucked on a cough drop and hoped for a confirmation. Pretending was also good. I would take pretending. One had a right to let a certain amount of complacency creep in by expecting (if often unreasonably) to obtain on time the support of one's friends. Ah, but expectations often lead to disappointment.

"No, darling, it isn't," my girlfriend said. The indistinct shadow of a smile crossed Rita's face as her eyes met mine. "Sweetheart, where might our relationship be if I didn't speak the truth and nothing but?"

"*Mmm-rrr-mm,*" offered Adam, planting his little furry behind on a rug.

In my mind, limitless possibilities, seductive with their forbidden sweetness, created a long line.

"Happier?" I ventured out in my screechy—sultry!—contralto after a somewhat prolonged pause. I happened to love our cordial teases that kept me on my toes and also kept my brain young, if one chose to trust the latest medical research on the subject.

Patrick lounged on the couch—a view I was unaccustomed to. He was a plastic surgeon in high demand, always on duty at either his private practice or

Mount Sinai Hospital, and being such a success often robbed Patrick of the luxury to dispense with his time the way he might like.

"Patrick," I rasped in my tactful way. "Ten minutes since you've arrived and you're still here. Your pager hasn't gone off. How odd."

"Shush," Rita said. "Don't jinx it."

Life being what it is, I could hardly recall an occasion when we had spent an entire evening together without his buzzer thing buzzing, nasty little bugger. Looking noncommittal, Patrick smiled, turned away from me, crumpled a napkin, and threw it to Adam. Only too happy to accept the challenge, Adam began to shred it with his teeth, but changed his mind and chased the remainder of the make-believe ball under the couch with a single move of a paw. Patrick reached for another napkin. Rita sighed.

Ah, Rita...to not envy her was verging on the impossible. All her life, she had problems—humongous problems—making and keeping female friends. The usual suspects—jealousy, rivalry, bitterness. One knows how it can go. All her life, she had humongous problems keeping male friends too, as men wanted more from her than just a simple friendship. I was immune to this sort of game myself, a rather fortunate detail, which made me a suitable candidate for friendship with Rita. My competitive gene was among my nondominant ones or missing, so even a weighty volume of *Competitiveness for Dummies* would do me no good. We had managed to stay best friends forever. A luscious blonde, her brow curved as a swan's wing, she was a classic beauty of Russian fairy tales, the type fit to be married off to the tsar himself, capable of stopping any guy on the street in his tracks by giving him a casual glance in passing—heads swiveled like sunflowers to the sun—though she lacked the Doric column of a customary braid, reaching to her ankles and beribboned with colorful silk treasures. The poor guy would be left standing disoriented, staring at Rita's back as she gained distance from him. And what about any woman who, after casting eyes upon curvaceous Rita, at once turned away and faked indifference?

After six years of marriage, Patrick still looked at his wife with an "I cannot believe she is mine" expression. Tall, slim, full breasted, with a wasp-like waist and feminine, generous hips, a long neck, perfect, glowing skin, and insanely long eyelashes, she was a delight for the eyes. To tell the absolute truth—there was, after all, a fair limit to how much the average person can be expected to handle—I envied this waist of hers: tiny, always mysteriously tiny, no matter what, when, and how much she ate. How could one not envy it? Would not you? Please remember that honesty is still a virtue.

My waist was a different animal altogether. No tantalizing mystery there; it refused to cooperate, preoccupied with constant change, caught in the flux, wax-ing and waning to wax again way too soon, each time receding a little less than it managed to gain—what a banal tragedy. Rita belonged to a class of a woman that was a basic nightmare to have as a girlfriend. Who would look at me twice when she was around? What a rotten bit of luck. I shared the fate of all other less attractive women. As a direct consequence, my puny self-confidence was ready to give up and retire to a monastery. For good.

No point in dwelling on the subject to no end. The one thing left for me to do was to accept this as yet another thorny fact of life. One could only hope such an ordeal would not be in vain. The even luminescence, kind and soft, emanating from Rita's eyes was addictive. If one had glimpsed it but once, one had to come back for more. I did and never regretted it. It has warmed my soul as long as we have known one another. The woman knew my heart and was a much-needed balm for my never-closing wounds. Over the years I had learned to trust her explicitly. Intelligent, confident, with the eternal mystique of a Mona Lisa smile wandering in the curved-up corners of her mouth, she was there to catch me when I was falling, which happened often lately.

"We've brought you the newest David Cooper novel to read," Rita said, and there it was again, this mischievous smile of hers. "I have my channels. It's a manuscript about to be published. I thought you might want to read it, so I've printed it out for you."

"Oh God Almighty!" I croaked. "How can I ever thank you? *Achoo!* The man is a genius. Genius! *Hack, hack, hack.*" I was forced to stop talking.

"*Ve-eeh.*"

"I'd sell my soul to meet him," I finished, ecstatic, and in anticipation of reading a new masterpiece by my favorite author, was in an instant renewed and replenished by an uplifting swirl of energy, my flu forgotten.

"Have you ever wondered why there's no picture of him on the back flap of his dust jackets?" Rita asked. "Is he so ugly?"

"He may want to avoid constant recognition." For the time being, Patrick stopped his interactions with Adam. The three-inch-high stack of napkins on the coffee table was gone. Someone would have to get up and go to the kitchen for the fresh supply if the game was to continue.

"Or he's very old and unattractive," Rita said.

"No soul-selling necessary," Patrick said. "According to rumors, this new book of his is coming out in two months. There'll be a signing in New York, and you'll be dying to go. Am I right?" He laughed. "The first time I see you speech-less. All right, let's get your flu cured."

Still laughing, he got up and went to the kitchen. Adam followed Patrick. Rita followed Adam. Eve was too preoccupied with stretching on Hannah's bed to join the spontaneous migration. With a spinning head, I froze, weightless, suspended between heaven and earth. My breath stopped. I was to meet David Cooper? Face to face? David? Cooper? And, like, even talk to him? Did I feel like fainting now or should I wait?

I sneezed. It cleared my head and brought me back to earth. Perhaps I would faint in a bit. Mmm-hmm, life sure was full of surprises. Some of them even pleasant. As I had no real reason to anticipate any menace—one can drive oneself to a state of madness if allowed to continue on such an unfortunate path—a nervous smile plastered on my face, I took a few steps on unsteady legs toward the general direction of where everyone else had gone, then stopped. But then a sudden sense of what was almost contentment came over me unannounced. My shoulders relaxed, and I proceeded to the kitchen.

My friends had brought a truckload of intriguing stuff to combat my flu. Patrick unloaded the goods onto the kitchen table—a battered outdoor bistro-type thing with two matching chairs—small square jars of potent manuka honey, endless bags with a variety of herbs, containers with smelly ointments, five cartons of fresh raspberries and figs. My kitchen began to look like a medieval witch's—a good witch, a no-need-to-start-a-hunt witch. From what I have heard, this sort of event rarely ended in favor of the individual being hunted; let us not start anything we could potentially feel sorry about later on, shall we? The only things missing were a caldron and a hearth.

Now, a hearth would be a more-than-welcome addition to our otherwise crummy, forever-dark kitchen, and a vast improvement on its existing architecture. In this modest, dowdy apartment the kitchen was a gloomy place where the sun never shone—not exactly a palace, devoid as it was of any hint at romance or alluring domestic smells, and with bad, bad mojo. The scabby, yellow-streaked walls could have used a fresh coat of paint years ago, and a plaster job too. The rust had eaten away through layers upon layers of paint covering the surface of the heating pipe, as broad as a fat man's arm. It pierced the room, beginning at the sinister-looking hole in the floor and ending at the sinister-looking hole in the ceiling on its way to the neighbors' habitat, with both openings being the gateways for crawly things with an overabundance of feet.

And what about the cracked, chipped, linoleum floor tiles, the color of crushed hope, that curled up at the edges? The cabinet doors, which refused to open or close? But our landlord was deaf and blind to my demands—deaf and blind!—he was happy to do nothing. In truth I would be of a more pleasant disposition if he took care of the leaking bathroom ceiling first. Or this moldy corridor wall. Or…Let us face it—I hated this place. Let us face it—I hated this place for a very good reason. I sighed. What if I painted the kitchen walls myself to liven things up a bit, say, something soothing like a cool dusk blue or periwinkle surprise accented with goldfinch yellow—very French—instead of this yellowed-gray, tired landlord-white that was there now? Would that help? Or a robin's-egg blue, like Tiffany's? Timeless elegance. Hope you were not thinking about a chartreuse green, now were you? Or should I torch the place now and be done with it?

Indeed, I had to remember to keep my attention focused on the present for it was essential to stay focused. I watched Rita with great care, memorizing the way she mixed herbs to make me some super-healing tea, hoping to recall the complete recipe later on, though I had my doubts I would. Meanwhile, Adam, who dealt with his own set of issues, galloped into the kitchen in a cheerful sort of way. He froze for a second, bounced sideways on straight legs, his back arched, tail puffed up, then stopped, growled, and charged out of the room. Eve also participated in the group affair by peeking with one deep-blue eye into the overcrowded room while the rest of her was safe, hidden around the corner.

"Curiosity killed the cat," Patrick said.

She seemed satisfied with the results of the up-close inspection, for she gave him a look, but said nothing and trotted away. A second later we heard a sound not unlike the call of a ship lost in a fog—Eve had voiced her thoughts on the subject.

Rita poured boiling water over the mixture of herbs, covering the mug with a lid to encourage proper steeping of the brew. The fragrances of a summer night in the south of France transformed our kitchen into something agreeable for human habitation. They covered up without a trace the permanent smell of onions—onions and disappointment—that had been burned to a crisp ash that our neighbors loved so much, and that I refused to learn to appreciate. Fuhgeddaboudit!

No room for us to sit down, and since there was nothing else of importance to do in the kitchen, we returned to the living room single file in the same order we had left it, those of us who were humans burdened with a full mug of tea each, while Patrick, being the only gentleman, was also entrusted with a plate of chewy oatmeal-raisin cookies.

Patrick placed the plate on the coffee table in front of him, settled on the couch with a tea mug in his hand, and asked me, "How's your book coming along?" He took a top cookie from the pyramid on a plate and bit off the bigger half of it.

He read anything I wrote, being my biggest fan. A blessed balsam on the gashes of my tortured soul, but then the validity of his opinion was questionable.

"I'm stuck," I croaked. "What started as a romantic dramedy has developed into my magnum opus, all happening in the context of a disturbingly depressing historical background," I squeaked in a falsetto. My voice's modulations were typical for a boy going through puberty. "It's flawed and hopeless. That capricious muse of mine is too unpredictable. Hence, a problem."

He chewed with thoughtfulness. "So?"

"The problem is you're too critical of yourself." Rita was my voluntary self-esteem coach. She was good. "Let it go. Have a cookie while there're some left."

"Are those the latest?" Patrick shoved the rest of the gourmet-baked item into his mouth, jumped up to grab the stack of printed pages with handwritten notes near my computer. His eyes sparkled.

"Take them if you want," I wheezed. "But expect no miracles. And no spitting into my eye if you don't like them either. *Achoo!*"

"*Ve-eeh.*"

Patrick nodded and reached for the next treat. It was gone in an instant. He reached for another one. Nothing was said for a while.

"Both of you are so quiet today," I commented. "Wasn't there something you wanted to share with me? Rita? Patrick?"

"No." Rita shrugged her shoulders, avoiding looking at Patrick all of a sudden.

"No." Patrick popped the whole cookie into his mouth, shrugged his shoulders, not looking at Rita.

An awkward silence ensued.

"Ah," I screeched. "I see. I'm going to ignore this performance and proceed with interrogation anyhow. So why doesn't someone tell me about your visit to the adoption agency? Anyone? Looking for a volunteer."

They shook their heads, not facing one another, and not looking at me either.

"Aha," I rasped. "You can play at silence all you want later, but I feel I've waited long enough for you to offer the information, so I'm going to ask for it directly. Rita, how did it go?"

Rita's grin came out lopsided. "As the prospective daddy and mommy, we're very qualified, if that's what you're asking. And we can expect to have a baby within half a year."

"Oh, guys!" I squawked, not sure how to interpret the sourness of her facial expression. "I mean, that's wonderful news, isn't it?"

Patrick said nothing, but crossed his arms on his chest and looked away, out the window.

"Yes, under normal circumstances, sure," Rita said. "Imagine, a baby! What baby? Would I be willing to be a working, *married*, single mother—that's the real question. I watched you juggle. It was too painful to watch."

I opened my mouth to chime in. "*Achoo!* Look—"

"You can stop working anytime you want to," Patrick said. "I make enough money to support us."

"Why should I be the one to give up my career?" Rita asked. "You expect this of me when you're not even willing to consider giving up one of your own jobs?"

Patrick's face grew gloomy, as if he had been taken aback a little. "I'm only trying to provide the best for this family. Which job would you want me to give up?"

Rita's voice was firm. "You choose. I'll support your choice."

"I can't give up either one," Patrick said. "They're both important to me."

"Are you saying your career is more important than us?" Rita asked.

"Don't put words into my mouth," Patrick said. "You know that's not true. I'm merely having trouble picking one."

"Fine," Rita pressed. "Then I'll make the choice for you. Give up the hospital. You have your practice. Be happy."

"Will it make you happy?" Patrick asked.

"Absolutely," Rita said. "You'll work regular hours, I'll see you from time to time, and *that* will make me happy. Ask Anna how many times I've complained you're never home."

"*Harrumph*—" I wanted to oblige, but this was as far as I got. As if to prove her point, the pager chose this particular moment to buzz.

With a guilty face, Patrick took it off his belt, glanced at the small screen. "The hospital. Sorry, girls, I have to go. We'll have to finish this argument some other time. Soon, I promise. Anna, get better. I apologize for the shortness of the visit. Rita, I'll give you a lift if you're downstairs in five minutes. I'll go get the car." And with a hearty hug for me from his left hand while he reached for his cell phone with his right, he was off.

"I better go with him," Rita said. "This is the longest I've seen him this week. He spends his entire life in operating rooms. I'm not sure if I'm married or not. A baby. What baby? The man has time to cut people open and sew them back together, but the one person he doesn't have a minute for is me, much less the time to get a proper lunch for himself—none—so that I can stop worrying about his health so much. I know a lot of women who envy my good fortune of being married to such a successful man. Me? I'm two seconds away from having an affair, I swear. And with someone who'll have room in his schedule for both me and lunch."

While Rita's lips were smiling, her chin had begun to quiver. She pecked my cheek, rushed to turn away. Her voice reached from a flight down the stairs. "I'll call you later. Get better soon!"

For the next three days, I drank the fragrant concoction, savored each tea-spoon of honey, rubbed myself with smelly ointments. Between all of them, they killed the bug that bothered me. Killed it dead. On a late morning of day number four, Mother showed up to check on me.

"The carrot juice." Mother always believed what she said. "I told you it'd help if you drink it *in tiny gulps.*"

"Yes-sss, Mother."

six

as an incurable optimist, I am inclined to mostly see the good in people…until proven otherwise. I believe everyone is capable of reaching their highest potential as a human being, and this capacity—mysterious, locked away in the dark womb of the unconsciousness, waiting to be birthed—is a powerful magnet for me. Though imbued with a certain hopeful significance, see how much good this particular belief of mine has done me. The wellspring of this deep-rooted conviction is in no way an expected consequence of my upbringing and it presents a riddle; in fact, it appeared at some hazy point in time in spite of it.

On occasion my unfounded optimism would pay off, though disturbingly often, this promise of a person's greatness failed to realize itself. So sad. This situation repeated itself many a time, and I—what an egotist!—inundated with disappointment, but stubborn, persisted to have faith in the general goodness of humans, thus overburdening them beyond the natural boundaries of their endurance with my naïve (to the point of being obnoxious) expectations. This unfortunate tendency of mine might suggest a learning disability on my part. Ah, the heavy weight of the truth. Perhaps I should look into it, and soon.

Quite upset each time, but nonplussed to find myself kicked in the butt to a place, the same hopeless place, where I did not wish to be yet again—a beggar on the street of loneliness—I could not stop wondering what I had done to deserve all this. What could be done to avoid making the same mistake over and over—a worrisome possibility—to prevent such things from happening in the future, and what exactly such a solution might be? I mean, without my transformation into Mother's double and expecting the worst from people a priori. Perish the thought. The bona fide state of affairs was that an imperfect union between two willing spirits was a good place to be, and that striving for perfection was overrated anyhow. How does one measure perfection? I will ask it again, because it is so important: *how does one measure perfection?* Aiming for it in a relationship automatically brings conflict, and when one adds their own little insecurities to the mix…*ticktock.* One of those things that goes *ka-boom!* And carried off by the wind, only small pieces of ash will float off into the night.

According to some, it is no coincidence when a particular person is attracted into one's life, as if by osmosis, since a partner was supposed to help with the work of *recovering* from old wounds. And one should be appreciative of having the privilege to meet such people (if only a thimbleful of gratitude) what with them going out of their way to bring all those educational experiences into one's life. Me, I would not exactly call those pyrotechnics "a recovery." Misstep after misstep, I had made mistakes in the arena of love that became clear only in hindsight.

Oh, how easy it is to see things in retrospect! I would like to say something about it. A tendency to calculate risks or profits while falling in love was anathema to me. I maneuvered straight from one entrapment into another, bridling my heart, which happened a number of times and was like halting a wild mare at a gallop while I waited for some person's potential to manifest itself. At this point, what did it matter how close to reality those wonderful latent qualities were, or if they were only something I hungered for so much that they had become tangible to me? To what extent was I actually able to see through humans to their essence, or was this merely a product of my imagination, the result of projecting myself onto existing people and situations? No, I am not mentally challenged. Not that I know of.

Without embarking on a full-scale recollection, allow me to briefly allude to the point—and why should I not admit this?—that all of the times I had been drawn to my future boyfriends, with their mostly fictive qualities, there had always been a steaming physical attraction, allied with some indication of this illusive power. For me, who never expected to walk a path of love carpeted with pale rose petals and accompanied by crying violins, this explosive concoction had been enough reason to get involved with these men. Did I love them? No, I loved them not (except for one). The magic of falling in love did not always flow without friction into the pain and suffering of falling out of love, with nothing worth mentioning in between. From hope to heartbreak, and heartbreak is heartbreak. Awful, even the predictable ones. And then I would spiral into a post-breakup depression—always.

In the very beginning, the sheer strength of such magnetism looked like a force powerful enough to surmount the obstacles in its way. Given a reasonable chance, it could have grown into love someday—who knew? The utter power of love, *n'est-ce pas? Oui, oui, l'amour.* A certain chain of events would have already been set off, and perhaps not the best idea in many respects—we would manage to move in together. Ah, but not *every* time. And it was mostly them moving in with me. I have no explanation for that, at least none that makes sense.

Though with the passage of time, the physical allure would lose its gravitational pull and fade away. The love well had never been filled up enough with tender and deep affections and had since dried up. The character flaws, which a short while ago had been innocent little habits, trivial in themselves, grew out of proportion, more annoying than adorable (however minor at the outset), turned into a giant squid wriggling in the dark, blotting out the sun, blocking the sky. The very differences that played an enormous part during the falling-in-love process now turned into a huge liability, a source of constant irritation and repulsion that did not help the relationship in any way. They would drive us both crazy and push us further apart. And again I would feel corralled like a horse. With each passing moment we would fall more out of love, and soon there would be nothing shared at all, nothing left to anchor us together, not a thread. The relationship would go sour and collapse in on itself. One would think that might teach me something.

According to my last therapist, I have been choosing the wrong mates for years to recreate in full the emotional deprivation I experienced as a child. And something about a fear of intimacy was thrown in there too. If such a disclosure was indeed the truth of the matter, one hardly needed to dwell on an entire new world of catastrophic alternatives opening up with these sorts of revelations popping up. Life is serious business.

Changing my therapist changed nothing about all of this and was not worth the trouble. Besides, I liked my current one, Alison. She was comfortable and comforting. We had a well-established routine—ah, blessed, meaningful sameness!—which took on a soothing rhythm. It gave me a nice feeling that everything was in order, everything secure, under control. I would like to add here—nothing derogatory implied—that while she was counseling me on my ever-dysfunctional relationships with the opposite sex, Madame Psychologist had gone through her own divorce with that fourth bastard of a husband of hers, a distinguished-looking gentleman with a white goatee, clad in dark clothes. The divorce came about after she showed up tipsy at some fundraiser dinner along with a buff, younger-looking gentleman who had his hand in the small of her back and introduced him as her fiancé. This came as a surprise to her longstanding husband, and he became rather prickly.

Ah, but Alison was also the one who insisted that the individual subconscious was but a part of the universal subjective mind, borrowed for individual use. How can one not respect such wisdom? As for me, I entrusted the precious health of my psyche to her. I will miss her. This emotional deprivation thing (without indulging in any further speculation than was absolutely necessary) turned out to be a powerful addiction, stirring the blood. Here be dragons. Fire-breathing dragons. Perhaps one can understand my growing excitement—those addictions would have to be vanquished at some feasible point in time, through a whole chain of brilliant but bloody battles, all while treading the path of healing toward the bright future. Considering the persistent residue of my ever-present bewilderment about the whole undertaking, I remain suspicious about how exactly this healing thing will be accomplished, and when.

I was grateful that Alison had done her best in taking me apart to put me back together again, though she did talk a lot. "You believe yourself undeserving of love," she had said. Familiar and homelike, like a pair of old slippers, this categorical statement was not devoid of verity. Alison had also said that, all things considered, the day would come when my attitude would shift from "Is he going to like me?" to "He is lucky to have me," or something to that effect. Imagine—that would be quite a change. While experiencing exhilaration mixed with a certain understandable amount of unease—why should I find the whole idea so daunting?—I reflected that I was a good catch, such a rare bird as myself! Though perhaps immodest, it did sound wonderful, did not it?

As Henry Miller said, "The one thing we can never get enough of is love. And the one thing we never give enough is love." With this short word *love* as the precious talisman pointing the way (call me an unrealistic romantic, which is in no way a deviation from the norm for a mentally healthy female of the *Homo sapiens* species), somewhere deep inside I was hopeful. I would have to dig for it, dig, dig, dig. I had nothing against that one day I would meet a man who would combine the good qualities of all my previous companions into one person—the fortunate amalgam of intellect and kindness, with a sense of humor and beauty. Economic stability would not hurt either. Ah, but it was a lovely dream. Perhaps I would be able to love once again with my whole heart, my whole being, and my life would change forever. What a marvelously delicious destination it was!

seven

Who is it?"

She took a long time to look through the peephole. *My God, she's right,* I thought when I heard a prolonged metallic scratch as Mrs. Goldfarb struggled to unfasten the third door chain. The door opened just enough for me to glimpse a dusty silk African violet on a small entrance table with a tattered tablecloth and plastic doily, yellowed with age, and the right half of a woman in a pink housecoat, knee socks, and pink slippers, the synthetic fur rubbed thin in places. In her long velvet robe despite the summer heat, she peeked out from behind the door with a cautious assessment and seemed startled to see me, though every day I left a newspaper at her door when I was done with it—our morning ritual. On the days I went food shopping, I rang her bell. Through the thin mess of white fuzz under the fine hairnet she wore, her pink scalp was visible, the left side of her bangs pulled tight in one big curler. At the age of eighty-seven, her movements were slow and labored. As always, she wore too much perfume.

"Good morning, Mrs. Goldfarb." I handed her the *New York Times* and a stack of quarters for the laundry room in the basement (two coin-operated washing machines, one always broken). "I'm heading to the store. Do you need anything?"

She grabbed my arm. "Have you heard? Mr. Schultz was attacked yesterday afternoon in our elevator. From *6C*? A bullet-shaped head?" She spoke with a slight lisp and a Yiddish lilt.

"How horrible!" Mr. Schultz? I had not even known his name until now.

"An old man—he can barely walk. He returned from the hospital with stitches and a nasty bump on his head. What is the world coming to?" She clucked her tongue. "His wallet was taken, with five dollars and all his food stamps in it. How is he going to eat? Since my Ira died, I haven't slept a wink, I feel so unsafe. In this apartment for thirty-nine years, and what should I do now? My sister, Edna—God bless her soul—wants me to move to Florida to be near her. What would I do in Florida? *Pfui.*" She flapped her wrist, flicking away the possibility, sighed, pointed to her left.

"My poor Ira died of a heart attack seven years ago on the floor of this bathroom, and I took a sleeping pill and slept right through it. I found him the next morning. He was a character, my Ira, but I loved him. He was mine." She hugged herself as if a sudden draft had brought an autumn chill into the July day. "This morning I asked Ira to come and get me. What's the point of my silly life? He answered. 'Bernice,' he said, 'Bernice, it's not your time yet. Have a little patience.'" Her lips formed a smile over her slightly protruding teeth. "Do I have any choice? Go, Anna, go do your thing. Don't worry about me."

With only a few customers in Key Food, the shopping did not take long. My first Pilates client for today had been canceled, which was bad since we needed the money—always—but it gave me an hour to make lasagna to freeze for later. Ground beef was on sale this week.

I dropped the shopping bags on the kitchen counter, filled the biggest pot with water, put it on the stove, and remembered that Hannah, my sleepyhead daughter, wanted to learn how to make lasagna. I knocked on her door. Silence and more silence. Almost nine. When had she gotten home yesterday? I had not heard her come in. The school was over, the prom with its prom-dress drama behind us. She had been miserable all last week, brooding on something. I had no idea what. How well do we know our children? How open are they with us? I tried so hard to know, to understand.

I opened the door to her room. The bed had not been slept in. I called Hannah's cell. Voicemail. Then Daniel's. Voicemail too. I called her girlfriends.

"Do you know where Hannah is?"

I got the uniform "No, Ms. D." I tried Hannah's cell again. A knock on the entrance door made me jump—a mailman brought a small package. The smell of Mrs. Goldfarb's heavy perfume was still in the hallway air. I called the police only to hear "In a missing persons case, we won't file a report for twenty-four hours." I felt a flicker of dread. Did she run away? I did. Many times. But why would Hannah? *Please call*, I thought. The phone remained silent. A terrible thing to wait for a call. I kept dropping things, could not think straight, ignored all other sounds, longing for that small ring, messed up all five training sessions with clients, and when it was over, tired, escaped to the kitchen.

The moon, stupid and pale and shriveled, hovered low over the building across the street. Dicing and mixing always calmed my thinking—nothing as calming as stirring a bubbling sauce—and the kitchen filled with the smells of a happy home, safe and sound, as if I created and maintained a fiction that everything was fine, everything would be, our troubled lives so simple and secure and sane.

The call came at nine in the evening when I was scrubbing the last baking pan.

"Maaa-ma, I'm with Daniel." Hannah slurred her words. "We took his aun-

tie's car. I bet she reported it sto-oolen. But his darling father is a bigger asshole.
O-ooh, yeee-ah. He gave us twenty dollars for lunch and gasoline to get back to
New—Hey! Wrong exit! Hooey!"

She sounded stoned. The thought of Hannah being in danger made me sick
to my stomach. "Where are you? Are you in Cleveland? Hannah?"

The call dropped. I was left with the phone in my hand, shaking, feeling the
sting of tears in my eyes. The phone rang again. I pressed *talk*.

"Oh thank God!" I said. "Where are you?"

"Anna!" My ex, the love of my life, barked it as an order, and the juggernaut
way he said my name sent a tremor of horror through me. I felt like a prisoner facing a firing squad. I used to love the sound of his voice, a long time ago. "Anna!"

My stomach slowly turned as I dried my hands on a dish towel. The front of
my apron was covered with tomato sauce and suds. I felt old and worn and sad.

"I'm kind of busy," I said, trying to keep my voice even. "What do you want?"

"How is your mother?" Sergey asked.

Oh, we are going to be polite. I used to be married to you. You never cared
about my mother. Or anything else beside yourself.

"Sergey...how are you?"

"I'm getting married."

"Congratulations." I almost meant it and forced as much polite sincerity into
my voice as I could muster. My voice sounded more despondent than I anticipated.

"Don't expect an invitation."

"I won't," I said.

"My swallow, why are you hostile?"

I was the aggressor? I hated when he did this, this tone of his—show no
mercy and spare no enemy. I felt like an unloved ex-wife, which I was. His remark
had nothing to do with hostility. It was about the pecking order. Fifteen years,
and yet the ghost of our marriage was still here with us, like a faithful dog. Old
habits die hard. Nothing changed. He had no heart.

"Hannah called," he continued in the same grim tone. "Drunk. You and your
unconventional ideas about upbringing. Dorothy says you're neglecting Hannah."

And as always, Mother could be blamed for everything. Now this was unfair.
How it was my fault that I had not raised Hannah right. I knew he would say
that. The son of a bitch.

"Is that so?" I smiled, shaking my head and managing to suppress a swelling
of nausea. I smiled as I had smiled all the time when we were married.

"Who's Billy?"

"No idea. Who's Billy?"

"You don't know who your daughter is dating? Dorothy says he's a loser."

I pictured his girlfriend, the insufferable Dorothy, with a throaty laugh. Both he and his Dorothy could rot in hell.

"He might as well be." I felt my hands curling into fists. "Whoever he is."

"Dorothy says he's after Hannah's money."

God, I hated arguing. The anger scrambled my thoughts. "And what money would that be? Sergey, your Dorothy is gold. Pure gold...Ask her to check her sources better."

"What? Do you let Hannah drink?"

I smelled something burning. Lasagna! The last batch was still in the oven.

"Shit!" I pressed the phone to my ear with my shoulder, shoved each hand into a red mitt, and pulled open the oven door. "Shit, shit, shit!" I fanned the thick smoke away from my face, grabbed the pan, and dropped it on top of the stove. The kitchen smelled of burnt Italian sausage and oregano.

"Sergey, you've made me see the error of my ways. By the way, you didn't send a check this month." And though I had this nagging feeling I was plunging across a great divide toward big trouble, I stood up a little straighter, picked up a stray piece of carrot from the kitchen counter, and popped it into my mouth. My heart raced at a ridiculous pace.

"What?" He paused. "Are you making fun of me? Everything is funny in Annaland. Forget it. Hannah was accepted to NYU? How much is the tuition there? I'll tell you what—you'll love this—I'll pay for her education if she gets away from you, say, to London. I don't want you anywhere near her. I won't reconsider even if you get on your knees and beg me."

A pause followed the stinging echo of his words. I let the uncomfortable silence stretch, which I knew he would interpret as an admission of guilt. I felt gutted. The anger arrived quickly. It flared, pulsed through me. I shook my fist in the air, started to protest, and then thought, *Twenty-five thousand dollars a semester?* Hannah would not have to pay out her student loan? Away from me? Ah, but also away from our beloved Dorothy and her big mouth.

"Fine." My heart hardened against the thought. "Are you done yelling at me?"

He was quiet for a moment. I bet he had expected an argument.

"You're an incompetent mother," he said.

"Funny you should say that. Where have *you* been all Hannah's life? And now e-mailing once in a while proves the effectiveness of your daddyhood and puts you in a position to criticize."

"Dorothy and I asked her to move in with us. When was it? A year ago? I wonder why she never told you about it."

Because she loves me, you snickering moron, and does not want to hurt me, my sweet Hannah. But he would not understand that.

"She swears like a sailor," he said. "That's your influence. She's motherless."

"This is becoming absurd."

"She's living with a crazy woman who goes to a psychiatrist. You're dangerous!"

For reasons best known to him, I assumed he felt he had a right to expect that the regular rules of social intercourse did not apply to him. I was no more than a thing, an irritating thing that still belonged to him, and who dared to want something that clashed with his wishes. My anger flowered again.

Steady, I told myself. We have been here before. He did not like the way I had smiled at him—he stopped paying child support. So what! It only covered one-fifth of the rent, and he would stop it in a month anyhow. But angry with me, he had taken it out on Hannah, a hostage caught in our bitter wars, a ghostly bond. And guess who would regret it later on? Another lesson learned. But people endure things and endure things, accumulating too many scars.

"A psychologist. What of it?"

"Quiet! Go…go work as a waitress!" he said. "It'll cure you fast enough."

We were not in the same room. He could not hit me anymore with his fist, but he could get me with words, and he looked for the most hurtful way. The more powerless he felt, the harsher his words became. Something inside me welled up, not unlike pity for the sad sod he was, though at the moment I was not opposed to the idea of smacking the vast expanse of his face.

"It's late," I said. "Let's continue with this conversation some other time. And please send the check. Goodnight."

He slammed the receiver down. *Hasta la vista!*

I was tired of being mad at him, and reeling with both guilt and anger. I had never asked him for anything. The girl's presence had always been an incessant thorn in his side. Damn him. Life's exigencies never end. They had asked Hannah to move in with them, and she had declined? Was it true? Was it true—would he pay Hannah's tuition, or had he only said it to get to me? I could not remember anything involving him and generosity. On my birthday he would drop a ten on the kitchen counter. "Buy yourself a pretty dress."

Nor had he been a doting father, involved in his daughter's life, not when we were married, even less so when we went through a divorce. In the beginning stages, Sergey would come to visit Hannah: he would eat lunch, then lie down for a nap for a few hours, while the little girl had to stay quiet so her daddy could sleep. I would have to wake him up at six so he would not be late for his date that evening. Why did I do that? In hope that there was a human being in there somewhere—a cold, intolerant man, but still a human being. Never pays to be nice in a divorce. I nodded my head.

The couple upstairs was bickering again. A man's voice yelled, "Doris!" as if it were a warning. I could hear him hacking up phlegm, then again, "Doris!" Something heavy slammed against a wall. A female voice shrieked. Not ten minutes later, the bedsprings would begin to groan and creak and squeak and moan, accompanied by a few generous farts.

I had made a lot of lasagna, six aluminum dishes. I looked in the packed freezer—no more room. Not enough cheese to grate on top, but I was afraid to go buy some and miss the phone call when it came. *Later,* I thought, and closed the fridge door. It was so like me to marry a jerk, to have a child with him and want to have more. Something must be done to protect myself from my own idiocy, but what?

I took a bite from my plate and grimaced. This lasagna tasted vile. I spat it out in the sink. Cats meowed. I looked down. The plate with my burned dinner was on the floor, the bowl full of cat food in my hand. Ah, well…I was not hungry anyhow.

I switched off the light and was about to leave the kitchen, but lowered myself on the chair instead. My back ached. I sat in the soft, formless darkness, pummeled with memories and regrets, listening to the intermittent drip of the faucet into the sink. How I wished I could treat those inconvenient memories as something disposable as a used diaper and keep only those which suffused my heart with a warming glow. A mosquito buzzed by my ear, giving out a high-pitched drone like an incoming aircraft.

Tonight was full of emptiness. A small surge of an old feeling, and my mind had raced and raced, dark and structureless and bad. The past could not be erased, shed, and left behind, like a snake's dry skin between the rocks. Why had not I left him? I hoped he would realize how wrong he was and change. I washed, cleaned, and waited on him, obeyed without a word, so undemanding, content with crumbs of attention and the miserly sums that were allotted for food for Hannah and myself. An angry man who was used to having things done for him, he had found a fool of a woman who asked for nothing and endured everything. I bet he had thought he had a right to expect it too. I felt empty. I felt unclean, day after day.

An invisible mosquito circled and circled my head. It buzzed and buzzed. I switched on the light again. Too bright. I squinted and tried to read. I read the same sentence over and over, but the words on the page made no sense. By one o'clock I had started the laundry because I could not sit still. But everything comes to an end, and after two loads I was done.

eight

i lay on the foldout couch, waiting for sleep. Sleep did not come. My mind raced, filled with a thousand shadowy things that made no sense but demanded attention, as if they were dangerous secrets never meant to be shared, but were on the brink of being exposed. Adam pushed his muzzle into my palm, licked my fingers, curled up at my side. The endless night hung over me as the sword of Damocles, with no relief, no escape, no last-minute reprieve. I kept drifting off and on the edge of unconsciousness, jolting awake again. In the end, I simply lay there until the sky lightened a little.

I turned over, looked at the clock. It was just after five. I got up, paced nervously, stubbed my toe, and hopped on one foot, swearing like a sailor.

The dark apartment was too confining, the waiting intolerable. If I did not get out of here I would explode. Air. I needed air.

I stopped at the all-night supermarket to buy cheese for lasagna. A lot of people were here at this hour, everyone in dark clothes. The tired, unsmiling people pushed their carts. I found myself in front of the freezer, staring at the boxes of veggie burgers I used to buy when Hannah became vegan in the ninth grade. My fingers snapped and unsnapped the clasp of a wallet in my pocket. Tears rolled down my face—when had they started? I wiped my eyes and went out.

I walked to the park, feeling strangely light despite the tug of fatigue. I looked at the sky the color of washed-out gray and inhaled the fresh morning air. A new day stretched before me. How privileged I was to be alive! The dark wall of trees, indifferent and eternal, silhouetted against the brightening sky. A police cruiser passed by as it did every night at about the same time, circled around the large flowerbed at the entrance to the park, and went down a side road, its tires rustling on the asphalt, its headlights useless in the perky light of dawn. The sun was low, and between the long shadows of tall pines, the grasses glistened, drenched with dew. The bees were out, weaving a secret net with their passes and making an awful noise in a flowery air. A little Pomeranian ran up to me, put its front paws against my knees, emitting a loud squeak of excitement. I squatted down to pet it. It licked my chin. The owner tugged on the leash, and the Pomeranian left, looking punished, glancing back.

I sat down on a bench. A squirrel darted across the path, climbed up, and sat near me. It shook its scruffy tail with fur missing in spots and jerked its front paws in short rapid twitches and squawked and squealed, demanding food.

Sergey. I tasted blood in my mouth again. The distant memory seeped into awareness slowly, like sands through an hourglass. I felt sick, and the crisp air became the thin air of a mountain. "He hits you, therefore he loves you," it is said in Russia. He did not hit me the first time. He had come home late in the evening, thrown his boxy attaché case on the floor at the entrance, stomped into the kitchen. His nose twitched, smelling the air.

"What the fuck!" He had grabbed me by the hair and pushed me down. "I work all day," he had said, looking at me from above, a wild light flaring in his eyes, "and I'm tired and hungry. You said you'll cook borscht, and what is this?"

And another time he had pushed me down, and another. He criticized the food I cooked after he had eaten everything on his plate and taken seconds. Sometimes he would appear behind me, grab my wrists, and press me into a wall, sweating and shaking and breathing hard.

When I was nineteen weeks pregnant with our second child, I had been doing dishes in the kitchen one evening. Sergey was watching a soccer game on TV in the living room, whooping and bawling and cursing.

"Get me another beer," he yelled.

"Get it yourself."

"Did you hear what I just said? Get me a beer."

"I heard you. Get it yourself."

Sergey walked into the kitchen, his head down, his eyes muddy. He glared at me under his brows, clutched me by the shoulders, and shook me.

"You do what I tell you to do."

I was trapped against the refrigerator. "Why?" I asked.

He hit me, his fist across my eye. I stumbled, hitting the wall. The pain shot through my left side.

I put a hand to my cheek, and my hand came away with blood on it. I staggered backward, clenched my teeth, righted myself, and covered my belly with my both arms, in a violent panic that he would harm the unborn.

He grabbed my wrist. I wrenched my arm away, ran to the bathroom, flinging a chair behind me to slow him down, and locked the door.

My knees gave out. I slid down the wall to the floor, trembling and breathless.

He did not follow me. He stayed in the hallway.

"I'm sorry I hit you, honey," he said, his voice deceptively sweet. "I love you. I didn't mean to hit you. I'm sorry. You provoked me. Honey?" Sergey made an indistinct noise in the back of his throat.

I pulled myself off the floor, holding on to the edge of the sink. The water pipes groaned and roared. My head throbbed. I blinked back tears, sat on the edge of the bathtub, staring into space and trembling. The pain bored through my belly.

"I know you're sorry," I said. "I know. Don't wake up Hannah." Our eighteen-month-old was asleep in the crib. A trickle of blood ran down the side of the tub, and I began to cry from the searing pain and a wave of self-pity and all the unavenged humiliations and for my lost child and for my lost marriage. I never asked if it was a boy or a girl.

Why did I stay? What made me behave as if nothing had happened, as if it was all going to come together, one big convincing lie? The scared person inside, the muddled decision point. From the sound of it, with these layers upon layers of misery, it may seem as if I was a morbid masochist. The truth was simpler. I could not say no to him. Could not say no to him for a whole year, a year of a hodgepodge of confusion and fear and trying to hold on to my very small shred of dignity. Two months later he hit me again. I told myself I would not wait till the next time, I would leave. I hated him, despised myself, and stayed. I had a choice in this world and stayed because of Hannah, as if this were the lesser of two evils; I knew how it felt to be fatherless.

How stupid and weak I was. Sergey did not care about Hannah. He never hit me again after that, yet I waited for it to happen. Terrified of him, with the simmering danger wrapped around my neck as a noose, I always leaned a little backward when he reached for me or came close. He never noticed. The present shrank. I felt like I was falling. I never stopped falling, living a half-life. And I still could not imagine my days without him. *It'll get better,* I thought. *You get used to circumstances.* Like so many things on this earth, there was no explaining it. All my senses dulled, I stayed for a year and left when I saw the look in his eyes—the same look he had when he hit me. It was back. I loved him a little less each day, and how could I ever forgive him for losing my baby?

I remembered that too. The blurry recollection swung into a sharp focus. The poisonous weight of it crushed down on me. If before I would let my mind drop a curtain over it, perhaps now I could tend to this fracture that still hurt, to transmute and dissolve it without fright of being banished to the shadows, never to return. I thought of my lost child and shivered. My pulse quickened. The nausea passed, and my vision cleared. How much time went by, I do not know.

Three long white limos sailed to the park's entrance and deposited a small, loud crowd in festive clothing. The breeze picked up, pressing long skirts to the backs of legs, outlining bottoms and demolishing stiff, complex creations on women's heads. Hands went up, holding on to the hats with silk flowers and colorful ribbons. The bride laughed hysterically, and the groom tried to bring her veil under control as it flapped in the wind. Little girls in pink clouds of lace held on to bouquets that were torn apart, and a whirling snowstorm of pink petals blanketed the pavement. An entire bouquet was ripped out of one girl's hands. She began to cry.

■ ■ ■

Hannah was home. She saw me, wound her hair around her hand, and tied it into a knot at her neck. Then she let her hands drop, and they hung helplessly alongside her body.

"How long was the drive?" I asked.

"Eight hours." Her nervous hands went up again, let down her hair, rearranged it into the same exact bun she had just taken apart. There were dark circles under her eyes.

"Did you take your vitamins today?"

She nodded. "Did he call you?" she asked.

"He did." I reached out, touched her hair. "We're having lasagna for dinner."

"Dorothy is pregnant. Did he tell you? Are you all right with that?"

"Not my problem." I opened the fridge. "You have to eat something."

"I'm not hungry." She glanced at my face. "I'll make myself a sandwich. Don't worry."

I watched her make a turkey sandwich, the vegan years behind us. She stood looking at her creation for several minutes.

"Bite." I snapped my teeth together twice.

Hannah took a delicate bite—nibbled, like a small, melancholy mouse. *Is she becoming anorexic?* I wondered.

She chewed thoughtfully for a few seconds. "Dorothy made everyone believe we were close friends." She put her sandwich down on her plate and wiped her fingers on the napkin. "And now she doesn't answer my e-mails or pick up the phone."

"And your father?"

"Oh." She flinched, her upper lip trembling. "Him." She reached for a tissue, blew her nose. "Sometimes he e-mails me a lot, and sometimes it feels like he forgets about me."

"So, so sorry. About London—"

"He wants to drive us apart."

"If the only factor guaranteeing our closeness is physical proximity, he had already won. Go, make the most of it. Go to King's. It's the opportunity of a lifetime—a great city and a good college. Let him pay for it. Andrew studies architecture in London, and his mom is there too. They'll look after you. I wish I had a chance like that."

"What about you?" she asked.

"I'm fine. Go get ready to be whomever you're going to become."

My words caught in my throat. The empty nest. I was terrified thinking about it. What was wrong with me? Now repeat after me: the empty nest is freedom. The empty nest invigorates women. I would have plenty of time to crochet. God, I would miss her!

Hannah put her arms around my waist and laid her head on my shoulder. We stood there silently, savoring the moment of unspoken understandings. Life was full of them.

She kissed my cheek. "Money makes the world go round."

"Yes?" I said. "And?"

"Beggars can't be choosers," she grunted in a noncommittal way.

"Life is hard. Look around you. Can we afford college? I'm grateful he's willing to pay. It's your chance. Grab it. Get a Eurail pass, see the world."

"He's talking out of his ass—he always does. Don't listen to him. I don't have to go, Mama."

"Yes, you do. Your life is waiting. Go."

"Mama—"

"Go!"

"I'll go, but do me a favor. Move into my room. You can sleep in the bed. Will you?"

"The second you're out that door."

"Ya think?" She laughed. "See, it's good that I'm going away, right?"

"Absolutely."

"And find yourself a good man. Promise me you'll at least try."

I smiled, nodded, pressed her to my chest, kissed the top of her head. In a minute there was the sound of the shower running. My heart sank. The place was beginning to feel empty.

hannah was right. While I would regretfully ponder the decisions I had made in the past, these decisions not inconsequential, I could not keep skimming along life's surface and letting my past fiascos scare me away from finding love. To cushion the blow of loneliness inevitable with the oncoming empty nest (these words made my mouth scrunch up like I had bitten into the whole lemon) and to honor my promise to Hannah, not long after the spectacular mess with Alex, I was about to try again.

But guidelines would have to be established beforehand and then reiterated a few million times. Say, settling for less was no option (when greater things were at stake), as entertaining as it was this settling had laid at the heart of a majority of my prior actions. I planned to do my best not to mistake the superficial for the essence, to keep levelheaded in my choices, and to not go gaga at the first cute face or whatever. Please stop laughing and keep your fingers crossed. It could happen. If I was to face no recurrent frustrations in the future, I should stick, stick, stick to the new rules. Stick, stick.

The sum of my past actions had brought me no closer to the happiness I desired, so I might as well try something else instead, and, as an experienced general in preparation for a battle, examine all possible angles. The landscape was still Martian—or was it Venusian?—but by getting in a proper pioneering spirit, with my determination unwavering, and resolving to stay undaunted by the undertaking, perhaps some hazards could be foreseen and avoided. If there were any justice in the world, now would be a good time for the God-smiling-upon-me moment. In the pit of my gut, I felt something extraordinary impending.

In all seriousness, was marriage something I might care for in the future? A union of opposites? For years all I ever wanted was to be happy in a traditional sort of way. An ordinary life, what the vast majority of people might find desirable: A husband (please notice the singular), children (yay!—plural), a place to call home, and a dog (maybe). Why did it often feel as if I chased the tail of a rainbow? Life was phenomenally confusing, hardly without its burdens, yet in periods stimulating. Some women had no trouble finding a good man—and it was tragic that I did not belong to that lucky group. And by "a good man," I meant that as long as the relationship had certain fundamental understandings between the partners, I would find it to be satisfactory.

How fortunate—we were in the computer age. The Internet this, the Internet that, which I heard was marvelous at bringing people together. If I would not go to bars, why not the Internet, the unavoidable tool, to rescue my situation? The whole world at my fingertips, yes? The miracle of all miracles. How thrilling. But first, in the shimmering haze of my excitement over the multitude of possibilities, I would have to learn to navigate the treacherous waters of popular dating sites. It made me wonder if it was customary to offer a sacrifice to the Internet gods—may they smile upon me and my children and my children's children!—before embarking upon this perilous voyage. If so, then would not following tradition be considered a form of fateful negligence, and would the offering have to be a virgin?

Oh to hell with it. *Start small*, I reasoned, feeling a new resolve, *then go global. Go ahead, live your life.* It did not have to end up in yet another disaster. As it was pointless to analyze things to such an unreasonable extent, after much hesitation, thus reflecting my unease, and talking to myself for some long minutes, I posted a profile on a popular dating site. Please think good thoughts. But we cannot always have what we want, I am sorry to say. Even if I had been feeling optimistic, this optimism was premature.

While probing the waters, I heard rumors how trendy it was in the present climate of our changing times for married men to look for innocent gay sex online, a rather unsettling development to learn about. How could one manage to keep up with all these innovations and avoid some prolonged moments of strangeness? I understood there would be a few compromises and inevitable adjustments of expectations during the transitional period. You may be amazed how reasonable I can be at times. As if to contradict the whole fabric of logic just for the sake of contradiction, the second and third glimpses into the dating scene brought no desired clarity to the picture, which looked forbidding, and the murkiness acquired a more sinister hue.

After the initial excitement wore off, I felt more confident in deciding whom I wanted to go out on a date with and the cases where I should not even bother. From the list of contenders, I picked a few that sounded promising enough. Though being a woman on the eve of turning forty myself and feeling a little like a dodo, how choosy could I afford to be? Right. A week later, after a number of e-mails had been back and forth, sensibly playing it safe, a satisfactory (within reason) amount of information had been exchanged, and some points of shared interests and values had been loosely established. I considered myself ready to meet the candidates face-to-face in public places. I lit a pink candle, said a short prayer for Cupid's aim to not to be too off the mark, and placed a pink Japanese love cat in my relationship corner as reinforcement. Look out, world!

So there I was, standing at the bar in an overdecorated Italian restaurant on the Upper East Side, expecting to meet a man five foot eleven and 190 pounds, as per the numbers stated in his personal profile. Yes, here I was, but my date was fashionably late. There was another, quite real possibility that he had already come in, disliked what he saw, and left. I had heard rumors of such instances. I would have rather not found myself in such a predicament, thank you. I was about to go away, but a promise was a promise. I had no choice. Then a purple-faced guy rushed in and more or less jumped on top of me. The good news was that my date was here at last, shaking my hand with vigor.

"Hi, I'm Roger." Well, I thought this guy was my date. The place seemed to be correct. The name seemed to be correct. The time seemed to be almost correct. I was looking from above at this Roger from my height of five foot four, thinking, *Huh?* Whatever he lacked in height he more than compensated for in width. When did he think I would notice the discrepancy in numbers? Had he thought it would be like a foot in a door or something? Not the subtlest of strategies.

All right, looks were not everything, never judge a book by its cover, we all knew these things. He had lied a little, but still he could be a caring person with a great sense of humor. *Give a guy a chance*, I thought.

A hundred mildly pornographic sentences later (all of which would have sounded better in French) that began with "I" and revolved around his innumerable successes in bed with predominantly filthy-rich women, though he himself was on the verge of being a tycoon, he asked to borrow money from me. I decided to be impolite, call it quits, and go home, too hungry to wait for a miracle to happen. Perhaps next time. One had to keep hope alive, right? I went home hungry but laughing about the evening. How did I manage to bring it upon myself? How?

Two evenings later I still sort of laughed when I met Warren, an eye surgeon with ridiculously thick eyeglasses that made his eyes appear enlarged and distorted. Impossible to say why the eyewear had not been featured on the picture he had sent me. And he was about ten years older in real life, perhaps twenty. Why someone would take the trouble to behave in such a way was beyond me. When did telling the truth become unfashionable? Was it something I might expect to encounter all the time from now on? Talk about adaptation!

Warren spoke little, but nodded a lot—what an adorable bubblehead, even if he was a bit frumpy. All right, a lot frumpy. This fact itself, though somewhat important, hardly took the highest priority for the moment. There were more consequential matters for me to contend with—namely, how long I would be able to keep up a monologue without getting more than a nod or a monosyllable in return, and, having my primary issues crossed, whether or not I might stumble upon a subject of conversation we would both be interested in participating in, and, if possible, at the same time.

He did not react to direct questions like "Where did you go to school?"—disproving my theory that geography was a neutral enough subject to discuss on a first date without it feeling like I was mounting a full-scale interrogation. It also subtly showed me as someone who is capable of taking interest in a fellow human instead of being self-absorbed, and *en passant*, it was a fine opening line too. So many advantages at once. It was easier to work with a theory that had already been proven to be true. Odds were I was wrong, as had been the case with many of my other theories. I noticed he looked bored. It was not going well.

Twenty minutes later I had beaten my personal record in reciting monologues and, as if possessed by a supernatural force, went a bit over and was about to give up. How was it possible I had been so off? Who had been answering my e-mails? Clearly not Warren himself. Besides "hello" in the beginning, he had uttered no other sound. A ghostwriter then. Could I meet him instead? I sighed. I ought to let go of my high hopes for Warren to be the sort of person who wrote poetry on occasion. Nurturing such hopes was plain silly.

But wait! Warren spoke. I could now stop wondering about the monologue issue—excellent!—only to wonder instead whether I had been the one who had somehow unknowingly encouraged him to divulge his most personal secrets, for how had we managed to get into the graphic description on the colonics procedure he had undergone last week? The effect of the story on me was close to what I imagined a terrified deer might feel about his physical reality in fast-approaching headlights, its cold-white eyes glowing, say, a bit on a paralyzed side of things, which could present a problem. There was also the all-important, urgent question of how long I would stay stunned, and how soon I would be able to get rid of the vivid picture monopolizing my brain activity in both hemispheres. I had no idea how on earth to make it go away.

Call me old-fashioned, but this was not what I expected to hear on the first date…perhaps on the second or third when we had gotten to know one another better, after we had established a list of immediate family members, or some geographical facts…or never. How dreary. But I have to give it to Warren—he was honest about his personal experience, which brings us back to the matter that now I knew more about him than I ever needed to know. Question was, where did we go from there? I would be going home. I had plenty of time to laugh at myself later on.

In a few nights, it was a guy with a sleazy shimmer of unveiled indifference in his eyes and ten thousand hands, with nine thousand nine hundred and ninety-six of them on my physical body. Boy do I know how to pick them!

"Please explain to me what's wrong with you women," he said with a nervous lick of his lips, confiding in me, looking for sympathy while he pawed my knee. "And what's with this sense of humor? Why do they want me to be funny?"

Just curious: should I have told him I was one of those unreasonable women? For that matter, as Napoleon Bonaparte said, "A woman laughing is a woman conquered."

So I had my heart set on romance, but life, alas, had other plans. What I found troubling throughout the whole undertaking was how little I could say to these strangers, hearing myself mumble, "Yeah, ha-ha, yeah, totally." And what about making contact on the level of souls, then? I went on a few more dates that were so unimaginably boring I will not even mention them here, making those three the ones that stood out enough to stick with me for a bit, even if it was the sort of memory not to last me more than a week, to eventually morph into an ominous and amorphous something to return and haunt me in my sleep as any other self-respecting bad dream would.

What had I gotten myself into? Might I be in need of a rehabilitation program afterward? Like a twelve-step ongoing recovery program at Desperate Singles Anonymous, which must exist somewhere, for the next twenty-seven years or so, if all went well. It made sense to quit while I was ahead, while there was yet some dignity left intact, before I got myself into serious trouble. Something of an inconvenience, that long line of boyfriends who passed like drab gray bodiless shadows through my days, like in the circles of Dante's hell, so some bitterness was inevitable. And now a few bad dates to add to the list. *Is it a genetic predisposition?* I could not help wondering. Was it me, or was it Zeitgeist? Was it the revenge of Internet gods because I had broken the tradition and offered them no sacrifice? Was it too late for that? As far as revenge went, was this it, or should I expect a hailstorm with individual hailstones the size of a small child's head right here in the coziness of my bedroom anytime soon? Where had I put my umbrella?

After I stopped laughing and faced reality—oh, the reality—I had no desire to talk about it. Please do not make me. On second thought, I do want to talk about it. After all, you are already here, so the least I could do is be considerate.

So…it was late at night. No question, I was blue. Desperate times call for desperate measures. I already had joined the countless army of evermore-blue people, so I might as well turn to an old, proven remedy. Would you care to guess what it was? No, not antidepressants, but you were close—please keep on trying. No, not some beverage with a high alcohol content either. I feel I should tell you that alcohol disagrees with me, but I do understand your logic and where you might be going with it.

To help mask the atrocious aftertaste, I turned to something else capable of enticing my palate and distracting my mind from the horrors and tribulations of throwing myself out there, so vulnerable and unprotected. Like any other self-respecting female under the weather, I modestly reached for a mere pint of Häagen-Dazs ice cream. Triple chocolate! Yummy-yum! Since things merited much rumination, I thought it would not hurt to add cookies to the mix, chewy double-chocolate chip, even if it was just for color.

I took everything to my sofa bed. I know nothing about yours, but as long as my freezer refused to freeze things into a solid-hard state anyway, on a good impulse, I opted to forgo the assistance of a customary spoon and scooped the ice cream straight from the container with a cookie. I was revived. The combination invaded my senses, provided a satisfying balance of tastes, textures, and temperatures for my body, together with undeniable comfort for the soul. What a fine way to end the day! By the time I was on my third cookie, I thought about what a splendidly brilliant idea the ice cream was. And my situation was not so desperate, if I considered all the possible angles, but pondering those angles required more cookies and more ice cream.

This could be addictive, I thought, calm and rational (make it "cool"), observing my case with detachment, surprising myself by not engaging in the thinking process with my inherent enthusiasm (overwhelming!) nor letting in swirls of emotions, which would cloud the picture. As it soon became evident, because of my being unengaged, I smoothly shifted gears from the emotional state I had found myself in at the beginning of the process (I almost felt like weeping) into a required, scientific frame of mind better suited for reasonability. Hurrah, I had done it. (Slow clap.) I hoped it would last.

Now I could chew over the situation endlessly while chewing on the treat. *And what a nice addiction to have,* I thought a little further, still rational, munching on the next cookie with a generous helping of ice cream heaped on top of it. *Soon I'll have another issue to deal with,* I thought, nonchalantly continuing to make use of my thinking apparatus. *There's the issue of expanding waistline, but should I worry about it now?* As any other regular human at normal room temperature, I could not be expected to worry about everything at once, no?

The front door closed with a bang. I heard the hushed cursing and an elf-in-sized person tiptoeing across the creaking floorboards. The door to my room squeaked open a bit. Hannah's head popped in, withdrew at once, and the door closed with a soft *click*. I heard her footsteps go to the kitchen, the silverware drawer yanked open, slammed shut. My baby stormed through the door, kicked off her shoes, and flung herself on my groaning sleeper sofa armed with a table-spoon. She said nothing, but shook her head, declining the offering of a cookie, and dipped her stainless-steel tool into the half-empty ice cream container. We ate in silence for several minutes. The phone rang. I picked it up.

"Hey, pumpkin, have you missed me?" Alex sounded tipsy. "Listen, whatever happened happened. You asked for it. The thing is, I need you back. What do you say?"

I heard a crowd in the background. A drunken female voice said, "Baby, hang up, baby. Let's go."

"Are you calling from a bar?" I asked.

"Pumpkin? Speak up. I can't hear you. I'm calling from a bar. I'll stop by later."

"No, Alex. No. Don't come here. And stop calling. Goodbye." I hung up.

"What a loser," Hannah said. She drank the rest of the melted ice cream out of the container, dropped her spoon inside, put it on the floor, curled up at my side, and closed her eyes.

I watched her breathe, even, deep, and soundless, like I used to do when she was little, and I could not help but wonder if I had ultimately gotten what I deserved...well, if one chose to believe Mother. Perhaps she was right and I should leave men alone. Think of it this way: I was no longer worried about my future dating fiascos. I had an infallible cure up my sleeve, and it involved ice cream. And with Hannah going away...I had better get up and write a note reminding myself to stockpile the stuff.

ot—the effective imitation of hell—it was too hot and sticky. A punishing heat, the kind that hit once every hundred years, fell upon the city without warning. Heavy, indifferent, relentless, it turned everything it curled around into somnambulists. Sweat-drenched, and with a damp phone receiver cradled against my ear, I tried to stay focused and found myself failing wretchedly. Bloody hell.

"…married? Stop pissing the time away. You aren't getting any younger!"

Obliterating the last of my thoughts, Auntie's overbubbly voice drilled into the pitiful remainder of gray matter inside my skull that had managed to survive being melted by the heat. Only a string of obscenities survived.

"You aren't getting younger!" she said, with the growing fierceness of an ocean gale that felt obliged to sink a fleet of warships like toys, strong enough to blow the flesh off bones. Don't you hate it when people repeat things they should have never said in the first place?

"Bella—"

"Let me finish. Just don't get offended as you always do by every little thing a person says—you're as skinny as a roundworm. You'll be blown away by the wind any moment. Now wait, what was it I wanted to ask you? Eh…Skin and bones!"

What energy! Forget the frisky gale—too impersonal. Bella mounted an attack fit for a rusty Soviet tank, clanking its caterpillar tracks, squashing anyone who happened to be in its way, leveling them with the ground with gusto. I could sense the turbulence in the hot air around her. Though today things were going no worse than usual, how I wished good Auntie would be less busy with my affairs! The same conversation repeated for the millionth time, hardly a novelty, no unusual elements present, familiar to the point of tears. To improve my single status so that there was a warm body lying next to mine in bed once in a while, she shoved me into marital bliss. Her well-meaning efforts were as effective as expecting a piece of cherry-flavored gum that materialized in one's hair to cure one's nearsightedness. How was I to get the resourceful Auntie off my back without quenching her desire to transform her bright vision of my imminent happiness into my everyday reality?

Considering herself a keen observer of people, she pressed on. "Find some-body, anybody, doesn't matter who, just not to be alone! Lower your expecta-tions. You're not *listening…*"

And here my attention wandered off, as it had gotten a good deal of prac-tice doing many times in similar situations, just prior to shutting down, never to return. I felt helpless, caught in the unfortunate pairing of ever-animated Auntie and the heat. With nowhere to flee, I gave in to despair a little. Soon I would stop protesting. While perhaps not the worst outcome, the path of desperation was hardly an appealing prospect. Like so many of us, I was in a habit of seldom choosing the best tactics to execute my present-day convictions, but to cling to a tradition for mere tradition's sake? Take for instance the custom of getting one-self married, which did not top the list of my present worries. At the moment, all males seemed unnecessary in my life.

The last mad days of July, almost August. Six years had passed since that divine summer day spent in the suburbs of Munich. Did it happen, or had I concocted it all, a treacherous falsification? With my mind's resilient tendency to idealize and embellish things, six years was more than enough time to make an ordinary outing look like an incursion into the ever-dreamy world of Shangri-La with its frozen-in-time essence. Memories mutate. In dreams I find myself on that distant shore, waiting…for what?

Five years ago I realized my dream man, Karl, was no more than a big crush with its broken hopes and embittered anxieties. Settling for anyone equaled beg-ging for a reprieve from the ever-present fear of loneliness, a daunting feeling I inherited from the line of female ancestors on Mother's side. Once I got over my initial reluctance, tired of chasing a fantasy, the more I considered it, the more giving up on the relationship frontier sounded less like a failure. I had known the ecstatic heights of capricious human love, only to ascertain that even in a caring relationship, I was alone, always alone. I was at a juncture in my life where I had abandoned the belief that turning to another human being could cure my aloneness—a point when, instead of incessantly beating myself up for real and imagined wrongdoings, I was ready to celebrate my failures alongside the victo-ries, to befriend and be befriended by solitude.

One cannot fail unless one has tried, so rather than perceiving any failure as a reason for regret, I decided to bless each one for the lesson learned as a stepping stone, each one bringing me closer to greater success. The rest of my solitary life in the unbounded world was looking better and better.

"…so, so stubborn," Auntie buzzed, a thorn in my soul. "Have you heard anything I said?"

She sighed. She tended to sigh a great deal. Her momentum was strong, and though it did not seem like it at the moment, it would wind down soon. It always did, as long as no one disagreed with her. Indeed, if I had learned nothing else in this life, I had mastered patience.

I howled inside. "Bella—"

"No, now you listen to me as to someone with experience. There's no love, it's a fantasy…"

Bella had not thought much of love, never been seduced by its siren song, had no patience for romance or poetry or teary-eyed reminiscences or any other passing fancy, and she took no trouble to conceal it. Such notions were classified as superfluous nuisances to only cloud the clarity of her vision, her sensible philosophy of life fortified by her cynicism and mistrust. But then Bella had not thought much of anything else—if she had given any thought at all. She read exclusively within the romance genre to have a good laugh at the misfortunes of silly, silly women.

The good news? If one tried dating in New York, being a female of forty, a fresh flower no longer, the mating habits of New Guinea's birds of paradise seemed less bizarre by comparison. The not-so-good news? The myth about the perfect mate was just that—an urban myth, nothing more. Yes, love was difficult. Yes, devoting myself to that wrong someone was an interesting notion, but to what end? Happy to report, my fruitless, lifelong quest for my soulmate was over.

"No point talking to you," she said, persistent as a chronic foot fungus.

Click. Bella, also known as Madame Inexhaustible, had hung up.

I bawled like an air raid siren. With neither Auntie nor romance pressing on my mind, life was relatively uncomplicated, if I did not call to mind that Hannah was leaving in a few short days, her things packed, all of her belongings had fit into one suitcase. Plain thinking about it plunged me into funk as dark as an eclipsing moon, and with that heat…I sighed.

An hour later things were back to peaceful. I sat in front of a computer, situated in my rented one-bedroom apartment on the third floor of a six-story building that still held together, situated in a not-particularly-glamorous Manhattan neighborhood. Adam entered the room with a pensive expression, majestic and flawlessly flowing at curving around the corners, his enormous, bright blue eyes wide open and solemn, all business.

"Rrra-ra-rrru-raaah-rra!" he said in the accusative tone of his high, boyish voice. My dwarfish cutie always talked in sentences. In our nine and a half years together, I had never heard a single "meow" out of him, ascribed by tradition to felines. He preferred everything with an *"RRR"* in it.

Turning my head to face the welcome intruder and contemplatively looking at him for about a minute seemed like a good sequence of moves. So I did that. Nothing else seemed to be forthcoming. Did Siamese have their own cat dialect, or was it a speech impediment? Think about this: it was obnoxious of someone who herself spoke English with an accent to be critical of others. Look, perhaps he was a lion at heart that had to voice out that little roar of his now and then.

As Leonardo da Vinci said, "The smallest feline is a masterpiece." If you want to know, I thought the cat to be an ingenious invention, ten out of ten for grace and elegance. It specialized in healing human souls and catching mice on occasion, with all this rodent-chasing business being a clever cover-up.

Adam scanned the room with an impish look, weighed the possibilities, and opted for my lap, gracious at first, but not two seconds later he became an inert lump, not a solid bone in its whole body. As if I had been in need of a shedding heating pad right about then, but had been blissfully unaware of such a require-ment, and—what was even worse—until it had been pointed out to me, had thought I might prefer a cooling gadget instead. My mistake, silly me. I apologize.

Adam's silky, living warmth felt soothing under my fingertips. He took his sweet time settling down with my legs slightly apart, then raised his little head, looking into my eyes with his deep, blue, wise, sparkly mirrors into a cat's inno-cent soul, generous in his readiness to reveal the ageless, well-guarded secrets of the universe if only I asked. Directed at me, the silent, warm adoration rose from the bottom of those bottomless gateways to other dimensions. Without fur-ther ado, he purred and purred away, working his feline eternal magic on poor, defenseless me. My little happy pill, Adam. He was worth his weight in salt. If instead of stealing slippers he would learn to bring them, he would be priceless. The other happy pill, Eve, was nowhere in sight.

I faced the screen and sighed. Persistent on staying empty, the page in front of me had become horribly irritating. *"The stingy sun gave forth little warmth..."* Then what? The release through artistic expression was not going well, though so far it was not enough to send me spiraling into the murky depths of despondency, not yet. But still, you know, unpleasant. I could almost feel someone's hand on my shoulder and hear a comforting voice telling me how sad—sad!—it all was.

Writing had been a true passion of mine my entire life, though this fact had been for the most part hidden from me as if I could not be trusted with it yet, and no doubt for a damn good reason. Mysterious forces were at work, the meaning of their lesson indecipherable. I would not go so far as to say it was well hidden, no. I would rather not be accused of neglecting to incorporate the important detail that over a period of years there were glimpses and nudges. I never realized the extent of these happenings until I finally began to write—things like the intensity of unconditional happiness it gave me, which I simply refuse to contain, and how much alive and fulfilled it made me feel. And nowhere in the world could be found the antidote to that poison. It took me forever to come to this point in time and space and this level of awareness.

In case you are interested, but too shy to ask: a talented and promising mechanical engineer with a bright, bright future, I emigrated from Russia with high hopes. To feed my little girl and myself, I grabbed the first American job that was offered to me, making close to minimum wage. It sucked me under like quicksand, and I got stuck, given the responsibilities and all. Several years down the line, the manufacturing sector hit a snag, and I was laid off. Since engineers were not in demand, only draftsman positions in New Jersey were available, so I commuted for two hours each way each day to a small town whose name has been lost in the catacombs of my memory, all for a salary that barely covered the rent and a babysitter. Ah, money, always money, always a juggling act—adding, subtracting, subtracting.

In a few years, I was lulled into a world of graphic design that seemed ideal for me. Nice office, mad hours. Fascinating, but not for me. It was a pathetic case of mistaken identity that took me eons to recognize. And when the speculative dot-com bubble burst, I found myself unemployed again. If I seem to be a slow learner (the unfortunate impression), let us concentrate on the important part—I got there, yes? Trial and error and error methodology. In my lifetime I had tried several professions, immersing myself to the hilt. Happy in all of them in their own time, I would stop feeling content when a mysterious itch came and took a powerful hold, and then I would find myself in a desideratum to make radical changes. My never-satisfied curiosity and my eternal quest to find myself and that blessed corner of the world where I would be understood at last—and track down some elusive happiness too—took me a few unexpected places, and brought me a few surprises along the way. Who knew that I was right *here* all this time?

The silent fever to write brewed under the surface for years until there was no room for it to ferment any further, so it had to and did explode. When it happened in the end, a violent event, it erupted overnight. Meanwhile, the majority of graphic design jobs got outsourced, and as I was busy nurturing and polishing my writing skills, giving birth to every page with pangs, personal training was taking up a huge chunk of my time and energy, but the whole personal trainer thing was more of a hobby-turned-profession a few years ago out of sheer necessity.

eleven

as happens nine times out of ten, I, like every person who eats their way through emotional pain, reached a point of annoyance with my persistent weight gain—ah, the pleasures of the flesh—a sad, sad, true tale of a battle lost to mammalian biology. Like a bad dream, it got worse and worse. The quest for a strong body, the vessel of the eternal soul, is a noble one. Out of desperation, I clipped a color image of Beyoncé out of a magazine, taped it to the fridge, slapped my own face on top of it to stimulate my desire for change, and increased the number of hours I spent at a gym. My weight gave a little, then went up again. Genetic predisposition is a tough thing to argue with and hope to win. You have been warned.

One day as the sky began to brighten, I was shown a way. Not without help from my wonderful Hannah, I discovered a new, exciting world, mainly by having my face shoved right into it while I batted my eyelashes. Pilates to the rescue—dare I say it?—I would be one hot mama. Farewell to the stubborn pounds that clung to my midriff and ate through the fabric of my confidence like a moth. Hidden away and almost silent, the endless generations of female predecessors in my genetic tree, which inhabited the chasms of my unconsciousness, resisted the whole idea. "Why is it sexy to be reduced to a skeleton?" some of them whispered, some hissed, unforgiving and otherworldly.

To feel comfortable in my own skin, I entered the world of glutes and pelvic floor and hip flexors. The workout was designed to throw me off balance, so I would ultimately find my center. Clever! It also was a godsend tool to deal with a dubious blessing—an evil curse bestowed upon the average Caucasian woman after forty, with few minor exceptions—a flat *derrière*, which under normal circumstances came in a flattering eye-candy combination with a flaccid belly. Just think, those long ballerina legs could become more than a pure fantasy. The change was in the air. I missed the exact moment when it happened, but I was hooked, and soon my core screamed to be stabilized. I had stumbled upon—Oh glory, glory!—the ultimate panacea. Bold, it promised a better quality of life and to increase the intensity of the Big O (please read, "orgasm") to make it even bigger, if I dared venture into the unknown. This was the last straw that was needed to make me dive in. Nothing wrong with getting in shape to look and feel attractive while boosting the pleasures of life too. May one live in good health with passion and joy!

One thing led to another. I rediscovered an unadulterated euphoria of existence on the earthly plane. Like a child with a new bicycle who rode it all day long, I craved to stretch and contract and pull and push and squeeze. Life turned into one continuous butt exercise. The pounds were coming off. As long as I was enraptured and longed to spread the joy, why not make it into a profession? Was it the hand of God leading me toward fulfillment—right?—to not only discover the miracle of Pilates, but also to realize that my newly acquired fetish could germinate into something lucrative at the end?

To make a long story short, for four months I acquired knowledge of the human body, spoke for days in a dead tongue, Latin, reciting the names for the body parts whose mere existence I would have never guessed. Overflowing with enthusiasm, I passed the exam and was certified as a personal trainer only to discover that my meteor of a career in the field of fitness was a catastrophe: I realized that whipping myself into shape was one thing, but pushing other living beings to conditions of better health was, well…less fun than I had anticipated it to be. It left me a bit flummoxed, not to say shocked, and this statement might not reflect the full picture of my feelings on the matter. Think of it this way: I had not thought of myself as "a skinny bitch." In my mind I was a caring person— and I say this with pride—in general well predisposed to people. Not to mention what a strange, unproductive way to express personal gratitude this was.

Imagine how I felt when I heard this undeserved phrase muttered through pressed lips behind my back on several separate occasions with an expression of envy, if not to say hate, blemishing the face of a talker who looked at me if I were the fat goose that had laid a golden egg, but was unwilling to share. After all the terrible things I had subjected myself to get there, it finished me. I struggled to regain my footing and grip on things. If one thought such a bad occupational move was something, please ponder this—according to Mother, I had also managed to flop my entire career as a devoted daughter. Now, *that* was unnerving. If, according to the chaos theory, a single wingbeat of a butterfly, given time, might cause unforeseen atmospheric changes somewhere else, like a devastating tornado or tsunami, can one imagine what rippling effect an action like being a bad daughter sent through the entire world? But this sort of thinking could take all the fun out of the business of living.

My enthusiasm over personal training as an indisputably clever career move died a slow, painful, but inevitable death. After a few wild pirouettes of flying sky-high, then plummeting way down, up and down again, bobbing, up and down, it stabilized at last and reached the level of a comfortable working environment, sparing my feelings from being dominated by a sense of total waste. It kept us afloat, provided a roof over our head and bread on our table, while it gave me a chance to explore my true passion—writing.

Which brings us back—I tend to drift sometimes—to me sitting in front of my computer in our rented one-bedroom apartment situated on the third floor of a gray-bricked six-story building somehow holding itself together in an unglamorous Manhattan neighborhood. I feel compelled to mention here that both the bedroom and the living room had eastern exposure, which was always a huge plus. Good ventilation too. You know the advantages of this natural light thing, supporting life and all that while keeping depression from settling in, and—alas!—what a bad thing it was to have, depression, if one was to believe in that sort of thing, which I do. I might also add that I had repainted the bathtub, torn out the stained carpet, and slicked the floors with polyurethane myself.

"The stingy sun gave forth..." The summer-drenched city melted under another oppressive heat wave—a hundred and six degrees in the shade and no relief at night. It was hot and humid enough to breed dinosaurs, though I hoped no one would. Beneath the flat sky, boxy buildings in eight shades of dirty gray on tired Broadway were being cooked, almost done, and were disguised by hot air currents, dirty-orange, thick, and rising. The crudeness of the view was softened by a haze that hung over it and was more reminiscent of a mirage than a dusty street that had been defeated by the suffocating July heat, the street in a real city under the washed-out sky somewhere in the real world. A complex and cruel deception—the *Fata Morgana*—quivered over the liquid blacktop and the roofs of parked cars. A perfect setting for an UFO sighting: a lot of people would see it, but no one would think it real enough to investigate. It gave a sense of doom, like the world might be coming to an end.

A secondhand window air conditioner that I bought a few days ago—how lucky we are to live in this age of electricity and marvelous cooling devices—dripped water the color of soiled bandages into the aluminum pan on the floor, rasped for an hour like it had emphysema, rattled, shook, and went silent, taking an undeserved day off, leaving me sitting like a solitary breakfast bun in an overheated oven. It took up a lot of space, blocked my view and daylight. Who could think of working up more sweat in this repulsive heat without air conditioning? Swimming in perspiration, forced to cancel my training sessions with clients and with no money to buy another one of those praised gadgets, I hoped this one day off would not become a week, but it might. God, have mercy upon me! I sighed and called the store that sold the gadget, which happened to be a repair shop too.

"Mamacita, you broke it."

"Please come repair it."

"Busy, busy. You bring one month." *Click.*

In view of it being the end of July with the whole of August ahead, the weather would hardly improve in the near future. The heat worked itself through the walls. Everything felt clammy. I was not a tropical bird. I hated New York summers. I lowered the shades and turned on the asthmatic fan. It whirred and screeched and made little difference. The ice cubes in my water melted away, but the sweaty glass was cool when I put it to my chest. The beads of water ran down my belly while small rivulets of perspiration ran down my spine and trickled down my calves from behind my knees. As I set about anticipating the days ahead in horror, a certain sense of doom came over me. In air rich with exhaust fumes, the humidity was palpable, the air itself almost visible. A set of gills would have been a more-than-welcome addition to my perfectly imperfect anatomy.

A young sparrow found refuge outside my open window in a tiny patch of a shadow, a small oasis of life on a rusty, misshapen fire escape plagued by a multiple personality disorder, as it thought itself to be a balcony on occasion and behaved in accordance with its belief. Imagine that. I followed its invitation once, twice, thrice, but each time ended up covered in soot and had to decline further temptations.

The disheveled birdie roasted with an open beak, not hopping, pretending to roost and ignore Adam, its round, black, beady eyes flicking. Adam, his pliant furry body slumped, was not in his gravity-defying mode at the moment. He was immobile, save for jerking his ear once, twice, his eyes more closed than open. From time to time, his eye slits grew wider when he threw a lazy glance in the general direction of possible prey—a pure disaster in the making looming over our heads—through the diamond-shaped openings in a security gate locked with a padlock. Adam had been created a predator, even if he did not look like it in this instant. If ever.

For a second, the sporadic awakening of his true predaceous nature distracted me from experiencing in full the sensation of being so cruelly overheated. Under the circumstances, he decided not to bother with charging or some other ridiculous-in-this-heat activity. *Yeah, maybe later on, after a nap,* he seemed to say. He sighed and averted his glance from the bird to look at me instead, his eyes opened wide for a millisecond and closed.

I sat in front of the screen in a state of lassitude and nurtured an ambiguous hope that my mind would kick in after it had been irrevocably fried. If I still had a brain. It seemed to evaporate in this hellish temperature, leaving no discernible traces. The current working hypothesis that the heat had something to do with it was my preferred explanation. I refused to consider the alternatives.

The descent itself had been gradual and silent, until one day I noticed how

exceedingly difficult it became to make my brain do tricks. Tragic. In one maneuver it excelled, and the brain used the inevitable passage of years to its advantage, polishing this stratagem to perfection—it was good at playing dead, and a
semblance of lucidity was appreciated.

In the last hour, not a thought crossed or was even remotely planning to cross
my dimmed mind. I was wide open to suggestions, anything plot-advancing, no
matter how minuscule they seemed to be. I looked at the bundle of fur on my
lap. The dutiful bundle pricked up one ear and looked back at me with one half-
opened eye. "Hot. Have pity," was written there. Besides, he already helped as
much as he could by sitting on me. At the same time, my computer, content and
cheerful, hummed to itself.

Without warning and to my mild astonishment, the recollection of a dream
I had many moons ago of writing a cookbook popped back into my mind. Not
one of my favorites, and I sensed there was no escape from it, no relief, and this
whole incident would go on and on to haunt me forever. Allow me to explain:
I loved having people over. I found it comforting to cook for them, to try new
recipes and perfect the old ones. People in turn loved my cooking, or at least that
was what they said. Time after time.

"Write a cookbook," my friends kept telling me, more like a summons to arms.

I'll write a cookbook, I had thought to myself. What a strange thing to bring
back to life from the long-lost archives, buried in the musty tomb of my memory
in a spot that had been unmarked on purpose. I had held that dream for years. It
seemed like forever. What a beautiful tale it was! I admit—not the most glorious
dream, not the most daring either, but a doable one, and what was important—
my dream. Though finding time for the project would be a major issue. While I
was working sixty-hour weeks as a graphic designer at the time, I was also a full-
time single mother of a teenage girl. You know how it is. One damned thing after
another and more. And one day I set myself down and began to write. That had
been a great day—what am I talking about?—such a magnificent day!

A short time later, in addition to ever-present pressures of time and life, somewhere past the middle of the new phenomenal book no cook should be without,
my flaming enthusiasm exhausted itself on its own, plain collapsed, and went
uninterestingly flat. That had been a sad day—what am I talking about?—such
a devastating day! The world had to learn to survive without this useful book. So
far the burning desire to continue with this project had never risen from the puny
pile of ashes left behind, which dragged a teeth-achingly boring, wistful existence
in the hidden nooks of my mind. Why had my mind, obviously the troublemak-
ing part of it, summoned this failed venture up, the silly thing? From the myriad

of memories big and small, happy and unhappy, my brain had to select that one. Annoying, yes. Let us hope it was not some bad omen. Please knock on wood.

Enough. Time to focus. "*On this crisp September day...*" I sighed and turned away from the screen to search for inspiration. On the table to my left was a stack of advertisements, deposited with kindness in my mailbox yesterday, which I had forgotten to throw away. I leafed through them, then glanced at the clock. How could it be just ten in the morning? The clock must be broken. I picked up the phone and dialed the time lady.

"*At the tone the time will be ten fourteen and twelve seconds. At the tone the time will be ten fourteen and thirteen—*"

I hung up. "*On this crisp day in the beginning of September, the stingy sun hung low and gave forth little warmth...*" I stared at this sentence in mute agony, gripped in the firm paws of creative nothingness while I suffered from severe case of infectious adverbanitis. Persistent as a termite, I squeezed a few words out, not one of them of much use, neither intelligent nor coherent. A notorious writer's block, I suppose. What self-flattery. The alluring mystique of a tortured soul, effective in self-imposition of suffering with its loyal companion—a nervous stomach, the meaningful gaze turned inward, desperate, searching, and the whole host of other lovely customary attributes. Oh, the divine misery of it! Oh, that horrible pit of hell!

It seemed harder to be the proud owner of this poor soul in this uncooperative weather—what an overall unwholesome idea that was—though this scorching heat would be a suitable setting for the certain notions of torment to be inflicted upon persons, especially if such persons deserved this despicable treatment.

This very instant, the lifestyle of a wandering minstrel sounded unattractive. I had no immunity to the common lethargy of the end-of-July day. It was unadvisable to move in this brutal heat, thinking included, unless it was crucial to one's survival. I began to drift away in a slumber-like state in this lulling heat. The cozy soundtrack from the vicinity of my lap that had been loud a moment ago had faltered, laced with longer and longer silence breaks—the fur face producing the whirring staccato was more asleep than awake, the inert weight of a curled-up, soft beast gently pressed on my lap. Then the purring, already faint, trembled on the verge of inaudibility, attempted to mount again, leaped across the entire length of the table, over the dusty philodendron plant in a terra-cotta pot, only to abruptly cease altogether. The gravitational forces have done something not unpleasant to my eyelids, and my eyes closed in an effortless shift. Tentative at first, but significantly more confident in no time, the initially formless shapes began a rapid transformation into a kaleidoscopic succession of vignettes of familiar but forgotten surroundings. *Roger, over and out.*

twelve

my fondest childhood memories have Grandmother Sarah in them, with her radiant eyes and smiling face, her hands, gentle and skillful, always in motion, always busy, and her gait, light-footed and youthful. She always was—and I believe still is—my guardian angel.

Grandma, my mother's mother, had an all-pervading aura of kindness surrounding her, so full of love, she lit up every room she entered. A feeling of peace, now twenty-odd years after her passing, descends upon me in soft waves whenever I think of Granny. Her everyday attire consisted of a faded floral-print dress, a requisite apron she tied with a bow in back, and worn house shoes. Her options were limited to two dresses: one she wore in attending to house chores, and one formal. That garment awaited its finest hour, smelling of camphor and time passed, snuggled among mothballs by caring hands.

While blessed with refined taste herself, Gran never complained about the scantiness of her wardrobe and seemed untormented by the coarseness of things she had to put on, as if it has not occurred to her to make this a part of her concerns. She circumvented the limitations pushed on her, laughed over them, though in her youth she had been accustomed to better quality clothing.

She looked poised in a plain midnight-blue dress buttoned up to her collarbone and a sole pair of old-fashioned, sensible-heel brown shoes with medieval-looking buckles. Such shoes must have been a high-fashion item somewhere at one time or another, but the truth of the matter was on the hazy side. These were exchanged for black *valenki*, * ugly but practical footwear at the time of year when the ground was blanketed with several feet of snow, resting in stillness, while the rest of the world, full of creatures big and small, was frozen without mercy, left to fend for itself. Shiny black rubber galoshes were put on over the *valenki* to prevent them from getting wet, making the soles less slippery on icy roads during Russian winters, long, snowy, and frosty. Regardless of decisions made on the appropriateness of footwear within the strict limits of nonexistent

---

* Stiff peasant felt boots. (Russian)

choices, Grandma Sarah put on a vibrant red lipstick, pinned an olive-branch brooch over the top button of her dress, covered her head with a shawl, took Grandpa Isaac's arm, and off they went to visit friends. Her brooch—dark, faceted garnet stones set in platinum—the one thing left of her mother's that had not been exchanged for bread in famine times. Grandpa, dressed for the occasion in his only suit and tie, would also be equipped with a pair of black stiff *valenki* with rubber galoshes for the harsher season.

Gran spoke fluent French and Yiddish, but struggled with Russian. Years ago, I heard Grandma was a brilliant pianist from her brother, Anatoly, but we had no piano for her to play. Anatoly, the conductor of a big orchestra, had been one of the three of Grandma's ten brothers who, by unexplained miracle, were spared the horrors of Stalin's hard labor and Hitler's concentration camps. Not many survivors were left in this once-huge, close-knit family. The rest—seven brothers and no one will ever know how many cousins, aunts, and uncles—had perished, brutally murdered, the majority of them in their youth.

She was the life of a house. Grandma's main reason for existence was to care for her family. It was her higher calling and she excelled at it, effortless in negotiating her days and tasks, with no reservations about giving herself—all of herself—for this purpose. She spent the entire day at the hot stove, cooking sumptuous meals out of a circumstantially limited list of ingredients, or cleaning the house to a spotless glow, or doing laundry by hand and hanging it out to dry on a clothesline stretched in the yard. That air-dried laundry smelled of wind and sun, exhilaratingly fresh. But hard, clunky like a thin sheet of metal and frozen flat in the winter, it would be hung out to dry in our small kitchen, where it had to thaw out first.

Gran would pluck a chicken for our family dinner, when there was a chicken to pluck, and with love and patience in time she gathered enough feathers for pillows and the customary, ever-luxurious though thin, down bedding for each member of our small family. And while the manna was still to fall from the sky, we were kept on a steady diet of diversely cooked potatoes, dark rye sourdough peasant bread, and homemade sauerkraut with cranberries, frozen to bring out the sweetness. The entire family participated in the jovial and noisy endeavor of dicing cabbages and grating carrots. The kitchen was a pitiful mess. As a result, after the sauerkraut had fermented under a wooden weight, we had a big barrel of crunchy deliciousness for the winter—oh God, my mouth is watering now.

We owned an orchard (nine beautiful trees) buzzing with bees, dotted with black currant bushes, all of which burst with shivering white-and-pink blossoms in spring to bear plentiful fruit later, the branches sagging with their weight. We considered ourselves wealthy, as besides the orchard we also owned a one-hole outhouse (built out of wood boards and not rotting plywood scraps) overgrown with stinging nettles on the sides and in the back. That secondhand lumber had been bleached gray by the elements, splintered and warped with huge gaps between the boards that were butted and nailed together. The outhouse was nice and breezy in summer, with sunlight peeping in through uneven slits, with a lovely smell and flies, but not that nice in the midst of notorious Russian winters with teeth that bit through layers and layers of clothing. So many winters.

We had running tap water *in* the kitchen—more trickling than running. Patience is a virtue. We did not have to go with buckets to the local water pump on a corner of a long—long!—street. Carrying buckets of ice-cold water that splashed and splattered was trickier than it looked during the winter months, when the treacherous ground was covered with a thick layer of snow and ice, presenting inconvenience when hand-transporting heavy, unstable loads while the ground wind entertained itself by swirling gossamer ghosts underfoot. Sad to report, we still had to do it, especially in the icy months, as during the winters the inconsiderate water pipe froze solid and burst more often than not.

The water in the tap was cold even in summertime, which was not such an enormous problem in itself since the solution was mind-bogglingly simple. If one insisted on having hot water, then—ta-da!—one could make some. One might want to put a bucket of cold water on a lit stove, cover it with a lid, and several hours later—*voilà*! For all other water amenities (if a written request were put in, I have no problem calling them "necessities"), there were the pleasures and conveniences of the always-overcrowded public baths.

Overloaded with pride, we had a chicken coop in the yard. Just two by two by three feet long, it was not big enough to be called luxurious. Relined with fresh, fragrant straw every evening, this primitive coop contained two tenants during the summer months who seemed content with their living arrangements. These quarters were for sleeping purposes during the nights and rainy days. During the fair weather days, the occupants could hide inside if they wanted to, but they were also free to roam outside, pecking at tasty worms or whatever, digging to their hearts' content, tethered by a long piece of rope for safety precautions, no animal cruelty intended. One line per hen, never extended by the inmate to its full length. The string was tied to the coop at one end and a yellow toothpick of a leg at the other to prevent the hens from wandering into the neighbor's abode and destroying the existing order of things—or worse, being caught, killed, and eaten prematurely by strangers.

Despite the widespread notoriety of chickens' intellectual abilities, those two knew where the water and the dish filled with grain were positioned and visited them often. It was the same millet that served as one of the main staples on our family table too, but we cooked ours. One of the lodgers provided a steady source of fresh eggs every morning, still warm for breakfast—one egg per any given morning but always on schedule, accompanied by much clucking. The other lodger had been there from infancy, but on a temporary basis, being fattened up for, you know…Hope such a revelation will not initiate a stream of mail from animal activist groups.

As a golden rule, whatever Grandma Sarah was doing was done in our multipurpose kitchen—the real heart of the house—the bigger part of the room occupied by a huge Russian wood and peat briquette-burning stove, which was used both for cooking and heating up the house. How alluring it was, with its live fire radiating warmth through the stark bareness of the house, austere and ugly with a general sense of dread. Each and every room was furnished with a bed, a wardrobe, a table, a chair, an alarm clock, and a small table lamp with plastic lampshade. Nothing but the barest necessities, though one room had a radio. Every morning as the first light broke Grandfather started up the stove with wooden logs, freshly chopped and fragrant.

For some obscure reason, I recollect no summers. My entire childhood seemed to pass in the twilight of everlasting wintertime. As if of another dimension, each morning, in unyielding darkness, I would be awakened by the wall clock striking six times—*dzing-dzang, dzing-dzang*—singing an unpretentious melody with aspiration, hitting notes with precision. Framed by the bluish-black shifting rectangle of a window, the pale sky would be luminous, the ghostly shimmer of pearl gray. A tangled cluster of icicles, as thick as anacondas, always hung from the eaves, blocking from view the upper half of heaven's vault. A blizzard would unfailingly burst from above. It would show its teeth and rule the earth. It would howl and cry as it would labor to breathe through the night, but by the morning, shrieking in powerlessness, it would lose its strength, subside, die away. The bare trees would still be standing, if a little dizzily, some oily black showing through a thick layer of clean, fluffy snow. They would knock on the window glass with their skeleton arms, nodding in cordial greeting, in good spirits at having survived the ordeal.

I would lower my legs to the cold floor, barefoot and holding my breath, fighting the urge to dive back under the warm security of a blanket. I would run like blazes into the kitchen to hide under the oaken monstrosity of a table, gloomy and silent. In the darkness outside, between the wailing and roaring and wistful whistling of the wind, I would hear snow crunch under the footsteps of a giant, inexorably coming toward the house. From what I had heard from some adults, the giants and witches ate little children, but never raw. The children had to be cooked first.

The giant would stop at the front door, stomp, and bang his boots against the threshold to shake off the snow stuck to them. The door would screech, and heavy, solitary footsteps would continue unopposed toward the kitchen, toward me. The floorboards would creak and heave and sigh and complain under his weight. At last, with a thud, he would unload the logs he had brought with him in front of the stove. Knocking against one another, the logs would be fed into the inky-black, hungry mouth of the old stove. A newspaper would rustle as it was wadded up and placed on top of the logs. The giant would grunt, light a match, and before long, as if by good magic, the evil spell would be broken as he turned into Grandpa Isaac. Logs would catch on fire, spit sap, crackle, and hiss. Thin flames would tremble, reach up, and illuminate him from the side. He would smile, extend his arms toward me. I would exhale the breath I had held till this moment and dash out from under the table and into the enveloping warmth and absolute safety of his tight embrace.

Grandfather Isaac was tall, dark, and handsome. He was very, very strong and kind. He was the one, loving and patient, who would cut up my food and the gargantuan outside world—everything that was too big for me to chew on—into swallowable, bite-size pieces. He was the best possible father figure by any standard, more so in view of the persistent absence of my biological one, and was the ideal prototype on which to base my search for a made-to-order mate (at least, this would be the case if we lived in an idyllic version of the world).

And on the surface, this was what I seemed to be doing in full awareness, only to discover, to my horror, the intolerable truth. I have got no credible explanation as to why I always ended up with partners that matched not Grandfather's personal traits, but my mother's—domineering, abusive, and needy. This was disturbing enough on its own, if not an implication that in stealth, behind the scenes, some faulty reasoning was clouding my perception of things. This deformed conditioning was imprinted on me with great success by the most important person in a little girl's world—her mother—and was so deep inside my being that there was no danger of any momentary sanity stepping in and intervening at any point of time. Nothing comes from nothing.

Exactly what this was and how that imprinting was done still eluded me. Even now, though I refused to admit myself beaten, I was imprisoned behind bolted gates in the citadel of Mother's indifference just the same, which inspired only despair and more despair. Speaking from years of experience on my shoulders, which, like Atlas's, became duly hunched after such an unbearable burden was placed upon them, I can say that Mother had remained the most central person in my life. Whether I liked it or not was irrelevant, and well…it held no significance just to Mother.

Grandfather was a carpenter, a good carpenter indeed. He had built the house with faded sky-blue shutters on its windows out of huge wooden logs with his own two hands, the house we all lived in—Grandpa Isaac and Grandma Sarah, Aunt Bella and her husband, Uncle Michael, my mother, Galina, and I. That tree-shaded house on the outskirts of Moscow had a ghostlike existence in the dungeons of my memory (or is it memory palace?), with all its anomalies, that was not always accessible.

Due to the indisputable necessities of urban housing development, its care-free existence on the physical level was interrupted with the utmost severity. The house was demolished, the trees cut down to roots. The roots were uprooted in turn, and holes filled in with rubbish and earth. Now a nine-story, grayish, featureless box of apartments towers over the endless pool of mud, standing next to another nine-story box in the same pool of mud, next to…like a parade. There was no stopping them. A simple flower, like a daisy or a forget-me-not, was painted over the number on each building so the children could know which building they lived in.

In the middle of the orchard, Grandfather had built a big woodshed with an attic, where he spent a lot of his time repairing things or making something new, depending on the current needs of permanent residents of the main house. The bigger half of the shed was occupied by an up-to-the-ceiling, neat stack of firewood, chopped to fit into the stove. It neighbored another organized stack of peat briquettes—all of which would be burned for everyday cooking and during wintertime keep the family warm.

In that woodshed Grandpa had made all the furniture for our house out of hardwood, thick and solid. He added elaborate carvings to the pieces destined to become mine, because I turned out to be the sole other member (besides Gran) of our living-together family group who was able to appreciate the gesture and the amazing quality of workmanship, which was done in accordance with proud traditions of carpentry. One might think this good furniture would last for generations—an ungrounded assumption in some cases, but not here—but it was the same furniture Mother and Aunt Bella threw away in a hurry to replace it with something mass-produced they considered elegant. It happened too soon after Grandpa's death from a second heart attack. Grandma was still alive—she went right after him, one within two months of the other. Her heart gave in, broken and lonely, and both of them were gone.

Ah, but what was deemed *elegant* was debatable, a matter of personal taste, and as it is known, tastes do differ. Uncle Michael sighed, shook his head from side to side as, silent and vacant-eyed, he handed two bossy connoisseurs the money. Smart move too. No sane person would step in and interfere to stop or reroute such a concentrated assault. The two hurricanes, Galina and Bella, had joined forces, and after exerting an inhuman combined effort to obtain these things (it was not as easy as walking into a store and buying the furnishings or anything else—the stores' shelves were empty), replaced it with a lacquered to a mirror-like gloss and spindly-legged something undeserving of being called furniture, which came apart each time one leaned against or sat on it.

And for the ironic twist—after buying it exclusively for its stunning looks, in order to prevent the newly acquired treasures from getting stained and scratched, both the table and sideboard were covered by a plastic tablecloth with impossible color combinations, cheerful to the point of inducing lasting nausea. In the end, this was the only clever move in the whole wretched furniture exchange, and a timely one too, since those pricy furnishings were as equally afraid of dust as they were afraid of moisture. The glossy veneer began cracking and chipping at once, but privately, under the cover.

In our small vegetable garden, Grandfather's loving hands had planted vegetables for the delight of our earthly bodies. As far as our souls were concerned, he sowed the fragrant, vibrant, flower borders, the preferred place for fireflies to hang around during a lightning-bug season. He tended to the garden every day from the early spring to a late autumn. Both unpretentious, the garden and the orchard fed us.

Helping Grandpa Isaac weed for hours or doing any other job he entrusted me to do topped the list of my favorite activities—right after reading a book, if not equal to it. The simplicity and monotony of manual labor added to the pleasure of doing something alongside that strong, kind, wise man. Ever since, there had been no sweeter fragrance for me in the world than the smell of the newly turned earth that had been warmed by the sun. Together with the aroma of cinnamon cookies Grandma used to bake, it permeated my soul and would always remind me of security of home, as long as I was I.

The sweet-treat baking would be reserved for afternoons. A bit taller than the kitchen table and proud of it, I would watch with wide eyes as Grandma Sarah rolled out flat the dough, dusting her hands and the rolling pin and the table surface with flour to prevent the dough from sticking to things. Next, she would cut out perfect round cookies, using a cup, make a little hole in the center of each one with a thimble, generously sprinkle her creations with sugar and ground cinnamon, and place them in the oven to bake. She made it look so simple, so down-to-earth. Those tiny cutout centers with extra sugar on top would be baked together with bigger cookies on a flat iron sheet and were intended for little people. The little people were me.

How I loved to watch Grandfather work in the toolshed smelling of freshly cut wood and apples! Ankle-deep in semitransparent, ringleted wood shavings, he would stand there making a new chair for the house, engrossed in his work, fully present in the moment. Tiny beads of sweat would glisten on his broad forehead. At the end of summer, Grandpa would pile up apples gathered from our orchard in the attic of a shed, and the apples would wait there to be put into the tiny cellar for winter before the first frost hit. This modest crop fed our family till anticipated with impatience times when the next crop arrived.

Grandpa would nest the apples among the curled wood shavings in small wooden crates he made himself. Filled to maximum capacity with fruit and neatly stacked, the crates wintered near neatly stacked sacks of potatoes, sacks of onions, and sacks of carrots in the cellar. The underground storage space was nothing more than a small pit dug under the house, its walls covered with bricks (if available) or lumber (if available), an ingenious solution invented by our great-great-grand ancestors millennia ago, as the wonder of the refrigeration technology had yet to be discovered. That cellar was our lifeline.

In the center of the kitchen floor made out of scarred wooden boards was a smallish door. Also wooden, heavy and thick, it lead to the cellar and was entrusted with a huge wrought-iron ring attached to it, the ring that would have looked more at home on the tall, unreasonably heavy gate of a medieval castle in Scotland's Highlands. Such a convenient ring was to be used as a handle or for any other purpose that could come to mind—for instance, as something for Mother to constantly stumble upon for the purpose of keeping her thoroughly entertained.

Grandpa would leave some of the apples to freeze out in the attic as a special treat for me since I found frozen apples such a delicious treat, but he gave me those contraband fruit in secrecy, away from Mother. Mother never approved of my eating them. Mother never approved of me eating anything cooler than the average room temperature out of constant fear I would catch cold.

thirteen

One of the biggest fears Mother had all her life always was, and still is, the fear of catching cold. This fear had no intention of leaving anytime soon (nor was there any subterfuge implied by my saying this, thus making it public), and if it did, what a miracle that would be—the change would be for the worse. No, Mother would still be Mother. She thought of the world as a vast, drafty place, with no safe corner anywhere. Drafts, the silent killers—every Russian knows that. Her mind, prone to periodic eruptions of hysteria, was ruled by a humongous collection of phobias, big and small, for every occasion, need, and taste. They were legion. A mere few were allowed to be verbalized, and often, without the panic of feeling intense dread and shame at admitting to have them in the first place. Yet those limited few made a long, very long, endless list of verbalized daily horrors to endure.

The youngest child, and a sickly one too, she had been overprotected, spoiled rotten (as much as the circumstances permitted), but more than the other two children, which brought forward a case of incurable narcissism while giving rise to a rich assortment of future fears on the side. How wise Grandpa and even wiser Grandma miscalculated so much was beyond me, as they only ever wanted the best for their children.

Sorely vexing, Mother managed not to be scared of elevators—one item on the top ten favorite frights list. What a miracle, considering the wild array of exciting, resplendent, vivacious phobias she lived with in her perpetual Armageddon-awaiting state. Shush—one must not give her any ideas. Otherwise, her cozy, static universe would be filled to the brim with the overwhelming, anticipated, catastrophic consequences of her treasured and nurtured fears. Danger, danger everywhere, and in everything. For the record, nothing had ever happened to her. Not. A. Thing. Bad tidings never came. If one was willing to work on it a little, one could talk oneself into being afraid of anything. And I say this not out of spite or to needlessly point out that she might have had a far worthier calling, nor do I wish to put under the scrutiny her lack of any sort of calling. The vocation of pessimist extraordinaire was no testimony of her neglect of other existing sets of circumstances, nor was it a momentary detour. She had *chosen* it from the vast variety of choices presented to her, as to many of us, and found it gratifying.

Even though in the duration of her life Mother had managed to catch cold a number of times—what a tragedy it was—she was still alive and well. That cold thing turned out to be an undeniably unpleasant sensation to experience, but there was little for the independent observer to report on. I was dead certain that if someone asked Mother her opinion of the experience she had undergone, she would come up with a horrific version of the story, at some point mentioning death as a nearly escaped ordeal, but why would one want to ask her in the first place?

A fragile flower she claimed herself to be (albeit a thorny one), and as such Mother was constantly subject to chills and forever obsessed with health issues. She was plagued by a multitude of internal ailments, major and minor (as if she only felt alive when she was feeling miserable), but thank heavens, nothing serious. Besides despotism, most of her afflictions were unexplainable, sometimes unmentionable, and thus close to being unmentioned. They were always hard, if not impossible, to diagnose, with the majority of complaints voiced each time with additional mention of her delicate digestive tract. Such a detail turned out to be not an issue by itself—Mother preferred all her conditions to be self-diag-nosed anyway. If one somehow managed to harness her to a plow instead of a horse, she would have the field plowed without breaking much of a sweat, and with no dawdling either. But the specifics of how one would manage to lure her into that harness and talk her into performing the task of plowing was entirely one's problem. I would be of little help here.

The obsession with her tender health, though occupying the biggest part of her waking hours, never interfered with her sleep. Nothing, I repeat, *nothing* ever made Mother lose her sound sleep, just as nothing ever disturbed her digestion given her iron constitution, despite her declarations. She had no interest in the outside world and its workings, and not a single thing out there might make her take interest (the rest of the world did not particularly give a damn about her either, so there). Heaven knows the woman raised the art of impenetrability to quite a degree, all while claiming herself to be the embodiment of good sense.

Everything I mentioned a moment ago must be taken into careful consid-eration, since it would be an unforgivable mistake, almost a crime, to ignore in-formation of such unprecedented value. The majority of her premonitions and prophecies, Cassandra that she was, had to do with the subject of her delicate health, inevitably ending in states of utter misery with a few subtle differences. That plenitude was more than enough to drive people around her to a state of madness. The fact that all her dismal predictions not once came to see the light of day was beside the point. In Mother's case, the adaptive mechanism had thought twice and in the end decided against developing entirely. It was better to make a mistake of giving a false positive in seeing danger where there was none than giving a false negative and missing the existing peril. Those who spotted the hazard survived, while those who screwed up were eaten. The traditional adage "evolution favors the anxious gene" still held strong.

In Mother's defense, she was consciously unaware of the majority of her fears, but to a lesser degree, in her defense, she wanted nothing to do with even a notion of becoming aware. I have got it—I do, I do!—she operated with her reptilian brain, with fear as its primary driving force. It must be pointed out that we *all* possess that part of a brain with its unsuspected treasures, but admit it, the thought of one's mother being a giant lizard was less than consoling. It always seemed so much easier to train a bear to ride a unicycle than to alter her judgment and set her a little bit free, so she in turn would set me a little bit free by relaxing her lethal grip, and preventing her from constantly filling my belly with fears. Any fortress might go green with envy at the splendor and grandiosity of the fortifications Mother had built around herself, all while digging in deeper and deeper.

Her personal, pancake-flat earth was propped up by four whales of general categories of anxiety-producing thinking errors: exaggerating, catastrophizing, overgeneralizing, and ignoring the positive. She was miserable when she operated on anything less than a grand scale. Well, as long as she was having fun. Just my luck these were the same valuable skills she was passing onto me with confidence, using the means she already had mastered, heard of, or was willing to improvise to assure I learned those lessons well—and what a Sisyphean labor it proved to be.

Along the way, Mother zealously nipped in the bud the things she thought potentially dangerous to my pliant and unstable young mind, which covered pretty much everything. That said, it was done with admirable consistency—consistency being a highly recommended trait in good parenting techniques. Even if some inconsistencies did creep in, they were also unconscious.

Time had no power over her. During my life the question of whether or not some deficiencies were at the root of the problem came up on occasion, followed by another disturbing question of whether those weaknesses were genetic in nature. If they were, what was the likelihood of passing them further down the family tree to unsuspecting descendants, and was there some sort of modification possible to bring them to a more manageable level? What were the odds, for instance, that a lack of nutrients was at fault, something that could get resolved one way or another with a good dosage of vitamin C or a strong laxative on a regular basis? Just a suggestion.

An infectious little bugger, the fear of catching cold was one of the lucky ones, as once let out of the closet, it roamed free. Ephemeral at first, the itsy-bitsy fear had grown up as if it had been fed some yeast, and truth be told, had had enough of Mother. So it thought of living on its own. It tested its wings, with caution at first, and they were good and strong—not exactly a wingspan of a mile across yet, but in due course, given time, they would get there. And so it began to lead a more and more independent existence. It always wanted to be independent, poor darling. It had people to see and places to go and serious things to think about, like the future, getting an education—what could be achieved in life without a good education?—perhaps getting married and having kids, girls, God willing. Fear was partial to girls.

Then there was a pension plan to think about too. Mother weighed it down a great deal. But it had bad news coming—Mother would have none of that freedom thing. Welcome to the club, little buddy. One day, eager to fly away forever, fear unfolded its wings, and…Mother caught it just in time. The wings were mercilessly clipped, and the sprouting of roots was enforced in a hurry. Cornered, doomed, and driven to utter despair, fear gave in to depression and developed a maddening itch in the early stages of a skin rash of nervous origin yet unknown to science (and therefore unnamed), but soon to become popular. In contrast, Mother looked like the act of disciplining fear and getting the upper hand made her feel better straightaway. They would remain together forever.

Most people tend to think of family legacies in terms of earthly items, like handed-down furniture, family memorabilia, and money. Me, I was predestined to be the involuntary yet the luckiest heiress to an untraditional, though vast family fortune—a fat fear portfolio. I would prefer cash, thank you. That is, if I had allowed Mother to reign unchallenged. Tenacious as she was, she was set to combat the opposition till the demise of the aforementioned opposition. Her energy would be concentrated on a singular point, ensuring the final outcome to her liking. I was not thrilled by the perspective of her prevailing in her efforts, and me spending my entire life against my heart, jumping at my shadow and weathering storms of despair.

As my destiny's contract stated with enough clarity, there would be no treading in someone else's footsteps for me, ever. Nothing but uncharted territories—uncharted by my family but not humanity in general, no, no—which turned out to be an exciting field for me to explore. If I were ready and willing, I was set for a multitude of consecutive lifetimes. The way I saw it, I was destined to take the road less traveled, to become a courageous pioneer into the world of illusion, cloaked in myth and mystery, a heroic adventurer into the unknown, and a lifter of veils. I was destined to give beyond reason, to care beyond hope, to love without limit, to reach, stretch, and dream in spite of my fears. And besides, I hated being told what to do. To Mother's greatest frustration, her free rein was somewhat limited.

fourteen

Starbucks: you must have heard the name before, considering how hard you would have to work to avoid hearing it at least once. Those coffeehouses popped up like wild mushroom colonies after a profuse downpour. Without further ado, in stealth and almost overnight, they overtook the city to become an inseparable part of New York landscape. The times and ways before the takeover were irrevocably erased from our memories forever. Gone. The coffee addicts' culture was reinforced thousandfold.

The café at the corner of Fifty-Ninth and Columbus was not big, but was not cramped, not overcozy, not too austere, but contemporary efficient, with a cluster of smallish tables in a slight disarray. I looked around. It was seven in the morning, but all seats were occupied, about a person per table. Someone with a newspaper, someone with a laptop, an idle someone staring out the window at passersby, one guy asleep. Whether you were escaping the reality of a crowded apartment, fancied being alone for a while, or were one of those lonely people craving to be with other people for a change, this was a place to meet live coffee addicts, outside of tripping in and out of the virtual reality of overpopulated cyberspace; how can one not welcome that?

Unintentionally, together with other food and drink establishments that had gone without prearranged agreements, Starbucks was involved in lighthearted matchmaking. Those French-bistro wooden tables for two were bound to inspire something—*ooh là là!*—as irresistible magnets for single people who wanted to meet other, equally single people in their neighborhood. Single guests to the area would do nicely too.

How it often happens—one is on one's own, content (not unhappy), nice apartment, nice job, nice friends (some of them). Problems seem manageable. And all of a sudden, like a clap of thunder in a middle of the blue sky, one realizes that flying solo is no longer fun. Ah, the longing for two lives to run parallel for a while. The eternal, unavoidable search for one's soulmate. The concept of soulmates had its origins in Greek mythology, according to which human beings were born first with two heads, four arms, and four legs. When these humans offended the gods, they were split down the middle and condemned to spend eternity searching for their other halves in order to become whole again and to acquire the ability to reproduce—an important option. So humans have been looking for their soulmates ever since. As far as the topic of offenses went, it was not just that humans were too often offensive, but that the gods were too easily offended. Not that I found myself in a position to criticize. Still, you know, for God's sake, gods—be gods.

It must be taken into account that those were the same deities who invented love in the first place out of boredom—just when one thought it was nice to be a celestial being—if only to introduce a new stimulus in their divine lives, and then they were never bored again. Ever. Then, on top of that, they split people in half. I do not know about that. What happened to all that nectar? Why was it all of a sudden so boring in heaven? If one were to disregard in its entirety the notion that those gods might forever be dissatisfied with whatever happened, then *thwack!*—this unattractive, violent behavior—going around and splitting people (not to say it was in any way exemplary) might illustrate how much the pressures of life took their toll on beings, even if one was a supernatural entity and immortal.

My presence in this café was incidental. You see, I drank no coffee. I am a traditional Russian tea person myself. Not that I was evil under normal circumstances (I have never considered myself a very good person either), but in working on projecting a more agreeable image, I thought I would bring a cup for my best friend's husband, since I passed by Starbucks anyhow on my way to my writing class in Rita's neighborhood, though I was passionately and resolutely against the use of addictive substances—except for chocolate, of course.

Every morning Patrick rushed to his workplace and disappeared there forever. Only the Almighty knew when Patrick was to resurface next. I had saved him ten minutes of standing in line. Let us not ignore the effect that scents play in the mood department, so now my friends could enjoy one another's company in the relaxed atmosphere of freshly brewed coffee. A good idea, yes?

So here I was, at the head of a patient, organized, fast-moving line, just one person ahead of me. In the midst of this euphoria brought upon by the overpowering aroma of roasting coffee, my fine-tuned nose caught a whiff of a different attraction, a whisper of a scent that made me dizzy—the seductive, assertive, bewitching power of an aftershave which men used to disguise themselves. I got lost for a moment in the scent. Smooth. A thick smell of success. A smell of money. Big money. A smell of power. Power. A tantalizing smell of a dominant alpha male. Interesting. Not that I was into domineering, goal-oriented males—I was not. And so early in the morning too. Been there, that hurts.

Disregarding this and bypassing the bit where I was supposed to scrutinize my motives and analyze the implications prompted by the dark shadows of my past, something clicked inside me. The *click* was loud and clear.

My heart plummeted in an abrupt drop to my feet. *Whoa!* Perhaps it wanted to know how my left heel was faring at this particular moment in time and was being plain neighborly. Things were swell in the heel department, and after a moment of hesitation, my heart came back, captured at once, about to blossom—make it, "about to open up toward the light as the bud of Japanese water lily unfurls, spreading white fragile petals, cultivated with such tenderness, and so exquisite, as the flower decides to forego the whole serenity bit and blossom wildly." *Ba-boom, ba-boom,* singing its own little tune in unison with a grand symphony of twirling stars composing the Milky Way.

They say—"they" being respectable scientists this time—it takes thirty seconds for a male and female to determine if they like one another. Imagine, less than a minute to fall in love, and just one glance. Now, how romantic was that? How very Romeo and Juliet! But scientists say something along the same lines about the decision-making abilities in the mating arena of a regular squirrel too. "Less than a minute," they say, nodding their heads. To overlook the obvious: I was all too ready to be razzle-dazzled into something regrettable at the end. And with me being an intellectual being (an unspoken assumption on my part that I was intelligently bestowed), I needed more than the average bushy-tailed squirrel might seek in a mate.

The man in front of me, the primary suspect as the source of the disturbing scent, was in his late forties, a head taller than me, broad shouldered and well groomed. He looked important and lost in contemplation. The expensive exotic-islands tan was becoming. So handsome, finely dressed too. So perfect. So devastatingly perfectly handsome. Not the sort of man who under the normal conditions crossed my path. I was ready to stay with him forever. His full mouth might under a different set of circumstances promise a smile, but he showed no indication of warming up to it at the moment. Something about the provocative curve of his lips suggested tension. His haggard gray eyes oozed intelligence, and something else, something I could not quite recognize, if one was to consider that I was viewing the man's back, a little stooped, with a minute glimpse at his profile.

Anyway, oh, almost-impossibly, too-irresistibly attractive. An impeccable, dark-gray suit, no doubt Armani. A tasteful tie, no doubt Armani too. Complementary to his broad forehead, his hair, with a bare touch of silver, was short and neatly trimmed. For an instant I imagined him naked and began perspiring a little. His masculine left hand with long fingers and manicured fingernails pleasantly shocked me right into the middle of next week—this gorgeous hand was worth Michelangelo's attention. No wedding band.

I stopped breathing. Was this even possible in real life? Here he was, the stereotypical lover-to-be of popular steamy romance mass-market paperbacks that sold for five dollars and ninety-five cents off the rotating wire racks at every drugstore, the sort of novels that cracked the foundation of many families by planting the ideas of ideals, poisoning the minds of unsuspecting housewives. That sort of hero—handsome, salt-and-pepper hair, with the accent on *pepper*— but a distinguished version.

But one could adapt a critical attitude toward anything if one was given but a sliver of a chance, especially if one was inclined to this by nature, and in addition, made a sincere effort. So…here he was, my dream man, not extinct, but in the flesh. Hubba-hubba, and hubba. Would he think of me as his nymph? Perhaps he was the answer to all my prayers, but it was too premature to tell. I was picky, you know. Ha, right! Spine-tingling goose bumps ignored the sane forewarning and were on their way. Right. Like someone this perfect was going to notice me. Wake up and smell the coffee, woman.

Time to take inventory. Was I even breathing? The tiny pheromones—what enticing, enslaving things they were!—flew, flew apart, twirled, exploded, flew. With levels of dopamine and norepinephrine elevated to such a degree I was practically getting an amphetamine bath and with heaven knows how many oth- er chemicals coursing through my brain, making my synapses fire, mad, mad, all circuits busy firing, firing, firing, my blood was about to boil in a furious man- ner…*Whoa!* How foolish we are sometimes.

The enchanting stranger with a bare touch of silver in his hair took his ex- tra-large mocha lite Frappuccino—the name itself a celebration for a mouth— from the smiling girl behind the counter. Ignoring this smile, he glanced at the page in the *Wall Street Journal* and walked into me.

The immediate result of this close encounter of the third kind was a choc- olaty-smelling silk blouse, designed as cream-colored, and a slithering, sickening sensation of hot coffee trickling down my body in accordance with the stringent law of gravitation. *Yukkity yuck!* As if served an eviction notice, the chocolaty smell did not linger and was soon replaced by something else less exquisite and not altogether palatable. As it was, dry silk was a different story, but wet silk did not fall into the category of aphrodisiacs.

To my sheer joy—please read, "to my utter horror"—in the shortest dura- tion of time, I emanated the intense scent of a healthy, but not particularly hap- py, wet dog from the general area of my breasts. But, as a higher realm's gesture of mercy, a smallish dog, say, a Yorkshire terrier. A note to know-it-alls: No, we do not have similar hairdos.

Now, when I could see man's face not sideways anymore but eye to eye, it was hard not to notice something steely in the intense gray of his bright eyes. I shivered. So much for the man of my dreams. Baffled by the unfair turn of events, I looked into his eyes, which at the moment regarded me wearily and warily, a little forlorn—the alluring gray eyes I could easily fall in love with, had I been permitted. Why are you smiling? Watch me. I looked down. His beautiful hand had a slight tremor; it still clutched an empty cup, which remained in a close vicinity of my dampened breasts. Was he a junkie? An alcoholic? Nah.

"Look what you've made me do! I'm sorry, but this is your fault," said the Adonis in a sudden outburst of fury. His eyes assessed me. His voice overflowed with anger, with no sign of incoming remorse, making yet another beautiful dream irredeemable in a blink of an eye—death to the dream!—and such a delicate water lily in its benign whiteness uprooted with crudeness, thrown into a compost pile to die. What sort of an evil person would do such a thing to an innocent lily?

The whole premature allure thing disappeared in a jiffy without even the most perfunctory of goodbyes. Pity. Ah well—still caught in a swell of elation I would adore him for four more seconds and then stop. A warm wetness turned into the cold wetness, sticking to my chest. Lovey-dovey-eyed as I was, the accusation surprised me. I had no idea how to respond to this.

"Pardon?" I said.

"You shouldn't be standing *there*!" he insisted.

"Where else was I supposed to be?"

As absurd as everything was, the incredulity of the situation intensified. The murmurs of disapproval behind my back became louder. A half-muted "Jerk." hung suspended in midair.

I glanced behind me and saw sympathetic smiles from complete strangers. A familiar stirring in the vicinity of my groin area caught me by surprise. Well, no. No surprise. There was some history, as one might imagine. The truth was—but let us keep it between ourselves, shall we?—you point me in the general direction of a jerk, and, attracted to him at once, I would hone in on him all by myself, no external help required. Worked every time—and I took no pride in this—like magic.

He honored me with no answer. In a hushed voice, he placed a second order for the same damn Frappuccino. Accompanied by the total silence and a bunch of hostile glances, he took his coffee and walked out of the store, his gaze glued to the floor, no backward glance. Perhaps not a total jerk. Ah look, what difference did it make? He had no plans to elaborate on his previous statement. He could have offered to pay for dry cleaning, but did not. The dry cleaning was not on his mind or in the stars for today. Neither was an apology.

I looked down. Even if those were events of no global significance, my favorite blouse was ruined. I thought myself to be the sort of person who would find the whole thing hilarious one day. At least I deemed myself to be not so despicably dumb as to be unprepared for disappointment. What luck that Rita's place was just around the corner. I could always borrow a T-shirt from Rita. Well, no need to cry over spilled milk, as the saying went, or over the spilled coffee with frothed milk.

It was my turn to place an order, so I asked for the unpretentious but well-rounded light and lively house blend with low-fat milk, no sugar for Patrick, paid for a bliss in a medium-size cup, and walked the hell out of there. So much for the notorious matchmaking powers of Starbucks. For an instant—an insignificant instant—it had seemed such an auspicious moment, so marvelous, so enchanting, and then that moment had slid by. What a dissonance between what was happening and what I thought might be possible to have happen.

fifteen

the midnight hour crept in, hiding behind the backs of its paler relatives. Taking matters into its own hands, it softened shapes and sounds, sharpened pains, veiled the distracting clutter, and encouraged revelations. The city quieted down as if a cease-fire had been declared, and given no choice, it dreamed. Such a decree infected my upstairs neighbors too. No yelling, no stomping, and the bedsprings were given a rest. Hannah was halfway to London. *Bon voyage*! We parted with her saying, "Mama, the sex thing…I didn't go through with it. Like you always say, 'Who knows what tomorrow will bring?' And please take all my posters down." My sweetheart.

I looked out the window. The sky was overcast, not a single star visible. I glanced at the *Star Wars* poster pinned to the wall over the bed, then the others—*Breakfast at Tiffany's, Witches of Eastwick, Dune*. All good movies. All loved by Hannah. Why would I want to take them down? On the opposite wall smiled a half-naked Sting. He could stay up too. I folded the quilt I had made for Hannah when she was in second grade, put it on the top shelf in a closet, and smoothed out Hannah's prom dress under the plastic in a corner. My things were already hanging there, brought in from the corridor closet, my entire wardrobe on twenty hangers. I propped up in the armchair the black-and-white Pierrot I had made for Hannah when she was four—he would keep me silent company. And with that, my move into Hannah's room was complete.

The room was small, but it had a bed. It felt strange to be sleeping in a bed that would not have to be folded in the morning. I stood in our apartment—my apartment—so empty! I would be coming home to this emptiness from now on.

I went down to the basement, and before getting off the elevator, checked the semidark space for signs of a rat. All clear. I dropped the garbage into the bin and rushed back to the door. It waited for me there, its whiskers moving. I pushed the elevator button. The animal advanced in no hurry, stopped, and sniffed at my bare toe in flip-flops. It sat high on its hindquarters, began to wash its face in a circular motion, rubbed its whiskers, scratched its side, pressed two tiny pink fists to its chest, and looked up at me with its black, beady eyes.

"I have nothing to offer you, buddy," I said. "Sorry."

The rat glanced sideways, dropped on all fours, and slowly walked away. Its tail, long, naked, and pink, dragged behind like a dead piece of rope. The rodent stopped at a distance, sat up straight, watching. The groaning elevator finally came. I pulled the heavy metal door, got in. The elevator went up, but produced a grating sound and stopped before it reached the ground floor. Someone was banging on some door with a vengeance.

"I'm stuck in here!" I yelled.

The banging continued. The elevator swung from side to side as if it were the car in the Amazing Adventures of Spiderman ride at Universal's Islands of Adventure, racing through the streets and climbing buildings alongside Spiderman, about to go into a four-hundred-foot free fall. It produced yet another deafening metal-against-metal grating sound, and then went up. The door on our floor was stuck again. I pushed it open with all I had and saw Alex banging his fist on our door.

He turned around, swaying a little and jingling money in his trouser pocket, then took a step toward me. "Pumpkin! Where the hell have you been? Have you missed me? I'm hungry. Make me breakfast." He broke into a contented grin.

I approached our door with caution. Alex grabbed my waist, bent to kiss my shoulder. He smelled of alcohol and sweat. His slurpy kiss on my throat sounded as if he were noisily sucking the marrow from a bone. An uneven two-day growth of beard scratched my cheek and neck.

"Alex," I protested, squirming away from him. "No one missed you."

He grabbed my shoulder, swayed, and snorted. "Hey, don't act surprised."

He jerked me toward him, and I stumbled. My stomach turned with terror.

"Don't touch me and don't shout. People are sleeping."

"Shhh." He brought his index finger to his lips and lowered his voice, but not much. "C'mon, open the door. Breakfast. Is Hannah at school?" He emitted a short laugh.

I felt queasy with revulsion, feeling each heartbeat behind my breast. I fumbled for keys in my back pocket, in no hurry to free them. And when I did, the key did not fit in the lock.

"Oh Christ, gimme that!" he said.

The hallway was empty. So were the stairs. I rarely saw people here. Alex pushed me against the wall, crushing me, one hand on my throat, another under my T-shirt, squeezing my breast. His kiss rough, he bit my lip. His knee forced mine apart, shoving his right leg between both of mine so that I stumbled again. The keys fell to the dirty floor with a loud thud.

"Why are you such a sourpuss?" Alex slurred, swallowing a burp. He grabbed my arm, squeezed it hard, and pulled me away from the front door.

I pushed him back with all my strength but achieved very little. His meaty palms pressed down upon my shoulders, then suddenly let me go for a second. Alex flexed his muscular thighs, grabbed my hair, and bent to kiss me again, his tongue stuck down my throat. I gagged and attempted to wriggle away, but he was too heavy. Then he released his grip. I caught my breath.

"We are over. Go home." I kept my voice even, remembering how easily angered he was.

He hit the wall with his fist, raised his face. His bloodshot eyes, like two loaded Kalashnikovs, came within a few inches of mine.

"You bitch—" He swallowed another burp. "You don't have a fucking clue. We are over when I say we are over."

I dashed for the stairs. He cut me off, holding my wrist, then picked the keys off the floor, and slid one into the lock. I could feel the hollow *click* with my body. He left the keys in the lock and pushed the door. It swung open. I wriggled to free myself. Alex let go of my wrist and squeezed my throat.

"Alex, no!" I clawed at his hand.

He pressed a knife to my ribs, as dispassionate as a butcher. I felt the cold blade through my T-shirt. Fear, a bone-deep, chilling fear, moved within me, slow, heavy, unclean, unseeing, like a bear disturbed in its hibernation by hunger. His lips brushed against my ear. "Be a good girl and go in. Don't make a sound."

A neighbor in *3D* opened a door just a crack, and right away the door slammed shut.

Mrs. Goldfarb opened the door too, the length of the hooked chain.

"Whatcha lookin' at?" Alex snarled at her.

Mrs. Goldfarb's voice was high-pitched and shaky. "I'm calling the police!"

An uneven rumbling came from Alex's chest, and I realized he was laughing.

"Stay away from her, you sonofabitch!" she said. "Are you all right, Anna?"

Still laughing, he pushed me hard against the wall with both hands, then released me and ran down the stairs.

"I'll be back!" he yelled.

I was shaking. *Breathe, just breathe*, I thought.

Mrs. Goldfarb unhooked the chain, approached the stairwell, and stared down intently. She was in her long housecoat and her pink-fur slippers, with a curler in her hair. "I think he's gone." She looked me over. "Are you all right?"

"Mrs. Goldfarb, thank you for saving me." I gave her a hug, and she hugged me back. She smelled of talcum powder. "I didn't know you could curse."

"That's the only word I know. I learned it when my Ira would lose all our money on off-track betting, my Ira." Her voice sounded shaky. "He wanted to show me a good life, to take me out of here. 'You'll be wearing silk dresses and gloves, Bernice. A pair of gloves for each day of the week. And one pair in lace,' he used to say. I wanted a pair of lace gloves. And silk dresses. He hoped we'd be rich 'till the day he had a heart attack. May he rest in peace. I loved Ira. I still love him. I talk to him every day. He thinks I should move to Florida." Her dentures clicked. Her laugh sounded like a creaky door, as if it was not often used. She pushed a finger at my chest. "Every week on the news, there's a story about a woman who has been shot by her ex-boyfriend. Anna, call the police."

"And tell them what? His threats? He didn't do anything yet."

With a pained look, she shook her head sadly. "God forbid!"

Amen to that. He might return. Should I take up kung fu? Buy a gun? Move? I would tell Rita nothing. Why worry her? And not a word to Mark. They did not need to know about that. Maybe Mother was right—I should stay away from men. I could live without them. I could not live without myself.

i plopped myself down on the couch, tucked my legs under me. "Let me tell you a story."

"As many as you want. Even with the familiar ones, I never know where you'll take me."

I had to give it to him, Mark always was my best listener, one among many of his redeeming features. If I suspected an element of banter hidden in the lining, it did not seem to be the case, for he looked genuinely intrigued.

"Yesterday in my Film 101 class, there was an interview with the director of a hit TV series. He talked about his dreams, his career, then mentioned the new bar he and his wife have opened downtown, so—why wouldn't he?—he invited everyone to come."

That piqued Mark's interest. Mark was my best friend turned boyfriend, then fiancé, then ex-fiancé, then best friend again. Good, right? We had quite a history together. Perusing the newest acquisitions, he had stationed himself at his usual place, near one of my crammed bookshelves that spilled here and there over all four walls.

He rubbed his left ear, pulled on the earlobe a few times, and without looking away from the books, said, "Free drinks?"

"No."

"Why would we want to go then?"

"Who said anything about going anywhere?"

"Am I to understand that free drinks aren't the main attraction of the story?"

"That's correct."

"I'm listening." He pulled a book from the shelf and leafed through it. "Go on. The bar."

"The bar—all in velvet, in reds and gold, all baroque. They're thinking about live entertainment, 'something experimental,' as he put it, but for now there's a live rooster in a cage. His wife, Elizabeth, designed the bar decor herself, and he mentions she's Russian. Then it dawned on me. Do you remember my ex-best friend Elizabeth?"

"No-ooo!" Mark rounded his *O*'s, his eyes wide. "You think it's her?"

"The world is a peculiarly small place. I remember someone mentioning something about her divorcing her third husband and marrying a TV director or whatever."

"Well, well, well. Who could forget Elizabeth? She was trouble," he said.

"You keep saying that."

He squeezed the book back into its spot on the shelf. "Well…what if I told you she repeatedly came on to me? The day after I proposed to you in front of everyone, for one."

"Did she. And what happened?"

He shrugged. "Nothing. I was with you."

"You never mentioned anything to me."

"I didn't want you to get upset. I warned you not to trust her, didn't I?"

"Persisting on telling me not to trust a person and omitting an explanation was upsetting."

"Do you want to see her?" He stretched out the last two words.

"What for? I had enough. And now new, interesting facts are coming up."

Elizabeth, Elizabeth. Strange what we can recollect, events so remote, abandoned, forcefully evicted from the mind, separated from the present by multitudes of scattered, half-forgotten memories, events that happened so far back in the past, they felt like another lifetime. I had first met her in my English language class for new immigrants, where we both struggled with English verbs at neighboring desks. As persons of the same nationality tend to cluster in groups, we too gravitated toward one another, she and I.

My marriage had thundered, soured, then fallen apart a short time ago. She had left her husband and was sleeping on a couch in a friend's studio. I invited her in; we had two rooms. Complete strangers, thrown together by fate, each with their own share of disappointment in affairs of the heart, we split the costs of meals and living quarters, weathered all stages of our divorces (Elizabeth had no children, so hers went faster and smoother).

Our compassionate camaraderie turned into a solid friendship. When our lives stabilized, she moved into her own space. Our bond frayed around the time Hannah and I were leaving New York for Germany. To the best of my remembrance, on the day in question, it felt like a wartime evacuation. Two short days earlier, it had been confirmed that the job I had applied for was waiting for me, which made me nervous. Jobs do not wait for people. It would be gone in an hour. In another two days, our new life would begin. If we were to have enough money to start anew, all our belongings would have to be sold. Some of the furniture was antique flea-market finds, and Elizabeth enlisted the help of her antique-dealer mother, Sima. What luck! Sima came.

"Don't worry, I won't cheat you and your little girl," she had said. "I'll give you the best price."

Something inside me screamed, "Mayday! Mayday! Danger!" I did not listen. I always trusted my intuition, but what could I do? I was short on both time and money. I was sick of being poor. The intuition? It was either this or nothing.

Lustrous like a magnolia in full bloom, Sima went around the place, pointing at things. "I'll give you fifteen dollars for that marble-top table. This mirror isn't worth more than twenty-five. You think that's real gold leaf? They lied to you, dear."

It was an antique mirror, framed in hand-carved wood that was gilded with twenty-four-carat gold leaf. Caught in the moment, Mark and I had bought this exquisite piece at an auction at Sotheby's to signify the beginning of a beautiful life together, our first joint possession.

Every ten minutes or so, Sima said in a syrupy version of her screechy voice, "Knock twenty off, would you? Knock another twenty off, darling."

It was a fraction of what she would sell it for. Right or wrong, I did not bargain, so pressed for time I was. I could have spit in her face, but I thought, *If she buys the furniture, it'll cover the move and rent.* I could breathe for a few months.

There was not even enough to cover one ticket. All my friends chipped in to pay for the rest. Things that were more or less valuable Sima packed in her car herself. The rest was picked up in a truck the next morning. The place was wiped clean. It might sound like I regretted selling those things, but that impression is wrong. I did not care about the material possessions. I outlined all of this to Elizabeth. She was so proud of her mother's achievement.

"She sure knows how to bargain, my mommy." 'Twas true.

Ah well... I sighed and looked up. Mark was silent, watching me.

"Years later, I still feel used, even...ah, well..." I bit my lip.

"Violated." Mark left my bookshelves alone, began to pace across my small living room. "And so unscrupulously, by someone you trusted, and at the time of need. I know, sweetheart."

"What a creepy feeling. Listen, I'd rather not bore you with my reminiscences."

"Never."

With all his shortcomings, big and small, one thing always stayed the same— Mark was loyal to a fault, like a faithful dog. A disarming habit.

Awoken a second ago, Eve came up to Mark, twined round and rubbed against his legs. He picked her up. Eve cradled in his arms, purred away.

I was quiet, slipping deeper into the bitterness of recollection. They were the sorts of memories, like small splinters in the soul, that were not quite agreeable, let alone desirable, and that upon entering one's mind, had no intention of leaving soon. They hopped into being from nowhere and took solid shapes, enabling one to sulk after pondering them thoroughly enough, and I was tempted to do just that.

I drew my knees up to my chest.

"Elizabeth never brought that yellow cat of yours to Germany," Mark said in a half-statement, half-question. "She told me she did, but he ran away later on."

"Orange. Azazello was orange. We agreed I'd adopt her cat too, Pizza. Never saw him again. I kept on confronting her, but she refused to talk about it. I think she kicked them out on a street. I can't even tell you how upset I was. We loved that cat, that sweet orange fluff, Hannah and I. It was the hardest thing for Hannah. I distanced myself from that woman, but there were more intrigues and betrayals. Let's learn from our mistakes."

I was filled with unsettling emotions I had not suspected I had, which had been lying coiled like snakes in the grass, dormant for years, awaiting their hour. Now evoked, stirred back to life through the unplanned resurfacing of unpleasant memories, they unhinged their jaws, dripping poison from their fangs.

Mark loved Hannah as if she were his flesh and blood. Hannah thought of him as her papa-mama group. What made Hannah upset upset Mark too. Mark's son from his second marriage, Andrew, two years her senior, became her big half-brother. They spent one weekend per month together. The rest of the time, Andrew lived with his mother, who disapproved of her son being in the company of any of Mark's women, no exceptions made.

Mark grew very silent, his eyes flashing. Per God's great plan, he was a nurturing guy. If he tried to suppress the outward display of such unmanly behavior, the suppression was done sporadically, in the rare moments when his image of himself faltered, as he thought his manhood questioned. Seeing the dark fire in his eyes, such anger at a person who dared to threaten people dear to him—for a moment it made me feel like a tenderly cared for potted geranium and brought the impulse to bud. I was almost in love with him again, easily impressionable as I am.

He put Eve down on my lap as a gesture of consolation. Eve did not protest the relocation procedure, her motor running. I stroked her velvety hair. Eve turned belly up, stretching her soft paw beyond the normal limit to pat me on the cheek. The continuous vibratory sound went a tone deeper, intensified.

We lapsed into silence. Our silence was effortless, familiar. Today, as on many other occasions, it was no heavily pregnant, awkward pause that hovered in the air between us as an obvious indicator there was an urgent need to change the subject. It also was not the loaded, uncomfortable silence between two people who, though no less than courteous, searched in desperation for things to say to one another, but could find nothing. Ours was brimming all right, but it was with the knowledge of what the other person was thinking. The sole anticipation was what form a thought would take when spoken at last.

Mark paced back and forth, rubbing his forehead. He stopped near the shelves, pulled out a book. "This is something new. *The Zen of Left Brain Development*," he read aloud, rubbed his thumb along the edge of the pages, put the book back. "Useful."

Hesitant, he stepped away from the shelf to return to it a moment later and turned to face me. "Why did you sell our mirror? Was it like 'I want nothing to do with you'? What did I do?" He spoke with gentleness.

"I sold everything, remember? How else was I to pay for the move?"

A slight pause. "I didn't know your financial situation was so bad. You never asked me for money."

"You never exactly offered."

No one said anything for a long moment.

"I was sure you wouldn't take it if I did. Would you?"

I allowed myself this terrible moment of cruelest satisfaction. "No. It was safe to offer."

"Now I feel like a total jerk." Mark's clenched fist struck his thigh.

"I'm all for self-flagellation, but please stop. You struggled for years to make ends meet. I did all right by myself." I raised my arms and spread them wide, in a hey-look-at-me-now gesture.

"I wanted to be the provider and protector. Ah, some protector. If it weren't for me, would you have moved to Germany? I wanted to live there, not you." He sounded plaintive.

"Indeed. And you were supposed to follow me. We were to get married in Munich. I waited for you to come, but you never did. *C'est la vie*. Despite the way it sounds, I'm not trying to rub it in. Trust me, Mark."

"I know, sweetheart. If you ever feel like rubbing it in, go ahead, rub it in. I deserve it."

"You could stop blaming yourself. We both know *why* I moved."

"Stop feeling responsible for what happened to you? What kind of a man would I be?"

We both paused, staring into space. It had not been me running toward something, though I did, but me running away from something else. I had fled from the tense atmosphere, I had to, away from my parents, the Stoic Ones, with a firm objective to block them from interfering any further with my life and messing up Hannah's as much as they had messed up mine, even if their intentions had been good. If physical distance was the only option available to me, then physical distance it was. And it worked. In the seven years we lived in Munich, Mother never came to visit, never wrote to Hannah or me, never called. Even if she thought it the best way to deal with a mentally unstable person—that would be me—there was something pleasant, if surrealistic, about the whole arrangement. But (a little rust spot) every other Saturday at two in the afternoon, I had to be home for the obligatory ten-minute call with Bella to discuss the advantages of New York versus Munich climatic conditions. New York always got the upper hand.

I took a sip of tea from a cup. Mark's fingers drummed "Macarena" on the table.

"Why is it we never talk about it?" he asked.

"Dunno. It didn't matter that Germany wasn't my choice. It was far enough from here."

Mark kept quiet for a second, mulling it over. "I was such an idiot, wasn't I? How I screwed things up. Do you think you'd ever be able to forgive me?"

"Nothing to forgive." And that was the truth. It was hardly his fault the university people changed their minds and decided against signing a contract with Mark at the last moment, thus unwillingly thwarting our joined plans to find a better life over there. Neither his in-depth knowledge of English and American literature nor his fluency in German, French, Italian, and Russian had helped much.

"Mark, I'd heard about the contract falling through."

"You knew?" The question mark of his brow became more pronounced.

"Andrew told me."

"You never mentioned anything to me."

"Neither did you. I didn't want to embarrass you," I said softly. "So you got scared you wouldn't be able to find another job over there, as you had every right to be. You don't have to be ashamed of that. Why should you?"

Mark nodded. Still, no acceptance showed in his eyes. He looked away.

"By that time I already had a job permit, a job, and a place to live. Hannah went to a new school. What was the point of coming back here?" I smiled. "Besides, you know my policy—one abandonment per customer, after which all the privileges are revoked. Think of it as a blessing."

"A blessing." He looked at me intently for a moment, like I was one of those soggy tea leaves left in a pitiful pile on the bottom of a cup from which he could try to divine the future.

"Yep. Besides, I already forgave you a long time ago for all your past and future sins. Please pay attention. You're here, right? You're my friend, I'm yours." I beamed at him. And I meant it in earnest. In one form or another, he seemed to be embedded in my life. Mark had already asked for my forgiveness at least a gazillion times too, though it was sweet of him to ask yet again.

"A friend, but not the boyfriend." Mark grinned, sat down, picked up the tea-cup in his hand, and with utmost concentration, turned it around in his fingers as if studying the design.

"So, how's—" We both spoke simultaneously, and we both laughed.

"You go," I said.

"How's Hannah doing at King's?" Mark asked.

"Loves it and loves living in London. Isn't it amazing how fast children adapt to a different culture? Besides, she has her big brother Andrew to guide her through both—the college and life abroad. How fortunate is that?"

Mark threw me a quick glance and nodded.

"Mark, what are you trying *not* to tell me with that significant glance of yours?"

"Do you think there's something between them?"

"Don't think so. The latest I heard, Hannah was dating a boy from a parallel class, Stuart, whom we suspect to be a playboy and a cheat. Every mother's delight. Why?"

"I thought I was getting a vibe from Andrew," he said.

"Define a vibe."

"Can't."

"Did he ever mention anything to you?" I asked.

"How much do you think he's telling me?"

"Hmm…"

"Exactly. Well…What did Hannah pick for her major?"

"Psychology," I said.

"Oh well, no surprise here, everything pointed to that. Are you happy with her choice?"

"Yes, but I wonder if it might be something that will need to be survived later on."

"Can't help you here."

Mark leaped up, kissed me on the forehead, and headed for the door.

"Mark?"

"Well." He motioned for permission to leave with his eyebrows. "An early class tomorrow. I'm off next Thursday. Would you like to spend the day together?"

"Do you have to ask?"

"Thursday, then." He smiled and left.

eye could see, the devastated fields…" Ah, what a peaceful late afternoon it was. Outside the windowpane, a town mockingbird paced the length of the air conditioner back and forth and rasped. From time to time, it stopped as if contemplating something, hooted like a mourning dove, and then walked on. Adam and Eve had curled up into a uni-cat ball for a scheduled afternoon nap in my bed. I was at my desk writing. Michael sat in the armchair, dressed in brown polyester trousers and a short-sleeved honey-yellow shirt, listening to his portable radio and escaping his wife, one earbud plugged into his ear, another hanging loose. Many an afternoon tumbled by as we, together like this, chatted a little on the subject of life. Some mornings too.

As if about to declare a war on some unsuspecting country, he pulled the earbud out. The station identification music bubbled out from there.

"This woman is unbearable," Michael said. "Simply unbearable."

"Which one are you talking about?"

"Eh?"

"Which one? Mine or yours?"

"Mine. Yours too." The wind seemed to whistle out of his sails. He went silent.

"Did something happen?" I asked.

"Er, nothing new. She never stops nagging me. Nagging, nagging, nagging. This or that. It'll wear anybody down. Nagging, nagging. Always unhappy. I can't stand her cooking anymore. I could never tell what it was before she cooked it to a pulp. No salt, no spices. It either has no taste—none!—or it tastes like a stewed soldier's puttee. Pepper, I like a little pepper on my food. Did you bake bread?"

"In the kitchen. Take the whole thing with you if you want. I'll bake more."

"No, don't give it to me. She'll throw it away. The woman can't stand anything edible, nothing that has color, texture, or taste. Always the same grayish mush. I wouldn't mind a little piece of that bread now."

"Do you want to put something on it?" I asked. "I could make you a sandwich."

"Thanks, no. Just want a taste of good bread, something I can sink my teeth into. Don't get up. I'll cut a piece myself."

On his way to the kitchen, Michael drew the window curtains tighter together.

By fortunate coincidence, Bella and Michael's bedroom window was five feet away and faced my bedroom window—what a dreadful comfort that was. Theirs was also two feet higher than mine, granting them a better viewing position. They were not inconvenienced to check on me when they wished, a golden opportunity Auntie never let go by, and no curtain in the world was to stop her. Amazing how much a person was capable of seeing when she set her mind to it.

A moment later Michael came back chewing, a sliver of bread in his hand. He settled back in the armchair, concentrating on putting both earbuds back into his ears one by one.

Ah, Michael...Let me introduce you to my pillars of stability, the esteemed Stoic Ones—Mother, Auntie Bella, and her husband, Uncle Michael—also known as Naysayers Inc.. They were Nobles clothed in a Mantle of Virtue, they were the Saints; only their wings were missing. Taken collectively, they constituted the formidable, the most influential of all entities—in common terms, "the family." *My* informal constellation. Some family, ours. So I was *blessed* with two mothers instead of just one. I am asking you, did I ask for it? How desperate was I to be born? But in all truthfulness, they asked not for me either.

Mother, a single dictatorial power, was the CEO in charge of Naysayers Inc., who were in charge of me, while Bella was a mere employee who on regular basis took grave offense with her boss's allegations. No secret to anyone, Bella plotted to overthrow the governing body and take matters into her own hands.

Michael...Michael, in general, operated under the misplaced perception he had to endure whatever life threw at him and endure in silence, so he stayed away from the main action in the hope of peace. He had an enviable capacity for endurance. But sooner or later, immersed without ability to surface in the muddy, turbulent waters of the ocean of negativity—and it was inevitable—he stopped resisting and was converted to follow in the proud footsteps of the naysayers. To his credit, he shied away from any leadership position.

The phone rang. I picked it up.

"Do you know where Mike is?" Auntie sing-sang.

"Ah...Didn't he tell you where he was going?"

"No."

I looked at Michael.

I'm not here, he mouthed and closed his eyes. The earbuds stayed in.

"Are you looking for him for a reason?" I asked Bella.

"There's something I want to discuss with him." Auntie gave a short laugh, an artificial sound. "If you see him, tell him I've been looking for him."

"I will." I hung up the phone.

Michael eyed me with suspicion.

"I lied for you," I said.

He shrugged his shoulders, closed his eyes again. The town mockingbird whistled for a bit and continued with its exercise regiment, a pittter-patter of tiny feet audible over the angry drone and horn-blowing of mushrooming traffic. Michael listened to the radio, his semiopened eyes focused in midair at nothing in particular. I stared at the computer screen, pretended to write. The sensation of someone's gaze boring my cheek was growing, and grew to an uncomfortable level.

I glanced at Michael. His eyes were fixed on me. I gave him a quizzical look. He pulled the earbuds out. The station identification music bubbled out from the piece.

"When I die, she'll manage to make my life miserable on the other side too."

"She might," I said.

"Nowhere to hide."

"True. Nowhere."

Michael set up straight. "I want to divorce her."

"Wait…what?"

"I want to divorce her." His right hand flipped an imaginary cigarette butt.

The dead weight of their shared past had clipped the wings off his heart, made his chest cave in, turned his hair to gray, caused his eyes to lose all the luster. Now they always looked tired. Haunted.

"All right," I said. "You want to divorce her. If that's what you want, sure, I'll support you. Is this what you want?"

"Yes, I want to divorce her." His tone conveyed this topic was exhausted. Bud went back into the ear.

"Why now?" I asked. So late in his life, how could I help him?

Bud went out of the ear. "Are you talking to me? I can't hear you when the radio's on."

"I asked why not years ago? You're eighty-six. I always wondered how you endured for so long."

"Ah…There was always something to be taken care of first. How were you able to endure them for so long?"

"I live on my own," I said. "Neither one of them is in here day and night."

"And you took a seven-year vacation to Germany."

"If it could be called a vacation."

"But it helped?"

"Where would you go?" I asked.

"Nowhere. Too late for me. She's my family."

He put the earbud back into his ear. Like a sack full of potatoes, Adam dropped off the bed with a thud, stretched his back and each paw, and jumped on Michael's lap. Eve busied herself elsewhere.

The saddest truth was, Michael firmly believed that whatever happened to him, he deserved it somehow—as if he had done something he needed to be punished for, and the gods of fate had contrived to make him pay for that horrible sin over and over. What an awful mistake it was, him sacrificing his life like this for nothing! This was not something to eradicate overnight, and by the stroke of misfortune, so far nothing, nothing I had said could make him abandon such an idea. "Only a piece of cheese in a mousetrap is free," he kept saying, shaking his head.

"Ouch!" Michael said. "Adam's licking me. No wonder Eve's hiding. What a smart girl."

"Don't you worry about that. She can't hide forever. He'll catch her eventually."

Michael nodded. Adam's tiny tongue, while warm, cute, and, well, tiny, was also as rough as they come—a formidable hidden weapon. The first twenty licks were divine, but everything after was a slow Chinese torture, and the spot under attack became sore fast. Right. Where was I? "...*the devastated fields...*"

"Nothing interesting's happening," Michael said.

"Do you want to move in with me?"

"She'll get me here. She'll get you too."

"I'll survive. Do you have a plan?"

"Ah..." He waved his hand, clammed up. Something dark seemed to take possession of his entire body. My heart sank.

"Do you have enough money to rent?" I asked.

"I have to think it over."

"Do us all a favor. Before you leave her, teach her how to turn on the TV, and how to use a vacuum cleaner, and anything else with buttons that need to be pushed to make it work. And every other basic skill."

He threw his hands in the air. "If I was able to teach her anything, I'd have done it by now. She's hopeless. She doesn't want to learn. She thinks I'll be around to take care of her forever."

A divorce. Life was like that sometimes. What was I to do with this information?

Michael switched on the radio, put one earbud in his ear, took it out again.

"I drove my Dodge to a junkyard yesterday," he said. "Hard for me to park it."

"Hallelujah!"

"It was a good car, big, powerful, steady on the road, built to last."

"All true, if you ignore the big hole in the floor on the passenger side, among other things. Don't feel sad. You haven't driven it in over a year, which was a good thing. It was too dangerous to drive anyhow."

"So it got a little old. Where will that guy live now?"

"What guy?" I asked.

"Jerry. He lived in there." Michael petted Adam on the head. "I used to give him half of my lunch too. He didn't mind Bella's cooking. I offered the Dodge to him, but he refused to take it. 'Too rusty,' he said. I gave him a little money to find a roof over his head."

"You gave him money?"

The phone rang. I picked it up.

"Oh, Mama…" I heard tears in Hannah's voice. "I think Stuart cheated on me again."

"You think or you know?" I asked. "And what do you mean by *again*?"

"Again." She sobbed. "And I know."

"You *knew* he did it before? I thought it was your suspicion."

"Mama, I don't have to tell you everything."

"All right."

"I'm a responsible adult who needs to learn how to handle my own problems."

"All right," I said. "I'm all for it. So…what now?"

"I have no idea. What do you think I should do?"

"Do you think it's time to let him go?"

"We're right for each other!" The sobbing intensified. "He cares about me."

"How's sleeping with another women a part of caring about you?"

"They mean nothing to him," she said through sobbing.

"Is that what he said?" I asked.

"Give me that phone." Michael snatched the receiver. "Hi, sweetie."

I could hear the amicable staccato of Hannah's voice.

"Oh-ho," Michael said.

More of Hannah's hurried voice.

"Sweetie," Michael said, "it's all grist for the mill."

Hannah's voice, insisting, insisting.

"Right." He hung up the phone.

I kept looking at him.

"She said she'll call you tomorrow," he said. "She's late for something."

"Do I have a choice?"

"She's so like you when you were her age. Who is Andrew? Isn't he Mark's son?"

"Yes. Why are you asking about him?"

"No reason. Grist for the mill." He shook his head, smiled, put both earbuds into his ears.

eighteen

Collective motion by organisms is common. Fish, insects, birds, bacteria group themselves into swarms, which favor no particular direction and move in interesting patterns. Swarming is an excellent survival strategy. Belonging to a large group also increases the chances of meeting a potential mate or two. Additional benefits of collective intelligence are indubitable, eliminating the need to elaborate further on the matter. Scientists go nuts with excitement in calculating behavioral algorithms for such formations. But what works for the primitive species is not always best for organisms higher on the proverbial evolutionary ladder. The incautious act of crawling out of the comfy ocean and growing legs comes with a long list of responsibilities.

Trained from the cradle to abandon individual needs for demands of the common good and infected for life with marching in step with the collective, the Stoics chaotically charged in a new direction after the rest of a faceless crowd, or, paralyzed, were carried by one. Is not stampeding fun? Not to be a total disappointment in one another's eyes like one of those organisms, adrift and predestined to become someone's lunch, in episodes they exhibited an unmistakable higher level of social development with rational organizational skills during the hunt, moving in unison, not unlike the efficient piranhas that eat their prey alive. Huzzah to those fish for implementing higher standards of freshness for certain food groups. Or was that an awful analogy? However impermanent, it moved them from a respected but somewhat boring herbivorous group into a category with a different orientation—that of predators. Blood! Blood!

Where and how nature discovered how to join organisms together for hunting was lost in the mists of time. As a demonstration of uncanny predatory brilliance is the behavior of hunters extraordinaire—the exuberant school of dolphins, rounding up the mother lode of anchovies, squeaking, screeching, and showing off a little. My pack was less like dolphins and more like giant hornets from hell in their splendor. Enamored with a metaphor, I was forever in search of a fresher one to describe the experience. But even the metaphor has its limits. Whichever way I would look at it, the whole commotion held as much entertainment value as any other typical freak show was able to provide and no more.

Out of convenience, the hunting season was officially open year-round. The Stoics were on continuous call, without time off for sick leave or vacation. An admirable but taxing lifestyle. For my part, I was on double-duty—I served as the preferred legitimate game and as the sacrificial lamb to the cutthroat gods of war too. No stone was left unturned, and they took no prisoners (the movie rights are up for grabs; it could also be made into a miniseries. And I am available for talk shows.). *Touché!* I was wholeheartedly glad they had an interesting hobby. Should I have widened their horizons by introducing them to something equally exciting with less bloodshed involved, say, bungee jumping? Me, I would have been happy to forego both experiences.

Life ran under the banner, "Ridiculous! Throw it out of your head!" It made my blood boil. Full of disrespect and tempting my fate, I would hum "La Marseillaise" under my breath while their arms flapped up and down, their faces turned red, on the verge of condemnation. I heard that phrase throughout the duration of solitary confinement of my life, as pragmatic form of endearment that was supposed to have a mild sobering effect on me.

"Look at that bulging vein at your neck! Look, look! Continue to be so angry, you'll die from a stroke for sure," Mother, the prophetess, would say all too often. "Mark my words."

The sad truth was that taking someone's power away was no act of empowerment, but the betrayal of one's inferiority. Mother had an extended version of this same banner, while reading a newspaper, crunching on an apple: "Throw it out of your head! Drink apple juice! And stop bothering me with this nonsense of yours. I'm busy." She would hide behind her newspaper, hiding in such a manner that unmistakably conveyed my existence was already forgotten. "Out of sight, out of mind," she turned her back, and things disappeared. The worst thing that can be done to a person is to make them invisible. There will be more newspapers to read and more apples to munch on. A bit of dog shit she picked up on her shoe had gotten more attention from her. She thought of a motherly kiss, or any show of affection, as a major weakness and was geared up to wean me off anything to do with it before I would grow accustomed to such things.

Lack of support was compensated by generous advice shoved down my throat with combined communal efforts. In our household joy was never a required feeling, but obligation was. Obligation trumped everything.

"Put that book down!" the Stoics said. "If we don't protect you, who will?"

"Who do you think you are?" the Stoics said.

"What did we do to deserve such a curse?" the Stoics said.

An ogre—me.

Ah, my watchful family, ever devout to the god of conformity. With the world being a complicated place that it was, they chose to fit in by becoming indistinguishable from the herd. After experiencing this concept for the duration of their lives and being satisfied with it, the Stoics insisted on putting this invaluable approach into practice as far as my life was concerned too. But had I not sort of been preplanned to be a uniquely gifted individual, with the headline to my life blazing like a marquee: "Original, innovative, fascinating!"? If I had been born into greatness, which was ultimately my birthright (even if it was to be my own unique form of greatness), why did I have to be conditioned into the grayness of mediocrity? My existential crisis was on the verge of toppling into the death-dealing pique.

Of course, I could always decide, yet again, to change my perception of the whole situation—to reevaluate, yet again, whatever truth was contained therein and take it all as a master's training course on how to handle difficult people. Perhaps it would put a more agreeable angle on the entire state of affairs, and even if this expectation was not exactly realistic or desirable, it was something to think about in the nearest future. Yet again…Ah, well.

nineteen

i paced back and forth across the length of the empty apartment, poisoned by loneliness. It twisted my gut, shallowed my breath, denied me sleep, and stretched my days. I opened and closed closets, cupboards, and books, tumbling through days and space, intent on immersing myself in housework or reading, yet focusing on nothing. My thoughts, jumpy and jumbled, plagued me. I worried about Hannah, how she was. Was she eating enough? Was she warm? Normal distractions did not work. And one late hour, when the world felt alien in the semidarkness that seeped into the room as I sat in a clairvoyant-like trance, a fleeting image of the stranger in gray tugged at my heart and reopened the old wound.

The night had cast a spell on me. I felt powerless before it. And before long, as soon as night fell on earth, I would abandoned reason and begin to brood over him. My isolation filled with shadowy premonitions, and my heart beat wildly. Why could not I forget those sad, gray eyes? What were they pulling me into?

The image was dangled in front of me like a worm before a baby bird. This obsession, called forth to torment me, intrusive and pushy, was becoming absurd, but when had my life ever been logical? What were the chances I would meet him again? Honestly.

Despite all my labors to feel content, I was sad. Lonely. Swooning from loneliness. The houseguest who would not leave had me by the throat. I pushed these fantasies aside and opened the browser. Internet? Internet. It almost felt like a comfortable routine by now. Wink, wink back, e-mail, e-mail, phone conversation, date. It kept my thoughts off Hannah. It also gave me hope. Funny how that was. To be optimistic, but not turn it into a hobby, I thought of the number of dates I wanted to limit myself to, and lucky number seven popped to mind. Seven it was. After that I would be freed from my promise to Hannah.

I will spare you all the details and fast-forward to say that the dates number one through six were no; no; oh no; no no no; um, no; and hell no. Nice to see that things had changed.

Then, date number seven, John, a lawyer, held hidden promise. He was cute, contagiously playful, oozing intelligence, bucktoothed, talkative, and in general an amiable fellow. He was fun and a half, unlawyerlike, and I was at ease, laughing while on a date, a wholehearted laugh. One might think I sought light entertainment and not a relationship, the responsibilities and all, but was unaware of it. And one would be correct to point this out. But that impression would be off—I was hoping for the whole package deal.

But back to John so you will not miss anything of importance, and just in time to witness his inner schnauzer puppy peeping out. For sure, Freud would have had something to say about that. Would there be any peeing on furniture involved later on this evening? Light leg humping? Should I hide my shoes? Did I possess shoes worth fretting over?

He charmed me into taking him home with me. *What the hell*, I thought. I dropped my guard and threw my usual caution to the wind. What a mistake. (I bet you knew that no good could come of this and saw it in the offing. And how right you were!) Later on he stripped for me…wait, not for me. For himself. Such a treat, and what a lucky girl I was—my own Chippendale dancer, and in the comfort of my home. Not that I had wanted one tonight, but in case I did.

"*R-r-r-ruff, r-r-ruff*," he said, in a state of agitation.

While I had admittedly wished for company, did it have to be a human imitating a good-natured dog? Every so often, with male confidence, he gave me a full frontal view, and I got a better look at his concave, hairy chest with a red, pierced heart and the word "MOTHER" in blue ink above it, and another one in purple ("FORVER!") a touch below the bleeding heart, all of this colorful art tattooed over his left breast. Lower yet, it was hard not to spot something else, barely there, pink, wrinkled, and limp, happily dangling from side to side with a periodic twitch. Absorbed in thought, John lowered his arm and scratched there. I understand; if it itches, it will be scratched. (So sorry to bring up a thing like this.)

I can assume that "FORVER!" was meant to be "FOREVER!" What a nice chest decoration it was, but then the whole concept of body ornamentation made me wonder what sort of lawyer John was, and upon pondering the subject a little further, whether it was consequential at this point. What were the odds that he was a seasoned jailbird released into the community a short time ago and, now living under an assumed name, was behind in his visits to his parole officer, and might have a decapitated cadaver or a flock stashed in the safety of his basement, hidden under the floorboards.

John was still caught up in almost rhythmic movement. It looked like he had a fair amount of practice. More was needed if he planned to do something with it as a second career. Who knows, perhaps it was his lifelong dream to become a performing artist. Who was I to criticize?

Sideways, full frontal, sideways, backside, backside. Impossible to say how aware he was of where the show was taking place, so carried away, so enticed in the moment he seemed to be. His face expressed, *Still got it!* and nothing else. At some point in time, he seemed to notice I was also present in the room and turned to me, smiling a knowing smile. "Do you like what you see?"

In all honesty, not so much, so I did not nod, even for courtesy's sake. For what it was worth—and it was not what one might have thought—the problem was less about any physical deficiencies and more about his behavioral oddity.

Now, we are all adults being frank here—I do not see why this should stop, do you?—so I do not want to mislead anyone into thinking I was a nun. I was no nun. Except now I had put myself in danger of giving a false impression that I was an easy woman, which was also far from the truth. You know what? This is uncomfortable. I will stop right here. If one were to consider Mother's view of me, I had been a full-blown harlot from the age of three, no doubt starting when I had refused to wear the Russian version of long johns under my summer dress in July, since no one else in kindergarten did. One must keep in mind that this opinion came from a woman who had had sex twice in her lifetime, and half a century later, still shuddered at the thought of undergoing such an excruciating ordeal, poor woman. Whatever. Let Plato say: "Be kind, for everyone you meet is fighting a hard battle."

I decided it best to let the matter go no further, so it was bye-bye to John. Hurrah for him, that he was so uninhibited by nature and stuff, if uninhibited is the word. That just was not my cup of tea, not at the tender beginning of a delicate dance of two complete strangers coming together for the first time, when maintaining the balance of forces was crucial. It was also possible I was too hung up on the romantic elements of a mating ritual and wanted to avoid the brutal reality of things.

If you must know, I did not think I was. Perhaps it was some innate female thing, that romantic bit. Though wait, because truth be told, with myself being on the receiving end of things, I can be candid in saying that size *does*, you know...

But I did laugh later on, despite everything going as wrong as it could. Guess what? The pink love cat had been useless. I had every right to be furious at myself and that pink love cat thingy too. And I was done.

twenty

thursday began as moody silver gray. It lost the silver fast. The light overcast turned into a bleak drizzle, then to rain. Soon the rain stopped, the sun shone a little, only to start sprinkling again. Then it plain gave up, clouded and leaden. By afternoon the blockage felt solid. The day seemed to be unable to make up its mind about what it wanted to be portrayed as, and being confused itself, it confused us.

Mark was late. When he showed up, two brown paper bags were nested in his arms as a peace offering—a big bag filled with white Asian pears and a smaller one stuffed with roasted chestnuts. He had calculated right, and the compensation-for-lateness bribe was accepted.

Though the plan to spend the entire afternoon at the local farmer's market had not quite worked out, if we hurried a little, we could still buy food. Shoulder to shoulder, stepping lively and sharing an umbrella, we made it to the market. It was closing time, and more vendors had cleared out than remained. Modest piles of unsold, discarded produce, scraps of newspapers, torn plastic bags, several broken umbrellas, and one perfectly good men's shoe were left behind in emptied spaces between the remaining vendors' tents. Presented with petty choices—a few root vegetables and five different kinds of apples—we brought home treasures which felt like spoils of war. Three ears of corn, one yellow squash, some baked goodies, a jar of honey, two local cheeses, and a potted basil.

Mark was distracted or reserved, untalkative again. He carried the groceries, held me firm by the elbow, and threw indecipherable glances at me. This week's Thursday was no different from last week's Wednesday. At my place, the bags were dropped onto the kitchen table, the basil found its place on a windowsill next to the African violet. I was led to the couch, handed a book, kissed on the forehead. Mark had been doing an awful lot of father-like forehead kissing as of late.

"Sit, read, relax," he said. "I'll take care of everything."

I opened a book and started to read, ignoring the clunking, slamming, thudding, glass-breaking noises coming from the kitchen. Soon Mark was back with a tray and a nervous giggle.

"Nothing's broken," he said, "and I put the groceries in the fridge."

I could sense his tension. He set the tray down in front of me, lowered himself into the armchair. The tray contained a teapot, tea mugs, small plates, a plate filled with pistachio cake and zucchini bread, both cut into little cubes, bite-size rugelach, a bowl with sliced sweet pears, and napkins. Service fit for a queen, minus cucumber sandwiches, which I did not care for.

"Have you heard from Karl?" Mark asked.

"Oh yes. Guess what? They had another baby!"

"Good for them."

"It's funny how detailed his e-mails are about everything that almost happens in that rural habitat they moved to, for the sake of safer child rearing, but fail to mention Martha's being pregnant—I assume her pregnancy was no two-day thing, too trivial to be mentioned between friends. Then, out of the blue, he drops it: 'We had a baby. It's a boy.' Maybe it's me, but I find it curious."

"Is it his second or third?"

"Second, as far as I know. I can just see it: It's morning. Martha bakes breakfast buns while Karl checks outside the entrance door for goodies delivered earlier by a milkman. He finds two bottles of milk, five bottles of yogurt, and a little Moses basket with a baby boy inside. Blond curly hair, blue eyes, rosy cheeks. A little angel. So they're having warm buns fresh from the oven with coffee lattes for breakfast along with a baby to keep for a while to see how it goes."

Mark grinned. "Well, that's the beauty of Karl for you."

We lapsed into silence. I got the impression Mark had been uneasy about something ever since he had come in last Wednesday night. As he was not about to tell me what was bothering him by himself—he never did—I had to drag it out, and it was not the easiest task. I thought the best way to bring the subject of conversation around to things more relevant to the current state of affairs of the company in attendance was to be direct.

"So tell me what's wrong," I encouraged him, "or I'll keep on talking."

"I like your stories. They keep me sane."

"Or the direct opposite."

"No, no." Mark produced a deep sigh, put down the mug he had held in his hand all this time, never taking a sip. "Why didn't you stop me from marrying Olga?"

How about that.

"I was told you married her half a year into your married life. Now what?"

I looked at him. With his strong cheekbones and dimpled chin, he was bewitching, startlingly handsome, with rugged good looks. The observation made my heart beat fast. In addition to possessing hard-to-live-without basics such as being intelligent, caring, responsible, and exciting, he had many other remarkable qualities I shall bore you not with, and all of them showed on his easy-to-read face. It was not difficult to fall in love with the owner of such physiognomy. The endless list of girlfriends and two ex-wives were living proof of that. Not dissimilar to buzzing flies attracted to a piece of succulent meat left unattended, so were girls orbiting in circles around him without end. I, being of flesh and blood (and hence frail and weak), could attest to that. Yep—been there myself. *Bz-zzz.*

Mark's position as a professor of English literature at Columbia University placed him under the auspicious circumstances of being a perfect subject of admiration, overexposing Mark—who somewhat, but not altogether, resisted these temptations—to the euphoric members of the opposite sex who longed for a subject to admire. If you ask me, this was like letting a fox into a chicken coop, but no one had bothered to ask me. Pity. I would have said something otherwise, but since no one seemed interested in what I thought, I would keep quiet.

Perhaps as any other mortal man placed in his too inviting circumstances, Mark on impulse, at almost fixed intervals, wandered off the right path—nothing more than a minicrush, never moving off the platonic level, an unsubstantiated threat of possible infidelity, but it was there. He never acted out on these insecurities and always regretted giving into temptation later on.

I continued staring at him. The pause had gone on long enough. Mark still gave no answer to my question and appeared to be studying the rug. I glanced over there too, but found nothing of interest. My concern for him ballooned—amazing as he was, he was a klutz sometimes—an important fact that could be relevant to the forthcoming conversation, though it need not take the highest priority at this instant.

"Olga's a bitch. How did I miss *that* at the time?" Mark declared straight off, the first one to break the silence. He shook his head as if warning me how convinced he was of the soundness of his reflections on life in general and on certain living things in particular, and that I should not bother to dispute it. For anyone's information, I was not planning to. Mark was back on his favorite horse, and as usual, he would not be climbing down from this stratum anytime soon. Fine by me. He could stay up there as long as he wanted.

I tried to sound casual. "You want my opinion or my approval?"

"Opinion." He stared at me with suspicion.

Set on stating my perspective in the most inoffensive way possible, I smiled wider to reassure him of my good intentions. "I don't know what you've missed. I can guess what your attention might be preoccupied with. Olga's a beautiful woman, smart, a bit on a paranoid side with her obsessive jealousy—and not entirely without a reason, we all know that—but she's no bitch."

"Yes, she is," he said. "And you're arguing."

"Be reasonable. Too bad about the way she left you, but you two were incompatible to begin with. You see that, don't you?" I did more of that smiling thing. Even if my intended grin had managed to placate him a little, it was hard to tell from his sullen pout.

He leaned back, interlocked his fingers behind his head. "What's your point?"

"Ah, the point. What did you expect when you married a woman twenty years younger?"

"I didn't expect her to leave me for another man. Did I make her jealous? Not on purpose. Did I cheat on her? Never." He combed his long fingers through his unruly hair, making it stick up. This innocent gesture was Mark's trademark for the times he was unsure of himself. That said—and I cannot be too certain about it—there was no trace of resentment in his eyes. Something was bothering him a lot, and though the nature of it was unclear, I knew better than to think it was Olga's cheating on him, for he had been over that for a long time.

"Ten to one, he made her feel special, while you—from what I've witnessed— nagged her to wash your smelly socks," I said. "You were never the kind of guy who believed a woman's place was in the kitchen. What happened to you? Mark, forgive me, but this conversation is long overdue."

He nodded, though it seemed his thoughts were somewhere else.

"You asked me to tell if you ever turned into a nag. You still want me to do that?"

He nodded again, but eyed me with hesitation, averting his glance.

"Mark, my love, please remember I'm on your side. Yes, I am. You're turning into a nag."

"I apologize for making you jealous." The adorable lock of black hair fell onto his forehead.

I sighed. "Mad with jealousy."

"Would you believe me if I said I'd always been faithful to you?"

"I know."

"We had eight good years together," he said, a strange glint in his eyes. "What happened to us?"

"Life."

Life. We never broke up as such. Time and distance, working at a snail's pace, dripping hours, days, dripping years took their toll, bled out all love, left us empty. I see no reason not to admit that, yes, on occasion, I often wondered to myself how things might have turned out had he come with me to Munich. What was it about this particular period that made it so vivid in my memory? Pathetic, I know. It was possible to speculate endlessly about such matters, but what purpose would this serve in the long run?

Anyhow, I could tell he was still warming up to spin his story, so I took several sips of tea to replenish my strength and continued to talk.

"Bless your heart, you and your laundry. You're a wonderful person. What is it with this obsession of yours? Were you punishing Olga for something?"

"She's a bitch. You know it as well as I do. Let's not talk about it anymore."

"I wonder, did you ever love her?" I asked, and as soon as the words left my lips, I was sorry I had said it. At once I corrected myself. "Never mind. Forgive me. You don't have to answer."

He did not, though I detected a certain strain in his face. This was not the first time we had had this conversation. For the past two years, it had been triggered by a reoccurring theme—not just a simple inconvenience—when a new girlfriend dumped Mark or he dumped her. This not-so-unorthodox mess had started with Olga, his wife of three years, leaving him for another man. They had worked at the same office, Olga and what's-his-name, she a paralegal, he an attractive, successful lawyer, both in their late twenties. She got tired of being jealous of Mark.

"Who did you dump?" I asked. "Or was it the other way around?"

He sat up straight. "How do you always know?"

"It would help if you stopped thinking of yourself as an unfathomable conundrum. So?"

"Lena. The most beautiful pair of legs I've seen," Mark said, barely audible.

"Seriously, legs? Your standards for the right partner have been raised even higher. A rotten end, if you ask me. Do you want an honest opinion?"

Mark nodded yes with serious reservation on his face, slouching back in the armchair. He seemed not to want an honest opinion, but it was coming regardless.

"Have you ever considered that you need to be fixed? What happened?"

His right hand jerked up and did that combing-through-hair bit again. "She wanted to go dancing at some hot new club that opened downtown."

"Shocking!" I said. "And why is this bad?"

He crossed his right leg over his left. "I don't dance."

"Take a lesson."

"I'd look too silly taking up dancing lessons at this stage of my life." Mark leaped up from the armchair, began to pace across the room with a spring in his step, holding his hands behind his back.

His disheveled hair added boyishness to his appearance. He never neglected to pay enough attention to the way he looked, not out of vanity, but common sense driving Mark's desire for a healthy body. It paid off. He looked good. This last observation caused a strange feeling to rise within me, a sort of nostalgia, more disturbing as it had been unexpected. The wooden floor creaked. I sighed. Ah, Mark. No wonder he had no problem picking up young women.

"And you don't look silly dating girls in their twenties?" I asked. "Are you trying to recapture your youth, which you find to be hastily slipping away through your fingers or something? Lena's not the first one. How many have there been now? Three? Eight? Do you notice a pattern? Those girls, what are they a substitute for? You think that over."

Mark raised his eyebrows, stopped pacing, his hands in the pockets of his jeans, his thumbs protruding. A little defensive, he turned to face me. "Oh c'mon, give me a break."

"Why should I do that?"

"Because you like me. Because I'm lovable." He jingled change in his pocket.

"Did you decide that all by yourself, or did someone tell you such a thing?"

"I was told," he said.

"You shouldn't have believed such outright flattery. It's a bribe. The person who told you that can't be your friend. They're conning you into something."

He cleared his throat, all innocence. "Is it? Well…I hadn't thought of it that way. But are you telling me you don't like me? Did I mention how beautiful you look tonight?"

I smiled. "I'll tell you what I don't like—you crying all over my place like this every time you get dumped by a girl you shouldn't have been with in the first place. I don't like you getting hurt all the time. I worry about you. Look at you. You're all bent out of shape. Stop setting yourself up. So tell me, what…why… no wait, let me guess. Laundry day, right?"

He shut his eyes and then reopened them. "Laugh all you want, but for some people having clean laundry is important. Well, I told Lena I didn't want her to go clubbing. She got angry, said I didn't understand her, and broke up with me."

"Of course. She wants fun and you're burying her up to her ears in a swamp of house chores. It sounds like there's a certain conflict of interests here, yet you're acting surprised. Tell me, what is it with you and laundry anyway?"

Mark cleared his throat again, leaning back against the bookshelf. "Am I not entitled to adopt new and interesting quirks in my behavior?"

"I'd have to argue with you about the 'interesting' bit."

He raised his eyebrows, hesitated a moment too long. "It's important for a university professor to look and smell good. I've read somewhere it promotes trust and enhances the learning experience for the students." He nodded a few times, panting indignantly.

"And why can't you do your laundry yourself? It won't kill you—trust me on this one. Are you marking your territory or something? Anyhow, that girl's too young for you. Deal with it."

Mark shrugged. "Well, if you insist on putting it that way...You don't have to look at me like that. You're right, of course. And I *am* dealing with it. Now you'll have to trust me. Do you have anything to eat besides cookies? I'm hungry."

I got up and headed for the kitchen. As far as I knew, he appeared to be relieved by the breakup. So it looked like he was not going to tell me what was bothering him, not tonight.

Mark followed me. "Do you think I need to lose weight?"

"Is this your new way of fishing for compliments?"

He held up his index finger. "I'll take that as a no. Thank you. You know, I meant it—you do look beautiful tonight." He threw a smile at me, and what a smile he had.

I smiled back, put a skillet on the stove, flicked on the gas under it. "How very charming of you."

"Did you know a pig's orgasm lasts thirty minutes?" Mark positioned himself in front of the open refrigerator with an innocent expression of thorough concentration, as if preoccupied with studying its contents.

"And I'm asking you, how is that fair?" I reached past him into the opening, grabbed the dish of roasted chicken. He did not flinch. "Mark, be a sweetheart, get the veggies out of the fridge and wash them."

Mark had too many issues he was trying to deal with all at once. Was he going through his midlife crisis, or was it something else altogether? The symptoms were there and not there at the same time. His faith in himself had seemed to take a sharp decline in the recent past, not that he had ever been brimming with self-assurance. Was that what the young women were there for—to restore his confidence? I was no certified psychiatrist, just an old friend who was uncomfortable at not being aware of the full implications of what was happening, but there was not much to be done about it. Or was there?

And he was right—I did like him. A lot. Even if he was a citizen of the dwarf planet Pluto.

twenty-one

ing, ring. At six in the morning. *Ring, ring.*

"Anna, he's here again!" Bella cried. "We don't want to let him in! Anna!"

"All right." I rubbed my eyes and reached for my jeans.

There was a shift in dynamics between the Stoics and me in later years, but not till I had reached the age when I could be called an adult by any state's legal system, along with its ensuing privileges, yet enough of a paradox, I was still deemed irresponsible by the Stoics. A lose-lose game. While we all pretended they were in charge, they began soliciting my aid and never stopped, blissfully unaware that their dwindling parental authority had already lost its potency, further undermined by a bunch of emotionally uninvolved psychotherapists, and beyond redemption. Guess who had to make decisions on every small and big matter and correct the consequences of some choices they managed to make themselves? I could shoot myself.

With many episodes forgotten, my all-time favorites were the persistent attempts to get evicted by writing checks guaranteed to bounce, fundamentally lacking the ability to grasp the curious relationship between the necessity of going through the motions of transferring money before sending out the check, the bank's unreasonable intention of collecting fees for unavailability of funds, and the angry landlord banging on their door at six in the morning, at which point they usually called me.

Today yet again the scene played like it always did: Without a word, I handed the check to the landlord waiting at the Stoic's door. He shoved it in his pocket and left. I used my key to unlock the door and entered never-never land. Its similarities with this curious geographical location was reinforced by the stained and musty, floral, plastic-slipcovered furniture that had served them well for the last twenty-odd years, which they refused to throw out, and which I will inherit when the time comes, but also by the absurd amount of clocks, which hung, lay down, and leaned against different objects and one another on all available surfaces, nesting among the yellowed plastic doilies and ceramic baskets of plastic fruit coated with fluffy dust. The clocks ticked loudly and showed varying times, allegedly all local, giving readings about an hour apart.

I was greeted by Auntie's bland eyes about to tear up, confronted with such an injustice of happenings.

"But I myself saw Mike writing him a check," she said.

I looked at Michael. He made a sound, a half laugh, a half sigh, and put the paper down. "She said she went to the bank, got some cash, and transferred the money," he said.

"And?" I asked.

Michael took a breath, shook his head, and made *tut-tut* noises for a bit.

"Why is Bella the one responsible for your bank operations?" I asked when he stopped.

Unable to destroy the evidence, Bella's uncomplicated face formed into a familiar expression of the Goddess of Haughtiness herself. "It's my money. My. Money. Mine. I can do whatever I want with it."

"And?" I asked.

Auntie's face morphed into her interpretation of Oliver Twist in the orphanage. "Please write our landlord a check and talk to him! I'll be careful the next time. I promise. You'll be a very rich woman when we die!"

As usual, Auntie took pride in her ability to read other people's minds. Michael folded the paper, looked at the ceiling, and made more *tut-tut* noises.

Suffice it to say that "very rich" was a relative term, if one was to keep in mind that the price for *any* item exceeding a three-dollar limit (imposed for some logical reason by Auntie on one of those clearer thinking days) never failed to extract a loud gasp from astonished Bella. The imposition of such limits was done not because of her misunderstood innate asceticism, the existence of which was unknown to her, or a certain mistrust of monetary transactions, but because she was implacably stingy.

Ah, inheritance, always the inheritance—what an incentive to keep the bond with your family alive. Exhausting and often infuriating, the situation was devoid of advantages. Like a persistent drip of water erodes the hardest of stones, leaving scars initially invisible to the naked eye, though getting deeper and deeper, so this arrangement changed me. I felt as though I were in charge of a group of obstinate kindergarten children. Behaving as if my patience were elastic, but detesting it, I had to correct the consequences of their activities, without the option to stand back and observe the unfolding events in peace. I felt myself wrestle with a wriggling creature that could not be slain. The general sense of calamity followed me around the clock.

Most days I felt I was hanging over an inescapable abyss, immeasurable abyss. On the rest I felt an intense yearning. If only I could yank out my magic wand...*bibbidi-bobbidi-boo!* At regular intervals, I wished I could end my participation in this whole family charade and set off in search of a more stable and pleasant setting. The world was such a peculiar place!

Beneath all these troubles lay their one persistent failure: being too delusional to grasp the simple truth that whatever they did worked neither for them nor for me. With no sign that this revelation was set to occur anytime soon, the way things were at the moment did not encourage a cheerful outlook for the future and did little to comfort me. When was I going to live my life? Keeping my sanity became more of a challenge. Could taking a pottery class to spend a peaceful afternoon glazing a bowl help cure my misery? Should I start drinking? Or should I be looking for aliens?

                                    ■   ■   ■

The phone rang.

"Mama? *Ciao*, Mama, *come stai?*"

"I think you've got the wrong number," I said.

"No, no, it's me, me, Marcello. I want to congratulate you on Hannah's birthday, Mama, and wish you long years and much happiness."

Mama? I thought. "Well, thank you!" I said. "I'm sorry, *who* are you?"

"Marcello. Your son-in-law. I'm going to marry your daughter."

"How marvelous! Does Hannah know about it?"

"Soon. I wanted to tell you my intentions are honorable. I'm thirty-seven, and my dear, dear mother doesn't want to die and leave me in this world alone. She wants me to marry. I have seven older brothers, but they're no good, no good. I have to honor my mother's wishes."

"Right."

"Mama, I'm in London for two weeks. My clothing warehouse is in Italy, near Laga di Garda. You've heard of Laga di Garda? I want to send you dresses to show my respect for you. Short skirts, long skirts. Everything's very nice. Tell me your size, please? And I don't want you to worry, Mama. It's *me* who's saying this. Hannah—she's my *bambina*, she'll never be naked. I'll make a good wife out of her. My mama—God bless her with long years—she'll teach Hannah how to cook pasta the way I like it. Now I wait for Hannah after her class. Oh, I see her. And this Andrew is with her. I don't like him. I'll call you later, Mama, yes? *Ciao*."

Ah, children, children...

twenty-two

On this crisp day in the beginning of September, the stingy sun hung low and gave forth little warmth. Autumn again. The earth was barren. The fragrant breeze had plenty of space to play over the flat expanse of irregular fields of prickly, yellowish-brown stalks of rye unevenly cut by hand sickle, punctuated by ragged patches of dry dirt that yielded not even the smallest blade of grass. The tattered remains crunched under Sarah's feet. The earth itself seemed to be in trouble. Aside from the occasional howling of dogs at nights and a distant cannonade, an eerie silence hovered over the land. For miles, not a bird sang. They flew away elsewhere as there was nothing to feed them here. The villagers, swollen from hunger, picked up each and every grain.

As far as the eye could see, the devastated land was interrupted here and there by tiny villages of five or six dwellings, the majority of them burned to ashes, some still smoldering. Then came parched grazing pastures, one after the next, followed by devastated fields of wheat, sprinkled with patches of arid dirt, the pale-gold of dried stalks fading to gray on the horizon. In a potato field it was pointless to dig for the few potatoes that had been missed by previous diggers, but Sarah tried anyhow. Nothing. Not that she had any matches left to start a fire to cook them over. No matter how careful she was with them, the matches got damp. They had been laid out in the sun to dry, but only hissed and refused to ignite.

The days grew shorter. For three nights in a row Sarah slept on the ground, hiding in bushes, a precious bundle pressed against her chest. The nights were chilly, and the young woman shivered through all three of them, though she collected straw to keep herself warm. The last night had been different. Sarah arrived at one of those faceless villages scattered through the countryside. It was a decent size, about twenty lopsided shacks, parts of roofs collapsed, the rotted structures standing due to some miracle. With the men gone to war, who was there to manage the repairs? The village had not been especially prosperous before the war began, and there were signs of poverty, years of hopeless poverty, everywhere. The ramshackle fences that had never known paint were short a lot of boards, used as firewood to keep the villagers warm, to cook scarce food. When the supply was exhausted, dry cow dung would be utilized for the same purpose. A cemetery she passed was marked by pauperdom too, with crooked crosses on even the recent additions. Sarah had seen countless newly erected crosses over countless fresh graves on her travels.

Eight shacks lined the narrow road, the rest scattered behind in chaos. A few sparse, sickly trees dared to beautify it with a sad result. A scraggly dog ran along the street. It kept close to the *neglected fences and threw nervous glances to the sides and behind. Starving people ate dogs, and this animal could feel the danger, but had been drawn to a village in hopes of finding something edible to put into its hollow belly before it itself became someone's unsatisfying dinner. It looked like a yard dog gone stray, used to being chained all its life to guard the house from intruders, and being fed for it. Nothing lavish, but fed. Poor soul. At these times no one cared about dogs. People died by hundreds of thousands, from bullets, from hunger.*

The news of her husband's death came a month after he was killed. The tidings had plunged Sarah into a state of stupefaction and insensibility. She completed the necessary motions without concentrating on any of them. She watched the dog absentmindedly. It dove under the crooked steps of a house nearby, disappeared from view.

Sarah walked the length of a dusty street to the last shack. It looked abandoned. A rusty pitchfork leaned against a wall among the tangle of tall brown weeds, the hovel's front steps missing, a part of a broken board hanging on a rusted nail. A dry tuft of grass stuck up a foot though a crack in the wood. Sarah stepped over the board and knocked on the door. No answer. She knocked again, more insistent. A shadow flickered past the window. A screechy door half opened, and a woman of indeterminable age peeked out of the gap, maybe nineteen, maybe forty. Barefoot, clad in rags, she sized Sarah up. The hard labor, hunger, and war reliably ages people too fast.

"Are you alone?" the woman asked after a prolonged silence.

Sarah nodded.

The woman gazed over Sarah's head to survey the surroundings, then gestured Sarah in. Three little children, barefoot, filthy, and snotty, hid behind their mother, clinging to her skirt. They looked malnourished. In all the villages Sarah had passed, the children were skinny and raggedy, regarding strangers with hostile eyes, like wolf cubs. The entire hut was one small room with a low ceiling and a dirt floor. The pungent air smelled of poverty and burned dung. The door behind Sarah was propped with a log to keep it shut. A Russian stove occupied most of the available space. A place to cook by day, it warmed the home up, and functioned as the family bed by night, the top of the stove covered with straw to serve as a mattress.

The woman, Ludka, dropped words sparingly at first, but then she thawed out, and her speech flowed like an abundant river through a valley. She told Sarah her husband had been killed during the revolution, and now she had no idea how she was to feed her children this coming winter. The crops were minuscule. With all this fighting, there were not enough hands to tend to the fields, and Mother Earth rewarded people with only a handful of grains. No wood left, and no dry dung either since the cows were gone, each one killed and eaten.

The cooking had to be done at night, with just straw to burn in the stove, and the straw gave out a lot of smoke, which could give their presence away. The counterrevolutionary Whites who had stationed themselves in the village had killed Ludka's one male piglet, which was supposed to feed her family through the winter. The Reds threw out the Whites, then the Whites threw out the Reds. Again the Reds returned, the last army to occupy their village, which had been abandoned by both armies for the time being. Unlawfulness was the new reigning law for now. The Reds, just like the Whites, were not shy to take whatever they could from poor villagers. The Reds, the Whites—Petlura, Denikin, Bolshevists, or God knows who else—all bandits, one not better than the other. They all pillaged, hanged, raped, burned people alive. The worst scum that ever walked the earth. The villagers could care less who was officially in charge as long as those in power were not present in the village to disrupt life, which was hard enough without any war.

It got dark inside. A weak light seeped in through the dirty glass of a single small window close to ground level. In the twilight, the corner of a neglected garden could be seen. Two low gooseberry bushes, bare of leaves, stood near leftovers of a tumbledown fence and danced like mad in the intensified, chilly wind.

The wind whistled, hissed, howled, moaned, bellowed, cried. Sarah, tired and hungry, not a crumb in her mouth since yesterday morning, was grateful to be out of it, in the relative warmth of the unheated hut. Ludka eyed the tiny lump at Sarah's chest, sighed, dug inside the stove's opening, and handed Sarah a cold boiled potato. Sarah nearly swallowed it whole without chewing, and the hunger let her be for now. She got used to sharp hunger pains day after day. They bothered her less and less, but she worried about not having enough milk to feed her baby. She wanted to give something to Ludka in return, though she had nothing to give but a piece of relatively clean cloth with several grains of gray salt wrapped in it, which was offered and taken.

Sarah untied the slate woolen shawl, knotted at her shoulder as a sling to hold the baby at her heart while she walked and cradled the boy in her arms. Her son. Tiny and weak, yet peaceful, he slept through the journey at her warm breast, lulled by her even stride. He made smacking sounds with his pink lips every so often. No whimper came out of him, not one since they had left. He took things bravely. Of course, he also understood little. She put him to her breast, and he took it with greed. She softly rocked back and forth. How was she to bring the boy up without a husband? The thought got her by the throat, but no sound left her lips. It would have to wait. Sarah was too tired to think or feel, in need of rest, of sleep, a few hours of precious senselessness. At the crack of dawn, she would again be on her way home.

Home. So far away, like someone else's lifetime. The bright house full of noise, the footsteps of running children, the laughter, the smell of freshly baked challah bread, candles flickering with the rhythm of a sabbath prayer. The daughter of a rabbi, his youngest child, Sarah had ten brothers. All eleven children had received an education, the brothers in Yeshiva in Vilnius, and though it was considered unnecessary for girls to be tutored, Sarah was sent to the Institute for Young Noblewomen, became fluent in French and could play a piano. Since she was supposed to find a good husband, she only needed to know how to cook, to clean, to give birth, and to obey her man. Home. How loved and protected she felt there! Would there ever be another time in her life when she could laugh so fullheartedly, so carefree?

The candle burned almost to the end. It flickered in the flat clay dish on a table, gave out plenty of smoke and stench, yet illuminated little. Ludka snored on an old blanket on the floor.

The baby dozed off at Sarah's breast. She put him up with the other children, asleep on the stovetop, pressed against one another to conserve heat. Her legs ached. She took her muddied boots off, climbed up on the stove herself. Her left boot came apart, the sole separated from the rest, hanging on by a few threads. In the morning Sarah would have to ask Ludka for a piece of string to tie it together, or she would not get far. The rainy season had already started. Unpaved roads were impassable, the mud reaching up to one's ankles. Several times she had fallen knee-deep into a pothole on the road, invisible under the layer of swooshing mud, too many of them present.

■ ■ ■

*Sarah woke up in the dead of night drenched in cold sweat, her face wet from tears. The room was pitch-black. She heard the even breathing of Ludka and her children, listened to the baby. He was deep asleep. Sarah pressed him closer to her body, and to shake off the recurring dream, recited Baudelaire in her mind, "…Il joue avec le vent, cause avec le nuage, Et s'enivre en chantant du chemin de la croix…" * but found herself in the midst of the waking dream.*

She sees the dusk taking hold of a small town. Sarah places a hat she just finished making on a stand in the display window. Fashion-conscious females lust after Sarah's creations, and women all over town come to Sarah's shop to buy hats. Given a gift of style—in the way she dresses and speaks—she knows where to attach a bouquet of fabric pansies, what color a ribbon should be, and how to drape it. She is about to close up shop, but tarries, everything taking longer with her growing belly in the way. Isaac comes to pick her up and walk her home as he does every day. How he wants to protect her from all the evil in the world. These are restless times. He hands Sarah a bunch of wildflowers he picked on the way, strokes her swollen belly with his hand.

On top of the stove, Sarah began to sob. She missed Isaac terribly, but it was not yet time to mourn him. She would do it later, when her little boy was safe back home. Glad to feel the dull needle of pain buried deep in her chest, she welcomed it. It meant she was still alive inside with death surrounding her. Another sunless day was breaking. Time to get up and get on the road again.

■ ■ ■

It was the third year of the civil war that was ravaging the countryside beyond recognition, the war started by the revolution, the country torn apart by both. The dictatorship of the proletariat's rise to power was bloody. Hunger and bullets claimed hundreds of thousands, as did the executions and correction camps in Siberia. Dark and tumultuous times. Life went on, weddings and births amid the grief and death. Sarah and Isaac had wedded less than a year ago, but their marital life was cut short.

A young doctor, Isaac was one of many recruited by force by the RKKA, the Workers and

---

* *…Free as a bird, he plays with clouds and wind,*
  Sings of the Passion with enraptured joy…(French)
—Charles Baudelaire. *Fleurs du mal.* Benediction

Peasants Red Army. With his assigned regiment, he followed the movements of the front line, if it could be called a "front line." Fights broke out everywhere when the White bands showed up, riding into the Reds' occupied territory for food and supplies. Isaac was stationed in some small town with a strange name in Belarus when the Whites took the settlement with all its inhabitants. He was a doctor, and people were people; his job was to treat people independent of the color of their political beliefs, and he treated the White Army wounded till the Reds liberated the town. The Reds declared the doctor a traitor to the revolution and were about to shoot him when there was another fight. More wounded came in, and the execution was postponed. In another attempt to free the people, the Whites gained possession of the town again. In turn they declared the doctor a traitor to God and the tsar and shot him without further ado, right before they killed every villager for sympathizing with the Reds. Such were the times.

The news of her husband's death had reached Sarah in the small town of Chernigov, where his parents had lived and where Isaac had taken her to give birth to their firstborn. Widowed at eighteen, she was having contractions by nightfall. The delivery was premature. She had not recuperated after giving birth to her son but decided to walk back home with the infant in her arms to be near her parents. Isaac's family refused to let her go. His mother cried like it was Sarah's funeral. A four-day walk under different circumstances, the journey through the pillaged country took Sarah a week, and she had only made it a quarter of the way on her road back.

It was safer to go around than to pass through, so she went around a few towns and villages, but got lost and had to turn back several times. Battles raged. The ownership of settlements by Reds or Whites changed from day to day, often several times in the course of the same day. The passage was tiring, but Sarah was grateful it was uneventful. So far she had met no fights on her way. What treacherous times. No place was safe. Death was everywhere. Sarah tried not to think about how she was to go on without her beloved Isaac. She had to be strong, had to survive, with their son to care for. She had named him Isaac after her dead husband and prayed to God to keep him out of harm's way. He would grow to be strong and gentle like his father. Sarah pushed on, but the feeling she would not make it lingered and intensified. She passed countless villages, which differed from one another only by the number of crumbling shacks. Towns looked likewise indistinct. They became one strange file in her memory, dreamlike and endless.

■ ■ ■

When the morning returned, in its ash-gray hours, Sarah was caught in a lashing rainstorm that dwindled to a drizzle. Surrounded by barren fields, she had nowhere to hide and turned her back to the icy, gushing rain, bent over the baby to keep him from getting wet. She was thankful it was a summery short rainstorm, a precursor to rains that would soon turn into drawn-out affairs, long, murky, and dank. She struggled to walk through the slimy, sloshing mud covering the road, slipped and fell twice. The light changed, brightened, and with shreds of pale mist draped over the wet ground, the sun cut through the clouds.

The day turned out to be warm for September, full of summer, but much colder closer to the evening. Autumn let everyone know its rightful reign had come. The smell of the moist earth brought tears of longing to Sarah's eyes. The mud dried, caking on her skin, hair, clothes, boots. The shawl was encrusted too, but her boy did not look so dirty.

Sarah arrived at the fork in a road and stood there, unsure which direction to choose. A lonely horse cart, loaded with several oddly shaped bundles and one chair, screeched, greeting the young woman and her baby. On top of the modest belongings, an old woman rocked. A thin mutt, no bigger than a cat, was curled up at her side. The horse barely moved its legs. An old man guided the jade by the rope, and two little boys lagged behind the cart, pale gloomy faces on all of them.

"Don't go there." The old man motioned with his head to the left.

"Who's there?" asked Sarah.

"The Whites," he said.

"The Reds," the old woman mumbled.

Sarah nodded. She continued her journey on the road that curved to the right. Yet another long day of walking drew near its end.

The young mother came to a small town, dragging her feet. The war had passed through here too. Where would they sleep tonight? Dead tired, she no longer cared, as long as she could lay down her exhausted body somewhere, anywhere, and plunge into the blackness of a dreamless sleep. She chanced to enter the empty town square with a well at its center, nesting among the ruins and surrounded by sparse trees bare of leaves. Water!

Where're all the people? she wondered. Two scruffy roosters pecked at something on the dusty ground, dug vigorously with their skinny, wrinkled feet, and crowed.

Sarah's throat was so dry it hurt. Glad to have an opportunity to wash away the road dust from her face and hands, she dropped the heavy wooden bucket into the gaping blackness of a well, heard a distant splash. Sarah pulled on a chain to bring the bucket full of water back up, but the chain was long and heavy, and the sleeping baby at her breast was in the way. She could not move him, but kept on pulling.

A bronzed, muscular hand caught the chain right over her tired, disobedient ones, yanking the bucket out of the well. Sarah had not heard the man approach. She turned to look at her rescuer. He smiled, his pearl white teeth in stark contrast to his sunburned face, his kind, brown eyes alive with golden sparks of a silent laughter. He made her feel strangely peaceful, safe. He took the thin metal mug tied at the well, dipped it into the bucket full of water, offered it to Sarah. She brought it to her chapped lips. The water was cool and fresh. It tasted heavenly. Sarah put the mug down and realized she was holding her breath. She forced herself to breathe again, and with some effort, each breath came out a bit less labored and a bit more even.

"I'm Isaac," the stranger said. "Come, you look like you could use some food and rest."

She learned to love this man, who became a devoted and caring father to her firstborn

Isaac—never differentiated from Isaac's own children—and who later fathered their two daughters. Loving him came with no effort. Before the revolution Isaac had owned a little manufacturing plant in a small town that lay in Sarah's path, but the Soviet power strongly felt that he should be relieved of such a burden and took it away from him, declaring it public property. He became a carpenter, building a house for his family with his own two hands—a house with sky-blue shutters on the windows.

Ever since Isaac had laid his eyes on Sarah for the first time at that well, he never let her go until the day he died. He loved Sarah deeply, devotedly. Sarah went quietly soon after Isaac's death from his second heart attack. Having been together with him for seventy-six years, she was unable to go on living without him. The two of them had become one.

twenty-three

*t*wo of them had become one…" I was out of the rut, happily tapping away on the keyboard.

Thump! Thump! The reality of communal living in a third-floor Manhattan apartment slammed into my cozy fantasy world with the force of a runaway M1 Abrams main battle tank, fully loaded with gasoline and ammunition. The thirteen-year-old ape of a boy from the apartment below was throwing a hardball against their ceiling. Again. Might such kindness be returned to him hundredfold. The effect was intensified by the interesting acoustics peculiar to old buildings, which generally made one feel like one was living in a drum. I was treated not just to the best in sound, but also to the sheer delight of the ball's physical impact too—the sickening sensation of a mini-earthquake in mindless, endless repetition till I was ready to bite and scratch and scream, red spots swimming in front of my eyes. Was he ever going to learn not to do that, one wondered?

I have heard a certain amount of discipline is a must for a growing child. Children need structure. An orderly life. For four years I tried to explain this to both of his mothers in matching "I (heart) NY" T-shirts—gabby Gigi, the massage therapist, and Trudi, on unemployment for years, which could be a sweet cover-up for narcotics-related activity. It was pointless to talk to them over both of their voices at full volume, luring as bullfrogs', *talking* together, lapsing into feigned cockney accents while two pairs of bloodshot eyes darted flirtatious glances at me. Nearing their sixties, they dragged with them the baggage of roaring junkies' years. I sighed. A potentially bright kiddo. *Bwahahaha!* I laughed like a bunch of cackling witches. With all this pandemonium, I could not remember if I ate children or not. Ah, well…I would play it by ear.

It was now after midnight. The thought of how long the thumping would go on entered my mind in vain search for an answer, found negligible resistance, and moved in wide circles. The duration of this pounding experience could be measured in hours. The boy possessed remarkable endurance. The notion of sending my inconsiderate neighbors a death ray bounced around inside my cranium, limped from the periphery to the center, grew in intensity—not because it received the necessary support, but because there was a lack of proper resistance.

It gained momentum, overshadowing every other thought I happened to have at that moment. You know, the *death ray*.

It was possible for such an idea to be a spark of genius, or it could be taken as a sign of derangement, though that would not be flattering, indeed. With all normal means that city dwellers commonly used in localized internecine warfare exhausted and proven to be ineffective, short only of sending in the marines, I was desperate. Dancing with danger, I decisively formed my index and middle fingers into the V-shape and pointed it at the floor. *Bz-zz! Thump! Bz-zz! Thump!* Nothing happened to improve the situation. *Bzz-zzzz! Thump!* Perhaps the intensity of the ray was wrong. Right. My mind was fried, and I had proof. A fate akin to death.

The next logical move was to begin talking to disembodied entities. Please do not ask me how I know this, but I was sure hallucinations were not far behind. Give it five minutes. Golden years devoid of boredom and loneliness were all but guaranteed for me. I waved my hand before my eyes, saw no trails, and yawned in relief. This barbecued-mind thing was more than an inconvenience to befall one, but as long as shimmer around the edge of my field of vision was absent and no kaleidoscopic patterns turned, I was not going to worry myself sick about the onset of schizophrenia and such. To think it had been triggered by an innocent boy playing with an unquestionably innocent ball. As one can tell, I loved my downstairs neighbors with a passion. God bless them.

A police helicopter, its roaring blades effortlessly slicing languorous air, made a pass overhead, circled, and ended up gluing itself to its usual hanging place in the skies to cast a watchful eye over our restless neighborhood. It would be parked up there for a few hours so the people down below could enjoy a peaceful sleep. Several bars of the ice-cream truck's simple tune rippled through the roll, adding a nostalgic note. The sanitation truck was not due till four in the morning. A group of freeloaders in hard hats with a sledgehammer the size of a small private army would show up at six to raise a dust cloud mimicking the one at Hiroshima in size and density, just before they would go on break till the end of the day, only to show up again next morning to repeat the same sequence of actions. One man drilling, the rest of the crowd onlookers—a high-efficiency group. One could speculate endlessly on the real purpose of such a regular gathering.

Trudi, smelling like overripe Roquefort and glowing with the charm of a mature, ready-to-breed cockroach, leaned over a windowsill to yell something cheerful in cockney English to the group of neighbors below who were relaxing at a barbecue on a beige velvet sofa at the bottom of the squalid concrete courtyard between many piled bags of garbage, two stained mattresses, a legless chair, a cracked avocado-green toilet, and a doorless, rusty refrigerator. Trudi's flabby body was squeezed into a rumpled, inside-out sweatshirt of unidentifiable hue at present, but formerly a gloriously fabulous color. Her unkempt, filthy hair twitched in the hot summer night breeze, faint and muggy. One of the neighbors down below yelled a few words back in Spanish. Then another one joined in. Trudi tried some Spanish, seemed to know none, and switched back to English.

The black smoke drifted off, rising from the overloaded grill, mixed with a dose of marijuana smoke strong enough to kill a horse ascending from the second floor. It wafted to my open windows and made me cough. All three voices trumped over the sound of the traffic on Broadway, which had thinned but was still a mess, along with the collective drone of hundreds of air conditioners and the thundering of the helicopter's motor. Based on extensive previous experience—as I was soon to rediscover—this animated discussion could go on and on.

Two of nine police officers, sitting in the courtyard of a local police precinct down below, briefly raised their heads, but did not seem to find the topic of conversation interesting, as they went back to their own exchange. The traffic light switched from green to red, and the gasping cars stopped to take a breath and a better look at one another. In the relative quietude that ensued, a weathered male voice broadcast from below: "This damn fruit soda always sprays me when I open it."

The victorious whine and whirring and grinding and gnashing of overworked ceiling fans—courtesy of my downstairs neighbors—changed into a loud rumble, holding strong in the general cacophony; as beside the sound, it contributed vibration to the scene. Three fire trucks with wailing sirens rushed by, chasing one another, making the glass in the windowpanes do a small, synchronized tap dance. The damp breeze, more of a waft than a wind, lost interest in playing with shaggy hair. On a spur of a moment decision, intent on messing with things, the breeze decided to coquettishly toy with my other senses besides my filled-to-capacity hearing, and brought the thick stench of death from the street below, stemming from heaps upon heaps of sunbaked, fly-buzzing garbage, crawling with hungry rats and emanating gas combinations yet to be studied and named. The odor of rot was so pungent that my eyes began to tear.

The puffing hot air shifted direction, as if unsure what else to offer, and delivered the stink of unidentifiable ingredients deep fried in mystery grease from a neighborhood restaurant downstairs, squeezed between an abandoned Laundromat (with an OPEN sign and grubby plastic flowers in the window) and a row of nondescript, tattered storefronts. The screeching sound of brakes as an asthmatic city bus, wheezing and coughing up exhaust, halted for the red light at the choked intersection, selecting this exact moment to break the monotony of the otherwise idyllic, if airless, night.

I headed for the shower. If I was in need of auditory stimuli, I had plenty to choose from in this wayward tuning-up of the biggest orchestra. The indescribable pleasures of living in a bustling mega-metropolis rental in a shabby-chic neighborhood! No wonder New York was called "the city that never sleeps," the land of sinners and an occasional saint—though the most prominent features in the world-famous night skyline were turned off at two at night, as if to suggest the city ought to give it a try since it looked sleep deprived. Given a fair chance, it would love to sleep and sleep.

Thump! Thump! Boom! Boom, boom, boom! Thump!

Good God! And the reggaeton reigned yet again. As if I did not have enough sensations as it was, the floor began to reverberate, shaking wildly underfoot, threatening, violent, rumbling like an awoken volcano on a verge of a major eruption and rendering life intolerable. Adding the final touch to the onslaught of my senses, my neighbors had reached the public concert stage, which usually meant they were stoned to the hilt. The whole neighborhood could enjoy this song. It would play at full volume for the next ten, eleven, seventy-two hours, till those ladies sobered up and joined the human race again, but with a mother of a hangover. It is a well-known fact that when a hangover dominates the scene, loud sounds are in smaller demand, so the music might get turned off then. Then the floor would stop undulating beneath my feet, return to a relatively immobile state again, taking into account the ongoing vibrations from old, too-tired-to-live ceiling fans in each and every room all year round. That was me being far too optimistic. They could go on for days at the time. And they did.

My already bleak mood turned darker. Though I could reminisce at length on a number of those unforgettable occurrences, freely initiated by my neighbors, that took place over the years, more than a few of them in recent times—no punishment was too bad for them!—I was over and done with here. I grabbed a pillow from the bed and the keys to Michael and Bella's place. Not the most comfortable couch.

In the inky blackness of the night, when the hidden crevices of the soul were finally revealed, I looked forward to a moderately deafer version of myself in the caressing embrace of old age as a beacon to hone in on, a thin ray of light on top of a lighthouse calling to wandering ships. On second thought, this one much clearer than the previous one, a little house with a rose garden somewhere in Connecticut would do nicely as my ultimate solace and reward.

Thump! Thump! Boom! Boom, boom, boom! Thump!

twenty-four

the doorbell. Three demanding rings, and the world stopped dead. Always an evil omen, as omens go. Long-suffering Mother and her hypochondria were here on her daily route to spread joy—like an invading army, trespassing on my time and life. Life-sucking procedures would be performed on me as, to sustain the illusion of love, I played the role she allotted to me in her little drama. If she stopped coming, I would not complain and would recall it with little nostalgia for the rest of my days. Years ago I vowed to have a place far away from her. What had happened to that dream? Why did I hope that someday things would be different—a hope that could never be fulfilled? What penalties did I risk incurring if I for once broke the taboo and told Mother how big of a lie it was to call our pathological attachment *love*?

A sinking sensation nested in the pit of my stomach as I opened the door. Mother darted in with no glance in my direction. Things were looking less and less optimistic. The foremost thing on her busy schedule was a task of great importance. Rain or sunshine, this time of day was the cats' naptime. They curled up together on top of a blanket in my bed with frequent episodes of jerking their ears and limbs and smacking their lips. Their slumber needed no interruption, but it was inevitable.

The cats lifted their heads a little and stared at Mother with deep-blue eyes, a total lack of curiosity in their crystal-clear depth. The ends of both tails barely rattled, a faint movement one was liable to miss unless one was looking for that sign of life.

Familiar with the drill, Adam and Eve felt no remorse for ignoring Mother. Two fluffy heads hit the blanket a millisecond later. Another millisecond swooshed by, and they were in a deep, dreamless sleep. My devoted companions, precocious little darlings, were user-friendly models, handpicked from the cat people tribes.

Mother looked confused, as if puzzling out something important. Then another expression crossed her face, but it was indecipherable to me. She reached deep into her pocket and pulled out a little baggie tied with a rubber band. In the corner was a teaspoon worth of something.

"Parts of the chicken I don't eat. Makes no sense to throw it away." She patted Eve on the head, cooing, "Good girl, Eve. I brought you nice chicken to eat, not like you're going to thank me. And you, Adam, go away. You never come when I call you." She pushed Adam off the bed.

Ignoring Mother with concentrated effort, Adam looked at me with reproach and contrary to what I would expect from the oratorically gifted Siamese, said nothing. I picked him up, put him back on the bed near Eve, stroked him. He curled up, closing both eyes, ecstasy on his little face.

Mother watched me with disapproval, her hands on her hips. "You can kiss him, kiss him," she said with a snort. "Like he loves you."

Not waiting for a reply, she spun around and left the room. None was forthcoming—what was the point? I knew I would be sorry for not standing up to her, but she would make me even sorrier for resisting. No matter what transpired, I would lose either way.

Next was her great technique for securing the perimeter, moving in a clockwise direction that demanded her undivided attention, in tandem with intervention. Great—if one was a Navy SEAL. For ordinary mortals it was on annoying side of things. Mother closed the windows, manipulating the crooked panes not without difficulty. With that behind her, when the feeling of a job well done registered on her face, Mother could relax enough to take her coat off.

As if there was a pressing need to annoy me with something else, she laid her coat across my small dining table instead of putting it on a hanger in the closet, which I happened to have. A closet. In the vestibule. And there were empty, reliable hangers, hanging loose, swinging in the draft from the open door, ready to shoulder whatever guests were willing to temporarily separate from. I would have to strangle her one day. Soonish. Should I practice my 911 call? Yes? No? Change my hair and skip the country?

"Leave it there. I won't stay for long." Mother's queenlike tone nipped anything suggesting a remote possibility of a discussion in the bud. She made a beeline for the couch, sat down, and made herself comfortable by throwing throw pillows onto the floor, so that some glittery dust hung suspended in the morning air, swirling and dancing. Mother pointed with her index finger for me to sit near her, and I did, not wishing to provoke a crisis. Trust me, there was no point in arguing with her. That would bring us nowhere and only end up in tears. My tears.

She sat straight and rigid on the edge of a seat like a young schoolgirl in a classroom with a strict teacher, her hunched back not touching anything for support. Her favorite shirt—white in a delicate pink pinstripe—was buttoned all the way up, her conservative straight skirt smoothed down to cover her knees, both knees properly together, her hands folded on her lap, pale white against the dark blue of her skirt, with her right hand on top. She was ready to take the center stage for the main part of the visit—Mother dropping in for a chat. The most pleasing portion of the event—the griping session with her longest list of grievances—was about to commence.

Should I add up the number of times she would call me "crazy" or forgo it for today? A dubious form of entertainment, it brought no satisfaction, though it shaved off a sliver of the duration of sluggish time, as I would imagine it might do for a prisoner etching marks on a cell wall to count the time passed. In five more seconds, the flow of information, presented in the liveliest way and filled with useful tidbits, would begin making its way into my poor, innocent ears. Mother, a woman of many opinions, was in her element now, oblivious to the rest of the world.

With her prevailing preference to chronicle the predicaments she suffered— her life was composed of such unspeakable griefs, *ay-yay-yay!*—the subject for complaints mattered little. She had an inborn and unflagging talent of finding faults with everyone and everything—the food, the weather, the people. When she opened her mouth, nothing else came out but a tireless stream of complaints. Her mind had a mind of its own, and with a single thought on the loose, flapping unchallenged in the plangent hollow of her skull, it had been plagued by the frenzied fear of getting stuck somewhere entirely boring. It darted from subject to subject, with her attention hopping off in random directions all at once. Yes, Mother, fire at will. Five, four, three, two, one…

"What a terrible weather we're having," Mother said. "I can't tell if it's hot or cold."

And so it began.

"I'm so tired," Mother grumbled. "Yesterday I washed two lace curtains, today my raincoat. I had to rinse it five times. Five times! The water was black."

At the tender age of seventy-one, she did her laundry by hand. To save myself from her fury at my mentioning dry cleaning to her, which would bring upon the uneasiest sensation of a solar storm raging in my gut, I said nothing. She would not touch a washing machine for all the candy in the world, or to make the expression more relevant to Mother, all the apples in the world, her irreplaceable staple and treat, all in one. Pinkish-green Empire apples were her unshared passion, the single nonrenounced earthly pleasure she allowed herself, the sole thing that could excite her…or not excite, per se, but produce an emotion with the closest proximity to excitement that she was able to work herself into. She was guaranteed not to get scurvy. I am all for that. Take her idealized fruit away and she would wither and expire. As for me, apples always gave me a stomachache. Besides, I had heard what happened to Snow White.

Mother glanced at the Chinese area rug with disapproval and tapped her head with a forefinger. "What a hassle to vacuum out those cat hairs. What use is a cat? You have no mice. They might pee somewhere in a corner. You won't even know it until it's too late." She continued to stare down. "This rug, aren't you afraid of tripping and falling down when you get up?"

Ah, what an interesting conundrum. Yes, why was I not afraid?

The naysayers are not the sort of human element any wise, progress-oriented society should encourage to further blossom into existence among the other human element. Yet life is full of their hovering presence. By a coincidental twist of fate, I had two perky and one converted beings with their collective eyes watching my every move. What horrible crimes have I committed to deserve this? It must be an unfortunate, divine, bureaucratic mistake. I was introduced to the world with an extensive set of forewarnings of impending dooms and glooms—the naysayers' equivalent of a big hug and a running start. Mine believed in the undoubted superiority of early inauguration into awareness of cruelty of the world, starting at home. The world—a creature too unfathomable, too fearsome, too immense. So, with those three descriptors in tow, I should have been able to turn a few mountains upside down, right? A molehill?

"I've finished knitting a sweater vest from that orange yarn you gave me," Mother said.

I had no recollection of giving her orange yarn. Mother's definition of "orange" did not coincide with how the rest of the universe saw it. It could be anything within the visible color spectrum, and, I suspect, beyond it.

My engagement was limited to gravely nodding in agreement. She glanced at me as if she had forgotten I was sitting next to her. This was as warm and intimate as it would ever get. She required no interaction, per se. Monologues are and always were the preferred form of communication for her. Mother left no holes in conversation to be filled by anyone else other than herself.

Contrary to the many ways of information exchange adopted by people from different tribes around the world, my involvement was judged as an unwelcome distraction and seemed particularly ill advised. The equivalent of atrocious diversion, like a botched derailment by someone deliberately placing a stone on the rail in front of her train of thought, traveling full-throttle and powered by locomotion, it would force that train to grind to a halt and cause a distressing incident she could be annoyed with and complain about with a guilty pleasure for years to come. Her determination was so strong that she would never stop any phase of socializing activity, even if her train of thought veered off and was permanently derailed. The otherwise brilliant tactics of feeding her chocolates beforehand to butter her up and mellow her out would fail right from the start, for she was terrified of anything containing cholesterol like it was the Black Death. She planned to live forever. Vampires often do.

For as long as I remember, Mother was always knitting something, knitting, knitting, carefully matching one stitch to the next, while mumbling, "Knit two, purl one, knit two…" for hours, always vests for herself or Bella, both of them fond of sweater vests, intentionally made two sizes bigger in case they gained weight. Mother was appalled by the thought of anyone occupying her time unproductively. An activity such as reading a book was considered a waste of time. I guessed teaching her meditation would not be a splendidly brilliant idea.

"Stop slouching! Sit up straight!"

Her bony finger made a measurable dent in my rib area. She poked a few more times to ascertain I had gotten the point. I got the point.

Adam ambled into the living room to check on what the commotion was about, perhaps to see if there would be any more pushing of creatures under a foot tall today, but was delayed a few feet away from the couch we were sitting upon by urgent cat business. His whole being was engaged in the pleasures of yawning and stretching, gleaming with the joy of being alive. I envied him, painfully aware that, given a choice, I longed to be someplace else—far away, high up, somewhere windswept—say, the Himalayas. Or a well-ventilated hill.

"Look at Adam!" Mother said. "Look! His nose is orange! Don't touch him, he's contagious!"

Hardly a logical thinker, she grabbed my arm, pulled me deeper into the seat to ensure I abandoned all plans of ever touching Adam again. Yes, Mother, this was how I loved to spend my mornings—pinned to the couch, waiting to die the horrendously horrific death brought upon by my soft furball friend with the polka-dotted underbelly. Imagine, Mother was saving my life—in her mind anyway.

In case you were wondering, no secret meaning was encoded in her message. Mother was a vast collection of life's no-nonsense directives. Not all of them were applicable, the majority plain bizarre. Her perpetually discontented state might have brought on some unwanted side effects yet to be reckoned with.

Two minutes passed uneventfully. I found myself still pinned down, Mother's anaconda grip strong, her eyes on the bewildered side. I took in a breath, thinking of the least provocative strategy to free myself. Ideas crowded in my head.

"What's wrong with you today?" Mother asked, vibrating with irritation. "Why are you wriggling like a garden snake on a hot skillet? Keep still!" She sighed and let me go.

Anger management classes would do her a world of good, but who was to undertake the Herculean challenge of dragging her, spitting and kicking, over there? Not me. Are you busy this Monday? Tuesday? Thursday? Right. Mother and I, her personal human *piñata*, continued to sit there in silence. She folded her arms on her belly, Adam and his menacing nose forgotten.

"I'm so happy you split up with that Alex character. Where do you find them? Men are after one thing. After they'll get it, they'll dump you. What do you need a man for, tell me? You already have a child. Calm down, get busy with your life. Crazy, crazy, crazy."

The whole avalanche of "crazy" comments caused an adrenaline surge of medium intensity in my body. Mother, *begone*. Voicing my opinion was pointless, and eventually I deemed it best to do it less and less often, if at all, a gradual process over the years. In those rare moments when, pressed against the wall (figuratively speaking), I tried to voice something, she would stare at me, deadpan, with empty eyes, and give a deep sigh, like I was Mr. Ed's big butt waving from side to side, or a vocalizing horse manure. Indeed, Mr. Ed—the talking horse from an early sixties American TV sitcom—was downright trouble, and problems were to be expected if one decided to keep such company.

Mother was right in her unwillingness to be associated with any horse, talking or not, especially its enormous rear end (even if the owner of that shapely end was amicable, intelligent, and had something to say). A major inconvenience in my life was that Mother loathed all my boyfriends. She had loathed all my husbands too. She did not share things, me especially. She hated men in general and each male in particular with an inexhaustible reservoir of hate—it exuded through her pores. Men in my life, individually and collectively, competed with her for my time and represented a tangible threat, which she considered an unfortunate curse to fight violently to the death (in our specific case, mine). She preferred to ignore me whenever I happened to disagree with her on that matter or any other matter too. Please see above under "Mr. Ed Syndrome."

"What is it, a book?" Mother asked with scorn in her eyes.

Her scolding voice was gaining strength by the second, until the entire living room was filled with it like a bottomless well, every cubic inch of it, drowning out the million other noises. Her wagging index finger came too close to my face.

I realized I was sitting there like a chastened schoolgirl, afraid to move, afraid to breathe, afraid to bring the teacher's wrath upon myself, the score for today's "crazy" comments wiped clean from my memory. Yep, strangulation.

"Wasting your time on books! What can cure you? You'll ruin your eyesight and your brain will dry up! We'll put you in a psychiatric ward. I won't visit you there, you can rely on that. Eat an apple instead, then go outside for some fresh air. Do you understand what I'm saying to you?"

I had an urge to tunnel. She clasped my arm and, for a split second, Mother looked into my eyes. Her fingers possessed an unnatural force one would never attribute to a frail old woman with twig arms and twig legs attached to a big, soft ball of a belly. My forearm began to hurt. That all was a mandatory part of our sweet standard ritual of her lovingly caring about my well-being. I needed this like I needed an ulcer. I longed to believe that on some level, she was a wise, angel-like creature. Oh, whom was I kidding? She had no other level.

"Are you still exercising?" Mother asked. "You *are* insane. Stop before you damage something important in your body! You'll get a heart attack. Mark my words."

This time I was somewhat prepared for the poking gesture, with a bare split second to move away to soften the impact. She anticipated it and compensated by moving closer to me in the blink of an eye. I sighed. My rib began to hurt. Mother resettled on the couch, fidgeting a little, smacking her lips, and clutching at her heart.

"You don't look pleased. Here I am, going out of my way to give you the best advice I have. All I've done was speak the truth. I guess I should never say anything. Never."

The too-familiar feeling that my life was worth nothing and the world was about to end tomorrow was here with me once more, a crushing defeat. As circumstances conspired, my past and present threatened to turn into a future that looked gloomier and gloomier. I lived in a bloody snow globe—hopeless and stuck, not a sliver of hope. With the infinite potential of the unlimited power of love that is in everyone's possession—such a power, beautiful, terrifying in its sheer enormity—and with us even a simple amicability was not in the cards. What did life expect from me? Not a rhetorical question. How did Mother, the incarnation of evil, manage to throw me off course every goddamn time? As a Chinese proverb states, "A crisis is an opportunity riding the dangerous wind."

An inhuman effort was put into convincing myself it was of little importance what Mother thought of me—it mattered. The need to be accepted was so strong! With such a void aching to be filled, it made an exceptionally convenient self-trap. Convenient for Mother; a self-trap for me. Being an outcast was a lonely business. I was an honorary president of the local branch of Renegades Unlimited with an emphasis on taking worlds apart, being less inclined toward building up on ruins. A confirmation that I was in essence lovable would not hurt and could have made a world of difference to me. To paraphrase an old joke, with a support system like mine, who needs enemies?

What would it take for me to dig myself out from under that built-up Mount

Everest of resentment stirring up more resentment and eating me up alive? A mosquito in amber with an ever-growing sense of entrapment, *how* would I break Mother's hold on me? Questions, questions, too many questions. At the end of my tether, the more the thought entered my mind, the more I appreciated that we were not locked in together between four walls day and night. Oh horror of horrors!

"Explain to me what you think you're doing with your life," Mother said, her irritation revived; all oxygen got sucked out of the room. "A writer. What kind of profession is this?" She turned up the tip of her nose with a fingertip. "You are...I don't even know the word for it. We can't look other people in the eye, we're so ashamed. Listen to your mother for once—throw it out of your head! A writer? A young woman without potential. You'd think you'd be able to wash the floors in here if you have so much time on your hands to spare."

She made a dramatic pause for emphasis and smacked her lips. "Wipe that look off your face. Do you know how it feels for a mother to be right that her child is crazy? Watching you deliberately making a mess of your life? How many times do I have to cry? Answer me!"

Shazam! This time, knowingly or not, all civility cast aside, she had tossed a hand grenade. And it blew. It was at moments like this when I wished rather strongly for a specific type of a miracle to happen: I wished for the skies to open up and drop something significantly memorable on her, like a grand piano. Wishing for Dorothy's house to crash-land here might increase the chances of success in resolving the issue once and for all, but it would be too big of a mess to clean up afterward.

"I have to buy cucumbers," Mother said. "I have no cucumbers left."

Bursting with urgency like the world was about to end, she got up and left in haste, slamming the door behind her. As usual, I was depleted of life force while having been driven to a state of insanity, unwillingly proving Mother right after all. I felt like a wrung-out damp old mop used for washing floors. It was the sort of visit after which one needed to lie on the floor for a while to recover. The worst of it? She would be back tomorrow. As a Taoist proverb tells us, "The glory is not in never falling, but in rising every time you fall." I say one should never have anything to do with people who manage to drain the life out of them.

twenty-five

On one of those airless nights, as muggy as a night in July, though it was mid-September, there was no comfortable position to lie in as I flopped and tossed in bed. Since the Hamptons or Côte d'Azur were not in the stars neither for me nor Eve, my choices were limited to the vast wasteland of my twin-size bed, while Eve summered in the mahogany armchair—a museum piece carved by artisans of Austro-Hungarian Empire. The brownish furball had impeccable taste. How that masterpiece ended up in my apartment was a mystery…well, not such a mysterious mystery. It had been left behind by one of my ex-boyfriends.

Now, *mysterious* would better describe the disappearance of said ex-boyfriend, who called late one evening, soon after the breakup, stated his desire to reclaim the armchair, was granted permission, but never showed up. While someone might have found such a disappearance disconcerting and might have felt the need to start an investigation to discover motives and such, I considered the matter to be nontroubling and was plain uninterested in it all. After letting an appropriate amount of time pass for the sake of appearances, I befriended the stranded piece of furniture and reupholstered it in ivory tone-on-tone silky fabric. Day or night, Eve looked good lounging on it, a diva in a shiny mink-like fur coat. The two things missing were a diamond bracelet and a slim cigarette in a tapered cigarette holder. No matter what could be said about her abilities or sensibilities, she was aware of her stardom.

Now Adam…Adam was another matter—Adam was all about loyalty. As long as I tossed, he tossed beside me. He had developed an innocent foot fetish and positioned himself strategically at my feet. Tonight, as fate would have it, he lay to my left. Things were fine within reason while I lay on my right side, pretending to be asleep, but when I turned to my left, my toes came into the zone of Adam's influence, to be licked with empathic concern and offers of comfort: "There, there." Contrary to what would be expected from someone of such a miniature stature, Adam never took his duties lightly: no one, two, three, and he was done. His meticulousness was on the excessive end of enthusiasm. One more lick and there would be no more skin left. *Merci beaucoup.* One day, in retrospect, I might recognize it as one of the precious moments in life, but today was not the day, though I appreciated the camaraderie.

To curb his enthusiasm, I pushed him off the bed to watch his eyes widen with betrayal, as if to say, *When will I be appreciated by some people? Not to point any fingers.* My ice cube of a heart melted, and I petted Adam on the head.

Far from being angry with me for his undeserved mistreatment, the little guy pressed his head against my hand and uttered something long and articulate, baring his wounded soul to me. He jumped back on the bed, into the same spot I had managed to force him off a moment ago, and did a few push-ups. He did not believe on skimping on his duties and went back to where he had left off—licking my toes. Oh yeah, baby.

· · ·

The night frayed around the edges, yet lingered, unwilling to leave and sticking to the corners. As if a conspiracy existed between them, nor did the morning want to come, but then it loaded up, bright, full of promise, lifting up all sorrows.

The invigorating stream of the shower was gratifying after a sleepless I-hate-my-writing night, a thought that proved impossible to fend off. My shoulders ached forever, glued to my ears with no neck to separate them. *Five more minutes,* I thought, *then I'll make a cup of tea and reread what I wrote.* Perhaps it was salvageable. Have you ever noticed how things tend to look better in daylight than the night before? Especially on such a cheery morning. I switched the temperature to hot, pressed my palms against the steamed-up tiled wall, lowered my head, put my shoulders into the midst of a rushing torrent, abandoning myself to its spell. Loosening the strain's hold, the blessed wave of relaxation changed its pace, released in the paroxysm, pleasurable to the point of pain, and my own tsunami of relief began at the base of my skull and surged its way down my body.

The key turned in the front door's lock with a loud *click.*

Startled, I turned the water off, grabbed a towel, wrapped it tight around myself, tucked in the corner at my left armpit. Was it Alex? Oh no. I rushed to face the intruder.

Mother was closing a living room window. I took a deep breath in.

"Why are your windows open? You'll catch cold," Mother said, looking displeased. "I keep teaching and teaching you. A waste of time. Like talking to a brick wall. I'm washing my hands of you. Why are you staring at me like that? Why aren't you dressed?"

"Ma, why are you here?"

"This was jammed in a crack between your door and the doorframe." She handed me a piece of paper, torn off from a takeout menu, handwritten and unsigned. "Are you seeing anybody? You'll be sorry soon enough."

I looked at it. *Pumpkin, do you miss me, pumpkin?* If she only knew how right she was. A chill ran down my spine. I crumpled the note and let out an involuntary sigh. Mother noticed nothing.

"Ma, why are you here?"

"What's this flowery smell?" she challenged, her mouth drawn up tight. "Is it your shampoo?"

"Ma, why are you here?"

"I *repeat*, is it your shampoo? For the millionth time—a perfumed shampoo at your age—inappropriate." She smacked her lips, heading to the next window.

I took a deeper breath. "Why. Are. You. Here?"

"What's that face? Are you in a bad mood again? Whenever I come here, you're cranky."

"Ma, how about calling to let me know you are coming?"

She shrugged one shoulder, not looking at me, and closed the window. "I won't get philosophical with you. You're saying it to make my blood pressure sky-high."

"Ma, look at me, please. Why did you let yourself in? That key was given to you for emergencies only. Is there any kind of emergency I should be aware of?"

"An emergency? I'll give you an emergency," she said, her hands on her hips. "Oh, what a bunch of nonsense. You sound like a nervous dame."

"When you hear me speak, what is it you hear, Ma? Any words sound familiar?" As if she ever bothered to listen.

"Nonsense." She squinted, looked out the window, pretending to find something interesting to watch in the empty well of the courtyard. "You don't like hearing the truth. This is absurd conversation. Nobody cares what you think."

Her capacity to ignore the wishes of others was nearing legendary.

I exhaled slowly. "How many times we discussed this already?"

"Bite your tongue." She waved her arm. "I'm not going to stand here and listen to this. *You* drag me into it. I refuse to discuss it. You're overreacting, as usual."

"Ma—"

"Who are you to tell me what's what?" she spat back with a scowl. "That's my personal key, and you're my personal daughter. Do you understand what I'm saying to you? I can never tell if you understand. You have an overactive imagination, always blowing things out of proportion. Ay-yay-yay! You're asking me, your mommy, to call you first? Just to *think* about it! Nonsense! Utter nonsense! I can come here anytime I want."

"You can, huh? You're right. Enough discussions. If you refuse to behave like a civilized person, you don't get to have the key. Hand it here."

"You twist things. I don't know how you got this way." She covered her ears and fixed her eyes on me, startled to find me here, as if trying to remember who I was. Mother sharply raised her hand with her forefinger sticking out and wagged it in my face. "I didn't bring you up to be like that. I brought you up to respect your mother. Is that the filial gratitude I deserve? Ay-yay-yay! We should've beaten you more often. You're rude! Rude!"

No amount of bracing would hold against her. "Ma, the key."

"You look as chalk-white as death himself. So pale, you're green. Have you eaten something bad?" Her feigned interest was unconvincing. "With the way you cook, I'm surprised you don't poison yourself more often. I can't think where you get it from."

"Mother, the key."

"No! Don't you speak to me in that way! May your tongue fall off. Who do you think you are, torturing your mommy like this? You're nobody. You amounted to nothing!"

The effect being cumulative, there were no more available buttons in me for her to push that she had not pushed already. My patience, stretched to the breaking point, was about to snap. We were at DEFCON 2. I was seeing fire truck red, half-expecting Mother—the same woman who gave me the wondrous gift of life—to burst into flames under my blazing stare. Spontaneous combustion was also welcome.

"Mother, the key," I said in a tone intended to sound disrespectful.

"Go to hell! No! You already sucked all my blood out! What else do you want from me?" She looked at me with a challenge and hate in her eyes. "Go to hell!"

I cared no longer whether she was in need of my protection. To hell with guilt. She could be fate itself, but with fury swelling up in my belly, I was ready to hit her.

I could tell she smelled murder in the air. She backed up a little.

"Mother—"

She jumped back as if a bee had stung her and shrilled, "Fine! Oh, what a nice daughter I have! This is my cross to bear. Some children must be drowned like newborn kittens. Heaven as my witness—you're psychotic! I should've had an abortion when I had a chance! You'll be sorry! You'll be very, very sorry!"

Mother hurled the keys into my face, spun around, and bolted out, slamming the door behind her with a bang that shook the walls.

Oh merciful God!

twenty-six

Why? Why was I feeling guilty?

As Mark Twain said, "Forgiveness is the fragrance that the violet sheds on the heel that has crushed it." Me, working out my destiny in my own way, I might be incapable of being so generous. The sins of parents are among the most difficult to absolve. Mine endured a lot of suffering, and preoccupied with the tragedies of their lives, I empathized with them, the mere thought of horrors undergone knocking me sideways. The wounded children with limited joy, limitless sorrow.

I was trapped in compassion to the point of paralysis, swept into the madness of anger, with parts of me broken, while unforgiveness, the strongest of poisons, contaminated my every moment—such torment for the heart to hold. The indignation accumulated for years, and with no memory of motherly caresses, my good intentions to feel no resentment came to nothing—a walled-in maze with no exit, and me becoming smaller and smaller. With the ever-present reminder of my worthlessness, far more explosive than nitroglycerine was the swelling anger in me, this thriving anger, an unmoving witness. What was required from me by life—to camouflage my identity and accept the fate, or stand up and fight?

I removed the wet towel, began to dress. Underwear—check. Jeans—check. T-shirt—check. I found it hard to breathe.

"Good girls don't get angry!" the Stoics restated often, sensing—rightly so— that their authority had been called into question. "Lower your voice! Refuse, and we have no choice but to put you into an orphanage. There you'll learn *how* to respect your parents."

Women did the talking. Michael, being predominantly taciturn, said little. He provided himself as a backdrop for Auntie's performances, but was in the habit of nodding now and again. "Listen to your mother. She knows. And be nice."

"Do what we tell you to do," the Stoics would say, proud of their much-coveted way of bringing the child this far and eyeing me as a disobedient brat who delighted in upsetting them, as if considering an exchange for a more agreeable, and therefore better, model of a child, the sort who would never dream of contradicting her elders—a worthy substitute, and do not think they would not do it.

"Nobody else will ever love you but us. With the shortcomings you have, and as stubborn as you are, ay-yay-yay! Mark our words."

Why would they think the enforced love would turn into love, or that I owe them gratitude? While the current episode unfolded, as in an endless multitude of other similar moments, I did my darnedest to pretend to be small, smaller, invisible, as lifeless as possible. Three against one. What were the odds of me succeeding? Ah, a brainteaser. I will tell you. None.

I would like to point out here how caring and thoughtful the Stoics were by giving me this precious forewarning, and how appreciative I was they decided against going through with the motions of a child exchange and kept me after all and also for not selling my organs on the black market; may I say here for the record what a noble choice this was. With the benefit of hindsight, I cannot help but wonder—under such tutelage, when did I begin feeling like a misplaced person? I would carry that feeling as a brightly lit torch throughout my life.

And here was a paradox. "Why was I coming back for more, like a thoughtless goat?" one might ask. An excellent, *excellent* question. I will tell you. Love was never given to me by the Stoics for free. I had to do something to deserve those pitiful crumbs thrown my way. The need to be loved and the deprivation caused by withdrawing it were so strong. What child would ever risk losing her mother's affection? There was nothing I would not do for those several crumbs, even if in the process of being given, they were spiced up with condescending frowns on both women's faces. The periodic outings I undertook, sometimes followed by more substantial attempts to disturb the existing order of things, were never encouraged and seldom left unpunished. The risk-reward ratio was never to my advantage, and this insight could be just the thing to account for my failures to raise the necessary enthusiasm on one or three occasions.

Were Adam and Eve rehearsing a duet? Ah no—time to feed them. I opened a can of cat food and dumped the contents into a bowl. Both cats materialized near the dish out of thin kitchen air and began to eat, making little chomping sounds. I petted them mechanically. My mind refused to let go. Why could not I submerge myself in the healing waters of forgiveness?

If the Stoics were the reasonable sort of people who understood the consequences of their behavior, I would not be here in the first place, untangling this chain of causes and effects in an attempt to bring order while still sliding toward chaos. And who knows? My life could have been different, fuller and happier from childhood, but it was not. If I could find a way to clarify things, they would be able to understand. *How could they not?* I reasoned with an ever-deepening sense of guilt.

And that was a mistake I went on to make, the creator of my own heaven and hell, imprisoning myself for life. Was there anything more devastating on this earth than a feeling of utter hopelessness? Why did I refuse to see they were unwilling to know? No one intended to venture beneath the surface of my life. Their repeated "I don't understand, explain it to me" lured me in with false expectations of intimacy, and was a way to throw a net over me as I stayed plunged into the sea of desolation, feeling spent and resorting to mysticism in search for peace of spirit. As long as there was a need to explain and receive the admission of their guilt and self-blame for the failure, I was entrapped. A failure was not a sign of a final defeat, I argued with myself. But every single failure?

A cup of tea would do me good. I put a teakettle on the stove, flicked on the gas. Teacup—check. Green tea inside the infuser—check. And now to wait for water to boil.

They believed that being wretched was an indispensable attribute of life, and they bent over backward to mold events to fit this conviction to be miserable at any price. Frightened souls silently screaming for help, they had created their reality and gotten lost in their creation. Driven by an unconscious need to maintain the fantasy that their alluring version of the world was tailored just so, they wedged me into the same mold that had been used to create them. Identical interests, identical dreams. Or more like the identical absence of dreams, a nonbeing, the bloodless world, the appearance of a living substance. Why did not it sound like a thrilling prospect?

"Nobody is happy," they said often, x-raying me with their gazes. "Are your friends putting ideas in your head? Trust nobody. Do you know happy people? We don't believe you. They lied. You've seen them being happy? You're lying too."

Set in their ways, any change terrified them more than death itself, as it meant chaos, abandoning the familiar for the new and unknown. "Better the devil you know than the devil you don't," they would say. Lives ruled by fear, their habitual way of being. Like many of us, it unnerved me too, but beset by nameless longing, how could I spend my life resisting moving forward?

As if a secret had been found at last, I came to know hunger, and such hunger, once revealed, made it impossible not to fell defenses, not to step over onto unmarked terrain full of possibility to transform lives, with hope never entirely extinguished. The dread of the unfamiliar, with no guideposts, at the mercy of strange forces, alien in their incomprehensibility—the terror of the unknown one perceived themselves as being powerless to control was overwhelming. Coming from the shadowy depth within ourselves, unable to hide anywhere…how threatening was that? Unfamiliar territories would do that every time.

Where was I? And what was that smell? Where? What? Aargh. The stove.

The teakettle had burned. Did I forget to pour in the water? Damn. The kettle was electric.

I would like to state here, if only for the sake of making such a statement by itself, or, if one wishes, for the record—I did not go willingly, not me. I was dead certain I was not taming material. I made ripples, I screamed, I kicked. Forever rebellious, I ran away from home several times, for too short a moment almost free as a bird, and have been on the run ever since. Always a fugitive, I belonged nowhere. The Stoics hoped that rebellious spirit of mine would calm down sooner or later, at some point wear off, wither and turn to dust, and someday, with a bit of luck, I would mature at last and go limp. They were so kind to protect me from myself. Ah, Mother, the loving usurper. Anyone know where I could meet a force capable of protecting me from them? It is urgent.

Was my T-shirt inside out? I took it off, turned it out, and put it back on.

The most horrifying part was the Stoics almost succeeded. The point where I stopped dreaming went unnoticed. When did I give up and give my life away? I was dead inside for years, my wings broken, both of them, if one was to discount the intolerable pain that little by little went from excruciating to mere nagging, but never went away in full. It became like a regrettably familiar ghost, almost affable, insane and unseen, that shadowed me around. I was like a tree that had been chopped down, longing and damning existence. And they, betraying their own souls and mine too, waited for some insignificant formality after my spirit's annihilation was complete—for me to begin toppling over, so they could yell in triumph, "Timber!" and we would be done. As a stroke of genius, ahead of time, the tree that was me had originally been planted in the wrong soil, and to make the job of chopping it down easier, they had been gnawing on the insides, hollowing out, destroying the foundation like a group of social cellulose-devouring wood borers.

At times it seemed like I had forgiven them, but no, things were infinitely more complex. That lay far ahead, like say, world peace. With a mammoth sense of entrapment and a flea-sized capacity for self-respect, how I wished to fling open the doors of understanding and breathe deeply the sweet air of forgiveness!

So enmeshed I was in worrying endlessly over the questions of good and evil, having sworn in my heart to do no harm, I deluded myself into thinking the hurt was gone. I ascribed a higher purpose to it, something I was simply incapable of comprehending just yet. If I but dared to look—there it was, a huge tangled mess. Wounds opened up, the pain dislodged from where it had been tucked until now, unearthed and loud. As the Chinese saying goes, "There is great disorder under heaven and on earth and the situation is excellent." The boundaries that outlived their usefulness and became tools of destruction—my destruction—began to shatter, and there was a chance, however slim, before one came to the point of no return, to establish a new set of functional rules. But just a chance.

All of a sudden, I realized the annoying, loud ringing in my head was not in my head, but the phone ringing off the hook.

"We want to go out for dinner. We haven't been out for ages. Would you like to join us?" said the voice on the other end of the line, one of my favorite voices in all existence, the lone voice of reason in this upside-down world. "Come on. Get dressed."

Ah, Rita. Still a bit shaken, I said nothing, but nodded with enthusiasm.

She listened for about two minutes to silence at my end. "Are you all right?"

"Mother." I nodded again.

"Ah. Do you want to talk about it?"

"No."

"Do you think you'd want to talk about it tomorrow morning?"

"Dunno."

"I'll ask you again in the morning. Come have dinner with us tonight. And please hurry before the damn pager goes off. All right?"

Bless her. I hung up the phone, looked around. The dusk was bleeding away, all packed up and about to leave, and the day was already long gone. I sighed and went to the bedroom to get dressed.

twenty-seven

anticipating a pleasant evening in the company of people I loved, I hopped into the calm belly of the lobby with its inviting spaciousness, ecstatic to leave the street drenched by one of the typical July thunderstorms, the crazy downpours that come and go unannounced and furious. Not that thunderstorms were common to New York weather in mid-September (they were not), but stranger things had been reported to happen. As I stepped in, the skies cracked open again, flooding the blackness outside with blinding light, making the oblique, striped wall of torrential rain visible for a split second. Behind it, floating, supported by nothing, towered an enormous glass-and-steel mass, seemingly alive, hiding and silent. The skies belched out the deafening thunder, and the city vanished again into the gaping void.

My stilettos clicked and echoed on the marble floor as I passed by an enormous arrangement of blue delphiniums and green button mums bathing in warm yellow lights on a marble credenza. I folded my dripping umbrella, happy to have it in my handbag with the rain that was forecasted for tomorrow and grateful that my new pumps were not ruined. It is an urban myth that women need a lot to make them joyful. On the contrary, sometimes it was little things that make us content. For a bit.

I waited for the elevator, humming a catchy tune that had spiraled on and on through my head for the last hour. I was about to see the people I wanted to be with, on top of the fact I was not to catch sight of Mother for a bit (this was a biggie!). It was things like that that could presumably put anyone in a pleasant-enough state of mind. One of the few peculiarities known about the mood was that little touches made it or broke it.

The tamed elevator door slid open with a soft *dzing*. A man walked out and into me, stepping on my new pump, light dusty-rose suede, with the sole of his shoe, big and muddied. He raised his eyes, met mine, and retreated back inside.

I caught the familiar whiff of bewitching aftershave and recognized the face of my favorite in this solar system Frappuccino addict in person. This time he had no cup of hot coffee in his hand. That was good. He had a bulky wet umbrella instead, an oversized Godzilla of umbrella that had made a nice-sized hole in my new stocking. What was heaven's plan for this guy's persevering presence in my life—to ruin my wardrobe piece by piece? I can understand its happening once. But twice? Hey, you—yes, you up there—how about showing some decency?

"What floor is this?" the man asked in a hoarse voice as he put his forearm against the elevator door to hold it open, ignoring my undeservingly mistreated foot and the newly acquired hole in my newly acquired stocking.

He looked with bewilderment at me, perhaps because of my unwillingness to answer him sooner, but lowered his gaze. No apologies were forthcoming this time either, I guessed, as it was not one of his widely practiced habits. All righty, I could live with that. As far away from him as possible, please. Those brilliant gray eyes, pulling me in…Oh, not again…Brilliant, ah…a bit sad, though. A slight chill ran down my spine.

And there, in that moment, a bit swoony, I lost it. The day had proved to be too eventful indeed. Besides, I could never be sure what the proper etiquette was in a situation like this one, or any other given situation.

"Excuse me, sir. Is this a personal vendetta?" I felt warm tears welling up in my eyes, astounded at the unanticipated depth of my reaction. "Something I should be made aware of, given my participation in it was so unceremoniously forced upon me? Please do tell me. Would you also notify me of your future schedule and whereabouts so I can know when and where *not* to be so as to avoid your presence, which had proved far too damaging to my wardrobe?"

His face paler by two full shades, he stepped back into the waiting elevator and pressed a button. The door butted in front of him with a soft *ping*.

My mystic side wanted for this to be a projection of some deeper reality while my material side believed it to be all there was. While both of them got engaged into an argument, things heating up, a familiar stirring in the vicinity of my groin area caught me by surprise. Seriously?

Five impossibly long minutes later, I was looking at Rita's kind face. She inspected me up and down and shook her head at the devastation. "Look at you. What happened to you?"

"Guess," I said.

"It looks like…Is this a footprint on your shoe? Who did this to you?"

"Would you believe the same guy who ruined my blouse?" I said.

"You don't say." Her eyes rounded with understanding. She gave me a hearty hug, in no hurry to set me free, and I heard a muffled giggle.

I furrowed my brow, but burst out laughing.

Patrick kissed me on the cheek, shrugging as he fought to resist a grin. His facial features arranged into a welcoming expression. One can only admire such demonstration of willpower.

"Oh, go ahead. Laugh it up." I made a wide gesture with my hand.

With the three of us guffawing, the evening was bound to progress better than I expected, taking into consideration the events of less than ten minutes ago, never mind the whole morning galore.

"Come in, sit down." Rita wove her fingers through mine, lead me to the couch, inquiring in a soft sympathetic voice, "Do you want to order in?"

"I'm sorry to spoil your plans for the evening, but I think we should, if you prefer not to see me as the laughingstock of the entire neighborhood." I lowered myself onto the couch.

Rita sat down right by me, and gently squeezed my hand. "Oh, don't be silly."

"Give *him* time to leave the premises," I deliberated further, not all the steam gone. "For my sake, I hope he's visiting here. I couldn't survive if that man was your new neighbor. The marvelous world of opportunities. I have several good pieces of clothing left intact and I'd rather keep it that way. I never want to see him again. He isn't a nice person."

"You don't have to see him again," Rita said soothingly. "I'd feel exactly the same way. Do you want to know what I usually do in cases like this?"

"No, I don't." I already knew what was to come.

"As you wish." Rita smiled. "I concentrate on something positive. Try it."

"You aren't going to let me enjoy my misery, are you?" I asked.

"Not if I can help it, no. Remember, relax and concentrate."

I sighed, but obediently folded my hands on my lap.

"Now, big breath in." Rita watched me take a deep breath as her hand moved slowly up and down my arm. "And out. Good girl. And again." She squinted at me. "You like him, don't you?"

"Who? Me?" I asked in a squeakier version of what might be called my normal timbre of voice, and blushed. What would she say if I told her I had been fantasizing about him?

"*Me?*" I tried again. Still too high-pitched, a mosquito.

"Oh dear. You always were a bad liar." Rita placed her palm against my cheek. "As Bertrand Russell once said, 'To fear love is to fear life, and those who fear life are already three parts dead.' Keep breathing. Look, maybe you'll meet him again under more auspicious circumstances. Now, what do you feel like ordering? How about Japanese?"

That was my sweet friend. She knew how much I loved Japanese cuisine.

"Great idea." I blushed harder; Rita's face went blank, as always was the case when she pretended not to notice something too obvious.

"I'll get the menus." Patrick left the room.

"That mother of yours, what does she want now?" Rita asked.

"Let's not spoil this evening by talking about her. I only wish the bloody free-dom from fear to follow my own bloody path came naturally to me, with less of this bloody struggle." *Bloody?*

Rita was about to say something, but not two minutes after he exited the room, Patrick was back with the whole stack of takeout menus. He plopped him-self down in the armchair and after a short search, handed us several menus to choose from. Rita sighed.

"Any news from the adoption center?" I asked.

"I'm glad you asked. We rescheduled for the seventh time. And you know who is on probation?" Rita turned around as if intending to look directly into Patrick's eyes, just in time to catch him in the act of trying—sideways, side-ways—to sneak out of the room. "For a week he slept at the hospital in hopes that somehow I'd forget he didn't show up the last time too."

He stopped dead where he was caught and produced a soft whistle. With a mischievous spark in his eyes, standing tall in his broken jeans, he smiled, though the smile was tortured. He rocked back and forth as if nothing had happened, slightly rolling from his heel to toe and back, his hands tucked in the pockets of his jeans. An air of defiance hung thick around him. In his frayed, faded, or-ange T-shirt with a little green ball of a planet on the front—its skinny arms up, thumbs near its ears, fingers spread apart, and sticking out a red, fleshy tongue at everyone—it was difficult to imagine him being a successful surgeon.

"Have you heard this favorite author of yours will be in New York in Decem-ber?" Patrick asked me. "They kept postponing it for some reason, but now it's actually happening."

"Oh?" I froze. My breath stopped.

"That's all you can say? I expected something longer and much, much louder."

All of a sudden, I felt so uneasy, I lost my voice—crap, why was I so bloody nervous? Again, *bloody?*

Capable of executing only pitiful control over my head, I nodded several times. Yes, yes, yes, that nodding function seemed to be working fine.

"Hold your horses," Rita said. "Poor darling needs time to recover from an-other encounter with that brutal man. Look, she's turning green. Anna, breathe."

Rita had been the mother I never had. Through an unfortunate chain of cir-cumstances due to a doctor's incompetence, Rita had lost her uterus when giving birth to her firstborn had gone horribly wrong, and two months later, she lost her newborn daughter to sudden infant death syndrome. She never recovered fully from it, and her first husband hanging the blame on her had not helped her heal. In a rush to separate from the circumstances and blame, she divorced what's-his-name, which turned out to be an excellent decision in all aspects. Marrying Patrick had seemed to bring her peace. Still, unable to bear children and with a heart too big not to give, Rita adopted those around her whom she felt might be in need of some mothering. In turn, we, the adopted ones, gladly accepted her care, became dependent, and thrived because of it.

"Anna, we're going, right?" asked Patrick.

"Anna wouldn't miss it for the world. But who'll believe you'll be there and not at work?" Rita looked at Patrick intently, then turned back to me. "Ignore him. Tell me, have you heard from Mark?"

"We...*Harrumph*. We had dinner together a week ago." I came around, thank God. Must have been Rita's presence, which could always be counted upon to work its soothing magic on me. "He broke up with his latest girlfriend. Well, she broke up with him, so he's sulking."

"Is he all right?" Rita was the mother Mark had never had either. "Hmm... Hypothetically, now that he's free again and you're not seeing anyone, would you consider giving it another go? Let's pretend to think it over for a moment, all right? I have a feeling he wouldn't mind."

"I bet he wouldn't." I eyed her suspiciously. "Look, don't even start."

"I'm starting nothing," Rita said. "Is it wrong to ask? To check what your intentions are?"

"You could've guessed," I said.

"Oh, what a pity. Such a good guy going to waste," Rita said. "I worry about him. I'm starting to seriously question his present-day taste in women. Has anyone seen this girl?"

Patrick shook his head, visibly relieved the potential squall had passed him by, but said nothing, as if by uttering a sound, he was liable to tempt his good fortune and attract yet another one of those storms upon his head, and soon. He might have been right about it too.

"Mark's a grown man," I said. "He seemed uninvested in this relationship and not that upset with it ending. You worry about him too much. He'll be a bachelor on the prowl in no time, Casanova that he is. Let's hope his next passing passion is a bit more mature than his last one."

"You mean his last several ones," muttered Patrick.

"How very true," I said. "Tell me, as a man, are you envious of Mark?"

"No, no," said Patrick. "What would I do with a young girl?"

"What?" I asked. "I give up."

Patrick grinned. "I'm having trouble keeping up with Rita as it is."

Rita nodded. "He tells the absolute truth. I'm considering hiring an escort service to accompany me to social events. My female clients are unhappy when I show up alone."

"Hey, why pay someone? Take Mark for free." I glowed, proud of my ingenuity. "He could use adult company for a change. You'll keep an eye on him. And you won't be ashamed of your escort like you might be with some mumbling idiot. He's still quite presentable."

"Anna, you're a genius," Patrick said. "And I'd have no reason to be as jealous of Mark as I'd be of some young hunk. What do you say, hon?" He looked at his wife a bit nervously.

"Shows how much you know women," Rita said. "For your information, Mark is very hunky. Well, I promise to think it over. All right, are we ready to order?"

I sensed things were not well in their kingdom, but could not quite spot it. The foreboding feeling inside me grew. It got so strong that I contemplated asking the involved parties.

But when it reached its highest peak, at which point being silent was considered the equivalent of committing a crime, the premonition vanished. Burst like an iridescent soap bubble with a *ploop!* There must have been a simpler explanation for my sinister hunches, as my intuitive powers had been playing dirty tricks on me in the past few weeks.

Hey, Rita had said Mark might like to try again? Was that what he had wanted to, but ended up not telling me? And how would I feel about that?

Tempting, though. Very tempting.

twenty-eight

my wake-up call—the proverbial straw that broke camel's back—blew in with the onset of chest pain. It had bothered me for a week and now worsened by the hour. With the inordinate volumes of negativity I had experienced over a prolonged period of time, caught in an endless loop of crisis management, something was bound to happen. One negative thought too many, and one evening I found myself in agony.

Appreciation of impermanence aside, I was not amused when my hair stood on end while my mind, like a proper drunken monkey bitten by a scorpion, raced through a thick mass of questions only to go blank from the mounting panic, till, with a relative calmness as the distractions vaporized, it zeroed in on the only important matter—the business of the meaning of life—what one might call a genuine existential panic. Perhaps prebuilt into human consciousness, this focal point appeared when a person found himself in an extreme situation. Why should I be any different? I went about exploring the subject, experiencing the blessing and opportunity in between the bouts of fear, breathless while the angry volcano erupted in my chest. And no, it was not indigestion.

Moving in and out of an existential crisis, searching for a meaning, any satisfactory meaning, I had no clue what it was. Hunting for it was like seeking happiness—both can be frustrating. I thought that meaninglessness equaled non-existence, meaninglessness equaled death. Making sense of it all would give me motivation and a reason for being—one of the most intriguing philosophical problems ever known to exist—but if I spent too much or too little time thinking about it, what I came up with was insufficient. No wonder world-renowned pundits dedicated time and energy to the issue of the ultimate question of life. For me it was still in the realm of abstract, but solving the riddle took on sudden urgency.

Was it possible each instant had its own significance, and if life kept changing like that—in the twinkling of an eye, no one knowing what it will bring—how important was it to make the most out of each fleeting moment? Could the meaning pertain to each single life? What if there was no single unifying formula to suit everyone? Or was the point of creation a multifaceted entity, showing different sides at different junctures in time? Was it encrypted in the learning process or the material absorbed? Would the answer ever become apparent?

Some say the meaning of life is in the search for divine bliss, in experiencing divine, eternal love. Should one take it even further and transcend the duality of love to come into the realm of absolute unity? Or was it becoming aware of being a pure consciousness and merely being, without seeking to define what this consciousness or state of existence was? Was it as simple (or as complex) as experiencing being alive, with everything it entailed? Ah, the allure of the ultimate mystery of being, of gaining knowledge of something that, in its transcending-all-thought way, was perhaps never intended to be known or named. What a deliciously illusive mystery it was!

Never mind. Back to pain. I had to go to the emergency room. Now.

Unwilling to be alone, I called Michael to ask him to accompany me—a raw neediness in my voice—a sinking ship transmitting the SOS. I knew he would be here in a few short minutes, as they lived in the next building. But nothing ought to be taken for granted—nothing.

Michael came in an hour. Bella had felt the urge to drink tea with apricot jam—my favorite!—before taking me to the hospital. As a gesture of compensation for the lost time, I suppose, Michael brought Madame, his wife, with him. On her short feet, she and her sardonic smile sailed into the room in a stale cloud of pronounced habitual falsity, as I lay on the couch on my side, my knees tucked to my chest. My insides felt not unlike I was engaged in harakiri.

"Fuck." I gasped and curled up into a ball like a grub, my head swimming.

Auntie cast a disdainful look at me. "Watch your language! How vulgar."

"Fuck!" I said with more conviction in a second, when pain mounted to the next level.

"I heard that." Bella's eyes were riveted on mine, the twisted gnome—evil, so evil. She produced a grimace of repulsion, her body rigid, as if now was a perfect time to clear up the issues between us, a form of incontinence. "That's what you get for throwing your mommy out of your house. Your own mommy! Explain it to me—how could you have done it? You deserve this. Endure! Endure! I hope you're in a lot of pain."

With a worried look, Michael took a step toward me. Bella, dedicated to grabbing every opportunity to seize the spotlight, raised her hand, blocking him, and he stopped.

"How could your tongue ever turn to talk to your mother like that?" dribbled from Auntie's lips. "You don't think I know what you're up to? You think yourself more cunning than me? You tried to get rid of her by dropping her in our lap.

Forget it! Don't even dream of putting her in our care. We don't want her either."

The pain, reinforced by a fresh portion of anger, caused tears to roll down my face.

A smug smile spread on Bella's physiognomy like a fungus. "I hope you're crying because you're ashamed of yourself. Pick up that phone, tell her you're sorry. And that you'll never do it again!"

But that failed to happen. I picked up the phone, called the ambulance, and got myself to the hospital.

Thank God, it was acute gastritis. The diagnosis itself was in question. Several liters of blood lighter for a number of consecutive tests and one cardio catheterizing later, I was told I had the heart of a fifteen-year-old and clear arteries, but I was to stay alert since life came with no guarantees. The rest was "inconclusive, probably gastritis." The puzzled doctors also gave me an x-ray, a CT scan, and a sonogram. Then it looked like they had run out of machines to stick me into, as they were quizzically shrugging their shoulders and raising their brows, and as soon as the general anesthesia wore off, I was discharged from a hospital. Two Extra Strength Tylenol pills were placed in my palm.

"If the pain returns, come here right away," they said, cordially parting with me. Nice, nice people. Next, a hospital bill. *Mucho, mucho dineros.* Did I mention I had no health insurance? Could not afford any.

An alarming experience. At this point in life, when the reserves of the blind and unbounded devotion of a child ran out, the reserves that were given in abundance at birth and which always seemed to be bottomless, I had to stop behaving like I was granted a never-ending procession of days to live and hand in my resignation, which was easier said than done. Where I came from, one did not get up, full of disrespect, and walk away when one felt like it, leaving the family behind. On the other hand, I had already been through a suicidal stage once, when I would rather take my own life and throw it all away than fail to live up to Mother's expectations.

When utter hopelessness welled up within me and the total of my life was a gaping emptiness, devoid of meaning and dark—terrible darkness!—too senseless and vain, intolerable, a farce, I closed my eyes and thought how easy, disturbingly easy, it seemed to slip out of this sorrow and loneliness, out of this life. What a way to put a stop to being perpetually lost, hollow, and defeated. The never-ending sadness. No escape. And as if a higher power intervened and made me doubt the validity of my convictions, I wondered to what extent the situation was irredeemable for me to act on such a decision. And what would happen to my daughter? Never a question in my mind—I would die for her. Would I *live* for her?

I was determined not to end up at this notable stage again. Ever. Once a decision was made and I was no longer a captive—how blessed I felt achieving this place!—a curious thing began to unfold, shifting and awakening a renewed zest for life. An unwanted child, always terrified of my own zeal for living, but not anymore. My heart was set on happiness. In dealing with something as unpredictable as life, mistakes would be made. So perhaps unlike the Stoics, always anticipating and finding catastrophes, I would have to always anticipate and find the hidden opportunities. Except I had already been practicing it when the Stoics were not watching.

Tea, anyone? One lump or two?

twenty-nine

i t was early morning. Such a nice morning too, if a bit on the gloomy side. I positioned myself at the desk, ready to write, a cup of hot Earl Grey nested on a coaster near the keyboard, within easy reach. The phone rang. I picked it up.

"Is it you? It's me." Bella began her morning rounds with her usual aversion to preamble. "Where were you yesterday? I called and called. Nobody picked up."

"In the hospital," I said.

"Where? Er...It rained yesterday, so we spent the entire day inside. It's sunny now. Accompany me to the park. Mike says he's busy, and I want company."

"No, Bella."

"How can you not want to go to the park?" She sounded cross, as if she had gotten up on the wrong side of the bed, mounted the wrong broom, flown off in the wrong direction.

"How can you not remember I was in the hospital?"

I heard cellophane crinkle while she unwrapped a piece of hard candy. Then she sighed, like an accordion collapsing. "You ask too much of me," she said with a laugh, a false sound. "So you won't go? Suit yourself. Why are you so touchy today?" She rolled around the piece of hard toffee in her mouth with her tongue, and it clicked against her dentures like a small pebble. She sighed again. "Tell me, do you remember Lenin?"

Auntie had never left the enlightening why-is-water-wet stage because her curiosity was never satisfied. And how could it be? She had never bothered to remember the answers. To hell with curiosity, she was never curious anyhow, but had learned that asking a question shone a light on her and made her the center of attention. So Auntie asked question after question, no end to it. The topic of inquiry could be anything; the subject did not matter diddly-squat.

During the years when the Soviet power was still in power, Vladimir Ilyich Lenin's embalmed mummy was placed in a glass coffin in the moodily lit mausoleum at the Red Square in Moscow. The unnumbered army of Lenin's statues gesturing to whatever atop the granite pedestals marched through the USSR, dominating each town square. The slogan "Lenin will live forever!" hung all over the country, flapping in the perky wind of a bright socialist future. With the dead body lying in there and an eternally living image that was always with us, fluttering everywhere else, in the absence of a forbidden God, he was a figure to fill the gap with, to officially worship, godlike, a living relic, though not exactly an option for freedom of choice.

Ah, the land of the Soviets. The mausoleum was open to the public at no charge, so after standing in the shuffling, pushing, unhappy, stretched-till-infinity line for hours, anyone could pay their respects to the great leader, the father of the socialist state.

"Comrades! The kulak uprising…must be crushed without pity. The interests of the whole revolution demand such actions…" he had written, ordering grain requisitioning and executions, calling out for the armed struggle to abolish private property and establish the dictatorship of proletariat. The party had shed a lot of blood for the sake of global revolution, a preview of things to come; the atrocities they have committed.

The human element has always been attracted to oddities. The great leader, the petrified mummy. The near brush with immortality. It was the tiny mummy of a man rumored to have died from syphilis. Everyone went regardless of the horrors of waiting in line forever. Liberated at last from the slavery of capitalism and delivered into the socialist abundance, united Soviet citizens (the disillusioned *Homo sovieticus*) stood in all kinds of snaking lines all the time, for hours. (Well, with chronic food shortages, there was the daily drama of food lines. The line for TVs, furniture, or apartments lasted months or years.) The lines, with their unique bouquet of smells of stale alcohol, tobacco, old sweat, sickly cheap perfume, along with squabbles with unprintable three-tiered slang curses, were a place to trade gossip and insult and get into fistfights.

There was a line to use the shared latrine in the communal apartment (clutching portioned pieces of newspaper to be used as toilet paper). The lines in Kafka-esque state-owned communal cafeterias to buy a three-course complexed dinner number one, two, or three. The lines to buy bread, shoes, meat grinders—you name it, there was a well-regulated line for it somewhere, the important question being where exactly was it, this life-sustaining line?

Pervasive Soviet barbarism blossomed. Anchored in a totalitarian reality, barely washed comrades were in the habit of getting into a line first, then asking what was being sold there and what was the portion per head present. With everything in perpetual deficit, everyone carried an *avoska* * in their pocket at all

---

* An expandable netted bag, stretchable to a very large sack. (Russian slang)

times in case they stumbled upon some much-needed item offered for distribution among the population.

So yes, the mausoleum. My whole family had been there, sans Mother but including Bella. The impact of it must have been significant if she managed to remember something about it many years later.

"What do you think?" I asked, but then it occurred to me I had better not leave her with such a vague answer and clarified, "Yes, Bella, I remember Lenin."

"Is there a lightbulb inside Lenin's head?"

"What? N-no."

"So how come his head is luminous? Oh, I have to go." And the line went dead.

We were guaranteed to never get bored while she was still with us. God bless her and give her a long, prosperous life! Forgive me if I lack the proper anticipatory joy to accompany this blessing. No one was without a blemish, and Bella was always amazingly proficient—gifted, that is what she was—at finding out what was wrong and with whom. An undedicated researcher, unwilling to waste her time on such an ungrateful pursuit as research, and in general acting as if her brain were an annoying incidental appendage, she assigned faults to people at whim. Though mainly it was her compulsive projection—ah, the marvel of the intricate art of projection!—of whatever particular human vice her mind happened to be preoccupied with at that given moment in time.

Since her memory was not much to speak of and she was incapable of concentration, she carelessly forgot the shortcomings she assigned others, which was not as tragic as it appeared on the surface, for Bella reassigned those damn faults with enviable ease. It made her happy too. Having been in close physical proximity to her and for a long time short of stature while she appeared to be a giant, I was her favorite target. I, the untouchable, went through every vice imaginable. The lengthy list of horrific attributes she was capable of concocting, driven by a pressing sense of revenge, demanded the deepest reverence. Whatever undesirable traits Bella could come up with, I had them all at one time or another. If you were looking for the worst person on this planet, you had found her.

I found myself standing at the window, staring at the featureless, filthy, concrete well of the courtyard, the cordless phone clutched in my hand. It rang. *Private caller.*

"Is this the state correctional facility?" The woman talked slowly, annunciating every syllable. I was not fond of people who upon hearing my accented English straightaway insisted on speaking slowly to me, and louder too.

"No, it's not." I put the phone back in its cradle.

The phone rang again. *Outside of area.*

"Hi, Mama!" Hannah said.

"Hi, sweetie! Marcello called me."

"Why?"

"To congratulate me on your birthday."

"But my birthday is two months away."

"He also informed me you're getting married. Who's he?"

"Oh, whaddayagonnado? Nobody, Mama, he's nobody. I meet lots of guys. Look, I was checking if you're all right. I'll call you later. Love you!"

Ring, ring. Private caller. Other people have lives; I had phone conversations.

"Hey, what are you wearing?" asked a masculine voice with an upscale New York pronunciation.

I hung up.

Ring. Ring. Unashamedly. Another private caller. I sighed and picked it up.

"This is the Police Precinct Sixty-Nine. We have a gentleman here we need to bring over to you." It was the woman who had called two minutes ago. If I set aside my suspicion of the telephone company doing this with the sole purpose of annoying someone, I still wished they would straighten out their entangled telephone lines once and for all.

"I understand, but this is still not the state correctional facility."

"So, we can't bring him over to you?"

"I'm afraid not. Unless he's very, very handsome."

"What?" she asked.

"No, ma'am, you can't bring the gentleman here."

The line went silent.

I pressed the ON button, and the computer awoke from its sleep with a reassuring hum. A chapter draft opened. What a nice-looking chapter, if a bit short. The phone rang. I picked it up, which was unforgivable stupidity, considering I was the semiproud owner of a fully operational answering machine.

"I'm very, very upset," Auntie declared. "Your uncle is scheduled for surgery on Thursday."

"Surgery?" I asked. "Wait, what kind of surgery? What's his diagnosis?"

"We don't know," she said. "He has a tumor."

"What tumor? What's his diagnosis?" I was going in circles. I closed my eyes.

"I don't know what he has, but I know what the doctor said he doesn't have," she said. "I know a woman—I meet her in the park often—she has it, and it's very, very bad."

I could see her, as I had seen her perform those moves many times before— the same way she was to inhabit my memory forever, here and hereafter—on the plastic-slipcovered chair, her legs too short to reach the floor, dangling like a little kid's, the tilt of her head evoking the image of an inquisitive, peckish pterodactyl foraging for food, her empty-looking eyes reflecting the even shallowness and banality of her mind. Auntie raised her legs up in the air in front of her, put them down again, and, wiggling her toes, filled in the gaping emptiness of yet another day with purposeful movement. From time to time, she would turn both toes a little inward, then outward as in admiration, her left toe peeking through the hole in an opaque beige cotton stocking, free at last, her thick stockings loose, half down, soft folds cascading around her knees and ankles.

I opened my eyes and reached for the pen. "What's the doctor's name and phone number?"

There was dead silence on the other end.

"I'll keep asking until I receive an answer. What's the doctor's name—"

Michael, who had been listening to the conversation on an extension all this time, caved in first. "You can stop. It's Dr. Schubert."

"Dr. Schubert," Auntie echoed. The name had a magical effect. "*Aaa-ve Ma-riii-i-a!*" split the air as she, I bet, stopped doing whatever she thought she was doing with her legs.

Not to worry, though, for I knew she would resume the activity soon, and her health would not suffer because of unfortunate interruption. The same guarantee could not be applied to my own health conditions. It might have been the insufficient lighting in the room this gloomy morning that was at fault, but something peculiar happened to my eyes. For a fleeting moment, an image of a bleating gray goat conjured itself up, perfectly formed down to cloven hooves. Expecting nothing of the sort, especially a thing bearing a remarkable resemblance with a pagan idol, I blinked. The curly apparition faded. Nothing like that had ever happened to me before. What could it mean, this sort of thing so early in the morning?

Auntie was infected with opera fever and torn between thinking herself Madame Butterfly or Isolde. With frequency she impersonated a little of both at the same time, taking stance on an imaginary stage, which she also used to express her strong political opinions. She sang arias for hours with her "*tah-rah-rih-rih-rah,*" Edith Piaf she was not. Auntie could never remember the lyrics, but the melodies—ah, those melodies!—were off-key and loud.

"*Aaa-ve Ma-riii-i-a!*" carefree split the air and the insides of my head.

"Anna, how do you feel?" Michael asked. "What did the doctors say?"

"She's fine," Auntie said. "How come you never ask me how *I* feel? *Aaa-ve*—"

"Bella, stop," Michael said. "You're giving me a headache."

"Take an aspirin," she said.

"Doctor said I have cataracts on both eyes," Michael said.

"Don't listen to him. The doctor said tumor. I'm not stupid. I know what's what. Why, why do these things always happen to us?" Auntie wailed.

"What do you know about tumors?" he asked. "Or cataracts?"

"I don't have to know anything about it to have an opinion," she said. "I know my rights. It's my right to have an opinion."

"I think—" I said.

"That's none of your business," she said. "It's between my husband and me."

"Bella, enough," Michael said.

"But it's true," she said. "Tumor." What spirit!

"A cataract is not a tumor," I said. "May I talk to the doctor?"

"Tumor. She wants to talk to the doctor."

"I can still hear, Bella. Okay, Anna, you talk to him." And they both hung up.

I could not recall walking into the kitchen, but there I was, staring inside the fridge. I sighed and closed the refrigerator door. The phone rang. A New York call. I picked up the kitchen extension. Good time to admit I was a masochist.

"I've got a recipe from a website," Katie said. "Roasted pheasant with chestnuts. I'll e-mail it to you." And she hung up.

Katie was an incurable collector of recipes she would never cook. Her culinary escapades were limited to horribly overboiling huge amounts of vegetables or burning a frozen TV dinner in a toaster oven. Time and again, she made a wobbly, cockamamie sculpture out of a whole box of spaghetti—the weirdest shape, tortured out of insane nightmares, a mystifying creation. I thought it inedible, but this was as far as she would normally go.

We had known one another for about five months. She was older than me, nudging fifty, unhealthily skinny, with a sharp, long nose—a defiant geographical feature on a face the color of oatmeal, stark and triangular with high cheekbones and short, curly, dark hair. The luster seemed to be gone from her eyes forever. Even if I had thought perpetual sadness the only thing to be glimpsed there, I had seen a little sparkle in her eye once when Katie and I stood in line in a pastry shop in Chinatown, but that unauthorized sparkle was gone in haste. She dispersed miserly amounts of kindness to people within her closed circle, but seemed sorry afterward, as if she had exposed a weakness.

I could see a few other explanations, but concluded that something had happened to her, and that whatever it was, it had instilled in her heart a permanent fear of trusting anyone. I could relate to that. Not exactly filling our relationship with warmth, an intense ache for secretiveness permeated the whole of Katie's being, harboring the deepest suspicion of things alive. I assume it would not be entirely surprising if I mentioned that people unconsciously picked up on it and, in turn, mistrusted Katie.

Katie wore one modest, neutral, beige-colored dress with a matching finger-wide fabric belt as her uniform summer or winter, which was peculiar on its own. She was in possession of plenty of other suitable clothing. She paraded it with pride in front of me one day. On hangers. No statement providing particulars to explain a one-dress preference was ever volunteered. Ferocious, she ducked direct inquiries, and after a few abortive attempts, I stopped asking.

In the bigger scheme of things, her wardrobe choices, together with the causes behind them, made no difference to me. Adding to the quirky riddle, Katie's feet in pantyhose always overflowed, squeezed into a pair of neutral-beige summer shoes, open-toed with orangey-brown stripy bits, supported by a high, square heel. She looked painfully uncomfortable in them, poor woman. My feet ached on her behalf every time I glanced at hers, and the feeling refused to dissipate. I had to remind myself not to look down when we were together. Perhaps those two unfortunate pieces of clothing presented the peak of sophistication in Katie's vision of herself as a sharp dresser. She was a conundrum for me, but it was not a riddle I had to solve as if my life depended on it. Still, everything about her was unfathomable enough to periodically raise a certain amount of innocent curiosity in a fellow human being.

Katie was a single mother with two girls, and even if I was introduced as her best friend to anyone who cared to listen, I had no idea what had happened to her husband or any other intimate detail about her life. Some best friend I was. Katie avoided the subject of her persistently missing husband at any cost. Katie avoided any personal subject at any cost. That was her privileged right, indeed, and I respected that. Meanwhile, I was as perplexed as I ever wanted to be with regard to her case, but also free to use my well-developed imagination to fill in gaps. A fun game, but that fun was short-lived, and the deceptive attractiveness faded away and fast. I preferred to know the real person and was not into imaginary friends anymore.

I wanted to give no one a false impression that Katie and I felt a pressing need to do girly things on a regular basis, except her pushing some recipes on me on occasion. Despite that, I found myself used to her in some way. She resurfaced in my life at almost regular intervals with an urgency and longing, unfathomable and intense, creating primordial havoc on her way in and in her wake, when she took a deep dive into her mysterious existence soon after.

Midmorning. The phone rang. *Private caller* again? What was the point of having caller ID?

"Am I speaking to the male or female head of the household?" the voice asked with a New Delhi lilt, but it was hard to say if it belonged to a man or a woman. "I'm delighted to tell you that you qualify and have been preapproved to receive our platinum package of telephone services. Let me tell you—"

"Did you say 'preapproved'? I don't deem myself worthy, but thank you so much for thinking of me and caring enough to call. Bye."

I hung up. The nerve of some people!

Late morning. The phone rang. *Private caller* again. It should be illegal.

"Piss off," I said, extended my hand, and picked it up.

"What are you wearing?"

I hung up. The phone rang again.

"Don't hang up! What are you wearing?"

I hung up the phone and quickly pulled my hand away from it.

thirty

a t last I sat at my improvised desk, staring at the computer screen. Of their own accord, my eyes swerved toward the phone. I forced them back on the screen. Things refused to register.

Ring, ring, said the phone. *Ring, ring.*

What was wrong with people? I picked it up. What was wrong with me?

"Tell me—" Bella's voice trailed off. Spring chicken as she alleged herself to be, Auntie was perky after her hearty breakfast, riding the wave of a post-sugar rush. She was no proponent of warming up to a subject of conversation and grabbed the bull by its horns. "When will you make us happy? A respectable woman must be married. Look at you—not much to look at, so skinny. You weigh less than a baby chick. You've been jinxed."

I giggled and let it hang. Now, say, had not we been here before?

"A woman in Brighton Beach removes curses for fifty dollars. I found the ad in the paper. I wish you'd stop laughing. Fine, laugh, for all the good I've done for you, as God is my witness. *T'foo! T'foo! T'foo!*" She spat in my ear three times to ward off evil.

My right ear went deaf. I switched hands, in no rush to press the receiver to my left one.

"I have good news for you," she cooed. "I know a man. He's an aid at the home for the aged up the hill. He's Polish, older than you, maybe eighteen or twenty-five years older, shorter than you. So? Don't wear heels." There was a long pause. "Wait, I forgot what I wanted to say. My memory isn't what it used to be. Nothing gleeful about being old. Ah yes, I remember. He could lose a few pounds. Listen, he isn't good-looking, but he's nice. I pass by him several times a day. He sits on the bench in front of the nursing home. He always says, 'Morning, Mrs. Klotzky,' or 'Afternoon, Mrs. Klotzky.'"

"And who's Mrs. Klotzky?" I asked.

"Some woman. So what if it's not my name? He wants to greet me."

Regardless of my resolve to stay uninvolved, it was better to settle the issue now or she would call time and again, making my life complicated until she was fully satisfied she had done everything possible—what an effort that might be. It was not unlike being held at knifepoint, but it made little sense to aggravate the situation. With the morning dribbling away, it was wiser to play along. I focused. Why was this guy always on the bench outside? Did it matter?

"Do you talk to him often?" I faked interest.

"Listen, no, we don't talk. He speaks no English. No Russian either."

"So how do you know anything about him?"

"A woman in the park told me."

The majority of knowledge Auntie had in her possession came from a woman or man in the park, where she spent her days strolling or resting from too much strolling on a wooden bench. Staggering volumes of valuable information, an instructional avalanche, along with stray scraps of regurgitated gossip were freely exchanged on scratched, discolored park benches (at nights, the place to buy and use drugs). Some of those informational sources had the intellectual capacity of a fence post, and the validity of obtained data ought to be approached with a certain degree of healthy distrust. Not that Auntie would notice the difference, even being overly suspicious from birth. Bella always treated those nuggets of intelligence as the absolute truth.

"How do you expect us to communicate?" I asked. "I speak no Polish."

"You're a smart woman." She sniggered. "You'll think of something."

I had already thought of something. "Thank you for your trouble, but I'll pass on your offer."

I could hear Auntie rolling her eyes with displeasure and could almost hear her think.

"A good opportunity," she snapped, resentful at this inexplicable turn of events, "and you throw it away like garbage. Go introduce yourself. If you hadn't noticed, nobody wants you. Meet him, then decide."

"Bella, thanks from the bottom of my heart, but I'll pass."

"So stubborn! Do whatever you want." She slammed the receiver down.

What a pity to let such a talent go to waste. She ought to be used as an ultrasecret weapon to infiltrate enemy cities to weaken their fighting morale. They would not know what had hit them. Though an insatiable spirit of activity possessed her, she was technically challenged and limited to local resources. Terrifying to imagine—I spent some chilling moments pondering on these thoughts—what unexpected turn my life might take if she had access to the Internet. At least today Bella had called. The last time she had tried to set me up with someone, one summer evening—may she live a thousand years—she showed up accessorized with her own stranger in tow.

"This is Sam. We've just met." Bella put a finger to her lips and looked at me with an air of disapproval. "Come with me to the park, you'll meet interesting people. Ah, smile all you want. Sam owns a shoe repair shop on Broadway not far from here. He wants to get married."

To her visible astonishment, I did not beam at my unbelievable good fortune.

"Do you want to get married, Sam?" Not waiting for an answer, she continued, flirtatious and silly, "Don't be shy, Sam. Come closer, take a good look at her. Listen, I've brought him here before someone else snatches him up. He's a good catch." She interrupted herself, drawing back in mock surprise. "Anna, have you grown a belly?" She almost sang it with sheer delight, one hand on her red, veined cheek, a smile splitting her face. "Oh, yours is bigger than mine! Sam won't mind. The woman should have some meat on her, right, Sam?"

Ah, insults, insults, petty cruelties. Auntie's face was not disfigured by thought or any evidence of unexpected flashes of wits, nor was it unnecessarily tortured by kindness. Her usual arsenal consisted of displeasure, indifference, boredom, and contempt, as if at one time in her life, she had experimented with various miens, and those four were deemed to be worth her while. On occasion a fleeting shallow wave of wrinkles crossed her forehead when she was preoccupied with the interplay of hesitation and fear. Tonight she wore her latest countenance— an eternal cherub, plucked, thread-thin eyebrows over her protuberant, watery eyes, her cheeks flushed bubble-gum pink, her face smooth and empty, glowing with the lightness of being irresponsible, carefree as an innocent child. She looked deceptively kind and even a little plain.

In an intense-yellow polyester blouse with pink and green flowers, stretched over her prodigious bosom, and a shapeless, eggplant-colored, clingy skirt, which hugged her protruding blimp of a belly and square hips but barely covered her dimpled knees, Auntie resembled an unappetizing mythological creature: a happy mix of a parrot with a fat guinea pig and a duckbill platypus. As for the parrot bit, she looked like no commonplace bird, but a disheveled one, with a rumpled, bushy tuft cocked to the side, a little maniacal, a cockatoo that had been startled out of its sleep, drowsy and confused, preferring to be left alone to settle down for a snooze. Her aggressive-tangerine hair à la Orphan Annie, but straight, streaky, and spiky, having been unevenly cut by Michael (she cut his), reinforced the illusion. The whole chosen palette was puzzling—she insisted her favorite color was pleasant, muted beige.

An aimless half-smile wandered on her face, completely devoid of purpose. Not quite as composed as an un-silent Dutch Golden Age painting of an exotic creature in her equatorial colors, Bella prided herself on her impeccable taste. She assumed the Peter Pan stance she favored—her sturdy legs splayed shoulder-width apart, arms akimbo, her chubby, dimpled fists planted on opposite sides of her...let us call it a waistline. She would deliver an unsolicited, logic-free view of life as she saw it. Not to worry, she was not about to fly off. Pity. Perhaps she would topple over. It was bound to happen sooner or later, so why not this minute?

Sam cleared his throat, raised his right arm, adapting an unnatural pose that reminded me one of the favorite stances depicted in Lenin's monuments, or of a Disney prince in disguise who was about to merrily break into song and dance, ready to serenade his beloved, but who had changed his mind and remained quiet.

The arm was left hanging in the air. I watched him with curiosity. With the inconspicuous force of gravity pushing on it, unnoticed by the owner, his arm came back down on a gradual descending arch, while Sam appraised the surroundings from under his droopy eyelids, the armpits of his shirt damp, the stomach sagging, rare dull hair of unidentifiable color stuck together on his forehead. Say, a shave would not be entirely inappropriate.

Unperturbed, with his mouth open and the collective melancholy of misunderstood Slavic souls peeping from his eyes, he seemed satisfied with what he saw, as if his life had taken an unexpected pleasant turn. It was my time to get appraised. Sam had no reason to suspect that the woman he was eyeing would have an attitude problem toward these matchmaking strategies.

The excessively enthusiastic cockatoo she was, Auntie smiled a mirthless grin. "Sam's wife and three children are in Kharkov, but they're getting a divorce since his mother-in-law is a bad witch. Right, Sam?"

Sam belched. Bella blinked, gulped, but the gulp came out not without an effort, as if she swallowed a worm that was too big for her to eat. Her brain visibly conflicted, a fragment of a thought scrolled across her face. Her paranoiac eyes bulged more than usual. She picked up a few printed pages near my computer and fanned herself. A hesitant expression of uncertainty began to form on her face, but seeing how much work it was to realize itself fully it decided against continuing, and abrupt and impolite, the expression dissolved, soon to be replaced with habitual empty plainness.

"A small inconvenience, that's all it is," she continued. "Listen, this is life. What can you do? You want them to be mature and not to have a wife and children? You're too naïve. Deep in your soul, you know I'm right. He's good for you. A steady income, he'll bring everything home. Will you bring it, Sam? Of course he will. What else could you possibly want?"

A million dollar question, it is. What *did* I want? After all, the last time I had gotten married...

thirty-one

t he place was Moscow, the day a Saturday in May, the year *Anno Domini* nineteen hundred and...the post-perestroika years. Enchanting May winds brought me an unforgettable offering—the wedding. Always a good thing. And it was my own, which was even better. So many years later, when time had smoothed out the memory, erasing details, erasing voices, too many echoes, I would still recall it as one of the happiest days in the course of my life. I wish I could remember more. A rare, precious gift from the mating gods—I was to wed the man of my dreams.

Did I mention this was my *second* marriage to the *second* man of my dreams? Yes, and in itself that might not be a bad thing. The first despicably short endeavor had burst like a huge soap bubble—*poof!*—in my face. My first love at first sight and my first lover. We had spent all three days of our honeymoon in a tent city on the banks of Moscow River, with guitars and bonfires and cheap fruit wine and a ton of baked potatoes. I slept in our small tent, he in everyone else's. He loved me too—a few short liaisons of his later, I ended up with crabs. A fabulously forgettable encounter. It should have been a lesson to me that nothing was ever as one imagined it, or at least serve as a fair warning to be cautious next time when choosing a candidate for a significant other. But as the unfolding events would directly implicate, I remained careless. The ditzy goose I was, the possibility of an unhappy ending to a great love story had no place in my world.

For such an occasion as marriage number two, I had my hair done in a hair salon for the second time ever. Two bouquets of white, fabric flowers were pinned to both sides of my head, hornlike. The layer of far-too-fragrant hairspray that killed all the flies in a half-mile radius would stay on for a month. It was a nightmare to wash it out—so thick, it would serve as a bulletproof helmet in case the need arose. I was not particularly eager to meet face-to-face with any insect this robust flowery scent might attract, despite the apparent appeal of such a level of intimacy, though I would be truly honored by such a proposition—but no. I knew beauty demanded sacrifices. I just wished those sacrifices were less smelly and less sticky—a momentary weakness on my part. As the immediate result of dwelling for some time in the midst of a perfumy cloud with no means of escape, gentle waves of nausea rose and fell, slow moving and rhythmic.

I was so proud and glowing in my long, secondhand, white dress made out of high-fashion, virgin polyester—goods in short supply!—the best dress I ever had, but so itchy. I was ready long before the appointed time and stood in the middle of the room, afraid to get the dress wrinkled by sitting down or making any other motion, like breathing, with my waist still deep-curved, a small bouquet of white roses in my hands. My fiancé had bought this bouquet from the central market at the crack of dawn—roses in Moscow in May—an unaffordable luxury and a cause for wonder.

Georgians—dark-haired and mustached guys with tweed, checkered caps the size of a modest private airfield—brought a variety of flowers to sell (grown in greenhouses) from the sunny Georgian Soviet Socialist Republic, along with tomatoes and tangerines for the enjoyment of ecstatic Muscovites and guests of the capital. (Tajik and Uzbek and Latvians and other Soviet republics' representatives also brought small selections of dairy, vegetables, and fruits—everyone contributed his ethnic produce to the table in the friendship-of-nations spirit. For rubles. The big Soviet family.)

Beautiful roses! From my new husband! I was on cloud nine, a delicious, melting sensation. With a galloping heart and a pleasant sinking feeling in my stomach, I waited to be picked up and taken to the drab city hall by my husband-to-be.

The marriage ceremony was indecently short and dry. For four minutes Sergey and I stood in front of a female clerk with colorless features, clad in a badly made, well-worn, shiny-in-places suit in suspicious medium gray. Sergey looked at me fondly. I had my trusting eyes fixed upon his gorgeous blue ones. The button on a tape recorder was pushed, and the triumphant Mendelssohn's "Wedding March" took a small room captive. The city clerk stumbled on every other word as she read the text of the civil ceremony in a nasal monotone, befitting the spirit of funeral rites. Crowded in the tiny room, the immediate family members breathed on our necks.

"The respected groom and respected bride! We are gathered…a new society cell…raise your children in the best traditions of Marxism and Leninism…your personal contribution to the Soviet society and the cause of Communism…Do you, Sergey…?"

"I do." Exactly as we were instructed by the gray clerk five minutes prior.

"On behalf of the Russian Federation, we congratulate…Sign here."

A button on the tape recorder was pushed, and the enthralling procession of *March* interrupted. An impatient couple peeked through the half-opened doors.

"Everybody, stand closer together!" *Wzhick, krtch, wzhick.* With two shots a perspiring photographer captured for posterity the blissful moment, to be looked upon with true joy through the years to come by the happy progeny of ours, which would spring from our loins as the result of this blessed, lawful union. Not that we had planned any grand-scale reproduction, just a modestly sized brood of children, the nice-looking ones like in the Sears catalog, keeping it responsibly in the single digits.

On the spot we were given the detailed instructions on where and when to pick up our wedding photos, black and white (we had photos—plural!—yay!) and how much to pay. One picture came out nice. The other was blurry, not far from being in focus, with an unfamiliar crowd in the background.

Those two bore a resemblance to Sergey and me, if I were to cut my hair this short. The portrait of squinting Lenin in a business suit, vest, and polka-dot tie on the wall behind the gleeful couple had come out hazy too, but that was him. His right hand was raised, outstretched toward...what? Who else could it be?

The confusing picture of almost us was better than nothing. We were so much in love! And I was married to the best guy in the whole wide world! Ah, Sergey! I was melting, melting. So young then, so naïve, so full of lofty enthusiasm, so optimistic. So stupid. But that was a given. The things we do when we are young. At twenty-two I believed I understood how the world worked. It was normal to feel bulletproof, immortal, and as the depository of all the knowledge in the world. Thank goodness it goes away.

When Sergey and I met, what hit us both was love at first sight. It could not be ordered. Love happens. Fortunately for everyone concerned, it turned out to be true love, with its energizing and curative properties, which ideally should have lasted us as long as we lived. Wonder of all wonders. I would never imagined it could pack such an all-around-shattering force. So *that* was how being struck by love actually felt! We joyously danced to the music of life in this fiery, sensual, cheek-to-cheek tango. I could not imagine my life without Sergey in it. Separating for a second was unthinkable, perfectly intolerable, the worst misfortune. A powerful sensation, awoken by the omnipotent, unbendable rule of the cause-and-effect game the cosmos likes to play: he would leave the room—I would stop breathing. So positively, mind-bogglingly simple.

The same was true for him too, or so he kept saying. Going to the bathroom was an emotionally excruciating ordeal. Was there a choice? In an astoundingly short time, as intuitive as these things have a tendency to be, we adapted a style of "together-together" monkeys, inseparable, two halves united to create a whole. An exhilarating sensation of flying in perfect harmony with the flow in this magical, humming-around-us universe. I was ultimately happy, very alive, and slightly delirious. We had met two months ago—considered an indecently long-term engagement—but true love was there, and we were ready to take on the world together. Ah, Sergey, my beloved, my *raison d'être.* *

Little did I know that a year later we would find ourselves in New York City as freshly arrived immigrants from Russia—congrats!—stateless refugees without the right to return, knowing no one here, with one hundred dollars in our pocket for all four of us. America! The land of opportunity! The city that never sleeps! We traversed the ocean, completing the rite of passage from one world to another (a completely different world), but already deep in the midst of the divorce battle, fighting over the beat-up, bristly, red couch with the seating pillows missing. The memorable piece belonged to a bigger corner set, the only part I had found in a garbage pile on a street in Washington Heights. So what if spiteful springs stuck out of half-disintegrated upholstery on the right side? The left side was usable. I dragged it upstairs into our nest, to cozy it up. The Salvation Army would decline it. In all likelihood it already had.

Frown all you want, we had to sit on something. There had to be a couch in a room called the living room, according to the unbendable principles of divine order as I saw them in my infinite wisdom.

After Sergey found out I did not want it, he did not want it either. Or the beat-up, equally bristly armchair in a hard-to-define faded color—pumpkin? ochre? gamboge?—found on another garbage-pile-digging expedition. Or a mismatched pile of chipped, yellowed dishes. The list of our secondhand earthly possessions was short. The days were made up of small, big, and bigger collisions over anything and everything, though none over the custody of our little girl. He did not want her. I did. It worked out to our mutual satisfaction.

I worried about Sergey's well-being, heaving myself through unnecessary torment, so when he left, I gave him my grandmother's heirloom down pillow and beige camel wool blanket, so he would be warm on cold, lonely nights. Engulfed by the strong spirit of sharing that did not obey the rules of higher logic or any form of common sense, which ought to have been more common but was not, I had also given him a copy of *Joy of Cooking* and a few pots and pans so he would eat well. My behavior can be explained by a spilling-over-the-top mothering instinct—a legitimate first suspect for the driving force behind uncontrollable bouts of feeling responsible for the well-being of persons included in my immediate family circle.

In my peculiarly imperfect world, the abusive ex-husband (a father of my child) fell into that category. Shocking, yes? Turned out Sergey was worried about

---

* Reason for existence. (French)

our daughter's and my well-being too, so when he left, he emptied out our joint bank account and hired a Madison Avenue divorce lawyer. On inspiration I stuffed a Hefty bag full of his clothing and sold it all at a flea market and never felt embarrassed about it. Perhaps at this point one might be tempted to say I had brought all of this upon my head. All I can say in return is, What had I ever done to you, and what sort of benefit was expected to be achieved from such a seemingly innocent remark?

But I am getting way ahead of myself here. Please forgive me. Let us focus on important stuff, shall we? Right—the wedding.

There was an elaborate reception at Sergey's parents' small apartment in Moscow, with two hundred people attending, or so I was told. One might ask, how in the world did they all fit into such a limited space? I will tell you: I do not know. I have heard about the notion of curvature of space-time continuum, but it was hard to visualize with reasonable clarity but without going completely bonkers and desperately needing to spend prolonged quality time in the ha-ha ward.

The scariest part of all was that almost everyone turned out to be a relative of some closeness to my new husband. Talk about extended family! And I mean that in the nicest possible way, but was I expected to get to know *all* of them? What time frame were we talking about? And how close, if anything, would we actually have to be? I became more nervous, as if that were even possible. From my side there were only Bella with Michael. We never had a big family unit to start with, and it was not unusual for only a part of it to show up for any given social occasion. Not a surprise—it could not be overstated—Mother had chosen to absent herself. A drop of tar in a sea of joy, though she did send me off with her special blessing.

"If you marry him," she said, "you're going to suffer. Ay-yay-yay! She's getting married. Against my wishes. This can only end in tears. Don't you come crying to me."

She was right. For the moment, let us focus on the fact she never attended anything of importance to me, with compliant acceptance of her persistent absence enforced upon me, mostly post-factum. I never learned to accept it, even now, years later and worlds away, but what options did I have? As long as we are on the subject of close family, I feel I should mention I had no idea where my daddy was (who so far had shown no interest in being a part of his firstborn's life) or what he had been up to for the last twenty years.

Now, with such a notable fact out in the open, I do not have to spell out that issues of abandonment were to play a major role in my life, almost predictably forming and transforming it any which way they could.

thirty-two

in accordance with admirable traditions of generous Russian hospitality, everything a man owned was offered to the guests. Central to any good celebration were the pleasures of eating and drinking together. One room contained a complex architectural ensemble—nearly but not entirely a maze—an enormous table fabricated from smaller tables, borrowed from neighbors, differing in width and height, with boards laid in between to increase the useful square footage of a surface. The whole screechy, festive contraption was covered with a wild array of fabric tablecloths in various sizes, shapes, textures, and motifs, but all of them shades of white.

The enormous composite table still was not big enough to fit everyone who desired to partake in our festivities, so eating had to be done in shifts while sitting on an eclectic assortment of chairs, stools, and benches, with boards wrapped in layers of old newspapers and tied with a string to prevent guests from coming into too-intimate contact with stray, over-enthusiastic splinters. As far as protection from smudges or other distinct markings from clingy newspaper ink went, the guests were left to their own devices. Each available space was occupied.

Never mind the tablecloths, for the table was covered with something irresistibly attractive—food. The table sagged a little under the weight. This was heaven. No one could chase me away with a stick from that thing (no one should have tried). I stood there, dizzy, enchanted by the interplay of colors, shapes, and smells, a delirium of smells. My stomach growled. I purred, unaware of it. More food here than I had seen in the last two years of my life. How had they gotten all this? It might be possible to go to the store and buy it, but it was not—the stores' shelves were empty. Did I need to know where it had come from? Eat! Enjoy! Celebrate! Oh, how wonderful—life could not get any better—there was an empty space near Sergey, like it was meant for me.

He caught my glance, waved. "Anna, I saved you a place!"

Engulfed by a rush of tenderness, I hurried to his side. Before squeezing my behind into the seat, I inspected the area to assure the name of the central communist's newspaper *The Truth* would not be imprinted on the snow-white fabric of my dress, angled in the sector covering my rump.

Sergey noticed my hesitation, interpreting it correctly. As if performing a sacred ritual, out of his side pants pocket, he took a white handkerchief with navy-blue border, as big as a tablecloth. He unfolded it, laid it down in the space designated for my butt. Ah, Sergey...Ah, food...food!

There were baskets of rye bread—sacred to a Russian soul—dark brown, sourdough, dense and hearty with a crunchy crust, gentle beiges of wheat bread, fluffy and pale inside, and mixed-grain bread covered with tiny hard seeds that stayed in one's teeth for eternity, long after one was dead and successfully buried. It was a fairytale time of pre-carb- or fat-phobia, pre-genetically modified organisms, and pre-mocha Frappuccino. (You poor thing—do not furrow your brow, my reader. Go ahead, dig in, please, and pat yourself on the back for courage.) Whitish-yellow, cold, and profusely sweating, cubes of real butter nested nearby on small serving dishes. Steaming yellowish-white whole potatoes that nicely accompanied just about everything created a lively contrast to the whimsical combination of the eye-pleasing greens of pickled cucumbers, mature reds of pickled tomatoes, pale intelligent yellows of succulent pickled apples, the careless playfulness of pinks of pickled watermelons. And there was sour cream, rich and smooth.

Silver herrings, covered with sliced onion rings, thin, crunchy, and white, drowned in sunflower oil, emanated a persuasive invitation to indulge. The "herring in the fur coat"—earthly language is too crude to describe it. Deep gold of eggplant caviar played its drama against teasing lighter shades of beige of squash caviar. Do not ask—try it. Not to worry; it only looks like it was already eaten once. Trust me, it was not. Mouthwatering varieties of colorful salads were worthy of the artistic brushes of famous Russian masters, those whose matchless, deathless masterpieces were displayed with pride in St. Petersburg's State Hermitage Museum, hanging alongside matchless, deathless masterpieces by some other foreign masters. And here was a delicate yet sinful delicious dish made with deep-burgundy beets, sweet and earthly. I love that one. I really, really do.

And the famous Russian salad, Olivier, could satisfy several senses at once and could coerce one into moaning aloud. It was French in its origin, but the French would have never thought of sticking pickles in it, would they? Juicy reddish-browns of thin slices of meats cured or baked with garlic were cleverly spread in sunburst formations, studded with roses cut out of radishes, promised nirvana while still in a body. The tasty mounds of two kinds of sliced cheeses led the way into the culinary ecstasy. And in tiny saucers, the king of any table—the dignified, firm roundness of precious pearls of caviar, bright orangey-red, which held in its partially murky depths the ancient secrets of dining with equally ancient royalty, now deceased. Indeed, not a single self-respecting Russian feast would be without it if one could get it, and—a not insignificant detail—if one could afford it too. And if one would insist on having not red but black caviar... Get it yourself and pay handsomely for it. Get real.

The offering was spread out evenly over the huge table, with everything within easy reach. Cold foods, hot foods, a combination platter here, the same assortment over there, and there too. And this was just the appetizers. Vodka and homemade wine flowed like the mighty Volga with its creeks. I ate and ate. Why was the human stomach capable of holding only a small amount of food? I, enviable or pitiable, could wolf down more with my eyes than my digestive system. I decided I had better stop eating while I was partially conscious. For some reason, with a full stomach, it was harder to remember I was a spiritual being, a being of light, having a bodily experience. The "bodily" sounded right, though there was some confusion with the "spiritual" bit. I should not have been preoccupied with such concerns. In fact, I found it hard to be preoccupied with anything at this moment as I had the uncontrollable urge to smile for no particular reason from ear to ear. Left alone, the confusion might wear off soon enough.

My new mother-in-law patted me on the shoulder. "Leave room for dessert. I bought cake."

Dessert? I looked around. The jaws of guests opened and closed in concord, chewing the generous offerings in sheer ecstasy, in a rapture of food-induced stupor. Next to me on my left, squeezed into a horribly tight, mermaid velvet dress in magenta, a woman of elephantine proportions was barely breathing. With her dress making small cracking sounds, I could not help but wonder where it would rip, which seam would give out first. I hoped it was her dress and not the woman herself that was the source of sounds.

Two long hairs, thick and black, stuck out of an enormous bluish-black mole located in the approximate center of a jiggling monument of her thousand chins, cascading in soft waves down and down into the too-revealing décolletage. Wait a second, had those two hairs just waved at me, friendly-like? The idea made me nervous enough that I had to pop a morsel of food into my mouth to help combat the oncoming uneasiness.

The woman's lips curved into a benevolent smile, a smudge of lipstick on her teeth, her mouth full. I smiled back at her, my mouth empty.

The nostrils of a man on my right one chair away quivered while he polished off a sizable piece of fish on his plate. I smiled at him too, but he paid no attention to me. The chair next to me on my right was empty—now, when had Sergey left again? He had been up and down all night.

No one seemed ready to fall away from the table. The simple, yet brief pleasures only food can offer (*wink*). Always ravenous, I had unresolved issues. In all fairness, how many people have a reasonable attitude toward food at all times? You just wait, hon. In another year I would emigrate to America and, fresh out of hungry Russia, at the peak of sinful sophistication, I would discover doughnuts. Behold, ambrosia. Alas, despite its appearance, I would be among the last to advocate a doughnut diet to anyone.

Walking about might do me some good. Where was Sergey? Had he eaten? Oh, what was I talking about, of course he had. Ah, Sergey...

Forever an explorer at heart, I began a survey of the immediate surroundings, the act which foretold the semitragic signature of a future *National Geographic* addict, already in longing even if I never heard of its existence yet, in a state of miserable ignorance of what mind-blowing marvels it would offer me later on in my life, altering it in the process.

I ventured into a room to the left—what joy! Never in my life had I seen so many presents in one place, insurmountable mounds in front of my disoriented eyes, piles and piles of stuff. Something like that was bound to make any head spin, to a greater degree if the head were attached to a human female like mine was. We had no place to live yet—I know, an uneasy task, something to work on—but we were the proudest owners of a tea set for six and a coffee set for six too. Imagine: everything matched.

The wedding progressed into the witching hours of night. The momentum revved up a little.

"Anna," Sergey said, "sing for me. That song, you know which one."

It was he and he alone who was able to make me do anything he asked. I was helpless before it, always thinking what a great idea the undertaking was and how much I enjoyed it. Indeed, there was always a dissonance between what was happening and what I thought happened in these scenarios.

At once the crowd created a small empty spot in the center of the room, cleared of furniture for the dancing part of the program. Some kind soul brought a chair for Sergey to sit down.

"Singing! Singing!" A fast-spreading, loud whisper rushed away, reached the far ends of the small apartment and came back as a stuttering echo. In a matter of minutes, it attracted everyone into one place. A loud shushing followed a route of whisper, dared a loop or two on its own, and satisfied with the results, came back too. Everyone quieted down. The crowd was packed tight. The unlucky belated ones spilled into the corridor, stretching their necks, trying to peek over the heads and shoulders of people in front of them. I was not sure if everyone was breathing properly. Strange, a Russian wedding, and some guests were still bright-eyed and alert, but everyone was smiling and cheerful, as if they were darling elves in a workshop about to burst into a song themselves.

I stood there so radiant, smiling cautiously in my bridal dress—every girl's dream—so damn itchy. What would our guests—tipsy and thus unreliable as witnesses—think of a bride vigorously scratching all over? Despite the sadistic outfit, I held my head high. *Drop-dead gorgeous*, I thought. Well, potentially glamorous, if one looked at me in the right light. Cute? All eyes were fixed on me. The most terrifying but magical split second, it made me aware of every palpitation of my heart. A gray-haired guy in a colorful short-sleeved shirt, whom I had never met before or since, was to accompany me on the accordion.

Per Sergey's request, I was singing his favorite in my repertoire, a song from a popular movie at the time—though on second thought, perhaps not entirely suitable for our glorious occasion: "*I was a young virgin once, but I cannot remember when it was.*" Unsuspecting, be warned. But at that time of night, reinforced by amounts of alcohol consumption that bordered on illegal, the "second thought" gear of the thinking process was a virtual improbability, a silly thing to talk about. It would not happen. The intelligence levels available were nearing the standards of the common shorthair house cat, with a promise to nose-dive soon.

By the third verse, the lyrics reached, "*I became a wife of the whole regiment.*" Sergey, smug and half-collapsed on a chair, nodded in approval. I was so happy he was happy! Still on cloud nine. Everyone applauded with enthusiasm. Russians adore amateur performances.

The tape recorder swamped the room with modern music that sneaked up on one and in stealth took control over the body—call it a conspiracy—violating one's resolve to remain still and dignified and making them shimmy instead. Perhaps it began with an accidental tapping of a foot, an involuntary movement followed by a twitch of a left shoulder, a jerk of a right hip, then both knees joined in. A moment later, the whole body was gyrating, arms pumping and windmilling—what was so undignified about that?—to the music that was appreciated only by a younger generation.

Switching gears, the overheated tape recorder was shut down by members of the older age group to make room once again for the live portion of entertainment. The one-man band, someone's uncle or…well, *a relative*, the same bright-clad, gray-haired guy, who had accompanied my unforgettable performance, played a quick-tempo, cheerful tune on the accordion. Everyone capable of standing relatively upright without elaborate external support was dancing. A slower, soulful tune followed. A disjointed choir of drunken, predominantly female voices formed and dissolved on the spot, to form again with a new vigor.

So many faces were glimpsed fleetingly in front of me, so many hands to shake. My head was spinning. But everyone wished us good health and happiness. I felt wonderful in this bacchanalian, yelling, chaotically drifting mess of a crowd.

A small thorn from uncharted, deeper regions of my consciousness picked that particular moment to surface and prick me—some power of observation I possessed. *Why does Sergey's mother keep changing her dress back and forth?* I wondered. Then a sudden slam of realization—could there be *two* of them? Deep breathing was always beneficial, like inhaling for a count of four while expanding the diaphragm, exhaling for a count of eight, inhale love, exhale fear—seriously, no time for that now.

But there was nothing to get alarmed about. It turned out Sergey's mother had an identical twin sister, though this fact had not been mentioned prior to the wedding simply because the sister lived far away or some other logical reason.

Another insignificant but sharp thorn poked and pricked at my insides. Sergey and I hardly spoke to one another through the entire wedding revelry. Too many other people were waiting to speak to him. After the celebration was over, eternity lay in front of us to be together and speak—nice long conversations.

One would think this should have been the exact moment when I realized trouble was stewing. It was not. Festivities carried on into the early morning. And so our happily-ever-after life together began, my hubby and I. Ah, Sergey…

And that was how I married my mother.

thirty-three

ing. Ring.

"How can you be so ungrateful toward your dearest mommy?" Bella sounded cross. "I don't understand, explain it to me. You should wash her feet and drink that water!"

Exactly how I wanted each bloody morning to start, with Bella devoting much energy into delivering her vitriol. Instead of reconciliation—ah, harmony!—I was withstanding a siege warfare. Efforts to meet the situation with calmness failed, and I ended up with clenched teeth and tension built between my shoulder blades. If I hung up, she called and called, addicted to invading and conquering. If I did not pick up, she showed up in person. Not opening the door was of little use. She caught me on a street instead.

She had nothing better to do, in a habit of plowing over the obstacles in her path with sheer force of momentum and fierce tenacity. The entire neighborhood would learn what a horrible daughter I was. Some other things too. Hard to predict what she might come up with to say while exercising her right of free speech, thanks to her complete inability to think about anything before she did it, navigating through life on a dimly lit autopilot mechanism. She would not go so far as to create a pamphlet and stand on a street corner handing it to people, but damage was damage. Sidelong glances were not amusing. Neither was the whispering behind my back, nor was I looking forward to a bit of stone throwing. Pity we had no naked savages in the neighborhood, no one to eat her—and how nice and plump she was.

Nowhere to hide, no money to move. No rest for the weary. Attempts to send Bella far away brought unsatisfactory results, though she fled a room in fear, breaking into a gallop. She operated on a boomerang principle. Her comeback was assured. This never-ending conflict always made Michael sad, and Michael being sad did nothing to advance peace in the family. I could not bear to bring anything into his life likely to cause his unhappiness, and, not above being selfish, I liked Michael coming over every other day. We both needed those afternoons, talking about everything and nothing, best of friends, often conspirators. If I moved away, where would he go? And where would I be without him, the only parent who loved me? The thought made me feel like the sky was falling.

"...dearer than the dear *mommy*? A lunatic, she gave her whole life for you! Hannah's a better person than you." With mock innocence, she stretched a probing tentacle, made a pause, monitoring for effect. A quick change of tactics, resorting to trickery. Ah, wickedness. "She's lonely! She can't talk to her neighbors. Their smiles? Phony. Like they wish your mother well, those bandits. You have a heart of stone. Call and apologize!" She hurled down the receiver.

No, not a heart of stone, but she was the stone in my heart. I savored the quietude. Not to worry—she would call in an hour to pursue her claim on me. I would like to emphasize the magnitude of responsibility in carrying on the family's banner. When was Mars scheduled to be populated? I went to the stereo, put in a Mozart piano concertos CD, and pressed play.

Ring. Ring.

"Mama? I need your advice. Marcello invited me to his house at Laga di Garda for a carnival. With dukes and duchesses! But I promised Andrew I'd go to a movie. It's an ancient castle, with a moat and drawbridge and turrets." Hannah's voice trembled with excitement. "On a top of a hill. The Italian countryside! How dreamy. I'll never get another opportunity like this."

"Go to the castle. Postpone the movie. I'm sure Andrew will understand."

"No he won't. Andrew and Marcello, they hate one another. Mama, what do I do?"

"Ask your heart?"

"But you followed yours and married my father."

I did. Of course I did.

"Oh, I know," she said. "Thanks!" And she was gone.

Ring. Ring. Ring.

"Do I have to remind you that we are your parents, and you must listen to us?" Bella was so mad she had trouble catching her breath. "You must!"

That was the sacred rule number one of our holy covenant—not to be transgressed under any circumstances. Sacred rule number two was to always follow sacred rule number one. Rule number three and all other sequential numbers were missing, both a mystery and a mercy in one. I say it helped to learn the rules *before* one began breaking them. Indoctrinated up to my ears, quite intimate with the rules, which had been drummed into my head without pity, I was meant to be struck by the irresistible simplicity of the logic and to succumb to the uncomplicated beauty of it, appreciating that chaos gave way to order.

This charming tradition began in my vulnerable period—the impressionable early formative years. This thing alone, being one of those memorable childhood traumas, seemed an insignificant tear in the fabric of a little person's existence, but was enough to put anyone in a permanent state of fight-or-flight till the end of days. I was guaranteed the endless blast to switch this response off over the years to come. The marvelous gift of hopeless ineffectuality blossomed and bore fruit many moons later, after such a viable seed was planted in atypically fertile soil, as became evident years afterward.

It was at this later point in life when my perceived competence in dealing with problematic situations through my total artistic freedom of expression could cheerfully skip through all possible anxiety states to advance to a depressed state of being. Or I could feel free to fluctuate between both states, or mix and match to my heart's content, with an order of agoraphobia as a side. As long as I was bobbing in and out of my unresolved issues, unable to sleep, why not go for the most dramatic experience of all time?—a full-blown panic attack, an amazing occurrence altogether, if one was inclined to enjoy that sort of thing.

Just think, I was free to pick from that smorgasbord of emotions while I grew hard as a diamond. Aside from having a bearable amount of social stigma attached to it, this entire buffet was widely accepted by society at large. Then the migraines came, the archipelago of migraines, and I joined the countless army of catatonic migraineurs, the multitudes suffering in silence. Given it was too much fun for one person to handle, I am happy to report I lived to tell the tale. Yes, everyone suffers. One can learn to live with anything. The foundation was solid and durable, this being the positive side. On the flip side, the foundation was solid and durable.

Ee-eee! Ee-eee! Ee-eee! All thoughts were knocked out of my head with no future plans of returning. What in the world was this ghastly sound? The thought of possible catastrophes that could befall one with such a forewarning system in place possessed enough power to make one apprehensive. *T'foo*, I spat, a little disoriented, and went to search for the ill-mannered source.

I found it in one of my least favorite places—the dimly lit, narrow corridor, a feng shui nightmare. A smoke detector. Deafening and strident, it shrieked like there was no tomorrow. I checked for telltale signs that would spell an immediate mortal danger. No fire. Nothing was smoking or preparing to. I got the three-step foldable ladder out of a closet, climbed on it, lifted myself further on my toes, and in one quick swoop, removed the battery I had replaced not a week ago. *Voilà!* It was quiet.

I could continue with whatever I was doing before. What *was* I doing? Blank. I had a senior moment. I climbed down the ladder.

The obstinate smoke detector made an inarticulate sound, as if clearing its throat in preparation for a long speech, and then went into a shrieking mode again. Bad, bad feng shui.

Baffled, I looked at the battery lying motionless in my palm. The alarm hit G-sharp of a second octave and went on and on. Powered by what? Another life mystery unfolded before my unprepared mind. Alas! It made no sense. I turned around and went away. I did not want to solve riddles. I was not Marie Curie. I was not intent on playing with strange invisible forces and would not be looking for radium. *Ring. Ring.*

"You haven't called your mother?" she snapped. "Call and apologize!"

"Bella, I've done nothing to be apologetic about. On the contrary."

"What wording! You should've been a lawyer. Who told you this nonsense?"

"My therapist, for one."

"May she burn in hell! Putting crazy ideas into your head." She snorted. "I'll tell everybody who she is. Now, call your mother and apologize properly."

"Again, I've done nothing wrong. She should be apologizing to me."

There was a terrible moment of dead silence on the other end, the silence of deep dark waters haunted by a big predatory fish. It lasted fifteen seconds.

"I never heard such nonsense in my life." Bella stretched her words. "You're spoiled. Call your mother. Apologize. Now." The line went dead.

Funny thing about harsh environments: negativity only begets negativity. Was it the desperate willingness to please, brought to life by the need to be accepted? Or scavenging for scraps of affection, the devastating unwillingness to face the suppressed pain in search to fix the most agonizing relationship in my life, the one with the Stoics—to find peace and manifest the impossible—being loved by Mother.

Ah, psychology! Knowledge is power. Sabotaged and sabotaging myself, it sucked me, all of me, into a difficult journey. A distinct malfunction was revealed when, terrified of attracting bad karma and upsetting the incomprehensible delicate balance, I invited in a larger catastrophe. A trespasser in my own life, or a forgery about to be apprehended, I was mostly invisible. My uprisings were of little consequence. Though the whole extravaganza of fleeing from screaming villagers armed with shovels and pitchforks did hold a potential of excitement.

The strident sound continued to reign. With each isolated shriek, cats jumped up and down. My movements belonged to a twitching category. The moderate exercise in general was a good thing, but this scandalous behavior had to be stopped.

I got my screwdriver, climbed back up on the ladder, lifted myself further on my toes, and removed the cover—nothing resembling a power source in sight. A small black chip, a square black thingy on skinny legs, a round beige thingy on equally skinny legs. What powered it, then? I got off the ladder and went away.

Ring. Ring. I let the answering machine pick it up. There was the click of a disconnection, which my machine recorded duly. We all knew who that was. Bella hated technology with a vengeance and never left a message even while she was in the full swing of a potentially life-altering mission. *Ring. Ring. Click. Ring. Ring.*

Never questioning the Stoics' behavior was a mistake. Encouraged to doubt myself instead, I would brood. I would mope. I would be angry. Upon entering a dangerous dimension of temptation to plan the imaginary revenge in my wrath, I would envision in vivid details what I would wear to their funerals. But after a few days the feeling would dull, and utter guilt would rise. I would beat myself up, believing that everything was my fault—the routine ending to each one of my silent uprisings on a path to self-destruction. I rebelled at regular intervals, and as "a rotten apple in a barrel of good," I had to be reprimanded—and was—but still did not succumb to the social pressure. On this unpleasant note, they would produce a deep sigh, spread their hands wide as if saying, "We've done everything we could," and feel justified to deny me love. I fought one losing battle after another and, at the end, for a lost cause.

Anger that becomes trapped hungers for nothing but destruction. It festers, feeding on itself. It grows to a critical mass to erupt in violence. The evil of this world has risen from it. As per psychological profile, I was a good candidate for, say, a serial killer, or the always-popular black widow personality. She mates, then she kills—bachelors, beware. To come clean and avoid entangling myself in a rapidly rising ethical dilemma before I choke on it, I will admit that from time to time homicide looked awfully attractive. Forlorn in the jungle of shame and guilt, I got close to crossing over to the bad guys while my imagination was effectively stimulated by the act of pondering the idea. So I had a dark side. Oh, sweet mysteries of life!

Ee-eee! Ee-eee! Ee-eee! I felt the onset of an oncoming headache. What was this horrible sound again? I called Michael. In five minutes we stood in the badly lit corridor, looking up. The alarm frolicked, whistled, coughed, choked up, and died. And there was silence. *Ring. Ring.* The answering machine picked it up. We gave it a sidelong glance and heard a click.

"Who are you hiding from?" Michael asked. "Yours or mine?"

"Yours."

"Hiding from my wife, are you? There's nowhere to hide from her. She'll get you, this one. She'll drag you back from the other side to state her point." He nodded and went silent. There was not much to add, so I said nothing.

A few minutes passed. The smoke alarm coughed and came back to life with a vengeance. We stared at the persistent peace offender. Then at one another. At the battery. At one another again. Then Michael scratched the back of his head. Soon the epicenter of scratching was relocated to his chin, which also helped little to resolve the issue. He shook his head and left in complete defeat. *Ring. Ring.*

To protect others from my ill-conceived behaviors since day one, the hypervigilant, always on duty, hard-to-bribe prison guard, guilt, was permanently stationed to stand sentry in my consciousness. It was sealed and solid that I, transfixed by the large colorful world turned monochrome gray, could never break out of jail.

Along with the punishment the Stoics came up with, there was guilt too. A sneaky devil, it crept under my skin and with time, tended to assist the change into a better person, became an inseparable part of myself. With this helper on my side, masquerading as a friend, I, now abomination, turned into my own jailer and punished myself for a small eternity. Darn clever! Ah, the damage I had done to myself. Enter sadness. I have to say that the Stoics' disciplining technique deviated from the common educational trap of praise and punishment pattern. The praise portion was withheld entirely. Why bother if the penalizing worked on its own?

If that was not enough, there was another warden: shame—the extreme end of penance, as both timeless witnesses stood their silent vigil. With the horror of exposure thriving, my resistance weakening, and the landscape of my confidence shrinking—what an antisocial emotion this manufactured shame thing was—I was growing up with a big secret. It was not just the guilty and apologetic, "I've done something wrong, I'm sorry," but the crippling, "I am wrong." Fundamentally wrong, from the moment of my first breath.

Boom! Boom! Bang! My entrance door was about to be taken down.

"Are you in there?" Bella screamed into the keyhole. "I can hear you. What's this noise? Open the door! I know you're in there. Anna!" *Boom! Boom! Bang! Boom! Wham! Boom!*

I had amassed enough unhappiness that no amount of analyses could alter. Have I mentioned Mother never wanted to have a child? But she was against abortion—it was not about respecting the sanctity of life and not killing me. She was worried the doctors would damage something inside her and she would end up crippled for life. And giving birth to me had been an investment in her old age. I forever remained her property, an object. And how do I know this? She had told me herself. How proud she was! What Mother forgot was a simple, "I love you," followed by a hug. In her pragmatic mind, the substitution of that foolish statement with something of educational value, like "I should've had an abortion!" worked better.

Ring. Ring. Click. Ee-eee! Ee-eee! Ee-eee! Ring. Ring.

My temper rose as mercury on a hot summer day as my patience plummeted proportionally. Even though I was pro-life, I climbed up on the ladder, a big hammer in my hand. And *whack*! *Whack*! The bits scattered everywhere.

The ladder back in a closet, I did some light sweeping and took the garbage to the basement. *Finito.* Ah, quiet. The phone was silent too. I brushed my teeth, went to bed. Adam placed his head in my armpit, purring away. Eve curled up on my other side in a neat little ball like a lady, purring too. Her front paw, light as a feather, rested on my belly. The three of us drifted into a sweet kingdom of oblivion only a deep sleep or death could offer.

Eee-eeee! Ee-eeee! Ee-eeeee! Our ridiculously short voyage was halted with a jolt. The hair on the back of my neck had risen. No hallucination. Both cats had heard it too. Adam's head was still in my armpit, but his teeth chattered, pitiful and loud. Another dreadful shriek cut through the stillness of the night. I am sorry to report I could not explain what was happening. Perhaps it was time to ask the burning questions that I had avoided asking for years. Was this place haunted? Were all ghosts hostile? I tried to think of one. Nothing but Edgar Allan Poe came to mind.

The lights on, I got the flashlight out too, and in the most thorough sweep, looked behind the forever-open living room door too big for a doorframe—it had belonged to a different set. It had to be pried to close it a little. In the permanent darkness behind it, a meager few feet away from the executed innocent victim, an older, outdated relative hung on for dear life, shrieking like there was no tomorrow. I was euphoric. The universe still loved me! The laws of Newtonian physics still functioned.

I squeezed the ladder into the narrow opening, climbed up, lifted myself further on my toes, took the battery out in one painless swoop. *Voilà!* At last the awful high-pitched sound stopped. Everyone could breathe easier. Time to sleep.

The next day, first thing in the morning, once my head had a chance to cool off and clear out, I bought a new smoke alarm from the hardware store on the corner and mounted it on a wall. *Better safe than sorry,* I thought.

thirty-four

*t*he lilac was done blooming, the bush as tall as a one-story house. For a few short weeks, it had been covered with dense clusters of white flowers, with hardly any green leaves showing through. Now most of this splendor had turned brown, but here and there the splashes of white glowed in the sun, its fragrance maddening. New life stirred—several blushing pink buds peeked out from the lush foliage of the rosebush, planted five steps away from the front porch as a living fence in order to provide a semblance of privacy from neighbors, if there was such a thing. A white chicken sat inside the coop. The other, a spotted brownish hen, was busy pecking something on the ground, digging in a recently seeded vegetable bed with its skinny, yellow legs. A torn piece of rope trailed behind, still attached to one leg. A noisy fight broke out— the sparrows nesting in the gables under the roof had sharing issues. It was the end of May 1937.

The days got warmer. The summer was arriving with its wild strawberries—the tastiest things ever, the way Sarah prepared them, crushed with sour cream and sugar if there were any in the house. The first berries to come each year, the season for them was short. Every summer Sarah and her oldest, Bella, went into the forest to pick mushrooms and berries, with a big basket for Sarah, a small one for the girl. Day after day for two to three weeks, Bella squatted near low bushes, peeked under the leaves in search of miniature treasures, aromatic, dark red, studded with golden seeds. Her little body quivered, anticipating the treat. She picked every berry off every bush, no more than an adult handful, some of them half green, stuffed them into her mouth before her mother could tell her to put some in a basket for her younger sister so Galina could enjoy the delicacies too.

It was getting dark. The breeze fluttered the laundry hung on a clothesline. A curved, uneven, brick path led from the house to a small orchard of five apple trees with blue, slanted shadows. On that narrow path between the gooseberry bushes, Sarah and Isaac stood with a strange guy, Vassil, the least talkative person they had ever met. He had showed up today at dusk, unshaven, in tattered clothes, and given Sarah a pair of old eyeglasses, two circles of yellowish clouded lenses, the flimsy frames tied with a string. She clutched them in her hand, crying, "And Fayva is dead. Fayva. They killed Fayva too. The whole family is gone. Murderers."

The family had short periods of relative peace in the general turmoil of Stalin's repressions that began before the civil war had the opportunity to end. By the end of the Roaring Twenties, people had disappeared into the hungry belly of Gulag by the hundreds of thousands, the political prisoner population significant, half of them without trial. Echelon after echelon of unheated cattle cars with human cargo headed east to corrective labor camps. The total count would reach around twenty millions in nearly four decades, and with harsh physical labor, meager food rations, inadequate living conditions, and almost nonexistent healthcare, mortality rates were high.

Sarah had ten brothers. Stas, Jakob, and Boris were military officers in the Red Army, Joseph and Simon doctors, Yuri and Nathan physicists, Anatoly the conductor of a big orchestra, and Alexander, who was fluent in twenty-five languages, worked as an interpreter for the Kremlin. They had a misfortune to live in times when the young Soviet power felt that intelligentsia was the enemy of the people and toiled toward physical extermination of this undesired layer of society. Stas, Jakob, and Yuri were arrested first, all three in the same week. Two months later it was Joseph's turn, and every three or four months, the family lost one more brother to the human meat grinder of Gulag. All of them, with the exception of three, died there. No dates were released.

Anatoly was allowed to continue conducting an orchestra until his death from alleged food poisoning at thirty-eight. Alexander was too valuable to be eliminated. Unassuming, he worked days and nights, and his life ended in a quiet death in his late forties. Another survivor, Nathan, went crazy. Both his illness and his occupation were a taboo to discuss. Sarah's father—a regional rabbi—faded of influenza, dying in his own bed before the Soviets could determine his fate, a month prior to when the first three of his children had been arrested. He was spared the lot of a father who had to bury them all. And though Sarah's mother outlived her husband and most of her children, she had not been the one to bury them either. She was deprived of her right to say goodbye— one by one her sons were put underground in unmarked common graves at undisclosed locations.

Fayva, the youngest, was a mathematician. He stayed away from politics, always with his books. He could not buy the correct prescription lenses for his eyeglasses, as everything was in short supply, so he wore them anyhow but squinted and wrote his formulas in larger symbols, like a diligent little boy sticking out the tip of his tongue. NKVD * took him in the dark of night, as a person deemed dangerous to the state, not unlike they took almost everyone else, and he was sent to Siberia, to Kolyma River. It did not take much to be sent to Siberia. An antigovernment joke sufficed, and it was not unheard of for people to get arrested on false information from a friendly neighbor wanting to occupy their living quarters. Ah, Fayva…Who could be so cruel to harm such a gentle soul, just to take possession of his closet-size room in an unheated attic?

Sarah could not stop shaking. She would have wailed, but she did not because of the neighbors. Isaac encircled her with his arms, whispering in her ear, "Shhh, shhh," to console her.

Vassil spoke in a quiet voice. "Fayva said tell no one you're a rabbi's daughter."

The neighbors next door to the left, Nastya and Ivan, peeked over the fence not ten minutes after Vassil had knocked on the gate, looking at Sarah's guest with disdain.

"Who's this, Sarah?" Nastya asked. She untied her triangular kerchief, vigorously flapped it to smooth out some of the wrinkles in the fabric, and retied it under her chin. "He looks like a criminal to me. You wouldn't be putting up criminals under your roof, would you, Sarah?"

---

* The People's Commissariat for Internal Affairs. (Russian)

Ivan looked at his feet, hands hidden in the deep pockets of his patched-without-care pants.

"This is my cousin, Vassil, from Crimea," Sarah answered in a soothing tone.

"The Jews called their son Vassil? Some relatives you have," Nastya said. "You're crying. Did he bring you bad news?"

"My brother died from pneumonia," Sarah said.

"Tsk-tsk." Nastya crossed herself. "You never told me you had a brother. Was he young?"

"Only thirty-one."

"Vassil, is he going to live with you?" Nastya asked.

"No, he'll overnight here on his way to visit our relatives in Minsk."

"Well, good day to you, Sarah." With her right hand, Nastya shielded her eyes from the sun and remained standing, holding on to the fence with her left.

"Good day, Nastya," Sarah said.

Ivan nodded, removed both hands from his pockets, and headed back to their house.

. . .

The sun barely had a chance to peek over the horizon. The day was still considering whether to dawn or not, promising nothing. The dew had dutifully turned up to silver the bushes and grass, but little Bella already sat on the very top of the three-step stairs leading to their front door. Her small elbows perched on her rounded knees, baby chin propped in chubby fists. In semidarkness she watched Vassil at the washstand in the yard scrape his soaped-up cheeks with a blade of Isaac's straight razor.

"Are you my uncle's friend?" Bella asked. "Do you also like math?"

"I'm bad at math," Vassil said. "But I'm a good thief."

"What's a thief?" Bella asked.

"Someone who takes other people's things without asking."

Bella jumped up and ran inside the house so fast, she almost knocked down Sarah coming down the front steps.

"I put a clean shirt and pants on the bed," Sarah said to Vassil. "The boots are old but mended. We don't have much."

He went inside to change and came out shortly, his wet hair brushed. The pants were too big, but he tied them down with a piece of rope as a belt, rolled them up at the waist. The shirt was big on him too. Vassil left it untucked, peasant style. He paused on the steps to button it up.

"May God keep you safe." Sarah kept her voice muted, but in the emptiness of the yard, it sounded like a shout to her. She handed him some food for the road, bound in a piece of cloth.

He tucked the shirt in, hid the knotted bundle at his bosom. Vassil's voice was hushed too. "Thank you for everything. I'll be off now. Arkhangelsk is a long way from here."

He doesn't look so scary when shaven, Sarah thought, but so emaciated. Her eyes followed Vassil to the gate, saw him close it behind himself. She lingered near the steps for several minutes, looking at the rising sun, but breakfast needed to be prepared. The girls were up, and her husband and son would be up any moment now too.

Two-year-old Galina, clothed in a worn out dress, walked out the door. Slipping off her Lilliputian shoulder, partially unfastened, the dress had used to belong to Bella. With a businesslike strut, the toddler intended to pass by her mother into the yard. She was detained while her mother's hands straightened up the dress, buttoned it up. Sarah stroked her baby on the head, went up the steps, disappeared inside.

The sun climbed up the sky fast. The clouds were engaged elsewhere, and the day had no other option but to begin its glorious journey through the land. Bella hid behind the half-opened front door, watched their guest walk out the gate, then Galina being caressed. In turn she too received a few strokes on the head. One kopek laid intact under her mattress. There was no urgency to rehide the treasure, but still, the girl waited a bit longer to be sure Vassil was not coming back.

Bella returned to her surveillance post on the front steps, settling down on the lowest of the three. She looked in the direction of the chicken coop, where Galina had squatted for the last quarter of an hour, as she did every morning, waiting for a chicken to lay an egg, her favorite food. As the youngest and the weakest, constantly holding on to Mother's skirt, Galina did not have to worry about getting to the egg first—Sarah would have given it to her anyhow. The toddler got sick and coughed often, and when Galina coughed, an unnatural trumpet sound elicited from her puny chest, shaking her entire body and making Sarah go pale each time.

The chicken clucked, lowered its rear end, and the white object plopped to the dusty ground. Victorious, Galina scooped up her warm prize with both hands and holding her breath, aimed for the entrance door. Preoccupied with her task, she ignored Bella, and that was a mistake. The unsuspecting two-year-old had climbed up the lowest step when Bella placed her hand over her sister's face and pushed. The toddler's foot caught between the steps, and she lost her balance, fell on the ground facedown, and bawled.

Sarah dashed out of the house, and gathered Galina into her arms, showering her with kisses. She checked the girl's forehead for the signs of fever. The remains of the egg mixed with dirt trickled down Galina's scratched cheek, between her fingers, from her muddied dress. Sarah brushed off pieces of smashed shell from Galina's face, frantically kissed the girl, repeating, "Oh my baby, you're all right, you are. Don't cry. There'll be another egg tomorrow."

Galina, tear-streaked and crushed, kicked her mother in the belly with her bare feet and tried to wriggle out of her grasp, shrieking, "Let me down! Let me down!" But she was carried inside the house despite her wishes.

Bella dusted off her dress, folded her hands on her lap, sighed. She envied her older brother, Isaac, who never had to put up with that bratty sister of theirs. Every morning except Sundays, he left for school. Sarah promised Bella that she too would attend school the year after next. The new personnel was being forged, the education was free. The young country was in dire need of politically reliable specialists to lead it into the bright Communist future.

thirty-five

entering Katie's apartment was an arduous challenge. The issue lay within the inhospitable door—a strict gatekeeper—that from its birth had a cordial predisposition toward people, but later in life had undergone a change of heart toward any visitors popping up. The permanent residents were not treated any better, but acted as if they deserved such a lot. Instead of allowing a breath of life to enter and flow inside the dwelling, the entrance door flung open just a crack—the worst feng shui ever—permitting a gap a foot wide, an unjust conduct, discriminating against people according to their physical size.

The truth of the matter was that it was entirely innocent. The poor door, while partial to the human touch, was a victim of unfortunate circumstances. It suffered over the years, its distress immense, creaking and warping at nights when no one watched, it kept it to itself. Behind the door, preventing it from providing a full-scale welcoming service, were piles of lumpy shopping bags on the left of, on top of, and behind the tangle of two bicycles, rusty and dusty, outgrown by Katie's children long ago.

Today, of my free will, in ineffable shock and awe, I bore witness as Katie and her youngest daughter, Tanya, unloaded a family-size shopping cart full of groceries. Katie squeezed bags through the constricted aperture one by one until the cart was emptied. Tanya, on the receiving end inside, had the honor of dragging everything into the kitchen via a long, narrow corridor, poorly lit and unventilated. No one talked. Only the clanking and creaking and groaning of the cart and rustling and crunching and grating of plastic bags violated the silence. Then Katie trickled into the opening herself, for an instant disappearing from view. Her right hand reappeared, folded the cart, pulled it inside.

It was my turn to enter. I exhaled the air from my lungs, sucked in my stomach, and—sideways, sideways—wriggled through the gap. Fanfares! I was on the other side, and into a parallel, forgotten, long-lost universe that no one wanted anymore. Or was it an alternate one, with one annihilating the existence of the other? I could see why no one wanted it. Very subterranean, clammy, and chilly, with an odor, sour-sickish, unfamiliar and unsettling. *A burial chamber inside a prefab*

Egyptian pyramid, I thought, *fake-aged by putting a vacuum cleaner on reverse.* Or a house of horrors. Well, congrats! I also seemed to slip backward in time.

Though I had briefly been here once before, it was still a shock. A naked, half-blackened, fluorescent light ring flickered and buzzed—the unreliable source of illumination shedding light on the situation—a sore sight in the center of a sooty ceiling. One thing I sensed I had nothing to worry about was the place being haunted. No self-respecting spook would be caught dead in here. Yet a living being inhabited this space with its thick air of desertion and called it *home.* So, where might those bold guys in dresses have placed the sarcophagus with a mummy?

The corridor—I could not shake off the vivid image of an underground tunnel—had a number of unmarked openings to the left. This passageway of considerable length spanned its dark, spooky miles and time in front of us. The invitation had been for tea, so I assumed we headed for a kitchen. Russians gravitated toward the kitchen as far as gatherings were concerned, where matters related to food were always involved—food being the focal point of everyday lives. With the Soviet standard of nine square meters of allotted living space per person, the living room was not in the architectural plans or a part of the active vocabulary of a modern Russian until they came to the West. In reality the apartments were too small, the families too big, with every room being a place for sleep. Accidentally, there is no word for "privacy" in Russian.

The corridor was to be treaded single file. Did I want to know what made the crunching sounds underfoot? To hell with "knowledge is power." Shopping bags filled with mysterious stuff and tied with a double knot crowded the thread-thin passage, on both sides. A lost treasure! Or some dull, dull stuff. With the macrocosm's obsession with recycling, the atoms—the stardust, the building blocks of life—that were trapped for the time being in these bags had once been forged inside the fiery furnaces of distant balls of superheated gas, or were an aftermath of the death throes of exploding supernovae. They had journeyed here to take a break from all this volatile creation business on a floor of questionable cleanness in a dingy corridor. Everyone needs a little vacation now and then. And everyone must have the option of whether to participate in this chaotic evolution thing or not.

The bulging bags were piled up high and seemed about to topple over. The poor lighting helped little to dissipate a deception. The bags became a permanent part of architectural ensemble, had no intention of falling, defying the known laws of gravitation. No one had looked inside the bags for long stretches of time; the thick layer of dust was virginally undisturbed. I felt I had to support my friend's freedom of self-expression while suppressing a strong urge to flee.

The sculptural wall of bags flowed from the corridor into the living room and every other room in the apartment. Almost, but not quite, identical lumpy shopping bags, tied with familiar double knots, were piled up on the floor, the chairs, the plaid couch. I thought there was an early-American-style couch covered by an orange-and-brown afghan under there, against that musty wall, though I was unsure what primary impetus made me think of it. I would not make a reliable witness. The double knots, presumably, were to prevent living creatures from getting inside the bags and disturbing the order of things, or else to prevent the items inside from escaping and disturbing the arrangement outside the bags in that marvel of organization called our universe.

Instead of taking stuff into the kitchen, Tanya unloaded the groceries near the front door. I offered to help, and the three of us got busy with the tricky task of carrying the load. Our magnified and distorted shadows crept from the low and scabby ceiling, once white, onto the scabby, flaky walls, once white, and seemed to avoid the dung-colored floor. No one spoke. After my initial acclimatization, every time I passed by, I noticed a certain number of bags on the northeast side of a room had been shuffled to the southwest, only to be found back northeast, but the width of a passageway in between the piles remained roughly the same. The access to furniture hiding behind the animated piles was denied in either case.

My natural curiosity about how things worked had its limits. I chose to stay in the bliss of ignorance as to the purpose of such an activity. There was always the slight chance those changes could be attributed to perfectly natural causes like seasonal migrations and such.

Tanya said goodbye and rushed off to see her friends.

"Sit over here." Katie pushed a kitchen chair closer to me. With a palm of her hand, she brushed off the rickety table a handful of dried crumbs and several dead flies, neither of which resisted the procedure of being relocated to the floor, and began putting things for tea on the suddenly bare, faded, and stained pink Formica surface. Ordinary things, such as cups, saucers, spoons, tea bags. One table leg, significantly shorter than other three, was propped up with a mystery object wrapped in a double-knotted plastic bag. Still, with the slightest of provocation, the table attempted to walk away on four drunkard's legs.

Over the table, a swath of yellow flypaper, overcrowded with long-dead flies, spiraled down from the ceiling. On the opposite wall, a flyspecked picture in a flyspecked, plastic frame hung on an angle from a bent nail, the picture of an uninteresting bridge segment going out of nowhere to nowhere else in particular. Cups rattled against the saucers while Katie set them down. The radiator hissed, the table creaked, and from behind the fridge came a squeak—the cozy sounds of home.

I relaxed a bit and sat, transfixed by the activity. Katie's nervous fingers fidgeted with the positioning of objects. Her fingernails, which had never seen fingernail polish, had been cut ridiculously short or gnawed away to the point of almost nonexistence, making the pink, fleshy fingertips seem deformed. Her mounting tension made me uncomfortable. I glanced down. The dead flies, newly dropped from the table, joined the impressive population on the filthy floor. No one said anything for a while. The silence was filled only with the weary buzz of a fly, trapped inside the room, beating against the windowpane in anger.

Projecting her chin, Katie placed a sugar bowl on the table. "I think you might like him."

"*Him* who?" I asked. Katie, a matchmaker? That struck me as odd. But then Katie was odd. I was unsure what to expect from her half the time. A little chill crawled up my spine.

"Oleg is special." She shrugged, a glint of uncertainty in her eyes. She was spared the explanations by the doorbell.

Enter Oleg. In his early thirties, tall, dark, and Top-Ten, Hollywood handsome, if one were to ignore that twenty-four-karat-toothed smile of his. After I had decided to give up men, the universe had thrown me another curveball. The chemistry was there—a light tingling, nothing sensational, but there. Not like with that Starbucks guy. I sighed. Was it worth it? Was I willing to scrape myself up off the floor after another predictable heartbreak, then nurture myself back to health and some semblance of sanity once again?

Oleg slipped off his red leather jacket and carefully hung it on the back of a chair. The tanned Greek god was in a white T-shirt and triple-white-striped navy Adidas sweatpants, unzipped at the ankles and dragging on the floor, with brand-new Adidas sneakers, no socks. His attire, relaxed on the surface, could either be taken as a testimony to his desire to project his unwavering fixation on fitness, or a high-fashion statement, the particular style worn by people in modern Russian criminal circles. Such a dress code could even be used to pinpoint the exact position of an individual within the group, if one was familiar with that hierarchy, which I was not. His knuckles were tattooed, which meant—I was told—time served in a jailhouse.

Oleg threw professional glances around as if casing the joint, produced a gaping yawn (all three of his gold front teeth glinted in a dim light), shoved both hands deep into the pockets of his sweatpants, and, not waiting for an invitation, flopped down in an empty kitchen chair. He cast more professional glances, this time at me, from head to toe, like an experienced customer might evaluate a workhorse he had been offered by a nomadic group of gypsies at a marketplace.

The air of general sleaziness around him thickened. His face took on the expression of a contented house cat. The whole weak chemistry thing vanished. The teakettle whistled impatiently.

Katie dragged her chair closer to Oleg's and hitched her skirt high above her knees as she sat down. I looked away.

"A husband and wife are sitting on the couch, and..." Katie poured boiling water into the cups while telling her favorite joke of the day.

The tea in my cup filmed over, rainbowed like an oil spill on the surface of a gas station's puddle. My hope that invitation to tea would not include the act of drinking tea shriveled and died.

Well, etiquette was etiquette. Its rules would have to be observed if we were to keep this society at the edge of civilization, which was the responsibility of every conscious individual. In that light, I scrambled some bravery and attacked the teacup, jerking it up from the saucer and grabbing the top cookie off the plate. And lo and behold, a juicy cockroach was hidden underneath it. It rushed to the edge of the dish but froze there, with its front legs, nasty and little, poised on the rim of a plate, staring in my direction, wiggling its long antennae. How perfectly disgusting. No one else seemed to notice its presence.

My whole courage evaporated without a trace. I put the cup back down and laid the cookie on the table, careful not to disturb the brownish visitor and provoke any sudden activity. I wanted to go home.

"What time is it?" I checked my cell and got up, ready to flee. "It saddens me to leave such nice company, but I have a previous engagement and must go now."

Katie looked startled. She blinked, several rapid flaps, pulled back her chin, froze, and stared at me with the blank stare of a cow.

Oleg placed his sweaty hand on my hip and hit me with that smile of his again, oozing nonchalant confidence. He lost no time. That was how someone used to victories, only victories, and hardly ever any defeats might smile, the sort of pleased expression that could charm the socks off someone even if they were barefoot. I had seen it before, and it did. Something small gnawed in my gut, but then something small had gnawed in my gut often in recent times. I tried brushing it away without success. The sensation was getting stronger.

"So, when can I see you again?" Oleg asked. "I predict a bright future for the two of us."

I pushed his hand off my hip. "Wouldn't ten years of age difference—I'm guessing here—put you off a little?"

He smiled the most seductive of simpers. "I don't mind older women. My tourist visa expired, so I'm looking for that kind of marriage. Catch my drift?

I'd also be appreciative, if you know what I mean, if somebody loaned me some money. But I promise to pay it back. You can have my word. Are you in?"

What a lovely idea.

Katie seemed to be happy with the plan unfolding to her liking, rearranging cups and saucers on the table. She looked up and met my eyes, and her expression soured into that of a semiblind chicken with incurable diarrhea. What a harpy had she turned out to be. God Almighty would forgive her of course, but why should I be so generous?

"A pleasure meeting you both," I said. "Katie, thank you for thinking of me. Don't call me again. Oleg, good luck with your enterprise."

I had seen and heard enough for that day. That was the end of a not-altogether-beautiful friendship. Pity. Or not.

Meanwhile, I was going home to have a nice, hot cup of tea. Perhaps with some tasty cookies.

thirty-six

a small piece of paper with "Call me. Don't go crazy on me. A." was taped to my entrance door. I ripped it off, crumpled it up, and aimed from the corridor. It sank into the garbage can. Yes!

Agonizing over those notes would be one way to go, or I could ignore him. He might get tired and stop. Five minutes later I had gotten into my sweats and blocked Alex from my mind. In a sulking mood, I grumbled to Adam, the cozy critter who had planted himself on the vacant kitchen chair closest to me. "After everything I've done for her... And that gold-toothed smoothie...ew, gross!"

Reveling in the attention, which, as always, he took personally, Adam purred.

I stopped muttering to contemplate for a bit on the state of things and to check if there was anything else I wanted to share with him. "She can keep her trust issues. I've plenty of my own. How do I always get myself into some predicament like this?"

My captive audience did not move or blink, just shifted in place, redistributing his weight from the left paw to his right and back to the left, eyeing my every move, eager to catch every word.

I searched and searched the cabinets for a box of cookies. But I knew there were no cookies. I had not bought any. To think of it, I did not need carbs to put me in good spirits. I had been around. I had heard things. I had heard I could be joyous if I decided to be joyous.

"Come here, cookie. Don't I look happy to you?" I pressed Adam's warm softness against my chest. The purring amplified. I could bend him into a pretzel and call him one too. He was only glad to oblige. That is true loyalty. True love too.

While I waited for the teakettle to boil, it occurred to me to call Rita to discuss at length my latest escapades, sans the note from Alex. A brilliant, brilliant idea. It was late, and the call could have been postponed till morning, assuming this place was still standing tomorrow and nothing hit the earth later on this evening. There were objects heading our way, you know. I decided not to wait.

The three scintillating beads of Orion's belt—the faithful guides of ancient mariners—were stuck in my window frame along with the rest of the constellation. And then, on that dark, ill-fated October evening, on Friday, my world crumbled. As John Lennon once said, "Life is what happens to you while you are busy making other plans."

The crumbling began in a friendly fashion. I put Adam down on the couch, interrupting his intense experience of rapture—life could be cruel—and reached for the phone.

The phone rang in my face, a loud demanding shriek with a nasty chuckle at the end, conveying a sense of urgency tingled with dreary, inexplicable longing. Did it always do that? I picked it up.

"Anna? My name is Susan." The female voice on other end of a line was unfamiliar, but sounded pleasant, nonthreatening. Still I felt a vague alarm. "I'm a triage nurse in the emergency room at Columbia Presbyterian. Your mother was found on a street. She fell. Her left arm and elbow are bruised and swollen, and so is the left side of her face. Something could be broken. She might need surgery, but she refuses to be checked, demands to be taken home, and requested I call you."

"So sorry for the trouble she's causing, Susan! Please don't let her go anywhere! I'll be there."

No cab in sight, I sprinted to the hospital, sixteen blocks, scared to imagine what I would find there. "Let her be all right. Please, God, thank you, God," I prayed. I ran into a crowded emergency room and stopped, breathless, swiveling my head left and right to spot her in the sickly lighting. And there she was.

"There you are! What took you so long?" Mother yelled in Russian as soon as she saw me half a room away. Perched upright on a gurney, her right eyebrow arched, she cradled her left elbow in the palm of her right hand. Her face was so puffed up, it was hardly recognizable, her left eye swollen shut. "I've been waiting forever. Take me down from here at once. I'm going home. Why are you in sweats, like a savage? To embarrass me in front of everybody here?"

"Hi, Ma. I was told you refuse to be seen by the doctors. Is this true?"

She seemed not to hear the question. Nothing atypical about that. I glanced at the silent nurse stationed near Mother. A hefty, indifferent-looking guy in scrubs stood behind Mother's back, also silent, his arms crossed on his enormous chest, as if waiting for something.

"Look at me. I fell." As if angry with the whole world, Mother lifted both arms a little, the left one, held up by her right, almost doubled in size.

"Let me see," I said. "Where does it hurt?"

"Don't touch me!" She squirmed in panic, true to her nature, stricken but not defeated. "If anything it should be looked at by the doctor."

"Why not let the doctors examine you, then?" I asked. "You know we're at the hospital, yes? Do you remember being brought here by an ambulance?"

"Brutes," Mother mumbled.

She stirred, twisted, began to slide off the gurney. The nurse, who was trying to follow our conversation in a foreign language, pushed Mother back on.

"She keeps doing that. Tell her to stop," Mother complained to me. Still in Russian, articulating each word, she addressed the nurse directly. "You. Need. To. Stop. Stop."

The giant uncrossed his arms, put a hand on Mother's thin shoulder. She shrank a little.

"I can't spend so much time with your mother. I'm sorry," the nurse said. "It's an emergency room. I have other patients too. She needs to be taken for x-rays and a CT scan now. Sign here." She lowered her voice to a whisper. "I think she suffered a bad concussion."

"Why do you think that?" A whirlpool of worry geysered inside my belly.

"The way she behaves."

"Ah no." My little laugh came out nervous and short. "That's normal for her."

The nurse looked at me, nodded. "We need to take some blood too."

"Let's do this, please." I smiled at both the nurse and her untalkative aide.

"Blood? They want my blood?" Mother asked in Russian, attempting to wriggle away from the giant's iron grip. "They aren't getting a single drop. Tell them. And how do I always bring such catastrophes upon my head? My envious neighbors jinxed me." Mother threw blazing, sidelong glances in the direction of the nurse's aide with her right eye, the only one available to her for the moment. "I was afraid this would happen. Didn't I always tell you one day I'd fall? I fell. And why can't I see with my left eye? Am I going blind? Look at me! They said my arm's broken. I don't want my arm to be broken. What am I to do now? Take me home."

"I will. But let the doctors check you first, all right?"

My heart was breaking. I looked at the nurse. She nodded. The silent guy in scrubs wrestled Mother into lying down in one effortless move and, keeping her pinned, wheeled the gurney away.

"What kind of a daughter are you?" Mother wailed in Russian, but switched to accented English. "Oh, I'm all alone in this world! Somebody help me! For God's sake! I'm being murdered! Help!"

■　■　■

Mother had suffered a small stroke, and her arm was broken in two places. Yes, she needed surgery. I am happy to report it was uneventful, which was always welcome news. Her arm was pinned together, put in a cast for the next six to eight weeks. Mother was placed in a bed in a semiprivate room to recuperate for two to four days until it was safe to send her home. In short, she was to live.

"How could you abandon me here in this condition when you know I don't speak any English?" Mother sounded outraged, for an instant forgetting she was ill and weak and letting her thundering voice carry far into the hospital hallway. "How did this not occur to you?"

Ah, why should not she execute her powers of control over another human being to a higher-than-usual degree when she could? She thrived under such circumstances. I glanced at the immobile body on the neighboring bed, lying on her side with a blanket over her head. The person stirred, almost an unnoticeable motion, more of a half sigh, half cough than a movement. A corner of a blanket lifted a little, and one dark, unmoving eye stared at me.

"Ma, but you do speak English."

Her face fell. "You had to find the moment when I'm on my deathbed to argue with me over such a petty subject?" She barely whispered as if she were, indeed, dying and attempted to clutch both hands over her heart, but with her cast in the way, she only clutched one. "All my labors in vain! How heartless can you be?"

"Ma, you aren't dying. You'll outlive all of us. It's a broken arm. It'll heal soon."

"Did they tell you I was to lose my arm and now you're hiding it from me?"

"No, Ma. You'll be fine. Dr. Adams is letting you go home in three days."

"Doctors! Why would you trust doctors? They know nothing."

"They fixed your arm, didn't they? I'll be back early in the morning."

"I've had enough of this conversation," Mother said, obstinate as a wall. "You do as I say. What if I need you in the middle of a night? I understand nothing they're saying. Oh, my head is spinning."

Maybe it was, maybe it was not. Who would be willing to suffer the consequences? And so my around-the-clock presence at her bedside became obligatory.

"This bed's so uncomfortable," she said. "I'll never be able to sleep in here. Get me another pillow. Now. The pillow, go get it."

Not three minutes later, I was back, a pillow in my arms, to find her sound asleep. A Herculean snoring shook the small room to its foundations.

I carefully laid down the unnecessary pillow at the foot of Mother's bed, lowered myself into the plastic chair, and crossed my arms over my chest, fidgeting a little to find the least painful position to settle in for the night.

The chair creaked. I froze, afraid to wake her up. Her uninterrupted snoring carried on. A loud sigh came from the neighboring bed. The blanket's corner rustled as it was let go, and the person turned to the other side. The bed squeaked. And then all went quiet. Only the snoring reigned.

thirty-seven

i n the blur of the next four days, I was too dazed from not getting much sleep and too wrapped up in a fog of worries, driving myself mad about the state of Mother's health, to recall with any clarity the entire chain of events. How much sleep could one grab curled up in a chair in a hospital room, inhaling the faint odors of illness, the repellent smells of fear? Days and nights were filled with efforts to make Mother comfortable when she was dead determined not to be on every level of her being. When awake, she complained about everything and everyone. In one day's time, she had alienated all the nurses in the ward, all shifts. One could have predicted with tolerable ease that the parting would not be full of mutual fondness, drowned in warm tears of separation.

The only thing Mother made no complaint about was the pain in her broken arm, as by some freakish accident of nature, her arm did not hurt. For the entire duration of Mother's hospital stay, duty and common sense—also known as a self-preservation instinct—were engaged in the bloody duel inside my ill-starred soul. Here she was, Mother—the victim and the torturer. How in the world did she manage to always force me into a situation where I had to choose between alternatives, all of them unpleasant? "*Nobody loves me,*" she said. And though she specialized in melodrama, it was all too sad. When compassion joined forces with duty in the fight against common sense, guess who won? That is right. I felt I had no choice. How could I let disabled Mother be with an indifferent home attendant to care for her?

She lay in that huge bed asleep, propped against the pillows, her skin an ecru color with broken capillaries on her nose, the injured bird, the defeated bird, so puny, so helpless, her bony arm with her nails kept short—a deformed claw that stuck out awkwardly, with veined, transparent skin, bluish-white, flecked with dark spots. The wrinkled skin on her upper arms hung down like empty sacs. Her face had acquired the bright yellow-green shade of a ripe cantaloupe supported by the thin stalk of a bruised neck. The wispy gray hair, the fragile shoulders, the jutting out blue-and-black collarbone. Through the thin, worn fabric of the hospital gown, which was too large on her, I could see how badly curved her spine was, and the bulging lump of the little bag with small cash in it that Mother had fashioned out of a folded handkerchief and always kept pinned to the inside of her underpants for emergencies.

I stood there, listening to the labored sound of her breathing. Each uneven breath broke my heart. I inhaled the reassuring medicinal odor, took the bait, and took her in. I must have lost my mind. A huge mistake. What was I talking about? Not a mistake—a disaster of epic proportions. One would have better chances at survival playing Russian roulette. Even if Mother could be seen as birdlike from a certain angle, she was no hummingbird. Wish me luck. Better yet, next time you see me behaving like this in the future, please stop me. Whack me on a head with something heavy, if you have to. *Please* do not be shy.

Everyone was only too happy to see her leave. I fed Mother her breakfast, waited for her to finish chewing, suck her teeth, and hiccup. I dressed her up, put her in a cab, and took her to my home. You only get one mother, right? But no good deed goes unpunished, I have heard. As could have been predicted but not prevented, if something was needed from her, one was to expect a fight. The reason for it never had to be big. It could be as tiny as a pill.

To prevent future strokes from happening, Mother would have to take two baby aspirin every day, and my job was to ensure they were taken. So I sat her down on the couch, propped her up with pillows to make her comfortable, and was about to give her the daily dosage of her medicine.

"Take this while I make you a cup of tea." I handed her two pills and the glass of water.

"How like you to think only of yourself. No," she rebuffed, cradling her casted arm with her good one. "Are you trying to poison me?"

"Ma, what are you saying?"

"I said nothing special." She shrugged. "You don't like hearing the truth. *Are* you trying to poison me? Do you hate me so much? Is it because I'm old and of no use to you anymore?"

"What in the world are you talking about?" I shrugged too.

"If I knew you had wanted to poison me, I'd had had an abortion long time ago, believe me."

"Too late for that now. Take these pills. You've heard what the doctor said."

"Ay, the doctor! And you believed him? I don't believe a single word he said."

"It's up to you what to believe." I handed her two pills and the glass of water again, resisting shaking her so that her head wobbled on its neck. "Take this."

"Get away from me." She removed the safety pin holding her jacket pocket closed, took out a Verizon envelope that was secured with a rubber band. It was full of tens and twenties. She counted the bills.

"One thousand, two hundred forty-three dollars. My life savings, all of it." She twisted the rubber band over the envelope. "Get away. Don't think I don't know the truth. You're an addict. For a young woman to numb herself with pills!"

"What pills? Mother? And why are you carrying all this money with you?"

"What's the matter?" She let go of her left arm, leaving it to rest on her lap, and waved her right, not a hint of resignation in her tone. "I call them pills, you may call them vitamins. No need to get picky with words. Those vitamins make you crazy. We lived our lives never hearing of vitamins. And look at us!"

I made yet another attempt to hand her two pills and the water. "Please take your aspir—"

"Take it yourself! I hate you." She pushed my hand away in a sharp, concentrated effort, some water spilling on the rug.

She was stubborn in excess, but this time it was more than a thoroughly annoying character flaw. She was hysterical, her body visibly tensed up. I looked into her eyes, wild, filled with primeval, palpable fright and hate. Her fear was real, so very raw; she was convinced I meant her harm. The self-love, the angst for her existence was so strong, that she fought me, ferocious, with the intensity of a fatally wounded, cornered animal fighting for its life. I was her worst and most lethal enemy. It did not occur to Mother that I was not. Unexpected, it was terrifying to watch.

As if I was witnessing the event not in the present, but had been sucked into a time warp, thrust into the past, the situation felt like a *déjà vu*, like a repressed memory. My throat closed up, and my heart sank, filled with dread. I was in a place where darkness overpowered light. From that edge of reality, the terrible revelation arose, crystalline-clear against the silence, flooding every fiber in my body with a grave chill. The same revelation that I, stubborn as a mule, had refused to acknowledge on previous occasions became a certainty—the only thing Mother always loved and valued was herself and her own life. She had not ever loved me. Her "I hate you" had never once been an empty figure of speech. What a thought to bear! Why was I still waiting for her to show any signs of motherly love?

My stomach felt queasy. I folded my arms across my belly. No tears! I had never wanted my worst childhood fears to be proven true, but there they were. No child at any time was supposed to go through this. There was no place to hide from such a feeling. And I accepted it, not knowing how to live with this acceptance yet. The thought left as suddenly as it had come, leaving a yawning abyss not of suffering, but emptiness in its wake. The eternal dusk in my heart had lifted as the whole world populated with my hopes had perished. The end of childish hopes, and one of those possible futures had terminated, giving way to another kind of future, full of new hope. What would a new one bring?

It took me forever to find my voice, but it came out calm and steady. "Ma—"

"I hate you."

"That's nice. Now you listen to me. You can stay if you take your medicine. If you won't let me help you, go back home with an attendant. The choice is yours. What will it be?"

Breaking the existing order of things was hitting below the belt, but how else to convince her? I hoped not to be considered a proponent of cruelty to old little ladies who would not listen to rationale. It was more productive to reason with a wall. Besides, a wall would not use tears as an argument.

Mother began to cry, but opened her mouth like a small child. A thin, wet path ran down her bruised left cheek but stopped before reaching her jawline, with one fat tear hanging there, about to drop. The other one quivered on Mother's eyelashes, ready to go. I put both pills in her mouth, handed her the glass. I could never stand to see anyone crying. It made me crumble. My hands trembled, but she did not notice.

She took a sip of water, swallowed it. Her tears dried up, more of a symbol than anything else, and her whimper, which seemingly had a staying power, was gone. Not overwhelmed with appreciation, she made an angry face, hit me hard on the shoulder with her good hand, clamped her lips so tightly together that they paled, and went into the bedroom. What had I gotten myself into? My worst nightmare was becoming my reality in a flash. Wait…This was way beyond anything I had ever been willing to imagine.

A watchkeeper of the night, I checked on Mother every hour. Hard to explain why I was tiptoeing around like a burglar when it was well known a grenade could explode right under her nose without waking her up. She snored in my bed, in the firm arms of Morpheus, with episodes of lip smacking through the night, projecting a tranquility that could be mistaken as a testament to her gentle nature. I was too exhausted to fall asleep, but I did at last.

Exiled to the lumpy couch in between my reconnaissance sorties, I dreamed of horrible, flesh-eating monsters, their bloodied jaws snapping, half-eaten body parts scattered everywhere.

The morning dribbled in through my closed eyelids. The monster dream was not about to simply go away. The images lost their potency a bit, then the edges eroded fast, as if, split in half, the monsters fell away from the center and vanished, leaving behind the sensation of something ravenous breathing in my face. The sensation lingered.

I opened my eyes. Mother hovered over my nose a few inches away, shining her countenance down on me, purple and yellow and swollen.

"Look who's still asleep at this late hour," she said. "A sleeping beauty. Get up. Get up."

"What happened?" I rubbed both eyes, glanced at the clock. It was five in the morning, still dark outside. Too early for the domination games to begin. The floor lamp near the couch was switched on, and irritated by the bright light, my eyes refused to stay open and closed again, my eyelids leaden. My mind declined to awaken too.

I was about to drift back to sleep, and a new monster, a chocolate-brown with minty-green spots—a real cutie if one was into that sort of thing—peeked into the newly hatching dream, started to crystallize, acquiring mass. A tenacious claw dug deep into my shoulder, and my shoulder was shaken. I was about to wake up screaming.

Ah...no, this was no dream. I opened one eye, attempted to focus it.

"Get me dressed and make me breakfast. I'm hungry," Mother said in her melodramatic voice. "Get up. Get up."

"I'm up. I'm up. Stop shaking me." I sat up. "Good morning, Ma. Did you sleep well?"

"I couldn't sleep at all. My eyes didn't close for a second the whole night."

How could I have missed it? The thought of her suffering brought my defenses down in one sweep. "Were you in pain? Why did you refuse a painkiller?"

"A painkiller? The sheet was wrinkled. It bothered me all night."

"What?" I asked, still a little concerned.

"Come with me, I'll show you." In her nightgown and house slippers, her left arm in a sling cradled in her right, Mother shuffled back to the bedroom. My eyes more closed than open, I followed her.

She switched on the ceiling light, pointed at the bed. "Open your eyes."

"They're open. Ma, those sheets don't need ironing."

"Stop being so lazy and iron mine."

I imagined myself lovingly ironing Mother's linens. Yeah, right. "You iron your underwear obsessively, but not your sheets, you never did. Why is this suddenly a problem?"

"You can't compare yourself to me. I'm old, I won't be in this world long. Look at how your household is maintained! Shame on you. You're still standing here? Start ironing."

What devil had seduced me into volunteering for this? This was another question hard to answer. Something about the story was familiar, though. Anyone? Oh, I know—but Cinderella had a fairy godmother and a glass slipper. And she was younger. And got the prince at the end. Whatever had happened to *my* fairy godmother?

I closed my eyes, and half-asleep, drifted in the direction of the kitchen. The day had not begun yet and I was already exhausted.

And there was evening, and there was morning—the first day.

thirty-eight

One domestic cataclysm followed another, the onslaught of events redoubling the unleashed chaos. Days took turns. The endless parade of unexpected exasperations and resentments rolled in the dull uniformity of Mother's bossiness as her perpetual misery settled over the place. "Where's this accursed girl?" blared throughout the rooms at all hours, the whole day long, discouraging any light development in our microcosm's dreary ambience, with another little piece of me broken. How could one fight a sick old woman? Let me ask you this: How could one accept her caprices? What new terrors would await me tomorrow? My heart and mind filled with mutinous intent, and my hands itched with a desire to strangle her, if only a little.

Her arm would heal, but the idea of Mother's health declining, putting her in need of the long-term caregiving fated with old age, stopped my heart, drenched me in a cold sweat, as the infinite universe with its multitude of suns folded into the origami of dread in my palm. In my reflection in the ever-truthful mirror, I saw Mother's face staring back at me and was repulsed by it, a troublesome consequence. I looked away, but the disturbing image lingered. What was the occluded lesson here?

November. The winter, filled with chilly loneliness, would be long. In a ghastly manner, over and over I was informed of my incompetence in everything I touched, that my life had been misspent, not that I had been complacent to begin with. No sense in presenting the entire list of my shortcomings since it would take a long time to account for the lot. All unpardonable sins. I also had nothing to say, and my head needed to be examined. Oh my God, for once she was right! I had sucked all the blood out of her, or so she, bloodless, insisted.

"Washers are for lazy people," Mother kept saying.

"When you're back home, wash anything you want by hand. Knock yourself out. Here we'll do it my way." An undutiful grin bloomed on my face.

"Don't put my sheets in there," she said. "Your stupid machine will ruin them."

"Ma, those are *my* sheets. End of discussion." I stuffed the linens inside the washer, added detergent, pushed a button.

"We never talk," Mother said after a minute-long pause, sporting the offended expression on her face. "You brush me off. I won't be with you for much longer. I could go anytime."

"That's very dramatic, Mother. What do you want to talk about?"

"Washers are for lazy people," she said, a tough old boot. "If you don't get it, there's no point in my explaining it to you."

She marched out of the kitchen. I stood watching the machine tumble the laundry. There was something comforting in the warm, sudsy water rhythmically sloshing around inside. I could hear Mother sitting herself down on the couch, fidgeting to get comfortable, then crying as loud as she could, projecting her voice over the living room boundaries. And it had used to work too.

Now it made me boil with anger, suspended on the verge of losing it. I chose not to follow her to the living room and hazard to console her. Who needed another big production number for a Las Vegas variety show, right? Mother and her artistic urges. I crossed my arms over my chest and watched the washing machine do its job. Besides, she would be back presently.

Mother showed up seconds later, her face distorted with anger, her eyes dry.

"Happy now? Is this the way I raised you? Her mother's suffering, and she's doing laundry. You want to put me into an early grave? I bet you'd like that. Nobody wants an old mother," she said with an expression of offended innocence and left. "I'll never talk to you again. Don't even beg me."

Adieu! Indeed, that expression would remain detectable on her face for a long, long while. A healthy dose of icy silence was always called in to bring my failing senses back to normal as fast as possible for a human offspring to process, while the enchanted Stoics' fortress held strong, impregnable, with turrets in the corners, from which the boiling oil or tar could be—and was—poured upon the doomed heads of the attackers. The skulls of unfortunate fallen enemies, long dead, grinned, displayed on pikes to discourage anyone's approach—so many dropped heads, such an accursed fortress! Mother was solidly entrenched, a frightful woman, and so was everyone else on Stoic's side. No renegotiations for existing treaties. Giving him his dues, Michael had acted as Switzerland often.

■　■　■

"Anna! I'm still waiting for that 'thank you for paying my daughter's tuition' call. I could always stop. Like I don't have better things to do with my money."

"Sergey," I said, "thank you for paying my daughter's tuition."

"I mean it."

"What do you want me to say? Tell me and I'll say it. Look, if you feel the need to punish me, then punish *me*. Why take it out on Hannah?"

The silence that followed was long and weird. *He could and he would,* I thought.

"Do you think I like having conversations like this one?" he asked.

It sounded like a rhetorical question, so I said nothing.

"You know what?" he asked.

"What?" I asked cautiously, after waiting for him to continue.

"A-ah!" He hung up.

Ring. Ring.

"What's your problem, Anna?" Sergey asked.

"My problem?"

"A-ah!" He hung up again.

There goes the tuition. And then I realized I was so mad, I was shaking.

■ ■ ■

"Mama, I'm not coming home for Christmas. Your place is too small for both Grandma and me. Kick her out."

"Hannah, don't talk like that. How can I kick out a helpless old woman?"

"She isn't helpless."

"She's suffering."

"Oh, Mama! You're too giving. She's using your big heart with its big compassion against you. She's horrible to you. Kick her out."

Mother floated into the room. "I hear a man's voice. Hang up!"

"It's Hannah."

"Give me the phone. I want to say hi." The receiver was snatched from my hand. "Hannah, is it you? Can you hear me? Your mother's sucking all the life out of me." She tossed the receiver back to me. "And what do you say now! I'll work on Hannah. We'll teach you how to respect your mother." And beaming with pride, she retired to the living room in a stately manner. I heard a *click* as the TV went on.

"Hannah?" I said into the phone.

"Mama, she's sucking all the life out of you. Kick her out."

"I'll never forgive myself if I do. What about my duty as a daughter?"

"Stop being so Russian and think about what she's doing to you."

She was right. "Have you heard from your dad?"

"Yes. He and Dorothy are off to the Virgin Islands for New Year's."

"What about you?"

"Mama, get real. Why would Dorothy want me around?"

She was right about that too.

. . .

December. So dark. Snowflakes, big and fluffy, drifted down to turn into brown slush. The pale wintry sun, like a proverbial stepmother, gave little light and warmth. It barely bothered to show up for the short winter days. The crazy ice queen ruled day and night with an iron fist, and I, her pawn, the object of her august control, was incarcerated in my home and losing my mind, on the brink of permanent madness, at last fulfilling Mother's prophecy. One of the many prophecies, the bane of my life for many years, it had loomed over my head since childhood, branded on my brain (both hemispheres), but so far had failed to manifest. For years, one would have looked in vain for some fulfillment of this prediction. Until now. With the addition of many signs, like a strong internal agitation and such, the evidence was hard to ignore, swarming about, laughing in my face, and the witnesses present and were but one in number.

One great distress to Mother, the warden, was staying at home alone, and I sympathized with her. I would sympathize with her more if her terror was not limited to times when I went to train my clients or—a monstrous joke in her eyes—when I voiced the intent to spend an hour with friends to improve my mental health a little, given my present state. But what if, in a state of extreme agitation, Mother had another stroke?

. . .

"Mama, I miss our conversations. So I bought the ice cream before I called you."

"Aw! What did you get?"

"Guess? My spoon is ready."

"Hold on." I reached for a pint of triple-chocolate Häagen-Dazs, grabbed a spoon, and scooped up a generous portion. "What's on your mind?"

Mother materialized in the kitchen. "What's that in your hand?" she asked.

"A bicycle," I said.

I was relieved of a precious carton. It hit the bottom of a trash can with a dull thud.

"Think of all the cholesterol in there!" Mother said. "And I know you won't thank me for saving you from getting pneumonia." Shaking her head with disgust, she left the room.

"KICK! HER! OUT!" said Hannah.

. . .

Perhaps. I might feel better if I avoided Mother, but considering we lived in the same, not-too-spacious apartment, that tactic had little chance of success, yet might be of some entertainment value. Small difficulties were apt to arise while people acclimated to new living arrangements, and allowances for such circumstances must be made. With us, Mother acclimated just fine. I, on the other hand, was lucky to save my skin and bones and would rather find myself three hundred miles away in any given direction—six hundred would be even better, though still not far enough.

What was worse, one by one my clients dropped out, refusing to come here. Mother, unburdened with understanding of the specifics of our living arrangement, barged in on each training session as if she were a police squad tipped off about someone in possession of deadly weapons and was prepared to requisition the whole arsenal with force.

"Why is that door closed? Are you exercising again? And you," Mother addressed one terrified client, "think of what you're doing before you damage something vital in your body. Go home!" She raised her broken arm a little, as if offering it as proof of her words.

"What does this fat cow think she'll get here?" she asked another client. "To grow herself such an ass! You should've stopped eating a long time ago."

"What?" The woman looked at Mother's right shoulder with squared eyes and left.

"Why do you allow yourself to talk to people in this way?" I asked Mother.

"Don't you get moral with me. They sucked your life out. Look how skinny you are."

"And how am I going to pay my rent now?"

Mother rubbed her thumb, index, and middle fingers together, a very Russian gesture. "Money! Money! Ay!" She waved her arm.

How *was* I to pay the rent? I always scrambled to make ends meet. The letter from management notifying me of the 8 percent rent increase added to the cold feeling in my chest while it put perspiration on my forehead. I was trapped, trapped, trapped. There was something not exactly right with my present lifestyle. It felt claustrophobic.

■　■　■

By day forty-eight of my strict confinement, Rita felt I must be rescued before I ceased to exist, reduced to nothing. An intervention maneuver, consisting of coming over to spend an evening with me, was planned at once. Rita was the courageous one. No one else wanted to stop by while Mother occupied this place. Could anyone blame them? So I was beyond ecstatic Rita was to visit. A pleasant conversation and a friendly face, while Mother staged a demonstration and stayed in the darkest corner in the other room, sulking but silent. She would give it to me later on, all of it, no reservations, and then some. Since Mother showed no interest in meeting any of my friends—a happy circumstance for me—I flirted with the notion that she would not make an appearance when Rita was allowed to come into the sacred presence.

The day dragged, dragged, dragged, the actual minutes slowing to a crawl; Mother grumbled, grumbled, grumbled; there was no end to either one. At last the day limped away to give way to the evening. After exerting a great effort in supervising the preparation of her dinner, tired Mother sat in stupefied boredom in front of the TV, commenting on the idiocy of the shows and dozing off. High-pitched whistling alternating with low rumbling came from her direction. I lowered the volume on the TV, to ensure a restful nap, and went into the kitchen to cook dinner for Rita and me.

Mother shuffled in a few minutes later. "What's this stink? *Phew!*"

With knife in my hand, I said nothing and kept looking down at the table, though the rhythm of the blade chopping vegetables, knocking against the cutting board, quickened a little.

"Butter?" She grimaced. "It clogs your arteries. *Phew!* What are you cooking?"

"I'm cooking Thai. Rita is coming for dinner."

"Rita? I don't remember any Rita. She should eat at her home. What's this, a restaurant? You always pick up some rejects of society and drag them in here to feed. That's so selfish."

No sound escaped my lips. Something unpleasant stirred, waking up, and tumbled into the pit of my stomach. Hard to say what it was, but it was…well, unpleasant. I gritted my teeth, but it went unnoticed.

Mother watched my hands. "Do you hear me?" she asked. "I don't want any Rita here. Tell her not to come."

I stopped chopping and turned to face her. "Why was I never allowed to invite friends?"

"Are we having a discussion? What is this, a General Assembly of the United Nations? There are no friends. What's with your face? If I hadn't told you what I thought, who would? You'll never learn the truth."

"Fine. You told me."

"The stink! I'm warning you." She used her thumb and index finger to close her nose, but remained standing near the stove. "I'm getting nauseous!"

"Ma, if you hate it here—"

"And whose fault is that?" She fanned herself with her hand.

"—You can always move back to your place."

"Go back? Why back? It's impossible to please you. I was only joking."

"Not funny," I said.

"Don't laugh. You sound just like your father. Tell your friend not to come."

"Do you realize no one wants to come here anymore?"

"You should thank me for that! Those people will only lie to you and let you down." She grimaced and fanned herself again. "You're too stupid to realize it. They feign smiles while they look around for something to steal."

"This place was already robbed by strangers once. Do you see anything left worth stealing?"

"Don't you worry, they'll find something. *Phew!* Throw it away! Oh, I'm ready to throw up. If you continue to cook like that, no man will ever want you. Mark my words." Mother, the part-time prophetess.

"What's with all this shit? Mother, you're hurting me."

"Such expressions! You have a way of putting things that has nothing to do with real life. Hold your tongue! How can a mother hurt her child? It's all in your head. Make a call."

Whatever had given me the idea there was some good left in her? I switched off the gas and made a call. Then I took my handbag, grabbed my keys, and stepped out the door.

"Don't even dream about coming back here!" she yelled into the stairwell. "And when you're back tonight, you'll find me dead! I'll go and die now!"

The door slammed.

■   ■   ■

Rita and I had Thai for dinner. I came back home in the dead of night. Mother was fast asleep, snoring in my bed, her clothing carefully draped over the chair.

"*Lucy, I'm home!*" I whispered. "*It's me, Ricky. Just got home from Club Babalu. Lucy?*"

The snoring failed to cease. I headed for the couch. Every night, ever since Mother had moved in with me, I had tried to fall asleep and could not, as Mother's voice chattered livelily in my head. Though not something unheard of in connection to my lifestyle, the power of those special effects was on the increase, gaining momentum, starting to reverberate, filling all my consciousness: *"HOW CAN A MOTHER HURT HER CHILD? KICK HER OUT!"*

My life had gone completely to bits. Planet Narcissia, population: two. Days slowly turned into weeks, weeks turned into months. As for the belief that God never gives one more than they could handle, I prayed God would help me to endure this! I would survive, I would survive, I would...

thirty-nine

january. A chain of bleak days. One late windy evening, when Mother was tucked in and snoring away, I tried to put the aromatherapy book that had collected dust lying on my table for several months on the shelf. It did not fit—an unfamiliar volume barred the rightful owner from its space.

I pulled out the intruder. *Self Matters.* Something in my head went *dzachung!*—soft, pleasant, and unobtrusive. Funny thing was, I did not remember buying this book. Had Mother been messing with my books? I tried to visualize the event. Possible, as in "throwing them away." Must have been Rita.

I opened it, and the strangest thing happened—I could not put it down, as if this were some "when the student is ready, the teacher appears" thing. I read it from cover to cover, and from cover to cover again to ensure I had missed nothing of even insignificant importance.

To relieve the mounting suspense, I will tell you now that my holy and noble battle for freedom received a better footing and a blood transfusion. *Vive la Liberté!* Wondrous things were afoot. "You can't change what you don't acknowledge," the book said—a good opportunity for consideration. With the resolve to change things around already within me, I had in my hands something priceless—the method for paving the road that would lead from hopelessness into the light. Oh mighty spirit of fear, set me free! Let me embrace you, so you will become my friend on the path of my spiritual empowerment and teach me how to achieve transformation! Amen. Ah, transformation.

The choked filters of my brain were unclogged, and my inner voice—almost silent, all transmissions jammed—came in loud and clear. With a charming quality of insistence to it, it promised serenity at the end of the journey. I wonder how long had it been yelling "Hello! Anyone out there? Hello-o!"? I hoped that inner-voice phenomenon was not a happy-go-lucky hallucination. Hallucinations—and mental psychosis—could occur with electrolyte imbalances caused by extreme dehydration, heat stroke, or kidney dysfunction. Knock on wood to ward off such evils and send them far, far away.

The feeling was electrifying, almost a religious experience. Yes, God, yes! I was immersed in the book to the hilt, taking notes. The uneven stacks of scribbled papers lay everywhere. As the Chinese say, it was "like adding wings to a tiger." I should have Dr. Philed myself long ago. What had I been thinking? No going back for me. But hang on—had not I been here before?

I had no option but to take up arms, considering the revolutionary-oriented, Russian heritage in the best traditions of Decembrists that nested in the marrow of my bones and would happily go on living in the next several generations of my poor unsuspecting descendants. If I was serious about developing a healthy dose of self-esteem, the absence of which proved to be a source of considerable inconvenience. I was very serious. The fever of anticipation infected my blood.

Something must be said here for the unfortunate fact that I, discovering much about the nature of things, had not the foggiest idea how to go about achieving such a state of mind—that holy and noble battle for freedom that has already been mentioned. Wondrous things. *Vive la*...A sense of foreboding galloped inside me, intoxicating and sweet. I had been in this rut for a small eternity—why would I want to delay? There I was, aching with excitement, my head filled with the thoughts of escape. I felt impatient, like a horse kept in a stable for too long. I needed to run. I needed my *oomph* back, my *joie de vivre*. I wanted to feel thrilled about life again. To stand tall and reach beyond today and into the happy future. I was done feeling like I was hanging over the chasm. In short, I was done. The genie had been let out of the bottle for good, ready to kick booty.

I read through the night. I cried, I laughed, I paced, I contemplated, took notes, and had to cry some more. When the first morning light, sober and timid, peeped inside through the slits in closed Venetian blinds and streaked the room, I was curled up in the armchair with the book on my lap. When Mother presented herself after an unhurried breakfast, bumping into the furniture and dropping things on the floor on purpose, I did not stir, though I tracked her movements in my peripheral vision and held my breath a little. Mother trailed silent Doonyasha, the newest home attendant, if the reinforcements were needed.

"She's reading again!" Mother, the major contributor to my poor breathing patterns, said in her casual loud voice. "I wonder, who could help us make a human being out of you?"

I ignored her.

"You'll ruin your eyesight!" Mother's voice changed pitch, her good hand on her hip, the one in the cast sticking out of a sling as a silent reproof.

I ignored her. Doonyasha trembled, paled, and froze, as if she had turned into a pillar of salt.

"You'll thank me for this someday!" Mother said in a very thin voice.

I ignored her. Nothing twitched in my stomach for the first time ever. Mother tapped on my left shoulder with an air of impatience, awaiting my response. My eyes were glued to the page.

She bolted out of the room, slamming the door. Doonyasha remained a motionless post.

Not two minutes later, Mother was back, in her favorite cotton housecoat with buttons down the front. Absurd in its roominess, the old piece of clothing had seen everything. Its fabric was frayed over her breasts, meticulously darned with a beige thread meant for mending cotton stockings.

In a half polka, half waltz, coquettish and sniggering Mother flitted into the room, stretched her hand—the disproportionally long appendage—snatched the book from my hands and fled with it. Then she seemed to change her mind, and to enliven the situation further, teasing and tittering and almost skipping, she cavorted in small circles around me. All giddy and giggly, fluttering, which was more appropriate for a fairy, but in a mad fairy sort of way. Her movements were hardly graceful, not fairylike at all, but Mother was not graceful under the best of circumstances. Doonyasha stayed rooted to the same spot.

I scanned the room with my eyes, but no, there was nothing in here to placate her. I should get in the habit of stashing cookies behind the books, but with a confectionery sprite on the loose, would I have to prepare for her possible post-sugar crash, and how exactly would that play out?

A vision to behold, in pale, innocent blue with tiny purple flowers, she attempted a pirouette, a Giselle. You have no idea how disturbingly peculiar it was. I wish I could say how adorable she was, but I cannot. It was thoroughly creepy, the worst modification ever. There was a lot to be wished for in the entire situation. Used to dealing with the chronic unhappy states she was always in, how was I to survive the Mother-is-happy catastrophe? No one had ever trained me for it.

I awaited the moment when Mother was directly in front of me, then stretched out my arm, relieved her of the book, took Mother by her bony shoulders, evicted her from the room, and locked the door behind her, which brought her into a state of fury.

She banged and banged on the door with her fist. "You'll be sorry!" she screamed. "You'll be sorry! You'll be—"

Dragon slayer! For a few minutes I stood near the door, amazed at myself, and ignored her with pleasure. I glanced at the motionless Doonyasha, went back to my armchair, and opened the book where I had left off. About thirty more pages to read. The day promised to be glorious after all.

That said, ignoring Mother was both an art and a skill. I knew nothing of either, so the celebration was premature. She had not invested years of her life into nothing, and my conditioning held. *Voilà*—not even half an hour later came the familiar tightening of my abdomen. I felt guilty about not feeling guilty.

That all-too-familiar anger began to seethe inside me. The wish to have an available mother was so basic, but I would never know it. Peace at any price was no peace. What a peculiarity. The attempts at negotiations had failed so far. The amiable agreement existed as a mere blueprint in my head and gave me something to do while aching for connection. As illusions go, it was a persistent one, a misfortunate thing, stirring old shadows, doing no service. What can I say...Welcome to Utopia! If I, her only child, turned away from her, who would support her? Well, she had a sister. As fate would have it, both Mother and Bella competed over one thing or another all the time, a bantering camaraderie, with no reconciliation in the works. The endless, endless dramas:

"What's this stuff in your pot?" one usually started.

"Spinach," the other retorted.

"It'll give you gout."

"Why do you say it? Like you want me to have it. So stupid."

"Why are you calling me stupid? You're stupid yourself."

"Of course I am. I'm putting up with you. You...you ate my bread this morning! It was right here, on my shelf!" With her fingertips, one sister would tap the empty space near a shoebox filled with ointments and medicines held together by rubber bands, organized in accordance to curious logic and stored in the fridge.

"Why would I want to touch anything of yours? Yours is caca."

"I'm eating caca. You're cholera! Why is it my fate to live with you all my life? She watches every morsel of food I put in my mouth. I eat so little! Watch what *you* eat, look how fat your belly is! I never want to see your face again!"

"Is the saying about you, then: 'She eats like a bird, but shits like a horse'?"

"*Feh!* Such a profanity! You're so vulgar."

"And you're full of culture. To think, she heard some operas once. I spit on your operas."

"Move out! Don't expect me to talk to you ever again!" At which point a plastic spatula would make full contact with the other sister's upper arm—*thwack!*—and bits of overcooked spinach would fly off in all directions.

"Don't expect me to talk to *you* ever again!" And one sister would spit in the other sister's face.

"Anna! I have something to tell you!"

"Anna!" And she would spit again. And both of them would feel superior to the other.

forty

Since June 22, 1941, six weeks since the campaign had begun, over three million Wehrmacht and half a million Axis troops went into action. Riga, Vitebsk, Lvov, Minsk (a key railway junction a third of the way to Moscow), and countless smaller towns and villages were occupied. This was only the beginning, a mere part of the territories that were to be taken into possession, which—according to Nazi ideology—were at the moment populated with Untermenschen * ruled by Jewish Bolshevik masters, as the land was intended to be used for the repopulation of Germanic peoples, all for the benefit of future generations of the Nordic Aryan master race. Russians were to become usable slaves, undesirables—exterminated.

Overconfident from a rapid low-cost success, basking in the glory of resounding victories in Western Europe, the Germans, who had the best-trained and the best-equipped army on the planet, were set on achieving a permanent mastery of the world. In high spirits, they marched over Russian land, carrying out blitzkrieg warfare, expecting a quick capitulation, prepared to crush and destroy the Soviet Union as a political entity.

By mid-July, the Army Group South penetrated the lands within a few kilometers of Kiev, and Army Group North Panzer Army broke through the Soviet defenses, and advanced within a striking distance of Leningrad, waiting for the infantry formations to catch up to begin their major offensive. The outnumbered Soviets inflicted heavy losses on Axis armies, mounted fierce defensive and counterattacks all over the invasion front, all while suffering massive losses of both personnel and equipment. The Red Army was left leaderless after Stalin's Great Purge, which had killed or incarcerated almost all competent military officers, along with millions of its citizens. On top of a complete breakdown of communication, the supply and ammunition dumps were destroyed, the army was widely dispersed and unprepared to begin with, ill equipped, without transportation, and facing a logistical collapse.

The Soviet forces were ordered to launch a general counteroffensive, but their uncoordinated attacks failed. The Germans prevailed.

Hitler claimed victory after victory, and the Red Army assumed a defensive position, focusing on a strategic withdrawal under severe pressure. The triumphant march of the Wehrmacht armies was slowed down by rainstorms typical of Russian summers, which turned the unpaved roads into impassable, streaming rivers of mud, confining the Germans to the very few that were

---

* Subhumans. (German)

left, where many bridges were blown up and land mines were laid. The undefeated advancing armies found themselves immobilized for hours, sometimes for days at a time, giving the defending army time to organize counterattacks. Forced to learn the art of modern warfare in haste in the middle of a battlefield, the Soviet defense proved resilient and surprisingly adaptable. It stiffened, became more and more marked. Still, the Wehrmacht *marched forward, unstoppable, until they reached Stalingrad, a year and a half away.*

While the Russian front's news summaries came on the radio irregularly, incomplete and often with huge delays, Nazi Germany applauded the victories by blasting "Les Preludes" by Franz Liszt (the official theme song for Operation Barbarossa **) over the government-controlled radio stations to whip up enthusiasm for military actions among the German populace. The last few Soviet radio newscasts included summaries of the ongoing month-long encirclement operation of the Battle of Smolensk; of the defenders who faced the Germans along both the Rivers Dnieper and Dvina in stretches of Stalin Line fortifications; of an attack made with seven hundred tanks by the Soviet Army's Mechanized Corps; of Germans having overwhelming air support; and of a three-day battle, in which two Soviet Mechanized Corps were nearly wiped out. The city of Smolensk—the site of one of the largest battles, which resulted in the highest casualties for Soviets and Germans alike—was an important command point controlling the road to Moscow.

In a few days, the radio brought an account of three Soviet armies trapped between the great pincers of panzer armies, and of the Russians who desperately fought to escape the trap, causing high German casualties. The news came that when a gap in the encirclement had been snapped shut by the panzer groups on July 26, huge numbers of Red Army troops had been captured, but liquidating the pocket took another ten days, during which time large parts of the Red Army managed to escape the pocket.

The radio was silent for the last several days. According to rumors, three hundred thousand Russian troops had been captured to join the three million POWs, two thirds of which would never return alive, dying from exposure, starvation, disease, or willful mistreatment by the German regime. Wehrmacht *units pressed forward with its spearhead of panzer groups in their all-out drive toward the heart of Russia, aiming to take the capital.*

One hundred thousand Soviet soldiers who had escaped the net around Smolensk now stood between the Germans and Moscow.

** Operation Barbarossa—the code name for Germany's invasion of the Soviet Union—is listed among the largest military operations in world history as one of the most lethal campaigns, in terms of both manpower and casualties. Seven million Soviet military members lost their lives either in combat or in Axis captivity, and though Soviet civilian deaths remain under contention, the most frequently cited figure is around twenty million. Though to a large extent unclear, estimated 4.5 million German military and almost a million among the Axis forces lost their lives either in combat or in Soviet captivity. Smolensk, Minsk, Kiev, and Leningrad were among several Soviet cities later to be awarded the title of Hero City for their heroic defense operations. I will leave all the details for the war historians, and ask forgiveness for any discrepancies that crept in.

. . .

It was just midmorning, but the heat was already scorching. Today, August 8, 1941—Michael's fourteenth birthday—had started out on the wrong foot. He had gotten into a fight with his brother about whether Michael was old enough to cross the front line together with Greg to join the Red Army, as if a four-year difference provided sufficient seniority for Greg to insist that his underage brother stay away from the adult war. He had always looked up to Greg, but today Michael's fuse was short. He stormed out of the house, went to the creek to cool off.

He was already sorry about the fight when the door slammed behind him, and as he headed to the creek, he thought of ways to make it up to his brother. His swim was brief. The cold spring water made his teeth ache but cleared his head. He got out of the water covered with goose bumps, and thankful for the heat, he pulled on his shirt and pants over his wet body. His clothes dried on the brisk walk back into town.

The unassuming Ukrainian town was in the new German territories, behind the front line. The victors themselves were expected to show up any day, but unsettling rumors multiplied and circulated ahead of them. No village had been untouched by Stalin's repressions, and the Soviet regime's brutality was emphasized by the Nazi propaganda machine in leaflets thrown from airplanes by the tons over populated areas. In regions such as the Ukraine, the rumors were confusing—some mentioned Germans as saviors and maintainers of culture, while some told of horrific atrocities.

"The nation of Bach and Goethe…how could it be?" Michael wondered aloud. He stopped on the path he was following through the golden field of rye. The sun singed the back of his head. "All right, who are you then?—part of the force that stood for always wanting Evil, but still creates the Good," *** *Michael cited. He listened to the echo of the words in his mind.*

On the outskirts, where dwellings hid behind the dusty green of abundant orchards, Michael's family house stood at the end of an unpaved street lined with poplars. This time of year, soft white hairs, blown off flowering spikes of downy catkins and dispersed by the wind, got stuck in all vegetation with foliage, adhered to houses and fences, and full of dust, pooled on the ground. The panzer blocked the short street. An awkward, heavyset construction of blackened metal, it smelled of overheated grease and gasoline. A piece of flattened fence lay crushed under its caterpillars, with not a soul around.

Michael sneaked behind the houses to the neighbor's woodshed in the thick shadow of apple trees and squeezed between the overgrown, prickly raspberry bushes. He pressed his back against the shed wall.

*** Nun gut, wer bist du denn?—Ein Teil von jener Kraft,
Die stets das Böse will, und stets das Gute schafft. (German)
—Johann Wolfgang von Goethe, *Faust*

The neighbor's dog, Tuzik, stuck his nose out of a doghouse, produced an uncertain whimper, and crawled back inside. A few weeks ago he would be barking as if about to burst, threatening to bite off Michael's heels, his chain unable to hold him and ready to break off. Since the war began, the dogs in town had gone silent, as if they sensed death and did not wish to provoke it, to anger it with noise and attract it to them. If they kept quiet, it might pass them by.

Michael's family house and the yard were in full view, the row of dense red currant bushes along the low fence separated their property from the neighbor's. Two German soldiers in mousy-gray uniforms were in the yard. The one in the strange-looking helmet rested his hands on a machine gun slung across his chest. The other, in unbuttoned shirt, suspenders hanging over his hips, caught a red rooster, holding it upside down by the leg, and both soldiers bellowed. The rooster hung still, his eyes filmed over.

Michael had a sudden hollow feeling, though nothing seemed out of the ordinary. They looked like everyone else in town—no horns, only well fed and well groomed. With more of a curiosity than fear, the youth observed the activities of the uninvited guests, listened to the parts of the conversation held in their foreign, brusque language.

A heavy motorcycle with sidecar clattered from the street into the yard, stopped not far from the porch, and Michael, who never seen such a beauty before, could not help but admire the powerful, shiny beast. The driver pulled the goggles from his face down to the top of his chest, turned off the ignition key. The motorcycle snorted, went quiet. The young, slim officer stepped out of the sidecar, took off his tall hat with the patent leather visor, and lowered it onto the seat. Unhurriedly, he patted his forehead with a folded handkerchief, removed his belt with its holstered gun, placed it inside the sidecar as well, took off the uniform coat, folded it lengthwise, draped it over the side door. Then the officer unbuttoned the collar of his shirt and rolled up the sleeves, revealing muscular hands covered with thick, red hair. He seemed at ease in Michael's town, in Michael's yard, as if he belonged here, as if he had a right to walk on this ground.

"Juden!" Three soldiers with machine guns pushed the two nonresistant men through the front door—one younger, one older, with their hands up in the air. Two other soldiers pulled out a woman's body by her arms. She looked lifeless. Michael wanted to yell, to let them know he was right here, but no sound came from his opened mouth.

Greg stumbled on the porch, was pushed with the tip of a machine gun in his back, and fell down the steps. Mother, a paraplegic, tumbled down to the ground as a sewn-up, boneless, rag doll, her arms and legs at unnatural angles, her silky thick braids in disarray, only her eyes alive.

The officer folded his hands behind his back, widely spread his legs in boots that looked as if they had been shined less than five minutes ago. "Alle, aufstehen! Schnell!" the soldier who had pushed Greg yelled. "Du dort, Russisches Schwein!" ****

Their father looked calm, swayed a little. Greg scrambled to his feet, took a step forward,

---

**** Everyone, get up! Hurry! You there, Russian pig! (German) stood near their father, his shoulder almost reaching the top of Father's ear. In the tumult the rooster was dropped. It limped to the fence, ruffled its feathers.

The officer said something in a lowered tone. All the soldiers except one approached the fence, stood with their gray backs to Michael. The one who remained in the center of the yard wiped his mouth with the back of his left hand and raised the machine gun.

Michael did not hear the shots. He did not understand why his brother collapsed to his knees, blood streaming from his mouth, why his father crumpled to the ground and moved no more. Greg was still alive. He yelled something. Michael strived to understand the words, but he was unable to make them out. Greg sagged near their father. Mother wailed. The officer nodded. Michael did not notice where the rope came from, but it was in the soldier's hands. Trying to make some sense of it, the boy watched in horror how the soldier tied the rope to his mother's long braids. Why was the other end of the rope being tied to the tail of the neighbor's horse? The soldier whacked the horse's behind, the horse kicked, charged along the dusty street. The wailing stopped.

Someone's hand was pressed hard against Michael's mouth, and the boy was thrust to the side. Their ever-grouchy neighbor, Mikola, who always threatened to remove the chain and let Tuzik loose on the neighborhood boys getting into his orchard, held an index finger to his lips in the sign of silence, his eyes made of steel. Shaking Michael was pushed inside the woodshed, and the man whispered in his ear, "Cover yourself with hay and be quiet. I'll be back." The shed door was shut. Michael was left in semidarkness.

Michael...the youth who never again went home, forced to become a man in one short moment, the youth who crossed the front line alone, lied about his age, forged his papers, and joined the Soviet Army. He was wounded, nearly died from the injury, but returned to his platoon and was one of the soldiers who took Berlin in order to bring the reign of the Third Reich to an end.

forty-one

help!" Mother's voice, frightened and squeaky, if a little muffled, carried across the apartment. "Help!"

Oh my God! Had she hurt herself? Half-dressed, I dropped my jeans on the floor and hurried to find her.

I found Mother in the kitchen, all in one piece. In her roomy, frilled nightgown, she was bent in half, her rear end sticking out of the wide-open refrigerator. Doonyasha was present as an additional ornament, silent, pressed against the wall, the stream of sunflower seeds flowing into her mouth interrupted, a lone empty shell stuck to her lower lip.

"Ma, what's wrong?" I asked the bony jutting-out part covered with small faded-blue daisies on a white background.

"Look who's finally here." Mother scrambled out, straightened up like a Greek tragedian, her right hand on her hip, her face puckered into a single point, and oozed my morning dose of slush, sharper ice shards yet to come. "It's my duty to tell you to your face—you're lazy. La-zy!"

What on earth…

"What are you talking about?" I asked.

"What's this stink in here? Are you trying to poison me? Smell it!"

I stuck my nose where Mother's had been a second ago and inhaled. No offensive odors were present.

She grimaced. "Something spoiled in there. Take it all out."

Arguing was pointless. One by one I lined things up on the table for a closer inspection. Doonyasha snuffled, looked away. Mother, the self-proclaimed owner of a delicate olfactory capability, brought up each item to sniff like an agitated dog, reached for a tissue, blew her nose, sniffed some more, the displeasure on her face in full bloom. What an old meanie! Doonyasha and I watched her in silence, like two accomplices in a horrible crime. The inspection over, in one august gesture—a wave of her royal highness's hand—I was dismissed.

"Put it back. Hurry up! Get me dressed, make me breakfast. I'm hungry."

Who was I to argue with royalty? *Salute!*

Her unsatisfied eyes dimmed, while an expression of relief failed to appear on her face. Mother was warming up to seize the day. Just another morning, and me again in a cockeyed position. Some days there was no point in trying. The more she pushed to control me, the more her heart seemed to close down and the less the void inside her was filled, for her need for power seemed to escalate to the point of insanity with time. This life of ours kicked off to feel like a bloody Mongol-Tatar invasion of Russia with all of its implications. That one that lasted over four hundred years and brought nothing but desolation.

How was one to avoid losing oneself to a constant fear of disapproval when such massive attacks to erode one's self-confidence were always on the way? The holiness of the title "Mother"—the Holy of Holies—so twisted that I could hardly breathe in its grip—and without fail I was always the one to give in by blaming myself: she could tell I did not love her enough, and this was why it was hard for her to love me.

She knew enough to wait for another slight relapse of my "craziness" to pass, and I would do the rest. Gentle reader, you cannot imagine how grateful I was for this lesson, though I would have given a lot not to be put in a position to learn it. Ah, she was what she was. Every persecutor was once a victim.

With each passing day Mother dug in more and more, conquering the entire territory for herself. On her demand I transported her belongings from her place to mine daily, and one cloudy day I brought over a full ten-pound jar of honey, which made me wonder—how long was she planning to stay here? At the precise consumption rate of one teaspoon of honey per day (Mother was in a strict habit of measuring things to match the recommendations in a nutrition book she revered as if it were the original Bible scrolls), this jar was meant to last. Even if she mentioned in passing that I too could partake a little of her honey, still, "Beware of the Trojan horse," they say. She could have this dump of a place if she wanted. Me, I was moving out. Give me ten minutes.

Two hours elapsed. The morning incident forgotten, things quieted down a bit. It was hardly a relaxed household, yet nothing out of the ordinary happened to break up the routine. I was left alone, a deceptive thing. In the kitchen, Mother and Doonyasha argued the finer points of the proper way to chop dill. Some light screaming was involved, which penetrated the closed door of my room in waves. Not to worry, for my exclusion from discussion was not to last forever. I would soon be summoned as Mother's champion, as she was a woman of iron principles. If I had the good sense to hide from her, there was no place here to hide. Mother had busted me in a closet once, crouching down between a box stuffed with scraps of fabric and spare buttons and a box full of Christmas ornaments with a blanket over my head, having a quiet moment, plotting insurrection.

Guess where she would look first? That and the fact that I am claustrophobic.

Events were heating up. *Poor Doonyasha*, I thought. *Poor me*, I thought a bit further, and sighed. The whole idea of having her here was to free me for several hours to earn a living. The first two unlucky home attendants—or very lucky ones—had been replaced within a week, as Mother had erupted a volcano of hate and would not let me live until they were taken as far away from her as possible, or she would die.

It was not a good time for me to deal with a funeral, so Doonyasha—a mousy, middle-aged woman, her thin, grayed hair scraped back into a ponytail—was assigned as the third woman to attend to Mother. She was loathed as soon as she showed up for the first time with a ten-pound bag of sunflower seeds.

"They'll clog your digestion," Mother said, foregoing the customary hello, a promise of bloodshed in her voice.

Nothing was in the way of the abhorrence becoming mutual, and Doonyasha might not remain the last in Mother's chain of home attendants. With a little time left before I would be dragged into the squabble, I felt free to dedicate myself to my life, to things like training, which I have not done in the last few weeks, and laundry, which I seemed to never be finished with. Laundry had become my life. I mused on my choices and went to the computer.

"Michael...the youth who—"

"Help!" The shriek almost brought the dead out of their graves. The door was flung open, slammed against the adjoining wall, rattling blue glass bottles on the windowsill. A big piece of plaster from the ceiling crumbled to the floor, and a network of hairline cracks ran from a hole in several directions. Mother barged into the room like a well-sized herd of Furies. Her right hand jerked up as if to tear out her hair, but Mother seemed to reconsider the repercussions quickly.

"This horrible woman wants my death!" she screeched. "I could only wish her upon the heads of my enemies! Send her away!"

"No one is sending anyone away. Keep that in mind." I headed for the kitchen, angry Mother hard on my heels. I was greeted by a lovely sight.

"Look at it!" In case I planned on missing the picture, her forefinger trained on the cutting board with something amorphous and green piled on it. "For heaven's sake, do you see it? You're useless. The dill isn't chopped finely enough!"

"You think? It looks too fine." I beamed at her. "It resembles a paste."

"A new trend—to insult your mother! My own flesh and blood—a traitor. Waiting for me to die to dance on my grave. Get out of the kitchen!"

I looked at Doonyasha. She was calm and composed. I smiled at her, nodded.

"The abuse I have to put up with at my age! Laughing at me, my own daughter—a godless apostate—and that horrible creature! Your neighbors are laughing at me too. Why doesn't the earth open up to swallow you, to deliver me out of my shame? I knew you were schizophrenic as soon as you were born. But don't you worry." Mother grinned, her hand on her hip. "I told all your neighbors you're psychotic, so they won't think it's me who isn't normal in our family. I won't let you tarnish my good name."

Oh, for God's sake, I thought. "How do you mean?" I asked.

The grin on Mother's face grew a little wider. I looked at Doonyasha.

"When you put her outside for some air with a chair to sit on?" Doonyasha half-said, half-asked. "She stops everyone passing by."

"Some building—a Russian immigrants' nest," Mother said with a sneer. "All incurable drunkards."

I turned and left the room.

"To torture an old, disabled woman so!" Mother whined. "A heart of stone! That's my greatest tragedy! Nobody would believe me if I told them. What I've lived long enough to witness!"

There was no indication that the screaming would stop soon. I closed the door to my room, slowly breathed out through my teeth. Where was I? *"Michael... the youth who..."*

Angry—that is where I was. I would give everything I had to be upgraded from being a closest relative to a position of a total stranger. What did she want from me, my death? Did I say *my death*? And in Mother's voice too, so personal, so knowing. I was possessed. The enemy was within me. Oh, horror of all horrors. Oh, look, another pile of laundry to be folded.

Half an hour later, I was sorting out laundry and moping. The whining from the kitchen was winding down, coming in bursts. The horrific images of Mother's untimely death were becoming sweeter.

The phone rang. *Private caller.* I let the answering machine pick it up.

"Pump-kin..." I heard, and held my breath. *"You're not returning my calls. That worries me, pumpkin. I said I love you, and that means I'll love you 'till death does us part."* He giggled. *"Oh yeah—I almost forgot—I won't tolerate infidelity. Be a good girl, pick up that phone and call me. Love you."*

Click. I breathed out, feeling uneasy. Should I call the police? Well, to hell with him. He was a coward. What could he do?

The phone rang again. I glanced at the caller ID and picked it up.

"Are you alive?" Rita asked. "Heard nothing from you for several days. You've got me worried. I'll pick you up in an hour. The book signing? David Cooper?"

"Oh right! Crap! Wait, you said Wednesday. Today's Tuesday."

"It's Wednesday."

"What happened to Tuesday?"

"What are they doing to you in there?" Rita asked.

"I can't leave. They've reached the point of not speaking to each other. Last I looked, Mother was eyeing a skillet for a weapon. She'd eat me up alive if I dared to leave."

"She's already done that."

"She might really hurt Doonyasha."

"Let them kill each other while you're gone," said the distinct voice of pure reason on the other end of the line. "Get out of there. This is so exciting! Guess who else is coming?"

"Patrick."

"Mark. Doesn't matter. I won't take no for an answer. You know me. I'll physically drag you out of your burrowing hole if I have to. David Cooper. David Cooper." She dangled the name in front of me like a carrot in front of a donkey. And what a nice carrot it was! "You have an hour. Let's hope your mother is too embarrassed to make a scene when I'm there."

"Don't count on it."

"It's David Cooper, your favorite! Be ready." The line went silent.

It took a Herculean effort to block Mother's whining out of my ears and focus. My anxiety mounted, promising to soon shoot through the roof. Ah, to be in his presence! I am sad to report my IQ was dropping with a terrifying speed. Silly Anna—what was I so agitated about? It was not like it was a date or something. Breathe! Inhale: one Mississippi, two...

So I donned bought-on-sale, dark-wash Donna Karan jeans (I could not recall buying anything *not* on sale, often pulled-from-a-bin kind. Hell, I refuse to pay full retail price, never could afford it anyhow, and was not ashamed of it). I slipped into a black wool V-neck sweater (sale!) and black Italian leather high-heeled pumps. Casual with a touch of sophistication, to project comfortable, yet very New York. The hair? Too short, no options. Like *he* was going to notice, like *he* was going to speak to me. With luck, half a smile. What if he *spoke* to me? If he said, "Hi!" what would I say? Something stupid, I bet.

Mother glided into the room. Her eyes rounded with an outrage, perfect orbs, which narrowed to hateful buttonholes as soon as she had processed the initial information.

"Abandoning your own mother with this woman! Ay-yay-yay! Don't expect me to speak to you after this, you vagabond. I'm warning you. You leave me now, I'll disown you."

I made a step toward the door.

Mother blocked the exit with her body. Her fingers grabbing the doorframe turned white. "Over my dead body!" she said in a tight voice. "You look like a slut. I can see the shape of your ass in those jeans. All that's missing is a red pompom. But you always dressed vulgar. Are you having sex for money? I'm your mother! *I have a right to know!*"

She could always be trusted to go right for the jugular. I turned away from her, took my purse, slung it on my shoulder. She let go of the doorframe, outstretched her hand, and grabbed my butt. *Woof!* No matter how much I wanted to push her away, she was an old woman in a cast. Nothing left for me to do but to shake my head.

I shook my head.

Her Highness pressed her lips together, managing to make her permanently unhappy face even unhappier, and stormed out of the room. What great dramatic talent was going to waste. Imagine where the world would be today if she put all that energy into Lady Macbeth, who later avoided suffering pangs of guilt for her part in the crime. Ah, the stormy drama of being her. She could wear that face as long as she wanted to. My insulted butt and I were out of here and into the world of humans.

forty-two

rita greeted Mother with "Galina Isaacovna, how are you?" The respectful form of address among cultured Russians is the first name and patronymic.

"Nothing to boast of," replied the honorable elder with a distinct lack of warmth, her strong jaw clicking from overexcitement. "I have one foot in the grave."

A fire kindled in Mother's chest. Her hungry eyes darted to a potential victim. Not entirely unlike a heat-seeking missile on a seek-and-destroy mission, her death apparatus on standby with no chance of self-destructing, she possessed an unprecedented talent to seek out the opportunity to humiliate me and found one every time. No encouragement was needed to loosen her tongue. But first things first. The stage had to be set for yet another unforgettable performance. The woman was predictable. Mother's ever-percolating animosity was live at all times.

At once, in a flurry of activity, Mother declined all offers of help. An experienced strategist, she kicked Adam out of her way, dragged a folding chair from the kitchen, tripped on it, placed it between the couch and the door, closer to the couch, to block the exit if someone dreamed up an escape.

Rita and I were ordered to sit on the couch, and we promptly did, as if held at gunpoint, clutching our purses, shoulder to shoulder to await the last judgment or whatever Chief's agenda was for the day. From the bottomless pocket of her housecoat, Mother produced a handful of tissues, folded twice, put it back. The stage set to her liking, she doubled over, perched upright on the hard chair, the very edge of it, and froze, turning into a stone statue of a gargoyle guarding a cathedral.

She held her broken hand in a cast with the good one, letting it play its role to the full effect. Only her eyes moved. She watched Rita as a cat watched its prey, about to pounce, yet hesitant to jump. An expression of extreme pain and suffering on her face, the epitome of martyrdom, looking at no one in particular, she came back to life and sighed. Hear, hear! Mother began her act.

"Why are your eyes sparkling? What do you think this is, a circus?" she said to me in her stage voice and unloaded things weighing on her heart—her plight and the losses she suffered, enumerating this and that, all her hardships—in one messy pile, reeling with pleasure at such a captive audience, which did not happen to form often.

Given little choice but to listen to Mother progress through the rapture of unburdening herself, mostly about what a bad daughter I was, poor Rita nodded innumerable times, not uttering a word to avoid pouring more fuel into the flame. Like it made a difference.

"You should be ashamed of yourself, Dina." Mother made a sharp turn, meaningfully fixing her eyes on Rita's face. "Dragging my daughter to questionable places when she should be caring for her ailing mother—Dina, look at me, I'm talking to you. You're a bad influence. I want you nowhere near Anna. She's already an empty-headed slut. Somebody needs to put salt on her tail, but no, there's no capturing her, always speeding away like a mare in heat with her tail lifted up high."

On a roll, Mother's fiery eyes darted to the left, hesitated as if in torment, then returned to Rita, but failed to burn a few holes in her, though the flames raged. "She has the madness of a uterus. All she ever wants is a stick. That's how she repays my generosity. God knows what's to become of her. She'll end up in a gutter, a prostitute." She flicked her eyes to me for a fleeting moment then back to Rita again, with a private smile and a sliver of self-satisfaction on her face.

Woof! If I were a dog, I would have bitten her on the ankle a few times. I looked around for a means of escape. There were none.

Mother did not bother with pausing to inhale now that she was on her fiery trajectory, breaking ahead, quivering with excitement—here I was in front of her, the live target, defenseless, unable to run. She was going in for the kill.

Mother took a tissue from her pocket, blew her nose with a battery of blares for what seemed like an hour and a half, refolded the tissue into a little square, and stuffed it back into her pocket.

"You've ruined the family's reputation." She brought her face within several meager inches of mine, her jaw thrust forward. "Ay-yay-yay! I forbid you to go. Ungrateful! How I slaved for you! Cutting back on everything for myself only to feed you. To kick your old, sick mother out in the rain and not be ashamed of it in front of your friends!" She straightened up and continued with her cold-eyed squint. "You should see your face right now! Shocked, are you? You'll live. You took after your father." To eliminate a remote possibility of this being mistaken for a compliment, she seemed to feel a need to clarify. "You have your father's tainted blood. Go have one of your psychotic fits. The crocodile tears." She dragged her bony index finger down her left cheek, then her right. "*W-e-eh.* See if I care. You always were a whiny little shit."

Rita stopped nodding, her eyes ablaze, throwing forked lightning bolts.

"Eve, Eve. Good girl. Come here. Here, Eve," Mother cooed at the cat, who entered the room and sat down a good distance away from Mother, watching the woman. Mother smiled with tenderness. "Take a look at those beautiful blue eyes. You, Dina—"

"Rita. My name is Rita."

Mother looked at her as if she were insane. "Is your name Rita? Am I saying it right?—She's so dumb that cat of yours, she never comes when I call her, but I like her anyhow. Right, Eve? Come here. Here, Eve. Dina, call her. Let's see if she'll come to you."

A terrible moment of silence followed. I recovered first—I have seen this show before—the comrade speaker rummaged through her brain, through a long list of things plaguing her, prioritizing, considering what to complain of next, which I took as a cue to leave.

Before Mother got wind of what was happening, I grabbed Rita's arm and pulled her out of there. We popped up, edged past surprised Mother, and leaped like racehorses out of the gate.

"It looks bad to admit wishing to do violence to a little old lady, but she could be the exception to the rule." Rita carefully stepped over something that in the dim, yellow light looked like a used condom, then another, and stopped walking down the stairs, despite being pulled. "Tell me she's into torturing small animals, so I can feel better saying things about her."

"She's into torturing small animals." I proceeded to pull Rita by the arm.

She wriggled from my grip, glanced at the stairs—filthy, chipped, worn down at their centers, studded with cigarette butts in the corners—then looked up at me. "I believe you."

I grabbed her by the arm again, resumed pulling her down the stairs. My only wish was to get as far from this place as possible. Rita sensed it, stopped resisting.

"I'm still shaking," she said. "You don't have to go back there. Stay with us."

"That's where I and the two furry hostages normally nest." I smiled. "But I do feel your love and appreciate the offer."

"Adam and Eve are welcome to stay with us too. You can change your mind anytime. I mean day or night. Holler when you've had enough. We'll come and get you. Promise?"

She stopped at the landing, glanced at the window that offered no view—the painter's brush must have slipped off the wall and continued over the glass, covering most of the surface. She glanced at the dusty popcorn wall, at the floor covered with discarded cellophane food wrappers, a dirty athletic sock, the impressive amount of used condoms, and continued on.

We passed by the elevator with the note Scotch-taped to its door: "I need to urgently borrow the flyswatter. Promise to return it in three days." The smell of urine got stronger. Neither one of us wanted to deal with getting trapped between the floors in that clanky thing, which broke with regularity. Rita glanced at me. A second later she gave me another glance, slightly cocking her head to a side. A small vertical line appeared between her brows.

"How come you never show any anger?" she asked. "Don't you feel furious?"

"Infuriated, seething, enraged."

"It means you're still alive." She whistled. "God, you hide your feelings well! My poor darling. Did she ever hit you?"

"Slapping was always a part of the educational routine."

"I see." Rita paused. "What does she mean by you wanting a stick? What's a stick?"

"A penis."

"She hates the whole notion of sex. Did your father do something to her?"

"Seriously, like I'd be her confidante?" I asked, then added, "Even if he was so inclined, which I don't think he was, there was no time for it. He was kicked out several months after they were married. And don't you go on thinking it was because he was a violent type. He wasn't."

"How do you know that?"

"If he had been, I'd have heard no end of it. She was upset with him liking to read books."

"But he got her pregnant."

I shrugged my shoulders. "A miracle, if you ask me. I can't imagine her doing anything resembling the things required of her to get her slightly pregnant, while all she ever wanted to do was to munch on an apple. Not that I want to imagine it. Anyway, it was nothing more than the same old missionary position, which she mistook for a deadly personal assault."

"So that's a good enough reason for her to call you a slut? Or shit?" Rita decisively spun around, raised her leg as if about to mount the stairs and go back for a kill. I jerked her a little and dragged her farther down the stairs.

"Relax," I said when we had resumed a walking-down motion. "I'm surprised she didn't say something worse. Woe is me, woe is me. She even promised to tattoo the word *slut* on my forehead several times, but as you can see, she was unable to find the time to do it."

"The Evil Queen. It's like she's avenging something! No wonder you blotted your entire childhood out of your memory. Do you want to talk about it?"

"What's there to talk about?" I shrugged. "I don't even hear it anymore."

"Should we talk about repressed hostilities and veiled aggressions?"

"Yes, but let's not do it now, all right?"

"All right," she said in a soothing voice.

In silence we advanced several steps down.

"The rape...what about the rape? Have you told your mother about it?" Rita asked.

"She said I provoked the guy, but afterward she told me it never happened, that it was a lie because I was a born liar, and she could never understand my perpetual need to lie."

"What a relentless bitch!"

"I fail to detect a proper reverence in your voice," I said.

"And now she's got you taking care of her. Even animals protect their young." We both stopped at the next landing. Rita leaned her back on a dusty rail of the banister. "The rape...can we talk about it?"

"Here? Now?" Was there ever a right time and place to talk about it?

I took a long breath in, let it out, steadied myself against a dusty wall.

"I met him one day in April on Tverskoy Boulevard, which was bursting with multicolored tulips. The leaves were coming out on the trees. He called himself Nick. Dashing, dreamy, with fire in his eyes, dangerous and hot, a well-dressed prince from fairy tales. Every girl on the street followed him with her eyes and held her breath a little. He'd chosen *me*. We had lunch in an expensive restaurant. Hand in hand, we walked along the granite banks of Moscow River. He brought me to his home, somewhere on the outskirts of Moscow. His roommate was there. My prince took champagne out of the fridge and shoved me in the bathtub, saying, 'Wash yourself, dirty whore!' And they raped me, taking turns.

"When they got into an argument, I grabbed my things, ran out the door, and hailed a cab. We drove toward the city. The car turned into a small birch grove just off the highway. The driver grinned, unzipped his pants. I remember his red, rough hands on the wheel and his lustful eyes staring at me under his low brows. I screamed and bolted out. I came home two days later, covered in bruises, blood on my clothes. No memory of where I'd been. The woman I was renting a corner of a room from got scared and threw me out. Nick's face was erased from my memory. If I met him or his friend on a street, I wouldn't recognize them, though my heart might skip a bit, knowing."

"Where did you live?"

"At the Belorussky railway station. I slept there on benches, between women from nearby villages with their enormous baskets that they used to bring produce to the market—how can old women carry such heavy loads? They gave me the leftovers that didn't sell. I showered at the university sports center and continued going to work." I shrugged my shoulders, half-apologetic, and bit my lip, suddenly very tired. We stood there, not a word spoken, not a sound made.

"It must've changed your whole outlook on life and on men," Rita said in a soft voice.

"It changed nothing," I said, but thought, *Be quiet, Anna!*

Rita stood looking at me.

I went out on a limb. "My outlook on life had already been doctored: If I wanted some love, I'd have to pay with my body. Simple," I said quietly. Why had I told her this? I had told it to no one.

With horror on her face, Rita had trouble phrasing her next question.

"All right, now I've really poured my heart out. Please don't tell me to go out there and hug a tree," I pleaded with Rita. "I'd obey you, as always, but that tree will be very unhappy."

Rita made an inarticulate sound, lurched toward me sideways, gave me a long hug, sniffled, and ran down the stairs. I saw her holding back tears. I followed, trying hard not to break into an ugly cry myself. Outside, the gentle breeze caressed Rita's face, fanning her bangs, messing with the rest of her hair, helpless to erase the determination in her eyes.

"Know that whatever happens to you doesn't define your essence. You're off the hook for now. We're late as it is," she said. "I'll just tell you one thing about your mother—it's not as hopeless as you think it to be. You can't direct the wind, but you can adjust your sails. But right now you could use something good to think about. Like meeting David Cooper. All right, let's move." Rita stepped into the street and raised her hand. "Taxi!"

forty-three

forty minutes later, Mark, pacing in front of Barnes and Nobles, saw us. "What happened?"

"A long and horrific story," Rita said.

"Mother," I said.

"Ah," Mark said.

The revolving door let us in. Ta-da! Behold, another world, where Father Time passed differently. The place had an atmosphere of reserved dignity and grandeur, gave off a sense of order, and wanted nothing to do with the push-push madness outside. It was crowded, but the din of voices was muffled.

I breathed in a lungful of air: the marvelous scent of new books. All around me was a labyrinth made up of thousands of volumes, so potent, so still, long rows after rows of bookshelves. Since time immemorial, the voices of countless generations who had lived, loved, laughed, quarreled, and hoped. The power of hope!

Born out of the thoughts and emotions of their authors, these books had traveled extensive distances to get here. Spine to spine, a silent procession, invaluable treasures concealed in their fat bellies, these user-friendly, rectangular objects were prepared to wait as long as it took to fulfill their destinies of stirring the minds and souls of their future readers and to find their way into a heart to become someone's best friend. Two minds touch—the author's and the reader's. The wisdom of ages, bits and pieces of frozen time, it was all here. Other civilizations and languages—here. What a mess! Babel—it was Babel all over again, but in this friendlier version of it, people understood one another quite well.

We were late for the reading, but the room was overcrowded, the signing still on. I paid for the book, clutched it to my chest like a baby. We got at the end of the line. David Cooper was blocked from my view. My anxiety was about to reach the Moon on its way to Jupiter.

"Anxious?" Rita asked. "Time for imagery work. Any image coming up?"

I nodded. "A bee."

"Describe your bee."

"Little. Yellow. Buzzes a lot."

"Anna!" Rita hissed. "Be serious. How does it behave?"

"Frenetically."

"Give it a rose to feed on."

In my mind's eye, a rose appeared before the bee, half in bloom, majestic and pink.

"And don't make it pink," Rita added. "Try white. White is calmer."

The obedient rose petals faded into spotless white, nice and fresh. The bee let out a frustrated shriek, not in a mood to feed. Its path became more erratic.

Rita watched me intently. "Smack it!" she said.

The bee gave a short buzz of outrage and flew off.

Rita patted me on the shoulder. "Good job."

When you want things to speed up, they slow down. The lazy line was unwilling to move. I savored the final moments of suspense in anticipation of rapture, my impatience tinged with guilty, torturous pleasure. One last time I envisioned David's face, but saw young Harrison Ford's instead.

For a short moment, the crowd parted a little, and I stretched my neck for a better view. My effort was rewarded with a glimpse of a man sitting at the table, dressed in a black blazer and crisp white shirt, its top button casually undone, a stack of books in front of him. Complementary to his broad forehead, his hair with a bare touch of silver was short and neatly trimmed. I felt slightly faint.

This can't be happening. The thought crystallized in my mind in slow motion.

He closed the book and with a smile gave it to the woman standing in front of him. A clear view of David Cooper's face finally fell upon my retinas. It felt like galaxies were colliding, with me caught in the epicenter of the catastrophe.

I took an unconscious step back, stepped on Mark's foot, lost my balance, felt Mark's hand catch and steady me. Then I stopped feeling anything and froze. My breath stopped. The book dropped out of my hands and crashed to the floor with a loud thud. Several people turned around, eyeing me with curiosity.

"What?" Rita seemed concerned. "Whatever it is, don't blame me, blame life."

I stood there blinking, unable to speak. Mark bent down, picked up the book from the floor, and shoved it into my unresponsive hands. I pointed at David.

"I know, it's David Cooper." Rita patted me on a shoulder. "That's why we're here—to see him, remember? Keep moving."

"It's *him*—the guy from Starbucks," I squeezed out without moving my lips.

"What? Wait a minute…" Rita smiled one of her most devastating smiles. "It's a huge mistake not to do his author photos."

"Humph," said Mark.

My unprepared support team took their sweet time regrouping. I had the strongest urge to flee, but to my horror, my body refused to cooperate. I sheepishly remained in the line, while Mark assisted me from behind by giving me little shoves with both hands, step by step, up to the scratched, wooden table with the man sitting behind it, the owner of the short hair and white shirt.

One look at him was enough to realize I was in deep, deep trouble. The chemistry was immediate, on a deadly scale. Almost a vibration in the air, it forcefully struck a chord somewhere inside me, resonated through my entire body, out into creation, then back into my body, settling as a warm glow in the vicinity of my heart.

I had learned to relish and cherish those warm fuzzies whenever they happened. With the strangest weakness in both knees and my head spinning in all directions at once at the speed of light, I came to the table, and like a badly oiled robot, handed the book to David Cooper.

He took it from me, opened it up, lifted his face. Our eyes locked. I did not look away. Neither did he.

He jumped up. "Here you are. I tried to find you but had no idea where to look. I policed Starbucks and that lobby for weeks, even if I felt utterly foolish. You were nowhere to be found. So glad to see you again. I'm David." He extended his open hand to me. It was shaking slightly.

As if in a spasm, I stuck out mine. His handshake was firm but not aggressive. Those radiant eyes of his were full of gentleness.

I said nothing, barely able to move. A crowd had gathered around us, growing denser with each passing second, eyes expectant. A woman in black with slick, heavy-framed designer glasses and a mane of hair leaned forward as if to see better.

"Please forgive me," David said in an undertone. "I'm very nervous."

My face aflame, I was given no time to ponder these new developments. He had been looking for *me*? *C'est moi*? Why? Was my mouth open? I could not tell.

Rita and Mark looked pitiful. Instead of helping me to get calm and focused, Rita gave the impression of being antsy. I could only hope I did not look as bad as those two did, but what were the chances of that? The faces of people around us indicated open excitement. All eyes were turned to me.

Mark recovered first. "Speak," he hissed into my ear, nudging me in my back. "Now."

I dutifully opened my mouth, only to close it. Opened. Closed. No sound escaped my lips while I did my guppy interpretation. The pressures of public speaking! The situation resembled something Shakespearean, yet the guppy was not Shakespearean in nature, which made me worried as to what sort of impression I was making and how to erase that conclusion.

Mark did not buy it, to judge by his repeated disrespectful gesture. "Speak now," he hissed into my ear, louder this time, and gave me a stronger nudge.

"*Aargh,*" I said. I was afraid I would say something stupid, and here I was. Panic-stricken, I thought I should clarify.

"*Ugh,*" I said, which to my shame was followed by, "*Aargh wryou?*" and a giggle. I ought to say nothing else, but I was powerless to control myself.

"*Hmpf,*" I added for good measure and nodded. I glanced at a guy near me, with his mouth open, pressed against the table, staring into my open mouth. I swallowed hard. Time to remobilize.

"Huh?" I concluded my improvised speech—not entirely unqualified as language. I wished I had just vanished then, but for no reason at all repeated, "Huh?" The horror! The horror! Congratulations, the nightmare had unfolded strictly according to plan, as conceived by me earlier. Its evolution had exceeded my expected levels of success, destined to bring me to previously unreachable heights—precisely the sort of thing to ruin a person's day a little. Which country was it best to emigrate to in a hurry?

Yet there was hope. Perhaps instead of thinking what a stuttering cretin I was, he would think I had pretended I had forgotten how to speak English and wondered what had been left unsaid. Or that I could speak in tongues. As long as he found a favorable explanation for my aberrant behavior.

My mind, despite the desperate plea from my beating-like-mad heart, participated as a mere observer. An honorable position to take, but the timing really sucked. My body had a mind of its own. Once it had gained the upper hand over my thinking organ, it was not about to relinquish the glory of power, acquired with hardship, and refused to cooperate. The treachery was complete. The only thing remaining for me to do was to stand there, silent, relatively upright, move my foot in short arcs on the floor, and blink at regular intervals. I had seen it done. So I blinked a lot.

Far from being crestfallen, David burst out in kind laughter, his eyes shining. He appeared relieved, yet unappalled by my absurd inability to articulate…well, anything. "I have apologizing to do, if you will let me. I'm almost done here, just a few more people. May I invite you to dinner, all of you? Please?" He positively beamed with joy at seeing me again.

"Huh?" I squeaked. "Sure."

Seriously? To admit, it was English, and two words were better than one, even if they came from the vocabulary of a summer squash (no, I am not anti-squash, not toward any variety). Some (questionable!) progress had been made here. What did it matter? I did not fit in. I felt the blood rise to my face and hoped, burning with shame, that I turned a pleasant shade of juicy beet red to the roots of my hair. But to attend to important matters at hand: When specifically was teleportation to be invented, how long was the waiting line to try it out, and how did it work, exactly? I would have plenty of time later to kick myself, sulking alone in my room with Mother whining nearby.

Wait just a second! What did he say? A dinner with *me? Me? Yowza!* From my neck up, I wondered what I was doing, while the rest of me was nearing bliss.

Mark grabbed my elbow, took me aside. "Breathe! Don't worry."

Do not worry? Easy for him to say. I was worried and baffled about many things at the moment, all of them attacking me at once, but two stood out from the crowd by far. First of all, how soon would the effect of being stunned wear off, and would there be any side effects for me to deal with? On the bright side of things—look at me—I was almost talking to David Cooper. Second, my idol was the guy from Starbucks. And the elevator. In a strict sense, he was rude, yes? Well, people do strange things. The guy from Starbucks…wanted to have dinner with me. God worked in mysterious ways, but this was weird. Was the world always like this, but I had been buried in my underground cave for too long and had plain forgotten this?

I turned to Rita.

She looked a bit perplexed herself. "We'll see," she whispered. "Don't worry."

Rita too? Good time to panic then, with such a nice prelude to imminent disaster. I turned around and was about to head for the exit when Rita grabbed my sweater.

"Close your eyes and think of England," she hissed. "*You* are going nowhere."

The crowd waited in anticipation for new developments, but nothing happened, and deprived of further entertainment, it began to dissipate with hesitation. A dozen signatures later, David was free to go.

I ran nowhere, and the four of us walked to an Italian restaurant nearby. Rita and Mark sauntered ahead, within earshot, as David and I followed. The illusion of privacy was there, but it did not take a genius to know that both of them were eavesdropping on us. They uttered not a word to one another, with the minor exception of a pair of shushes each. I did not mind their spying—the level of it too amateur for two sophisticated adults—but were getting the complete story firsthand to save me from telling it later. But if I would find narrating the tale in any way pleasurable later on, while dwelling on the finer bits—what were the chances of that?—I would have plenty of opportunities to retell it. As nervous as I was, I would be lucky to recall anything afterward. Between the two of them, accuracy of a report on the event might be higher, every insignificant bit of it, this assumption based on the pure speculation that they were capable of spinning the story.

David seemed to know about them listening on—how could he not?—but had an air of being unbothered by it.

"I'm generally not a rude person." His hand touched me on the elbow with delicacy. "If you give me a chance, I'd be only too happy to prove this to you. Please? When I saw you for the first time, I liked you so much it was scary. I shouldn't be telling you this, but I'll trust my intuition and chance it. I wanted to run away, but felt paralyzed. Never happened to me before."

I knew exactly what he meant, thawing out little by little myself. Distrusting my voice to give me away, I thought better than to open my mouth and nodded.

David smiled. There was something disarming in his manners, so incredibly gentle about him, so warm and charismatic, and the Don Juan bit evaporated. "Later I realized how irremediably ill-behaved I'd been. Hope you can find it in your heart to forgive me and think me likable once you get to know me better. I'm having trouble believing you're here. By my calculations, I owe you a whole new wardrobe. You'll have to meet with me again to get it." He touched my hand.

David's hand was warm. My head was spinning from this gentle touch of his big hand, from the sound of his voice. Was this really happening? Boyishly attractive, oozing intelligence, and with a shy smile, he had an air of innocence like a child, but with the smoothness of Don Juan—an invitation to trouble. Do not forget (please) the unapologetically hot body. Hubba-hubba.

I wanted to jump into his lap but nodded my head instead. It all looked very promising, so perfect, too perfect, and should have raised some suspicions, but did not. The conversation flowed without any awkwardness, which was an un-avoidable attribute of first dates. Can I call it a date? Please? Yay, I was on a date with David Cooper! Even if he was unaware of it.

"You're the most silent woman I've ever met." David touched me lightly on the shoulder. "And you never told me your name."

"*Ugh. Harrumph.*" The laugh came unexpectedly easy to me. "Didn't I? So sorry. Anna."

Mark turned, threw a quick glance at my face. Rita grabbed his arm and jerked him back.

David smiled, crinkles gathering in the corners of his eyes. "Anna," he re-peated as if savoring the sound, and beamed at me. "What a wonderful name. Anna." His fingers brushed against my hand again. "I'm going to Peru tomor-row. Have you been there?"

Unable to restrain herself any longer, Rita turned, blowing her make-believe cover. "I'm glad the pressure will be off us and on someone else. Anna's been driving us mad with her obsession about Machu Picchu and the secret temple and the horrible sacrifices of beautiful little children. If you take her with you, I'll be willing to help her pack."

"A friend of mine who's an archeologist is taking a small group there in a few months," David said. "We could all go together. Would you like that?"

"I'd love it," I said.

"Oh no," Rita said. "Count me out."

Mark pulled her away from us.

"How wonderful to have met with a kindred spirit," David said. "Did you know that the Incas' constellations aren't the groups of stars but the black void in between them?"

Well-traveled, he was also a gifted storyteller, a fortunate combination which did not fall into one's lap every day. He laughed easily. I would be boring you to quite an extent if I mentioned that the familiar street grew broader, the streetlights shone brighter, the pedestrians seemed to be happier, bursts of laughter came from all directions, there was a vibrant halo around the trees, the snow sounded delighted to crunch under one's foot, the air was crisper, and the sky was full of fat stars. So not to worry, I will not mention any of this.

"...a small reminiscence of Vietnam," David said. "In Hue, I was waiting to cross the road, and an old blind lady sidled up to me wanting to be taken across. She trustingly took my hand, obviously realizing I was a foreigner, and allowed me to guide her. I was so moved by her trust after all she must've been through, much of which was doubtlessly caused by us Westerners!"

He stopped talking and looked at me. What a captive audience I was, my eyes wide, catching his every word. I felt deliciously wonderful—forgive me for the banality—like a kid in a candy store. After ten more minutes, not totally unlike that old blind lady, I trusted him too. He could do whatever he wanted with me. I was available for dates if he was so inclined and would welcome all his advances.

Later, as the night deepened, the four of us found ourselves sitting in a restaurant, active participants in the Manhattan nightlife and unwilling to part with one another, listening to David spin the magic of his stories. I was happy to discover it was not just me who was mesmerized and looked at the storyteller with head-over-heels-in-love eyes. I looked at Rita. Her eyes sparkled. I looked at Mark. His eyes sparkled too, spellbound, if a bit uneasy. I turned my attention back to David.

"...Arthur and I took a bus from Hue to Vientiane at some deserted garage, where we and four other travelers clambered onto an alarming-looking vehicle. The crew consisted of three guys, who seemed rather sinister, plus a dolled-up lady. I took my seat on a sack marked 'Rice,' Arthur on a box marked 'Noodles,' both of us wondering what these items really contained. Anxious glances with other travelers were exchanged once the doors closed, and we were on our merry way toward the Vietnam-Laos border. Once there, we realized the function of the dolly bird. She sidled up to the customs official and disappeared with him into the customs house, while we were left unmolested on our boxes and sacks and off the hook in what otherwise could've become a tricky situation—how might I have convinced the customs officials that the rice sack I was sitting on and its contents didn't belong to me? The rest of the journey proved uneventful, except for a breakdown, though the motor or whatever was eventually fixed with a piece of string."

The storyteller was rewarded with joint laughter.

"More," I said, completely absorbed. "I want to hear more, please."

"More," Rita said.

Mark nodded.

"Let me see," said David. "Yes, I have it. The next episode happened in Nepal, when I was involved in a development project with my two other friends, a mother and daughter, Ingrid and Kati, in a remote part of the Himalayas. We were there to teach the local people, still living in the Stone Age, new skills—how to wash, how to build clay ovens. Our 'lectures' were poorly attended. After all, these people had better things to do, like making a living and such. One of our fellow workers was a sex therapist from California. One day she decides she'll round up all the women from the surrounding villages and give them a lecture on sex. We were horrified, but she went ahead, with the help of an embarrassed young male translator. And to tell the truth, this was the best-attended lecture we had ever organized!"

I had a head start—by reading David's books, I knew a little about him. His stories proved to me once again that he was a gifted dreamer. His overflowing passion for life was so infectious that it transformed everything it touched, infusing things with a vibrant spirit they had previously been devoid of. Even inanimate objects were not entirely immune to it. He was worth heartache, even a chronic one. As for the subtle nuances of the cursed and blessed daily reality of being together with a forever adolescent incurable dreamer...

One by one the stars got erased from the sky, when the rising sun found David and I stepping out of a cab in front of the building I lived in. He held out his hand to help me out. My hand remained in his as we walked toward the door. It felt like we had known one another forever—at ease, yet excited.

He stood on the decrepit steps at the decrepit door with cracked glass that lead into the decrepit building, not letting go of my hand, as out of place as an impossible dream. "I'd like to see you again. I'm out of town for the next few weeks, but how about the seventeenth, Friday? Dinner? I'll call you with details."

"Yes, please," I said.

Everything seemed right with the world. For an instant, it felt as if he might lean down and kiss my cheek. He squeezed my hand, a light squeeze, leaned down and kissed me on the mouth. It was a sigh of a kiss, barely more than a touch of his lips to mine—soft, yielding, unexpectedly tasting like wild honey—and left.

And what a touch of the lips it had been! A silent explosion, the singular enchanted kiss of fairytales. There I was, the sparks between us flying in all directions, feeling all dizzy and wonderful. Or was it my imagination in overdrive?

In eight steps David turned, smiled broadly, waved, hurried toward the waiting taxicab, and he was gone.

Anything could happen now. It was even too perfect, but I would take what I could get, since I was not one who would want to mess with perfection, not me. He was a guy every mother would love for her daughter. Oh God, Mother. I had forgotten about her. The soft breeze caressed my face, moved across my neck, causing goose bumps to spring up, and bringing back to life some scraps of memory, some old longings and pockets of sadness deep inside my chest. I shivered. And that was exactly how it all—the golden future—began.

forty-four

minutes prior boarding his plane, David called. "I've made reservations, so I'll see you at eight on the seventeenth?"

"At eight on the seventeenth. Have a nice trip."

"I'm asking your forgiveness in advance. I can't promise to call you for the next few weeks. I'm going on this dig to get away from civilization. If a truck goes into town for supplies, I'll hop on it. I'll miss you." He apologized for the shortness of the conversation and hung up.

This statement, so simple and amicable, put me in a state of panic. While I sequestered myself in a closet to hold counsel with myself, my heart went *ba-boom, ba-boom*, as if I were fleeing in terror through a haunted graveyard in the dead of night. When it was only us—he, the world-renowned author, and I, the local idiot, with my provincial ways—what would we talk about? Art? Philosophy? Space exploration? As long as it was not my small life, which was not the most intriguing subject on this side of the Himalayas. Would he be put off by my too-limited knowledge of dining etiquette? And there was a matter of delicate quality too: some sources mentioned his being married, but others placed him on lists of the ten most eligible bachelors in New York City.

"This girl's never around when I need her." Mother's voice boomed outside the door. "You better not be in that closet again."

The skies lightened and darkened eleven times, days and nights circled, the luminaries rose and set, the seas rose and fell, some kingdoms too. Hopes fluttered in my heart, doubts rocked my mind, and something leaden nested in my belly. I did my damnedest not to despair thinking about the seventeenth, Friday night, with variable success, despite Mother's extensive efforts to keep my head occupied and spinning. Friday declined to come, but if one waited long enough, everything would come to pass sooner or later. The date approached, and my fears refused to disperse while my agitation increased.

∎ ∎ ∎

"Mama, are you busy?"

"Sweetie! I was hoping you'd call. How was the carnival?"

"I never went. Andrew made an amazing dinner for me. Even the dessert, imagine. Pear clafoutis. Delicious. Isn't it seductive?...Would you get upset if we became more than friends?"

"Why would I be upset? Honey, if it brings you joy, I'll be joyful with you."

"Would it make things awkward between you and Mark? If you two—"

"We won't. In fact, I have a dinner date this Friday. With David Cooper."

"As in David Cooper, your favorite author? For real? Like he asked you out?"

"I went to his reading," I said, "and yes, he did."

"Awesome! That's my mama. You must be excited out of your mind."

"Terrified is more like it."

"He'll love you. This is superb! So...are you sure about Andrew and me?"

"Look, Mark and I, we both want you to be happy. And Andrew—we already know the guy from a good angle. We also know he's from a good family, a good gene pool too."

"And he's so sweet! Mama, what if I'm making a big mistake?"

"If you're afraid to make mistakes, you'll miss out on life."

"An ancient Chinese proverb."

"Exactly," I said. "Columbus set off to find India. Look what happened. So..."

"No, nothing happened. Just thinking out loud. I'll call you tomorrow."

. . .

Friday was here, the evening almost upon me. All efforts to contain my excitement went to waste, and at noon I began preparing for the date—now, for a clever twist, with compliments of the management—no hot water to wash my hair. Too often hot water was just an abstract idea. What might one do in a situation like this? Me, I had extensive prior training, the irony. Still hate it. I put my biggest pot, full of water, on the stove...

Someone knocked on the entrance door. I opened it to see Mrs. Goldfarb in her mandatory pink housecoat, a curler in her hair.

"I hope I did the right thing," she said. "Alex was hanging out in the hallway ten minutes ago. He was drunk again. I talked to him through the door and told him you have a boyfriend, and that he should leave you alone. Anna, be careful, I'm begging you! Something is very wrong with him."

Holy shit! "You did the right thing, Mrs. Goldfarb. Thank you so much!"

She patted my right shoulder and went back to her place. My mind was preoccupied with more important matters. I could not think of Alex. As Thomas Jefferson said, "How much pain they have cost us, the evils which have never happened." I shook like a Chihuahua in the midst of winter and forgot to ignore

Mother, who punished me for not paying attention to her by not speaking to me. It all worked out to our mutual satisfaction.

In a mental fog, excited and terrified, I will never know by what miracle I managed to get myself dressed and out the door. I walked into the restaurant and into the bright white, pleasant smile of the *maître d'hôtel* clad exclusively in black. Both he and his smile reflected a thousandfold in endless mirrors covering the walls.

"Mr. Cooper's table, please." I relished the sound of it.

His impersonal smile grew broader, displaying all of his forty-two teeth. "Yes, madam. You've been expected. Please follow me."

The room was packed. An army of waiters in black hovered around the tables. The place commanded certain behavior from a lady, a classy sort of behavior. Swooning inside and nauseated (that would be classy—to vomit here), I swallowed. My knees executed a move, inappropriate and strange, but carried me further. The black suede pumps with high stiletto heels I had on discouraged the feeling of stability. I felt a blister forming on the sole of my left foot. Thank God and Chanel for a little black dress that made a woman look smartly dressed no matter the occasion. I hoped that mine, à la Chanel, silky and above the knee, was smart enough for this joint, and that I was able to pull off—did it have to be so hard?—an understated simplicity of elegance.

Each step gave me a little thrill, bringing me closer and closer to David. Dressed in a tasteful black suit and crisp white shirt unbuttoned at the top, he awaited me at the table, stood up as we approached. My dress was color-coordinated with his attire, as with all the waiters' uniforms in this place—not on purpose, but who would know? And then all at once, there it was, the quickening of blood in my veins, sneaking up on me like that.

David cupped my hand in both of his in greeting. His eyes sparkled. "I'd like to say how happy I am you're here with me tonight."

"Are you kidding?" I said. "Wouldn't miss it for the world."

My knees could take it no longer, about to give way. Without a sound and with a bowed head, a waiter appeared out of nowhere, pulled out my chair for me. I lowered myself into it. The soundless waiter helped David, stepped away from the table with his hands behind his back, and slipped away. Classy, indeed. Which reminded me—be classy.

"I took the liberty of ordering for us," David said.

"I'm grateful you saved me the embarrassment of mispronouncing unfamiliar words." For no reason, I lulled myself into thinking that this style of conversation was expected of me, and I was proud to deliver the expected in a sophisticated manner. Not the first time I would set myself up.

"Hope not to disappoint you in the tender stages of our acquaintance."

"I wouldn't worry about that. I'm sure you've made excellent choices."

The elegant tool of seduction—flicking back long, golden hair cascading softly over the shoulders. My hair was too dark, too short, and refused to get flicked. What if I crossed my legs? Like so, offering a glance at my high, black, ankle-strapped heels to signal an intricate cultural message. And reserved as a trump card in a woman's arsenal was a breast brushing against a man's arm or something, but we sat too far apart for that.

The waiter returned, filled the glasses with imported water from a big bottle, placed it on the table, and left again, silent and unobtrusive.

I looked at the table setting. The array of matching silver, laid parallel to one another in front of me, had more pieces that I happened to own at home, matching or not. I slipped my left foot out of the pump and felt immediate relief.

I tried not to fidget. "I have to tell you, I was unable to put your latest book down. It kept me on the edge of my seat. I can't imagine what you lived through to reach this level of insight into a human soul. I find your descriptive powers, your dialogue, your attention to detail irresistible. I'd read anything you'd write. I'd read your grocery list. All of it true."

There was a mischievous twinkle in David's eyes. *Anna, drop the tone*, I thought, and recrossed my legs. I could not think of a thing to say. Should I tell him now that I had read each one of his books at least ten times? Later? Never? I mean, what do famous people want to hear, exactly?

"I'll take the compliment," he said, straight-faced, but with the faintest pucker at the corners of his mouth. "Leave a man alone with only his computer as his companion and no one knows what will come of it."

What a golden opportunity to ask! "I don't mean to pry, but I've heard you're a happily married man. If I recollect correctly, you were college sweethearts? How romantic." I trembled inside.

David smiled, looking slightly puzzled. "Good thing I never read what's written about me. The reality isn't always what the press presents it to be. My soon-to-be-ex-wife is seventeen years younger than I. She'd be upset to learn we look the same age to some members of the press. It could be amusing. I was happily married at one time long ago. Times change, people change. Seven years later, and my divorce is almost finalized—my lawyer has been saying that for the last six months."

The waiter placed a plate with carpaccio in front of me first, then he served David. David cut off a small piece of raw meat with his knife, picked it up with his fork, loading a bit of shaved parmesan cheese and arugula on top, and sent it all into his mouth.

Divorce? A bead of perspiration ran down my spine. I nodded, studying his table manners so I could monkey them. *Change the subject*, I thought. "Here's a question you're probably tired of hearing, but I'm genuinely curious about, if I may ask. How was it at the beginning of your career?"

"The very beginning? As a young aspiring writer, nurturing delusions of producing the great American novel and secretly believing myself to be a bohemian wunderkind, I thought it would make me look more distinguished if I wore black, or picked up smoking, or grew a goatee. Being the middle brother out of three and longing to be unique, I didn't know which one to choose, so I did all three, and to finish off the look, added loafers."

"You *are* a celebrity," I said, quick to laugh tonight, "so it helped."

"I'd like to think so, especially the goatee. Otherwise I looked foolish for several years. It might be better if I come clean now and tell you that my first novel was never published. The second one was, but by then, if I remember correctly, I shaved every day."

Compelled to absorb every little detail of David's face, yet embarrassed to be obvious in my intentions, I allowed myself a few miserly glances. He in turn had no trouble studying me and seemed to be amused by my embarrassment. I shot another quick glance at him to find a glint of laughter in his eyes, but he offered no comment, which I thought kind of him.

Realizing I had been caught, I bit my lower lip, lowered my gaze, and fixed my stare in the space between our plates, which was filled with wide assortment of glassware, silverware, and a candleholder with a burning candle. Opposite to my first, automatic impulse, this was not time to be one with the flame, dancing and bobbing, having out-of-body episodes.

In a rush of panic, I traced the plate's edge with my finger, raised my eyes to meet David's, and asked, "Does it get easier with experience?"

"Not to scare you off, but it gets harder, as long as you don't let any complacency creep in. I'm more aware of my deficiencies now than I ever was. The more you grow, the more critical you become, the more you strive for higher and higher standards. And as we know, absolute perfection can never be attained."

"And the rewards, like a sense of fulfillment?"

"The rewards are proportional to the efforts extended."

"What sort of advice would you give to someone who was starting out?" I asked.

"Advice?" He thought for a moment. "Do the best you can, but don't strive for perfection, or you'll set yourself up for failure." He shrugged, drank half a glass of wine. "Don't be afraid of failure. Embrace it as the crucial part of a growing process. Now, something tells me I might be in the presence of a fellow writer. Am I?" David's hand traveled closer to mine. His fingers brushed my hand lightly, then retreated, but not too far.

"If you'll be willing to stretch the definition of the term."

"I imagine that statement isn't totally justified. May I inquire what you're writing about?"

"My family saga from the times of the October Revolution 'till the present."

"May I read what you already wrote?"

"Really? Oh yes, please." *What have I gotten myself into now?* I thought.

"I'd be delighted. I find the subject fascinating. It could be a captivating read."

"Why, thank you." I beamed at him, my insides a liquefied mush.

"What better way to find out all the secret thoughts, otherwise hidden from inquiring eyes, in the shortest amount of time than by reading what someone has written? In all fairness, you already have the advantage over me in that department."

"It gives me better leverage. Not that I need it, but in case I did."

"I detect trickery," David said.

"What sort of human would I be if I didn't resort to trickery now and then? Besides, information is often a more valuable commodity than gold."

"Ah! Well said."

"Can I hope for an honest opinion?"

"You must be hinting at the possibility of outright flattery."

"Imagine that," I said.

"Even where that flattery is due?"

"No, I'll be grateful to take everything that's due, including flattery. But it usually comes in two sizes—too much or too little—and quite frequently hand in hand with ulterior motives."

"And if I promise to be fair?"

"How good is your word?"

David laughed. "I'd like to think of it as reliable."

"Then you've got yourself a deal."

"Excellent. I'm serious, please don't hesitate to bother me. I'd be glad to be of service to you. Besides, I already have an ulterior motive—I'd like to get to know you better."

I tried hard to keep a straight face and failed. My smile blossomed. The harder I tried, the wider it became. If that was not enough, I could feel my entire physiognomy bursting into bloom like a poppy in springtime. David, on the other hand, had no problem keeping his face straight, but his sparkling eyes gave him away. And how thrilled I was they did!

"I also have a selection of books that might be of interest to you," he said.

"Thank you. *Ahem*…Now it's me who's detecting possible trickery. It isn't by any chance a subtle attempt to drag me into your dark cave, is it?"

"Could be. Always a pleasure to deal with a smart woman, especially if she's as beautiful as you are. Though, fool as I am, I know better than to declare an early victory. I'm afraid I'm rusty in the art of seduction. How I wish now that I weren't."

"Then I suppose you wouldn't suspect how seductive that last statement was."

"You mean I'm doing something right?" He burst out laughing.

"You have good reason to be pleased with yourself."

"Ah! The offer stands. I always wanted to know more about that period of history you're writing about. Russia fascinates me. Never been there, not yet, but I've wanted to go for a long time. I took Russian in college but had little practice and would be glad to take lessons from a native speaker. Must be the gods that sent you my way. Tell me more about your story."

I suddenly noticed the waiter to my left, more like a shadow, taking away my empty entrée plate.

Throughout dinner, food and wine kept appearing and plates kept being cleared by a soundless waitstaff. I had not noticed what I was eating, but whatever it was, it was tasty. To give you a heads-up, the dessert was something pink in a chocolate cup with raspberries and the obligatory sprig of mint. If you were wondering, no, the date was not all about me and my writing, nor were there quizzes to test my knowledge of literature, or art, or any other sorts of subject. Word by word, sentence by sentence, open and trustful, he told me a thing or two about himself.

"You have a gift of being an extraordinary listener," he said. "So easy to open up to you."

We talked and talked. In the deep of night, David took me home and at the door gave me a gentle kiss on the lips.

"I'll call you," he said, with tenderness in his eyes.

And I believed him. I believed him so much, with complete abandon, not caring if and what would I get in return. It would be a privilege to have my heart broken by him. I believed him because I wanted to believe him, because I wanted to surrender myself to him. Yet, glowing with the feeling of liberation that surrender brings, and taking into consideration all of my previous history with relationships, I could not help but wonder how painful it would be to fall from this height.

forty-five

though I had not thought of him for years, I had the sudden urge to fill in the empty rooms in my heart and search for Father and Alyosha and Alyona, my half-brother and half-sister. Enough of ghosts. Ever since I could remember, I had wanted to have a sibling, and to think this entire time I had been the older sister. I was not resolute on this manhunt thing, curious yet perplexed, in the process of contemplating the necessities, possibilities, and hidden dangers. Knowing one's roots was a good thing. Or was it best to let sleeping dogs lie? Was I digging an early grave for myself?

What had tipped me off today, midmorning, around ten, was the enthusiasm with which my ever-disapproving mother, flinging her good arm about her head as if she were a malfunctioning windmill, said, "You're just like your father, that bastard! His spitting image." Her words resonated with deeper truths inside me. I felt a rush of cold wind in my face. Could I be so immensely stupid? From the cradle I knew the woman to be of a retaliating temperament, with hate and unhappiness as the deepest of her passions. Did it mean he *was* a bastard? Could be. Let us avoid falling into any delusion here.

Still, there was a chance he was a decent human being. If he turned out to be who Mother claimed him to be, the goodbyes would not be prolonged, teary in excess, or heartwrenching. As far as I knew, he had never made any attempts to locate his wonderful, firstborn daughter—that would be me—but in all honesty, the guy had been married to Mother, for however short a time. He might have a vast variety of reasons to keep his distance. It seemed like Ma was not missed. I bet he had been so happy to be out of there that the mere thought of coming back gave him heebie-jeebies for life. He could still be running and jumping for joy, who knows? Yes, I oversimplified things a little. I know, I know. Parental responsibilities and so on.

It was pure speculation that Daddy had been intelligent enough to realize the fabulously glorious advantages of being married to Mommy, but how dumb would one have to be not to? Any offspring of a blessed union must be put under intense scrutiny. A daughter may turn out to be the exact replica of a mother—the apple, the tree—for better or worse, and there would be two of them, a scenario for a horror movie, creepy yet promising to be quite lucrative.

Poor, poor Papa! I had dreamed of seeing Father again for years, but then I would get busy with life and forget about him. On, off, on. At vulnerable moments of occasional visions, the picture that came up looked not entirely dissimilar to this: We are running toward one another, Daddy and I, the girl with scrawny braids, sans ribbons, in a polka-dotted windblown dress, la-la-la, across the field of blossoming crimson poppies—No…white daisies. No…who cares? (Yellow buttercups?) I have trouble catching my breath. Excitement tightens my throat, and my heart pounds. My cheeks are flushed from running so fast. So are Daddy's. He clutches me to his bosom.

"You're so beautiful," he whispers, tearing up with joy—No. "You're so smart," he whispers—No. "So beautiful." Anything, as long as he is proud of me, meeting my needs and satisfying my yearning for self-acceptance, and as long as it is nowhere near, "Don't you find it rained more this spring than the last year?" or "Do you think the corn crop is going to be bountiful?" I would sob and forgive him for abandoning me all those years back.

I had met Father once, long ago on a windy May afternoon. The entire procedure lasted about two hours. I was the one to cut it short. The event itself took place during those great times in the history of emigration from the Soviet Union, when it was necessary to pay the government enormous sums for otherwise free higher education, and to obtain written permission from both parents in order to leave the country for good. To acquire the latter, that important piece of paper from Papa, I would have to go to his hometown, to his natural habitat, and introduce myself to him.

A week ago I had had no idea if Father were dead or alive. In truth, I had not had any recollection of having a father. Cheerful within reason, I had been busy living my life when my innocent-looking mother coughed up his latest telephone number—a bit unexpected, but I did not have the luxury of feeling shocked for long. Nor did I indulge in wasteful presumption—well, perhaps a little, nor had it been an expectation of a hopeful kind. I had to hop on a train and, fingers crossed, go get that vital piece of paper.

The only thing I had known of the man prior to meeting him face to face was what could be gleaned from a well-established "That bastard!"—a rather vital piece of data to occupy the center of a solid informational sphere pertaining to Dad. Over the years, all my attempts to get more details from Mother were rebuffed, always rebuffed. Once she slipped and let go of the fact his hair was red, a crucial item, but not exactly the type of particulars I was looking for. So when I went to meet with him—the red-haired bastard—I was nervous but also curious.

I was also terrified of anyone who wore the title "blood relative." Almost twenty, already a responsible adult, I had obtained enough experience to pass the unwavering judgment that any *relative* was likely another bloodsucker who would insist I was nothing and that I should follow his directives on how to live my life.

Dad had thought it would be a jolly good idea for me to meet with the entire family, sort of my family too. A whole gang of new relatives were about to enter my life. They gathered around me once I arrived, flapping their eyelashes, some producing nervous smiles. My hand got squeezed a little and shaken while they sized me up with suspicion and whispered unintelligible sounds behind my back. My heart grew heavier as the murmurs grew louder. I eyed the group in terror, and as soon as the first chance presented itself, I ran away like a headless chicken. *Je ne regrette rien...** Ah, but I did, with a bitter taste in my mouth. In the years to come I would be given a chance or a hundred to experience the thorough enjoyment of ravaging regrets, as there was much to be regretted.

When it rains, it pours. Would not you know it, not even three weeks prior to this pivotal meeting with Papa, freshly restored to me, I had met man of my dreams number one. Ah, *l'amour*, before which the world kneels in awe, and for a very good reason. The nightingales sang in my soul. My head was preoccupied with more significant, if different, matters. (Shhh! Please keep it to yourself— Mother can hear you.) My heart and all my other key body parts were somewhere else at the moment, buzzing, a fabulously memorable time in my life when my ovaries handled the majority of the thinking.

The conversation with Papa had been short. He began with a revelation that he was sorry for what happened between him and Mommy Dearest, and it looked like he was to weep with sentiment. *Sorry?* I had never encountered relatives uttering "sorry." I was hardly trained for it, drilled on how to hold my upper lip stiff. No idea, not even a hint at what had passed between them. Somehow, somewhere, I was somewhat ashamed of my ignorance. Why could not I open my mouth to pose a legitimate, straightforward question? It would have been so easy: "Dad, tell me what happened."

I was also preoccupied with the crucial but puzzling fact that Pa's hair was not red, as I had been so authoritatively informed. Could Mother get at least one thing right? Now, free from any expectations of discretion, had she simply been spiteful when she mentioned "that bastard" along with her timeless advice? With things too confusing to take in, seeking the place where I belonged and finding none, I was certain of nothing but my wish to not be there talking to Father. He

---

* I regret nothing. (French)

sounded unexpectedly human, and *human* was exactly the thing that frightened me. My whole cosmos collapsed. I was not ready for interaction. It was not until years later that I realized he had tried to reach out to me, that my forgiveness and understanding had meant something to him. Unable to guess his real emotional state, I resorted to pushing him away. For what it is worth, I am sorry, Dad, I was not open with you. So very sorry!

When the center of the power vortex so prominently occupied by Mother all these years had shifted at last, I breathed freely for the first time on my own. I claimed that freedom, no further persuasion needed. Intoxicating and exhilarating, it felt so strange and wonderful! "Better late than never," as they say. I hoped it was not too late for Father to still be alive and willing to talk to me. That would be quite a conversation, if only Mother's voice in my head would keep quiet for a few minutes.

"Non! Rien de rien...Non! Je ne regrette rien..." ** I sang with all my heart, but since it came out less like Edith Piaf and more like a sick rooster, I stopped, went to my computer, and opened my browser. Now, how would one go about locating a person?

** *"No, nothing at all... No, I regret nothing ..."* (French)
—"Non, je ne regrette rien."

forty-six

the kitchen outlet was unhappy. It had started to blacken on the outside. I fought off the thoughts that weaseled through to offer an explanation, things like a fire hazard or an equally unpleasant plan for the future. As Albert Einstein said, "Logic will get you from A to B. Imagination will take you everywhere."

The motif spread at a steady rate, a study in muted earth tones. This was the only outlet in the kitchen. No crystal ball was needed to forecast how grim the immediate future was, as I was addicted to boiling water for tea in the electric teakettle and the refrigerator keeping food relatively cool around the clock. I could live without a toaster.

I sighed. I needed help. The thought produced an involuntary clench of my gut. The proverbial damsel in distress was in need of a knight in shining armor. As for the candidates for that shiny knight, my options were limited to a guy better suited for the part of a man with a dark pencil mustache sans Brilliantine, concealing a dagger, decidedly shiny in his purple nylon shirt, but not a knight.

I sighed again. The hunt was on for the most elusive guy in the building—the superintendent, Pedro, *numero uno*, habitually running around like a young deer. Based on experience, I was in for a long haul. The end results were moot, with an inclination toward the final conditions being worse than the original problem.

About that: I was still impressed with the way Pedro pushed his inhibitions aside and let his inner beaver shine through to repair my bathroom door. Bravo! See, the door had wanted neither to close nor open, hopelessly stuck either way. It was old. The screechy upper hinge was no longer operational. Instead of replacing the ailing hinge, with impressive speed, the super chiseled off a huge chunk of the opposite side of the door, a loud and messy procedure. He did not do it bare-handed—he brought an electric beaver helper.

A month later, another huge chunk of the door got chiseled off. At the present rate, the door would soon resemble a barbecue skewer, no need for opening or closing it—people could squeeze by with reasonable freedom, especially the persistent ones. There might be a privacy issue on the near horizon, but that was not a mechanical problem. Just one complaint—the door still refused to open or close.

Or consider this unrelated, but likewise unforgettable event, since I am already in Memoryland—the world of echoes and shadows, with me buoyant, floating with clouds over the rivers of oblivion, the hills of hopes, and the occasional swamp of despair. The picture of the jinxed bedroom radiator remains too vivid, and I suspect the horror of it will never leave me. This steam radiator was not such a hot friend to have. Forever angry, it clanked, knocked, rattled, hissed, dripped, and spat boiling water. A reliable bucket kept it company over the years, used to catching dribbles and the sporadic trickle without a single complaint.

One day, out of the blue, the radiator developed delusions of grandeur. It presumed itself to be a distant cousin of Old Faithful, and was proud of this kinship, with aspirations of becoming its equal one day. Go figure. The small plastic bucket, which had weathered all other caprices of its metal comrade, had had enough. As had I. Unsure of how to deal with the irrational device, I naïvely called Pedro. When was I to learn?

I reasoned he was more qualified than me to find the satisfactory solution, as between the two of us, he was the one with the heavier toolbox. Neither the hot water geyser in the middle of winter nor the small-scale flood met his criteria of being an emergency, but because I would not stop nagging, he showed up three days later with his assistant, Bernardo.

Bernardo picked up one end of the radiator-geyser, and Pedro shoved a broken piece of lumber under the contraption. The fountain hesitated and sort of dried up, if a little drippy. The repairs were complete. Twenty dollars, please. Cash.

Though this particular methodology, to be presumed as tried and true, did nothing to cure the problem. Not half an hour later, the jet of hot water was operating again with a newly acquired vigor. As an added bonus, now I had a controversial piece of art in my bedroom—a lopsided sectional radiator with blistering paint peeling off it in strips everywhere in an unpicturesque fashion, a whimsical touch, conceived and born out of the mind of Salvador Dalí. Ah, the reality of surrealism, with a hidden, wise message lurking in its depths. Should I be calling an exorcist instead?

I had to call Pedro again. And again. After another three days he showed up with Bernardo and another broken piece of lumber. The same rehearsed procedure was performed again. Now the left corner of the radiator stood on two generous sources of splinters that fit together badly—and my worst luck—this was no optical illusion. This time the intensity of the fountain changed little, but the angle of the trajectory of scalding falling water did. Instead of targeting the old and cheesy dresser, it went two inches off from my pride and joy—my Mac.

Let it be known that I really, truly did not like anyone messing with my Mac.

My enthusiasm for repair techniques employed had peaked to its absolute maximum, and I voiced my displeasure. Well, I tried to voice it in a polite way, but the words failed me. I wailed like a banshee, an atypically angry banshee. With unsuspected agility, the super shut down the thing. No hot water fountain, thank you, but with the entirely unwelcome side effect of no heat in winter. It only cost me forty dollars and one overcooked dresser. *Domo arigato.* In half an hour, crystalline frost rimmed the edges of the bedroom windows. I lit the oven in the kitchen, but it helped little.

The handyman in question was a man busy to the extreme. Bernardo and Pedro moved cars from one side of the street to the other daily, except on Sundays, per strict requirements of alternate-side-of-the-street parking regulations in the city of New York. Fifteen cars had been entrusted into their loving care, though my gathered data was based on improperly made scientific observations and could not be considered reliable evidence.

Pedro had a heart of gold. By providing the service, he helped out unfortunate neighbors who would otherwise have to deal with the unpleasantry of paying parking tickets. No matter how much the neighbors paid him, he never felt he was paid enough, his dissatisfaction in plain view. Lately a mysterious epidemic of missing car stereos was on the increase, but in our neighborhood...Whaddayagonnado? Everyone affected was grateful the rest of their car had been spared.

With an air of carrying out a sacred duty for society, Pedro chased every woman fortunate enough to pass by our building, only taking time out for sleep. The age or looks of the lucky woman made no difference. He had made Mother giggle a few times, and Mother giggles for no one. *Que hombre.* *

The man had no time for me and my petty outlet issues. I had to keep bugging him, as remembering things was not Pedro's forte, and these just happened to be the rules of the game too. Strange forces were at work in the known universe at this time, and an unprecedented something went awry, so five weeks and fourteen reminders later, Pedro showed up at my door one early morning.

My eyes misted over. On my first impulse, I was ready to kiss him, but it occurred to me that exercising restraint in showing my true emotions was an infinitely wiser path to take, if this case were to be analyzed closer. He would mess up soon enough, then I would be forced to decide whether to show or hide my reaction, and choking him would be frowned upon. And he still had yet to discover the wondrous powers of deodorant. I settled on exhibiting a lukewarm happiness.

A minor issue demanded my immediate attention—Pedro was under the influence of a mind-altering, widely sold, legal substance, and it was not coffee.

---

* What a man. (Spanish)

Smelling like the bottom of a huge old beer barrel that had outlived its usefulness and was about to be thrown away, he gave me the best (if distorted) smile he
could manage. He grinned and swayed, grinned and swayed, and then he had to
do some more of that grinning and swaying.

Indeed, he had come *to repair* my kitchen outlet. Not right away, mind you. We
were at the second stage of the game. He gave me the look, almost succeeding in
focusing on my breasts for a moment, and declared there was a major water main
break in the building, then said something about shutting down the cold water
supply. And something about Friday. But there was always something about Friday
in our conversations, so I ignored it. His English was more Spanish than English.

His bloodshot eyes worked their way up to my mouth, failed to focus there
too, and toured back to my breasts. He tried to stand erect, but miscalculated the
angle. A wide sweep with a hand, which threw him off balance, was done purely
for my benefit, with the intent of clarifying things. It did not. He followed it with
several unsure steps in the same direction he had waved his hand a second ago,
his face strained. In a matter of moments, Pedro almost balanced himself. He
sighed, grinned, and swayed.

So, the water—he had to deal with that first. He would be back at ten. The
seemingly unexpected water-feature twist was always included as a lively prelude to round two of the game, but one could never know, and I hoped that this
threat developing at the speed of light was inapplicable to *my* living conditions.
Anything was possible. The absolutely improbable stuff would also be possible
in the end. In Pedro's impaired state, I worried less about him turning the water
off and more about him being capable of turning it back on. In one thing I was
confident—he would not be back for hours, and there was a slim chance that the
matter of the beer smell would resolve itself in the meantime.

The game continued without any unanticipated events interfering with the
grand plan, and round three had now begun. At ten Pedro was nowhere in sight.
Eleven came and left. I called his home at twelve. He was there. He needed
ten minutes. Ten minutes? Fine. He materialized at twenty-five after one, stared
unblinking at the outlet for a while, and left without uttering a word—all of this
well-charted territory. I returned to my chores.

Pedro returned in an hour, dropped a brand-new outlet on the kitchen table,
and whistled out. Alas, three hours later he showed his face and his toolbox back
in my apartment to indicate the beginning of all-important round four. The per-
vading smell of beer had been given no opportunity to diminish, and was mixed
with the aroma of burned onions that was a permanent attribute of my kitchen,
creating an unwelcome bouquet. At this point of the story, I feel a strong need to

clarify that I had nothing to do with the onions, burned or otherwise.

I frantically reviewed in my head whatever limited knowledge of CPR I possessed, to be used when Pedro managed to electrocute himself. But I could not back out now. We were at the point of no return—he had brought tools. The insignificant matter of the actual repair was the only thing left. Unrestricted to just my stomach, butterflies fluttered all over my body.

I situated myself in the kitchen doorway to watch the master at work. This was the same position one was advised to take in an earthquake type of emergency, which this was not, but what the hell. Ever-confident Pedro started by chiseling off layer upon layer of paint that had built up over the years, covering my ailing outlet. He concentrated on the immediate area of the outlet itself but failed, and a big piece of the neighboring wall was chiseled off instead. The kitchen was unprepared for this invasion. The evident simplicity of the procedure was deceiving.

While the super attempted to remove the paint, he was on his cell phone talking in rapid Spanish. Pedro was an important man. The phone rang the instant he hung up. Most likely, these were drug deals being made, as this was a popular, respected way to pass time in our neighborhood.

A man of decision, Pedro fixed his fiery gaze on the wall and renewed his efforts. I could have sworn he gave off a little smoke. The unforeseen visual effect intensified. In a matter of minutes, a heavy miasma, grayish with a mustard-yellow tint, hung around the kitchen. Did I smell sulfur?

In a state of growing panic, I looked at his feet, half expecting to see hooves. Pedro was wearing paint-spattered sneakers, tongues lolling. Keeping his other dubious qualifications in mind, I could not imagine him as a fully licensed demon. Perhaps a trainee. *Muchacho del Diablo.* **

I could not watch any longer. My built-in curiosity, giving no warning, suffered a meltdown, while my built-in caution went into overdrive at once. May the force be with me!

Meanwhile, Mother and her home attendant sat on the couch side by side, quiet as two scared mice, demonstratively ignoring one another. The ringing silence hung between them like an executioner's ax, rusted and double-edged, ready to fall down and chop off a head. Whatever Doonyasha had done, Mother had fumed about it for hours. It seemed she had enough fuel to keep her going a few hours longer. The help's constant companion—a ten-pound bag of sunflower seeds with hulls, erect as a national monument—dominated the landshaft of the coffee table. Doonyasha's hand visited it with expedited rhythm, popping the hulls like firecrackers with her teeth.

** A boy devil. (Spanish)

"They'll clog your digestion, I said." Mother eyed the steady stream of seeds entering and empty hulls leaving woman's mouth, the silence broken as temptation prevailed.

Doonyasha chomped away: *hrroomvst, hrroomvst.*

"What a suspicious character." Mother addressed me in a loud half-whisper with a worried look, her hands clasped at her chest. "That's the face of a hooligan. How he stares at you, he's planning to rape you. Stay away, but keep a close watch, or he'll steal something. Why are you looking at me like that? I never liked him—a beer-drinking thief."

The other woman, an equally worried expression on her face, stopped chewing and nodded in agreement. Glances of complicity were exchanged. Here they were, Mother and Doonyasha, united at last, however brief it was to be.

The phone rang. I went to the bedroom to get it.

"Who was that on the phone?" Mother wanted to know when I returned smiling. "Why can't they leave you alone?"

"Rita called to say happy birthday."

"It's your birthday again? How old are you?"

"Forty, Ma. Forty."

"Forty and still irresponsible. To date a married man. Ay-yay-yay! I remember how much pain I was in on that day, giving birth to you, so you'd better not expect congratulations from me."

"When did you ever congratulate me?" I asked.

"Ah, the pain! Don't you expect a present."

"When did you ever give me a present?"

"And don't expect me to start."

Loud banging and rapid Spanish burst from the kitchen, interrupted by the cheerful sounds of salsa coming from Pedro's constantly ringing phone. There were two or three seconds of deafening silence, followed by a single deafening bang, then spine-chilling quiet.

Moving sideways like a crab, I inched my way back into the kitchen and could not believe my eyes. A new outlet was nested in the middle of the wall, dented and indecently bare in places. Happy birthday, Anna! A hostile smell of sulfur drifted in the smoke-filled air. No sign of Pedro anywhere.

A warm wave of relief began to spread from the center of my chest on its jubilant way to my extremities. I held my breath, poured a mug's worth of cloudy water into the teakettle, plugged it in, and paused to see if the overhead lights would flicker. The kettle coughed in protest and went quiet. In ten seconds it hummed and gurgled. I switched it off and plugged in the fridge. The refrigerator rattled, but then it always did. Hallelujah! Let there be light! I headed for the shower.

Half an hour later, I walked into the kitchen to celebrate the new outlet by making myself a cup of tea and saw that Mother was having trouble containing her joy. I had never seen her smile so widely. A happy Mother? What would it cost me this time?

"Who was that at the door?" I asked. "I heard the doorbell."

"I thought he was a Jehovah's Witness in his black suit," Mother began to relay the encounter. "But when I realized who he was, I told him to leave you alone." She pointed to a bunch of long rose stems sticking out from the garbage bin. "Sex, sex, sex—that's all you can think about. Oh, you should see your face—it's a corpselike color."

She squared her shoulders and kicked the bin, beaming as if the tinkling clatter brought her satisfaction. I gasped and ran to the front door, but Mother was faster. She turned the lock and blocked the exit with her body.

"You schizophrenic—you're going nowhere," she said.

I pushed her away and ran downstairs. She was a few feet behind me, sniffling and muttering something uncomplimentary. I saw David's back as he was getting into the cab.

"Wait!" I yelled.

He turned around, holding the door open, saw us, smiled.

Mother clutched my arm, dropped on her knees, and wailed, her voice high, her eyes sparkling. "Let the neighbors see how your old mother begs you!"

I jerked my arm free. David paled a little, put his hand around my shoulders, and helped me into the cab. The cabin smelled of air freshener and curry. The cab lurched forward.

"I don't believe I've made a good first impression," David said. "I didn't quite understand what your mother said. I think she said she couldn't move her bowels. Are you all right? You're shaking."

I was shaking with silent laughter, though I had a terrible impulse to wail.

"I thought I'd surprise you." David gently squeezed my knee. "I came to invite you to dinner."

He was dressed in an elegant black suit and a crisp white shirt. I was wearing a black T-shirt and jeans, and, as usual, was barefoot.

"Champagne?" From the brown paper bag, he pulled out a dark bottle and two champagne flutes. "Not every day you turn forty. Rita and Mark will meet us at the restaurant."

And we both began to laugh. The cab turned right on the light, and slaloming between delivery trucks and city buses on Broadway, we headed downtown.

forty-seven

bella and Michael had returned from another European tour—three countries, eleven cities, in seven days and six nights, informative and entertaining. Planes, trains, and buses, packed mostly with elderly couples. They had traveled with a Russian group and a Russian guide, with transportation, hotels, and tours included in the package. Bella and Michael adored packages. They went on each trip determined to fit a proper tourist image and have fun if it killed them. Their necks got a solid exercise, providing an excuse to complain of pain in their necks for a prolonged period, which was also an important part of the recreational program.

Michael had dragged a video camera with him to document life experiences encountered on the trip. He remembered to take the lens cap off, but he was in the habit of checking the camera settings often. He would fetch his reading glasses from his breast pocket, put them on, check the settings, and put his glasses away—all with the camera running. I was treated to shaky close-ups of carriageway's cobblestones in one of these European cities and someone's scuffed shoes. Michael had forgotten to write down which city it was, so we would never know. Then shots of random shaky buildings on a weird angle came up and stayed on the screen, only to be replaced by more shots of equally shaky buildings at disreputable angles, followed by cobblestones and scuffed shoes.

The movie plot was brilliantly uncomplicated. No one could recollect what the buildings were. I recognized Bella in front of the architectural wonders or bushes, patiently standing still for the video shot. That was, I recognized the clothing Auntie had worn for the trip and the overall silhouette of the short and plump female in navy-blue polyester jersey bell-bottoms, which only reached to the top of her ankles, exposing familiar multicolored socks. The socks belonged to Michael. They had been expropriated for the trip and added to her flowered socks collection, never to return to their rightful owner. Post-trip, these attractive hosiery items would complete her skirt-stockings-socks-Keds ensemble.

Her sunglasses hung around her neck on a multicolored cord. Bella's face was hidden under a wide-brimmed sunhat. On the soundtrack, Bella's voice commented on facts of life not necessarily related to events being documented by Michael at this moment in time. This movie, as any reputable movie, was two hours long.

They had the nicest recollections of public bathrooms they had been to, and sweet buns they had eaten, happy to share these experiences with me. I was enlightened by what they thought of locals in a country they visited, and the quality of dairy, cottage cheese in particular, how much they liked their bus driver, and the weather conditions during their stay. I was glad they had had a good time, but was terrified at the thought that they had brought me presents. I was already the proud owner of five souvenir ashtrays from foreign lands, all with the name of the city they had been purchased in printed in bold lettering, though the gesture of presenting me with ashtrays was no disguised hint I ought to pick up smoking. A sophisticated touch, they were useful containers to fill with things such as paper clips, fruity candy in rustling wrappers, or loose change.

I was also presented with a collection of seven imitation eau de toilettes—from Paris!—and a promised-to-grow collection of six cheerful decorative kerchiefs. I do not recall ever wearing a kerchief, but that was beside the point. As if I deserved to be advanced to something bigger and better, from this trip they had brought me a black leather jacket, lavishly decorated with enormous scarlet leather buttons and enormous scarlet leather appliqué work in whimsical patterns loosely resembling stars. Bella presented the gift with pride.

"Feel it. We were told it's *real leather*. We paid a lot of money for this gorgeous jacket, a lot of money. The moment I saw it, I thought of you. It's your size too."

The size was Bella's—twelve sizes bigger than mine in case I gained weight, after which the Stoics could stop complaining about my poor eating habits and enjoy life. ("It's painful to see how skinny you are! A sardine!") But I could not put it in the closet and forget about it. Auntie's daily routine consisted of strolling up and down the street for a breath of air, with frequent incursions to the local park. Wearing a sun visor during all four seasons, she promenaded after breakfast till lunch, after lunch till dinner, and, weather permitting, after dinner too. The chances of me not bumping into her were slim. She would notice if I wore something other than my new, expensive garment.

"Throw those rags away," Bella kept saying of my favorite black jacket. "That color washes you out and makes you look skinnier than you are. Nobody will say it to your face, but you're a laughingstock of the whole neighborhood. No self-respecting man would ever look in your direction."

I could not figure out how *not* to take the gift without committing a deep offense. The moment was palpably intense. My mind raced back and forth, back and forth, getting absolutely nowhere.

Then, a eureka moment hit me.

I faced Bella. "Can you try it on? I want to see how it looks on you to admire it in full. Please?"

Suspecting no evil, dying to show off, she put on the jacket, pushed the big bowl of wax fruit on the dresser a little to the left, picked up a hand mirror lying near the bowl, patted her hair, then fluffed it out and studied her face, turning left and right. Auntie then spat on her index finger, tilted her head slightly back, smoothed out her thread-thin left brow, put the hand mirror back on the dresser, and marched toward the nearest full-length mirror.

Drumroll, please. Eat your heart out, Jessica Rabbit! I was looking at a 3-D silhouette of SpongeBob SquarePants, all five feet of him. Bella apparently thought highly of her reflection draped in the bright outside garment. The floral-motif socks added a much-needed punch to the look.

"Do you think I could borrow this from time to time?" she asked.

Bingo! "Of course you can!" I said, trying not to laugh. Another *eureka* came up, so eager it almost choked me. "What people will say when you wear it to the park!"

Bella happily nodded in agreement. "Ah, I completely forgot to show you! Where's my head today? Look, it's for my neck, a personal massager. We bought it in Amsterdam."

She reached for her purse and took out an object—a ten-inch vibrator in psychedelic purple. Auntie's face was beaming.

Should I tell her? I thought. Nah. Let her have a little fun.

"Ask Mike what he bought," she said. "Go on, ask him. He bought a Ziploc bag full of herbs, which give a smoky flavor to foods. *Phew*, they stink, taste bad too, and give me a headache. But Mike puts it in his soup and is very happy. I'm happy he eats soup."

Go Michael!

As for the jacket, we lived in New York—a city of opportunities—and in New York one could express whatever one felt a need to express whenever one felt it. Since it was not considered entirely safe to inquire out loud, "Who moved the rock?" she would be all right.

forty-eight

mother stood still in front of the darkened, cracked bathroom mirror.

"I can't go to the doctor looking like this!" she said. "I look too old. My hair's all gray. I don't want to get old. I'm scared. About to die, and I haven't lived yet."

Her wrinkled face was not drooping, no—it was sliding off, halfway there, about to run away. It pained me to see her aged so much. When had it happened? My throat tightened. I hugged her.

She pushed me away. "What are you getting all mushy for? Leave me alone."

"Ma, today is a good day. The cast is coming off. We could dye your hair."

"Never dyed it, never will. Don't you argue with me."

"Have it your way."

She clutched my shoulder, examined my hair, smacked her lips. "Will it be the same color as yours?"

For the first time in her life, the dame had sacrificed herself for a beauty call—a historic moment. I wrapped her in my hairdressing cape, in earth tones depicting falling leaves, and positioned her on the toilet lid, where she sat squiggling, wriggling, and complaining as I applied the color. Then she sat with a pointy, aluminum-foil cap on her head, complaining and waiting for the dye to do its intended job. For the victorious finish, she stood under the shower, her head sticking out of a hole in the pale-blue, transparent garbage bag draped over her body to prevent the dye from staining her skin as I labored to wash the gunk off. The squiggling and complaining intensified, and water traveled into Mother's eyes and mouth. She spat it out.

"Stop splashing," she said. "You've got me wet from head to toe."

At some happy point in time, it was over. She had survived the ordeal. I blow-dried her hair, arranged natural curls around her face. She peered at herself with suspicion in the old mirror for a few minutes and said nothing, but her reflection, fifteen years younger, attempted a smile.

Later at the hospital, in an office smelling of disinfectant, upgraded Mother and I waited for her cast to be taken off—another historic moment, two on the same day. Her brow was furrowed as ever, her foot beating nervously on the floor.

"Listen carefully to what the doctor says," she said. "I know he wants to kill me!"

Dr. Adams walked in. Mother rushed to him, all smiles, glowing with enough luminosity for one to read a newspaper by. Her hand flew up to her temple and adjusted a curl.

"Doctor, I don't know how to thank you," she cooed. "You saved my life!"

The all-business doctor did not waste his smiles. He nodded his head in greeting, shook my hand, and removed the blue cloth from the side table. There, on sterilized gauze, were displayed the medieval instruments of torture, I am guessing the complete set. Mother stopped beaming and looked worried.

The doctor glanced over his treasure collection, grabbed a shiny thing in the middle—something not unlike huge garden scissors—and five minutes later the cast was off.

He was as serious as a statue. "The bone healed. Goodbye."

"Goodbye." I smiled.

"*Dr. Adams, Dr. Adams, please report to eight-oh-one,*" came over the public address.

It was official. She was healed, my job was done, my conscience clear. As for Mother, she and her home attendant could…(use your imagination please).

Mother and I returned home. I made her a cup of her favorite Lipton black tea with orange pekoe, just the way she liked it—the teabag briefly dipped once, then saved for future use. I left her in the kitchen to drink it in leisure, went to the bathroom, put on my makeup, came back into the kitchen. Seated across the table from Mother, Doonyasha shelled sunflower seeds with her front teeth: *hrroomvst, hrroomvst.*

"Let's pack your stuff," I said to Mother. "You've healed. Time to go home."

Mother inspected me from head to toe, brought her attention back to the cup of tea in her hand. She sipped the pale-yellow liquid and gave me sideways glances.

"Call Bella," she said. "She was looking for you."

"Why?"

"Ask her. She pulled a book off Mike's shelf. Behind it was hidden a piece of chocolate. She pulled all the books off the shelf. She found a lot of chocolate."

"And?"

"Nothing," Mother said. "Call Bella. Oh, and I told my landlord I won't rent from him anymore. Hannah no longer lives here. You have an extra room. Why waste money? I'll stay."

I jammed both hands into the front pockets of my jeans so I would not strangle her in front of a witness. "Don't worry, I'll call him and tell him you've changed your mind. Now, packing."

"I can't stand how profligate with money you are! Like money burns a hole in your pocket. And now more shame on my head—all dolled up. You just saw him a week ago. Stop running after him!" She stood up, sat down again, flicked her wrist. "Ay!"

Doonyasha dropped a Chinese slip-on, studded with tiny mirrors, off her disproportionally big foot. She scratched the bare calf of her other leg with a callused heel and shelled her seeds—*hrroomvst, hrroomvst*—her eyes as calm as a grazing cow. The chair creaked as she leaned back.

I went to the bedroom, pulled a suitcase off the top closet shelf. Mother trotted behind.

"Entangled with the married man!" she said. "He'll never leave his wife."

"He's getting a divorce." I placed the suitcase on the bed, opened it.

"You see—what did I tell you?—he's getting a divorce." She got excited. "First they get married, stamp out children, and then they abandon you, just like your father did years ago."

"You said *you* kicked him out." One by one I pulled Mother's skirts off the hangers, folded them in half, placed them neatly in the bottom of the suitcase.

She wagged her index finger at me. "Yes, I kicked that bastard out, but I don't remember him resisting much. Listen to me for once. This playboy of yours will never leave his wife for *you*. Take a good look at yourself. You're nothing. His wife is beautiful and rich."

I opened the dresser drawer, picked up the stack of Mother's folded shirts, tidied it up a bit, and placed it in the corner of the suitcase. Mother's eyes followed my every move.

"A man will never leave a rich wife. Forget it. Come back to your senses, throw him out of your head. Shame on you! Wash the floors here, it'll do you good."

I picked up the stack of Mother's vests, placed them near the shirts. The stack fell apart. I left it as it was. "That's it, Mother. That's enough out of you."

She crossed both hands over her heart. "I'm saving you a heartache. I'm begging you."

I picked up Mother's underwear and dumped it inside the suitcase.

"And stop kidding yourself," she said. "With your shortcomings and your character, he'll dump you too."

I tossed in her toothbrush, slammed the case, zipped it up. "Done," I said. "I'm off."

"Ay-yay-yay! Throw me out because you have no use for me. You'll be ashamed to look people in the face. I'll tell everybody how you treat me."

"Be ready to move back home tomorrow first thing in the morning. Ask

Doonyasha to help you pack the rest of your stuff, and you'd better start being nice to her."

And I left.

. . .

The old joke says it best:

A man comes to a rabbi.

"Rabbi," the man says, "we live in small quarters, my wife and I, along with my wife's parents and our seven children and another one is on its way. We're on top of each other all the time. Life is unbearable. Rabbi, tell me what to do."

"Bring in a goat," the rabbi says, "and come back to see me in two weeks."

Two weeks pass, and the man comes back to see the rabbi again.

"Oh, Rabbi," the man says. "I respect you almost as much as my own miserable life, but I'm not sure you gave me good advice. My wife—a smart woman, I should've listened to her— told me not to, but I listened to you and brought in the goat. Oh, Rabbi, the noise, the smell! What have I ever done to you? Tell me what to do now."

"Get rid of the goat."

And she was gone.

"La la la," I sang with no particular song in mind, twirling in space. "La la la." And still twirling. A cartwheel? A cartwheel.

"La la la." Hop, hop. *"La la la!"*

1 forty-nine

ove came out of nowhere. Like thunder in the clear sky, it encountered little resistance and enveloped me in its hot, protective mantle. Stealing a moment here and there, David and I managed to meet once a week. Time between the trysts, awaiting the next rendezvous, seemed suspended. The entire creation was filled with David's presence. It breathed a higher meaning into all things I did, gifting me with rapture at his being in my life, as fierce as his physical absence was devastating. I walked a foot above the ground. Life was full of purpose, and days flew by.

Time was our worst foe, formidable time, along with Mother. While time faked indifference, Mother thought our passion scandalous, watched my every move like a hawk affected with partial blindness. No blood had been spilled thus far, but soon the Hudson River would run red with it, diluting the sludge. Still, love, especially the crash-landing type, has been known to surmount obstacles hurled in its way, accepting no preconditions or boundaries. It cannot be restrained, cannot be held back. I am talking true love here. I had felt no remorse in sneaking out, or on occasion, busting out of the apartment like a teenager revolting, being the horrible harlot I was who deserved to suffer the consequences of her despicable behavior. The less remorse I felt, the more Mother tried to suffocate me with guilt, and in too short a time, the effect nearly reached its dangerous apogee.

Yet today was different. Today was the first day of my freedom. The siege was laid off, Mother reinstated in her place. My place was once again mine, my life returned to me.

For over a year, ever since he had moved out of the apartment jointly owned with Joanna, David had been settled in a hotel. Last month he had bought a two-bedroom on the Upper West Side with an eat-in kitchen and high ceilings—an amazing space. Despite efforts to be neat, he resided among barricades he had created for himself out of four thousand books—piles and piles, quite a few leatherbound—and tall stacks of *National Geographic* on the floor and any available surface. While his was a comparatively spacious two-bedroom, it was too small a place for such disaster, disorganized in an organized sort of way. He barely had any furniture except for two black leather couches in the living room and a king-size bed made up with black set of sheets in the bedroom (perhaps in tribute to his freshly reacquired bachelorhood). The majority of his stuff was still in unpacked boxes, some sealed, some opened.

The inquisitive visitor might glimpse at what I found safer to think of as good-quality reproductions of pre-Columbian artifacts in order to avoid tiptoe-ing around them. Next week his custom-made bookcases had been promised to be installed. For the third time now, David had heard "next week" while awaiting the carpenter; until then it was chaos. The books had taken over the space. The only room that felt lived-in was his office—his laptop in the center of a gigantic antique wooden desk, a green-glass banker's table lamp to the left, also antique, a picture of me in a streamlined silver frame to the right, an enormous black leather swivel Aeron chair standing by, and an all-in-one LaserJet printer riding on top of the black file cabinet on casters.

A cocker spaniel, Toby, the gleeful object of shared custody, ran around, busy, busy, busy licking guests. Rita, Mark, and I sat in the kitchen. The host en-countered pitfalls making us tea, though these snags were of the foreseen kind—while the cupboards were well stocked with different teas, some of them herbal, closer inventory revealed only two cups.

"We have a choice," David said. "I can run downstairs and get us some tea from Starbucks, or we can wait a little and order it together with lunch. Which would you prefer?"

"This place could use some curtains," Rita said. "Some furniture too."

"Lucky for you, Rita is a woman with ideas," Mark said.

David nodded happily. "Excellent. Ideas are indispensable. I would have cooked, but there are no pots or pans here. No dishes or cutlery either. So we'll not only have to order in, my treat, but eat from disposable plates with plastic forks. Hope you'll forgive me."

"We'll survive," Mark said. "But how will you be able to live with yourself?"

David smiled. "Remains to be seen. On a positive note—there're two bath-rooms, though I have no idea why would I ever be in need of a second bathtub."

"Where else do you think we'll be pickling cucumbers for winter?" I asked.

David smiled wider. "Ah, but then we'll need plates for that too, and I antici-pate to be entertaining often. Anna, do you know anything about pots?"

"Pots?" I echoed.

He nodded. "And dishes. And don't forget napkins. We must have napkins."

"Er...I can crochet a doily," I offered.

"A doily." He seemed to consider this. "Hm. I could learn to live with those."

"No doilies," Rita said. "Anna doesn't want them."

"Other people have the right to indulge their free-flowing creative impulses too, you know," Mark said.

"What about cups?" David looked at me with hope. "And plates. Are you likely to want plates?"

"Plates?" I asked. "I have some knowledge of how to use them, but not which ones to buy. But Lady Luck is on our side—I know someone who does." I pointed at Rita.

"What's going on?" David asked.

"Anna belongs to that almost-extinct breed of women who don't like to shop," Mark said.

I nodded and pointed at Rita again.

"Rita, would you mind helping me?" David asked. "I need help."

"I thought you'd never ask," Rita said. "How about tomorrow? Anna?"

"I'm babysitting," I said. "Doonyasha asked for a day off."

"Already? What about the day after?" Rita asked. "Wait, I'm with a client then. I could try to reschedule."

"Don't," I said. "I have little to contribute on the subject of dishes and will only be in your way. You'll save several hours by going alone."

"Which way is the bedroom?" Rita headed for the door.

David and Mark's eyes followed her out and then turned to me.

"Ps-sst!" came from the corridor. *You,* Rita mouthed, pointing at me, then motioning with her head for me to follow.

Single file and silent, we walked into the living room, and moving via the corridor, passed by the office into the bedroom. Rita went inside, while I hesitated at its entrance. She yanked me in.

"What are you doing?" she hissed. "He'll get tired of chasing you. So many women are waiting in line to snatch him out from under your nose like that." She snapped her fingers. "If David asks you to play house, you feel excited and play house. Go out there and be excited. Go!"

We returned to the kitchen just in time—the food had arrived, so we settled down to eat. I mused over Rita's warning, not following the surrounding conversation, and with a sinking feeling, caught David watching Rita. I felt a stab of jealousy and shuddered at the thought. But then David turned his eyes on me, his expression softened into such tenderness. I instantly felt ashamed of myself for thinking such things. And then, all at once, there it was again, the quickening of the blood.

He bent over to my ear. "She's lovely. Like watching live art." David looked into my eyes. "But sweetheart, to me there's no one more beautiful than you."

I nodded. But thorns of unwelcome jealousy pricked me all over, and to hide it I turned to Mark. Now I was watching Mark watch Rita. How could I not become paranoid under such incessant circumstances? I concentrated on my food, so when Toby came to investigate, it was too late—my plate was scraped clean, and he stood by with a forlorn look on his face.

David's phone rang. He glanced at the number, excused himself, went to another room, and returned visibly upset. "Joanna lost her keys walking on the beach and has only her cell with her. I have a key to the Bridgehampton house. I'm so sorry. Please wait for me here?"

"I have to finish my laundry," I said.

"We'll help you," Rita said.

David sighed. "Let me give you a lift. I'll drive right back. Can I come by later?" I nodded.

. . .

Rita settled on my couch. "This Joanna sounds like trouble to me."

"I've heard she's one good-looking broad," Mark said, taking the invisible pipe out of his mouth. "Enchanting, enchanting."

"Oh, well then," I said, the opposite of relieved. "Thank you, Mark."

"It's better to know your enemy than be up for an unpleasant surprise later on," Mark said.

"I wonder," Rita said, "if those keys are in her pocket and she's tricking David."

"Then she's playing a dangerous game," Mark said. "Those tactics are known to backfire. David doesn't strike me as a fool."

"Are you saying she is?" Rita asked. "I don't see David marrying a pretty cow."

"Maybe she's desperate," Mark said. "Who knows? If someone tells you he understands women's motivations, mark him off as either a perpetual liar or a total dunce."

"Say, did David ever tell you why they're getting divorced?" Rita asked me.

I shook my head.

"Why didn't you ask him?" she persisted.

"I want him to tell me on his own," I said. "He will, when he's ready."

"All I'm saying is that maybe it's something you should know about," Rita said, "and it could be used to your advantage. I wonder, who could I ask about it?"

"He bumped into me at Starbucks," I said, "on his way to meet with Joanna and her lawyer. I thought he was angry at the entire world, but no, it was her."

"Wouldn't surprise me a bit if she was doing this on purpose," Rita said. "If only a part of what I've heard about her is true...Well, don't panic, we'll figure out something."

. . .

Rita and Mark left. I put on jazz, lit candles, switched off the lights. On windowsills, on the low coffee table, on the floor, the flames flickered in unison in the velvety darkness, twisting and righting themselves, orchestrated by gusts of the late-spring breeze coming from open windows. Pale tongues of melted wax crawled down and pooled at the candles' bases. Twirling shadows danced on the walls. Louis's hoarse voice wove its magic, restraining those seeds of jealousy from budding for a moment and kindling a fire in my blood.

The doorbell rang. I pushed up my black-lace bra and opened the door. David stood there, beaming, so desirable. He stepped over the threshold, wrapped his hands around me, gave my ear a soft kiss, looked at the candles.

"Hope I'm the one you expected. My first time in here, and the first time we can spend the whole night together—a moment to be written into the annals of history. Celebration is in order. I brought champagne." David lifted a bottle and smiled, sending a series of light tremors throughout my body. He gently kissed me on the lips. "Would you mind if I stay the night?"

"I'd be angry if you left."

The song ended, the pause filled with the scratchy sound of an old record playing and the faint whiff of David's aftershave. We stood in the corridor a few inches apart; no need to hurry anything. Barely touching, the tips of his fingers brushed against my cheek. I shivered, surrendering. The sweetness of anticipation rushed through my veins, exciting the blood, warming the soul. I took a little step back, forced my eyes from David's face, glanced at the bottle.

"Dom Pérignon? You'll spoil me."

He leaned forward. "Nothing wrong with that. I was saving this bottle for a special occasion. I think tonight qualifies."

I put the palm of my hand to the front of his white shirt, felt the warmth of his body through the thin fabric. "I'm flattered," I said.

"It needs to be chilled." He took my hand in his, and we went into my dingy kitchen. With him in there, it became a different place, almost acceptable.

"We'll have to drink it from mugs," I said. "This was something I preferred to hide from you a bit longer, a terrible secret, but now it's out—I don't have champagne flutes. Don't bother to search for two matching mugs either."

"Looks like we'll have to buy a lot of dishes. Will you help me buy them?"

"I will."

"Any other secrets you've kept from me and want to tell me now?"

"Yes. I'd like to reveal that since it's almost midnight, I may turn into a small orange pumpkin, but that could be too much to spring upon one person without due mental preparation. Instead of verbal revelations, how would you like a guided tour of the place? As they say, 'One picture is worth a thousand words.' You never know—more secrets might be lying around in the open."

"Absolutely." David stepped toward me, closing the gap between us. A flicker of a smile shot across his face. "In the morning. For now I have something else in mind. Come here."

His hands pulled me closer, I felt him against me, already half-drunk from the sweetness of his breath. He ran his finger under the strap of my blouse, around my left breast, down the side of my body to the inside of my hip, causing a sweet ache to arise and swirl and stream up through my body. I raised my arms. David's eyelids half-lowered, he pulled the blouse over my head. His hand lightly traced the curve of my neck, then his warm fingertips moved down my upper back, filling me up with tremors. He unhooked my bra. I closed my eyes.

d avid went to another one of his meetings with his lawyer. He left without waking me up, and I overslept for the first time in years.

The morning began like any other. Though it had a suspicious colorless quality to it, it was way too early for me to attribute qualities to things. On this specific morning, even if it was color-deficient, I was making myself breakfast in the kitchen as usual, both cats in there with me. In our household they were responsible for creating cute obstacles underfoot. With Mother and Doonyasha gone, this place felt almost, but not entirely, like paradise. And with Mother not speaking to me, it was a well-deserved vacation. Mother gone! David…Morning. Mother gone! Should I write a little poem about it?

My whiskered buddies were already done munching on their crunchy food pellets. I dealt with some pressing cheese issues. Content Eve played hide-and-seek, just the black tip of her skinny tail showing from under the piece of fabric covering the presence of the forbidden, but handy and overused washing machine. She stayed undercover—the adorable little lump!—until the glorious moment when with lots of fuss, I would stumble upon her "by accident." If discovery was delayed, she made insistent, squeaky-snorty or cawing noises (a little bizarre for feline lexicon) to remind me that, enough already, it was time for her to be found. I would stick my hand under the cover to scratch Eve's soft underbelly in hopes it was Eve's underbelly and not some uninvited visitor's. Loud purring was produced in acknowledgment of a job done well.

Adam—a copycat—was pathetic at the hiding game. His entire body was exposed, sticking out from under the cover, hind legs far apart, his proud tail shooting up, his head hidden. Like a little child playing peekaboo, he believed himself invisible if he could not see you. I had already had the honor of finding Eve, and Adam was in the preparatory position to hide under the same discreet piece of fabric. Mother gone! David…Mother gone! The morning had begun superbly well.

Ring. Ring.

"Mama, how would you feel if Andrew and I went backpacking through Europe during the summer break? Would you be all right by yourself?"

"Sure. Go for it!"

"Yay! Love you." She hung up.

Love you too. I felt a lump swelling in my throat and sighed.

All right, breakfast. I took a bite of my sandwich, about to take a sip of tea to wash the sandwich down, when a sudden commotion made me look behind me. Adam, done with the hiding, was having an awfully good time with a suspicious object he had discovered, which from here looked like a dead rat, though giving it closer inspection might prove to be a mistake. I gulped down whatever was in my mouth, put the mug down and went to investigate.

It was a dead rat. My sails set on being happy today at any price, I refused to let anything spoil such a wonderful, motherless morning. I ignored pissed-off Adam, picked the rodent up by the tail, dropped it in the garbage, washed my hands.

The doorbell. A long, insistent ring. Was Mother back already? I opened the entrance door—oh, splendid—an importunate scarecrow. The backside of it.

My heart skipped a bit from excitement, though it was an oddest thing to get buzzing about. The creature turned around. Nothing thrilling, but Mr. Brown-spot, my honorable landlord, in person.

Even though he stood just five feet tall, he had mastered the art of intimidation well enough to be taken seriously. Was that plastic-covered, two-foot-tall black hat supposed to deepen the illusion of the owner's unconquerable strength? But if his primary intent had been to blend in with the environment, it had not worked.

This landlord had volunteered to come to me—an implausible event of astronomical proportions. This could not be good. The usual scenario was that I chased him and he would run away from me fast, fast, fast, simply to vanish into suspicious nooks and crannies. There were evil spirits among us. To think of it, and one could never be too careful, those suspicious gaps in the building could be hiding something with a long, sharp set of teeth, watching from the shadows, waiting for an unsuspecting victim to swim by. (Imagine, some adorable toothy creature affectionately nicknamed "Big Tooth" by its well-meaning mother, and who, being of a tender sort, would never disappoint its mommy and would attack interlopers without fail.)

The whole landlord quest would always have a surreal quality to it, like in a nightmare. I must confess to a slight sense of alarm that would nestle in the pit of my stomach and grow stronger as the familiar surroundings turned stranger and stranger in the growing darkness. One of those dreams where one would be running, running, lost and confused, through dark, abandoned streets full of rubble, along grayish-brown walls, black gaping windows, empty doorways, amid dead and carnivorous-looking rare trees—which way was out? And with the strangest terrain, a maze that kept shifting, with one's legs getting stuck in a gooey, unidentifiable substance with a foul stench—a bizarre backdrop. And one would want to scream, to call for help. The mouth would open, but no sound would come out, and no one could hear one scream. Nakedness was obligatory. A perfectly good recurring nightmare.

Mr. Brownspot was an expert in avoiding tenants who wanted something from him. Those nooks were seemingly gateways into other dimensions. I had followed him several times and had always ended up, aghast, at a creepy, dead-end brick wall. "Open Sesame!" did not work, I had tried it a few times.

But now here he was at my doorstep. Then it hit me. Silly me—he had come because I had stopped paying rent.

When repairs needed to be done, like the leaky ceiling in the bathroom so I could stop taking an umbrella with me every time nature called, he was nowhere to be found for years. But with a money matter at hand, he was here in two days, in person (plus the hat, of course).

Forgive me. Let us start closer to the beginning.

I was on a warpath. May the force be with me, please! Renegades Unlimited. My holy battle for freedom. Wondrous things afoot. A little revolution now and then could be healthy, even if overall they were not, and this was more of a family squabble than a real crusade, unlikely to cause bloodshed on a global scale. Under the circumstances, which had developed at an alarming speed, it was advisable for everyone in relative proximity to hide at once. I refused to consider myself responsible for what might happen to those who did not take my warning seriously. I was one of those unpopular people who, against all common sense and the sound advice of trusted friends, took no prisoners.

This unrest, as with any war in the history of humanity or elsewhere, had gotten a simple but flying start. It began with a book, in the wake of Mother investing all that energy into preventing my mind from being littered. I had told Mother off in no uncertain terms, and she had flown at me like a mad chicken. But away with garden-variety egocentrism! Time to rejoice! Over and done with, her complaints would soon be a mere memory. Or so I thought. Life is funny, just *too* funny sometimes. Mother would never let me get off easy. My blood would likely be involved at some stage, buckets of it. No secret that after that woman dies, she would surely come back to haunt me.

Mother's unconventional ghost, personal and intrusive, will not waiver from the path she had spent her lifetime treading. She will be dead set on continuing to give me step-by-step instructions (while my lifespan will be shortened by this repetitive action) and spitting in my face, but from another plane of existence. I will be unable to lock the door behind her and have a small break. Giving me a permanent chill, she will be there yapping incessantly, always within easy shouting distance, and nothing could be said about this inevitability that would raise my spirits.

I would not be surprised to learn that her ghost had mastered materializing at will to perfection. I would totally expect a scented and pale apparition, pulsating with cycles of phosphorescence, if a little blurry, to pop up every so often and linger around. I would be left with no choice but to call in a whole group of people in caftans called demonologists to clear the place while I had my fingers crossed. But knowing how stubborn Mother always was, nothing would ever be able to bring me comfort. (You cannot see me now, but I am holding both of my thumbs up and grinning a mad grin from ear to ear.)

Let it be known, if I was going to be building barricades, I was going to go all the way with it, till it looked like a Great Wall of China. It was my noisy downstairs neighbors' turn to pay for their crimes. Ah, the downstairs reggaeton. As if under penalty of an unimaginably horrific death for doing otherwise, the neighbors had to play it at top volume, as their stereo assumed the role of public announcement system. Those sounds were accompanied by the reverberating floors underfoot, the sensation of a shaking and booming bed, couch, and other odd pieces of animated furniture. The chosen times for such entertainment were closed to negotiations.

Lo and behold, after additional deep thinking, I wrote a new letter to Mr. Brownspot to follow the other unanswered letters, and stopped paying my monthly rent. Full of honor and hope, a short time after I set off on my perilous warpath, I was in slimy, smelly waters with a weight tied to my legs, unaware of most of the underwater currents and dangers.

The landlord spurned my offer to come in and stood in the moodily lit narrow hallway with its unappetizing pink walls covered in grime. The stale brown air was spiked with the stench of spoiled cabbage, pot smoke, urine, and industrial-strength cleaner.

"I got your letter," he said, amiable as a tarantula, shifting a toothpick from one side of his mouth to another and giving me a stare for longer than I was comfortable tolerating. "You know how I always take good care of people, and I wanted to satisfy your wishes"—he jutted his dandruffy chest forward like a pugnacious rooster who was about to announce dawn—"but my lawyers say I must take you to court. So nothing for us to discuss."

He picked a few teeth with the toothpick, left it alone, wrapping his mouth around it. He looked me directly in the eye and stopped blinking.

My knees got despicably wobblier by the second. There never was a dull moment in this place. I shrugged, only with one shoulder. Court was fine with me. Warpath. Wondrous things. The Force.

And so we parted on that bleached melodramatic morning. Do you think I should have gone through the initial acclimation stage to test-drive this new-and-improved-me persona prior to embarking on this perilous quest? Ah, well...This too would pass.

fifty-one

everyone wants a happy ending. She did not wait for the customary month of icy silence to pass. One fine morning Mother called. "I'd like to hear what you have to say."

This was a huge departure from her negative world of no possibilities. My old dream to make things good was revived. Humans could change if they wanted to, or if circumstances forced people to abandon their ways and adapt new habits. Would that belief remain a childish dream of a perfect world?

This could be a life-changing moment for both of us. An obstinate little voice in my head, which sounded a lot like my therapist, Alison, reiterated, "She won't change. You're wasting your time. Give it up—she won't."

In anxiety's clinging claws, I rehearsed the opening lines in my mind over and over, my words chosen with care. Language is a devastating weapon. I had no intent to cause Mother unnecessary pain. My wants were basic. How does one give up the hope of having a loving mother? What a funny thing, hope.

She came. The conversation was short.

"Ma—" I said in my friendliest voice, forcing myself to stand still near the open window.

"I never heard such nonsense in my life," Mother snipped, her usual mix of contempt and indifference on her face. "You were an accident. An accident. I should have had the abortion."

Ah, yes. My wants would remain untold. As to the fundamental need to be heard, which is forever lodged in a human heart, I was to be denied it always. No peace, no rest.

"I don't feel a pinch of guilt about anything," she announced. "You're delirious as usual. What have I done? How could a mother hurt her child? You've forgotten whose bread you've been eating for years. Tossing me aside because I'm old. You're a monster! A monster!"

Her voice trembled as if she were about to break into prolonged crying. Her eyes sparkled with cold rage. I, her property, was the root of the problem, always at fault. Her conviction was overloaded with the potential to cause nothing but misery, and it did. Slicing me open till the last drop of blood had been extracted, she would keep me dangling over hell, another small death. It felt like an execution. My desire to gain a doting mother was an image far removed from reality.

"Ay-yay-yay, why did heaven reward me with such a daughter?" The tremble gone, she regained her footing. "It's my curse, my cross to bear. But I'll show you what a good mother I am. I'm ready to forgive *you*. Beg for my forgiveness!"

The sky, about to drop, lost its color. I stood in a stupor, yet again unwanted and abandoned, and stared at the woman in front of me. A few yards of lead-heavy silence separated us.

I glanced at the round face of the clock. Five minutes to three in the afternoon.

The tingling spread from the ends of my fingers to all over my body. The quiver intensified, as if my legs were to give out on me. The unsteady ground breathed heavily, it rose and fell to rise again. The ticking of a chatty clock—the sole sound, soullessly ticking my life away—pulsated in my head. The fickle minutes slipped through my fingers, the epitome of impermanence, hurrying, running away, in endless, faceless multitudes. Where were they running to, or what from? My heart strained to leap out of my chest, pounding over my echoed, tormented breathing. The world was a vast, hollowed blur. The feeling of aloneness came as suffocating spasms, in waves.

And I remembered.

I am standing in a white enameled basin, the one used for laundry, and if I hug my knees and roll myself into a ball, I will fit inside it. I am four, maybe five. The room is cold, the water lukewarm. I am soapy and shivering. Mother slaps my wet butt, the *thwack* loud.

"Stand still," she says. "For God's sake. I'm not done yet."

She reaches for the soap, lathers up her hand, shoves her fingers inside me and rubs hard. Her fingers are big and rough. It hurts. My underpants will be stained with blood again, and she will slap me for soiling them.

"No matter how many times I wash you, you're still stinky," she says and rubs harder. "What am I going to do with you? Stand still, I said!"

I squeeze my hands into fists, clench my teeth. I must stand still, I must. But I begin to cry, push her hand away, "You're never again to touch me, you hear?"

Mother throws a small towel at me. "Dry yourself off! Ay, it's urine coming out of your eyes."

The memory faded. It is as if a wheel had turned inside me—nothing would make this memory go away. I stopped fighting and let the pain take me, all of me, in its suffocating embrace. The time suspended, and the desolation was so excruciating, I could hear or see nothing. There it was—a ravenous black hole, and I was sucked into it. The world was shattered into a million shards that swiftly flew apart, but were caught, devoured, and belched into nonexistence. A thin ghost of a line divided different realities where things came together but also parted. The loud ticking of a clock—*ticktock, ticktock*—impersonal, indifferent, sterile, washed over me. All the times and no time came together into one spot as if on the fine point of a needle, focusing on this split moment of separation. The string that connected me to the puppet master snapped. I was free of her.

The crystalline clarity came, imbued with a singular richness of insight that brought with it calmness. I was floating, falling, falling, floating, falling, gliding, utterly weightless, afraid no more. The eyes of my soul opened, and all illusions vanished at once—the mind-blowing discovery of the true nature of the relationship between Mother and me. All along, I had been obsessed, wasting my life proving to her something she had no interest in knowing, as she ached herself, drowning in fear of being proven inadequate, over her head in denial, and sabotaging the only thing she ever wanted—the affectionate bond with me.

She is what she is. That is why I am the way I am. The impossible heights to which she had cultivated her brutal narcissism could never in a million years let her anticipate that her strategy of emotional battering could backfire and that I would be willing to retaliate. I stepped out of the lifelong trance and into a state of awakening.

Enough forgiving—it got me nowhere. I wanted out. The illusive myth of a perfect mother? As a contrasting shadow was cast on the facts, it revealed that mine was tormented by her inner demons, and it looked like only death would do them part. The hope was gone, but I was still standing. It had not killed me. There was the strangest sensation between my shoulder blades, as if two wings were unfurling—now I could fly.

I felt an incredible lightness as a tiny seed of peace gently stirred deep in my belly. Thus began my road to freedom, out of the world of fantasy in which I had crowned Mother with a halo of holiness to create a more palatable appearance, as the reality was so unbearable, the resentment forbidden. Why was I so reluctant to relinquish the past? How thin my protective crust of excuses was. Layer by layer, the shadowy forms shriveled up, faded away. My emotions leveled out as objectivity entered the picture. The tsunami of pain had passed, followed by tremors of anger and hate, and in its wake my heart was tranquil. My lifetime search for unconditional motherly love in the midst of the more-than-conditional relationship came to an end, and in a flash I was given the gift of a complete cessation of suffering. No more lies to tell and to live; the moment of absolute truth outside space and time.

There was silence, and enveloped in its bubble, I was at peace with myself, knowing I wanted nothing else to do with this woman. The decision would come back to haunt me, torture me. I knew it would. Ah, the magic of acceptance—it would not be cured by a good night's sleep. I no longer cared what was right or wrong by the standards imposed by society. Never again would I be willing to go through such intense pain.

I found myself back in the room, standing still near the wide-open window. How much time had passed? I glanced at the enigmatic clock. *Ticktock, ticktock*—precisely as expected of a chronometer—filling an eternity, counting a different era this time. The minute hand still showed five minutes to three in the afternoon. Outside the window, the sun, ruling the day, was the only object of interest in the absurd azure vastness of a shamelessly cloudless sky. On this side of the wall, Mother looked at me with the mixture of contempt and indifference on her face, her hands on her hips.

"You'd better leave now," I said quietly.

"You're dead to me. You'll plead for me to come back, but I won't." She spat in my face and slammed the door on her way out, so darn eager to run away at a speed that would put a stray bullet to shame.

I did not lose a mother—I never had one. She had lost a daughter.

When some lucky people close their eyes to revisit their safe place—there it is, the image of their mother, her face turned toward her child with love, warming their heart through the hardships of life. When I closed my eyes, there was Mother's face, all right. The image burned into my brain with such force, I thought it would never fade away—her face turned toward me, contorted by contempt, the ever-bottomless pit of her contempt, her words drilling into my soul. "W-e-eh! *It's urine coming out of your eyes!* W-e-eh!" A childhood revisited, indeed.

A portal to a different dimension had opened up, and through a refining fire I had been lead to the other side for initiation into a higher order. Enough forgiving. No more reconciliation, but liberation from painful dependency. A path had been cleared, and the change was so profound that I would be unable to go back to the way it was. The price to get here had been high enough, and I had paid it in full. I was not about to categorically say "Never in my life do I want to see her again," but that is how it felt at that time. A lot could happen between now and never.

And something else came through, another revelation, seemingly small and yet so big. Had I really been fighting Mother's image of me, or the flaws in my own perception of myself? Where was my unhappiness stemming from? Who was my true opponent? With a thankful heart, it dawned on me that from here on, I could face my life unafraid.

ardly ever the silent type, tight-lipped Rita had patrolled the length of my living room for the last half an hour. I watched her from a couch, also quiet. "We need to talk," she had said on the phone. "Can I come by? Er…I'm downstairs." It was my job to be the perturbed one, and her normal state was to be the ocean of serenity.

"How about some tea?" I offered in a loud whisper, trying to be helpful.

It startled her out of her trance. Rita stopped marching, faced me. Hoarse and unstable, her voice gave away how nervous she was. "I'm not proud of what I've done. Please forgive me. I'll make it up to you any way you want. He slept with me but is in love with you. It's so very sad."

Rita, what have you done? I wanted to take off, but remained sitting instead. To run, run, but where? One could not run away from oneself. Cold sweat trickled down my spine. Numb with disbelief, I stared at Rita, who started pounding across the floor again, flushed, with blazing eyes.

A wave of rage rushed through me, washing away everything else on its path. If my boyfriend was in love with me, but had slept with someone else…well, such things were not unheard of, but what would I be fighting for? To think that happiness had been so possible, so close. I felt like the lead character in a trashy novel.

Ah, trust…The funny thing about it is that it is too fragile a thing to rely upon, too easily abused, too relentlessly shattered. Whether to trust someone or not was forever a touchy subject with me, with mistrust leading the odds by far. Not once had I thought it could come to this.

I suppressed the urge to flee and hide. *All right, make it quick*, I thought.

Feeling as though I were flinging myself into a yawning hole in a thick layer of ice that covered a river in winter, I asked, "How long have you been sleeping with David?"

"What?" She stopped pacing. "Why would I sleep with David?"

Oh my God! "Then who are you talking about?"

"Mark. He went to bed with me, but he's in love with you."

"Mark?" I tried to take things in.

"Twice. We did it twice. Maybe two and a half times. And I want to divorce

Patrick. I've thought about it for a while." Rita sat down near me on the couch. She was shaking like an aspen leaf.

I took her hands in mine. "Why didn't you say something?"

"I'm doing it now. You had too much on your plate already to worry about me too, sweetie."

"My plate will never be so full that you can't come to me with your problems."

"In the last three weeks, I've seen Patrick once. I was getting out of bed, he was getting in, and he just nodded at me, no kiss. No matter what I say to myself I feel unwanted."

I put my arms around her. She lowered her head on my shoulder, hugged me by the waist as if she were about to drop her guard and to give in to the blessed release of tears. One escaped. Lonesome, quivering, it froze just past her eyelashes, surprised it had been called into service. I wiped it off with my thumb. We held the embrace, delaying the moment of separation from one another. I could feel Rita's tension easing up a little.

"Is he having an affair?" I asked.

"No." She sat up straight. "It might be better in some ways if he was. At this point, what does it matter? I'm tired...so tired. If I'm married, I want that person to be around."

"For the moment, let's suppose you do want a divorce. It doesn't explain you and Mark."

"To remind myself how it feels to be desired. We're not in love, just having mindless sex. Are you angry with me?" Rita tapped her lips with a finger, looking at me expectedly.

"God, no. Enjoy! Mark's fame and glory are not without good grounds."

"Should I tell him you said that?"

"I bet he'd like to hear it. When are you telling Patrick? Will you tell him about Mark?"

"I don't want to hurt him like that. I'll ask him for a divorce the next time I see him. Whenever that's going to happen." She tilted her head to the side. "Let's not get into the details now. Just know, Mark still loves you."

"Oh, Mark. It's so sad. But why would he tell you? That doesn't bother you?"

"Nope. It makes things simpler. If I never broke his heart, it might save me a guilt trip later on." Rita smiled, but her smile looked forced and unconvincing. "It was supposed to be a one-night stand, a mercy service, if you will. Why did he tell me? Who knows why Mark's doing anything. Maybe he thought he could take on your other boyfriends. You have to give it to him, he's realistic in his estimations. Only now he feels he can't compete against David for you."

"Aha. *Realistic*. As a couple we were a disaster."

"I know. Mark knows it too. I guess deep down inside, he was hoping it was somehow possible. Until David showed up."

"Should I talk to him?" I asked.

"No. Let him deal with it himself. He'll be all right. So, you thought I slept with David?"

"I watched him watch you more than once. And today, with an opening like yours, what am I supposed to think?"

"It was a bit melodramatic. But I'm good. Just everyday trifles."

"I'd be in small, quivering pieces all over the place," I said. "I admire your calmness. Can you teach me to be like you?"

"I've tried. You'll die like this. So, where is that tea you promised?"

We moved into the kitchen. I filled the kettle with water, plugged it in. "David and I are going to Hamptons for the weekend," I said.

"Will his ex be there too?"

"Good God! You think? David said a romantic weekend for two."

The teakettle made happy gargling sounds.

"*Ooh là là*. I think he's head over heels in love with you. Mark and I crashed into him at the party we went to last Friday. The guy wouldn't stop talking about you."

"Strange. David never mentioned a party."

"He came in with a gorgeous redhead. They could've bumped into each other in the elevator. He spent the evening with us and talking to other people. She flirted with every guy in the room, fishing for his attention, even when she was glued to the eager ear of Melinda Gloss, throwing glances in our direction and giggling. Melinda—the gossip columnist, remember her?"

I shook my head.

"A stick insect with a heap of curls on top?" Rita said. "Large teeth, predatory eyes? We bumped into her at one of my functions? Was it last year? You said her face looked equine?"

"Did I?" I fiddled with the teapot. "I have no idea who you're talking about."

"She remembers you. If there are things you wanted to keep private from the all-seeing public eye, Melinda knows them. New York is the biggest small town in America. You and David are the hottest gossip of the year. You're public property, sweetie."

"Splendid. No matter how I present myself, the version told behind my back will always be more interesting. Should I be worried about the redhead?"

"Only if you absolutely have to be. Otherwise, what's the point? Come to the next party with me. We need to broaden your circle of acquaintances and have some fun. And David knows everyone who is someone in this city. There was a line of people waiting to talk to him."

"We'll see," I said.

The kettle whistled.

Rita took the plates out of the cupboard. "Tell me, this romantic weekend of yours. Can Mark and I drag along? I could use a day in a nice house on a shore."

"Behave. Hey, won't David suspect something if you and Mark show up together again?"

"Oh, he'll suspect nothing. He already knows about us."

"He never hinted a thing to me," I said. "So everyone knows except Patrick. Poor Patrick."

"Don't you start feeling too sorry for him. It was his choice to put us last as a couple. Are you in love with David?"

"Way over my head."

"Good for you." Rita gave me a quick, happy squeeze. "What are you planning to wear?"

"Hopefully nothing," I blurted out and felt myself blush.

"I thought I was bad. Now, why do you always have to hide the honey?"

fifty-three

She stood motionless at the wide-open window in the living room, as if unaware of our glances—waiting for something, poised, willowy and tall, she had folded her right arm across her abdomen, the left resting against her flawless, curved hip. The afternoon sun stopped to play with the fiery orange of her glossy hair, caressed her statuesque shoulders, then proceeded to flood the room with light. The tender color of her cheeks, a fragile sheen of innocence, the vulnerable angle of her bent head—young and perfect. Perfection personified, she was a vision worthy of being immortalized by someone great, be it in poetry, or prose, or stone, or whatever.

The disturbingly beautiful stranger in the white, flowing dress made out of light-as-air fabric regarded our approach with a faint smile, a mysterious melancholy in her look. Almost but not entirely matching the splendor of the white of her dress, the wind-billowed, translucent curtains created the best of frames around her with soft folds. They curved, quivered, flying up a little at the whimsy of a breeze, reluctant to fall down only to fly up again. The white of the nervous curtains—though this seemed intentional—almost but not entirely matched the white marble of the fireplace and the sparse furniture in the spacious room, which had been decorated with passionate understatement exclusively in shades of dazzling white, pristine as the frozen world of Antarctica.

Everything about her commanded attention. I could not speak for David, but this work of art—her hair ablaze, the insanely alluring daughter of Eve—seemed aware of the effect she had on me, and looked entertained by my surprised face. There was a certain air of astonishing self-confidence about her, as if this was a place where she belonged, as if the place belonged to her. Her left eyebrow arched slightly higher than the other on her perfect, Botoxed forehead, in the manner of saying, "Amazing, eh?"

It's decided then—when I grow up, I want to be her, I thought.

Amid this entire dreamy ideal, I could smell trouble arising in what had otherwise been an incomparable weekend, until this *crème de la crème* showed up.

For a split second, I let myself wonder if the woman was real or a vision that had conjured itself up in my overheated head. One could never know what a hot day, spent without a hat under the intense rays of summer sun, might make one see. I tried to suppress the idea of possible hallucinatory effects as ridiculous, but it refused to be brushed off and insisted on playing with my head a little longer. The warm, smelling-of-the-sea breeze gusted through the room, and the curtains leaped up and out, about to fly away into the blue, empty sky, higher, higher, longing to dissolve in it forever.

An oblong, caramel-colored blur ran into the house, yelped, and charged toward the apparition, the yelping changing to whining. Exaggerating the arc of her wrist, the semigoddess made a gesture, which could be interpreted by anyone intelligent enough to interpret things as a command to sit. The blur came to a sudden stop in front of the woman, emitted a mournful bark, sat down. In a flash it formed into a likable dog with amber eyes and a soft mass of silly curls, yelping gaily and making an awful noise with his tail whipping the hardwood floor. He could not stay still after the invigorating run on a beach.

Toby ran up to David, licked his hand, put his paws on my hip and licked my elbow, wiggling and whining with excitement, then hesitated as if he was about to run off to the kitchen, but lay down at David's feet, panting.

Based on the dog's reaction—why should I doubt his sincerity?—Toby had seen her too, but that proved nothing. Was not it true that dogs, cats, and other critters could see supernatural beings as clearly as ordinary humans?

I glanced at David. This lollapalooza was indeed a creature of flesh and blood—he saw her too, his face no longer aglow. Though she was one of those fashionable people, it was not a fond look he was giving her.

So she was not a vision or an apparition, and I knew who she was, heaven help me. How was I to compete with her? What did he see in a tramp like me?

· With an air of being forever perfect, she glanced at me. Sharp chips of ice burst out of her eyes and fanned around her, refusing to melt. A chill of dread rushed up my spine. An unspoken word, *perfect*, left a sour aftertaste in my mouth.

Vanish! I mentally commanded and snapped my fingers to fortify it.

"I'm Joanna," the vision in white said in an unparalleled musical voice, a voice one could listen to all day long without getting tired of it—angelic, with a posh British accent, a strained one, but strangely not off-putting. "David didn't tell you? I'm his wife. You must be Anna."

Oh, how nice. She had heard of me. *T'foo!* I spat, in my mind and not on a whitewashed floor. Things like that could ruin one's day. You know what? I hated her. Was it my imagination, or did that voice of hers sound like a cat in heat? No, it was still angelic. What a voice! Life was not fair.

She hardly moved. Only her lovely, thin arms performed a flying, bewitching gesture, folding across her chest—pure poetry in motion. Alas, finishing the exquisitely executed move, she miscalculated a little, gripping both arms with her hands tighter than intended. Her knuckles turned white, creating a contrast with her tanned arms. Joanna caught the mistake that same instant and relaxed her hands. She stayed right where she was and smiled.

"Yes, I'm Anna," I said. "David did indeed tell me he was married. He also mentioned getting a divorce. Was I in any way misinformed?"

"You're funny." She gave a short laugh, more like a single bark, after a moment of strained silence. Something behind that smile of hers, not so much seen as sensed, made me cringe. The chill crawled over the floor, filling the room, pooling into the corners. If only glance could kill.

Her knuckles changed to the color white again. "Hi, David. Did you miss me?"

"Why are you here?" David seemed calm. "It's my weekend at the house."

"Is it?" She smiled. I almost felt a breeze as she batted her eyelashes. "It's too hot in the city. You know how uncomfortable I get when it's hot, Pookie."

Joanna stretched some words, like a capricious young girl who knew she could get away with anything. Tasteful and understated, her elegant white dress gently hugged her foxy figure, leaving bare her provocative shoulders and arms. Etched into my memory forever will be her long, suntanned legs and her tiny, perfectly formed, feminine feet in delicate, strappy sandals, the kind of sandals that the queen of fairies, Titania, might wear, and in all probability had been wearing. Breasts, waistline, hips—all ideally proportioned, of course.

Here she was—the ultimate woman amid a flawless setting. A vision, indeed. All I had was "funny." She had not even meant it. Well, "funny," and an overabundance of sand where I did not exactly want it—never conductive for inducing a pleasant disposition with anyone—and the taste of a sunny, salty, and long kiss on a beach just moments ago.

"I could recommend a personal trainer," la Belle said, looking me up and down. "It'll take work, but he'll get you in shape. David prefers women in shape."

David winced. Joanna looked directly into my eyes with a not-quite-kind smile, which could be interpreted as almost concern with a very big effort. From where I stood, it was hard to tell if her tongue split in two at the end, or was it another one of those unfortunate illusions brought on by the afternoon light playing tricks with my mind.

A pox on thee! I thought.

"You're too kind," I said. "I'll take my chances with what I have."

I felt unpleasantly naked in my bikini; it was not much, but was better than nothing. I would prefer the protection of knight's body armor, visor down, lance in hand. I wanted her to disappear forever. It did not have to be overly dramatic, like in a puff of smoke or anything like that.

"Joanna, whatever it is, please stop." David came to my rescue, his expression closed off, fists tightened. "You'd be interested to know Anna's an excellent personal trainer herself, if you find yourself in need of one in the near future."

She lifted one dreamy curved brow a little and made a tiny movement forward, almost a step. "Are you going to offer me anything cold to drink after this murderous drive?"

"You're welcome to check the fridge," David said, a bit frosty. "You have to excuse us. We're about to shower. Let yourself out when you've cooled down enough. Bye, Joanna." He moved past her toward the stairway streaking up and up to the top floor, but stopped at the bottom, turned toward me, and smiled. "Are you coming?"

"I am," I said. "Bye, Joanna. A pleasure meeting you."

I turned to follow David, but glanced over my shoulder at Joanna. Her smile had faded, and she was looking at me with naked hostility.

David waited at the bottom of the stairs. He put his arm around my waist when I joined him, as he usually did. I put mine around his, and we went up the stairs into the master bedroom suite. Toby was the last one to start up the graceful staircase, panting and squealing, his tongue out to the left, his ears spread like airplane wings, which put him in immediate danger of becoming airborne. He was the first one to reach the landing and sprinted until he disappeared behind the door of the master bedroom, slightly ajar.

She would not plan on staying, would she? I crossed the fingers of my free hand and continued walking up.

fifty-four

She did not stay. I swear (with my hand over my heart), I was not upset. The sun, the everlastingly solitary traveler in the boundless emptiness of the sky poured melted gold over the ocean, and light fairies danced on sparkling crests. It slathered the highest-quality crimson, dramatic bloody reds, and fiery oranges over the endless vastness of the dome. Tired after a long day, but disciplined, the sun paused to contemplate its creation and added generous strokes of saturated royal purples to contrast the flamboyant oranges, all of this splendor mirrored and glowing and swelling and sinking into the burning waters. Then the hectic luminary ran out of time, and either on inspiration or out of desperation to do something else grand and meaningful before saying its final goodbye to this world and going away for eternity, as if awaiting total annihilation, it thought of correcting bird plumage, originally conceived and executed in an aristocratic snow-white-and-gray combo. The whole chaotic gang of unappreciative seagulls, yelling, bustling about, riding the wind, was stained an absurd hot pink, perhaps fifty-five birds all with wings ablaze. The diffused light of the weakening sun lingered a little as the fiery globe dropped below the edge of the world.

David insisted on cooking the meal by himself. I sat at the counter, feeling like I was inside one of those shiny illustrations in high-end designer magazines. The white of the wood cabinets, interrupted by the stainless steel of appliances, the white of the granite counter, the iridescent white of glass backsplash tiles, the white of the marble floor. What was it with this woman and white? The northern kitchen wall incorporated built-in display cases, which reached up to the ceiling, a total of three in number. Two of them contained sets of exquisite dishes in white, and the third, a whole herd of cow figurines, in white with black spots. A hundred cows, bigger and smaller, stood in rows, all silent, all facing due east. Toby lay on the floor on his side, his head resting on my foot.

David took something bundled up in wax paper out of the fridge and unwrapped it. "How do you feel about redecorating this place? I could handle color for a change."

"I wouldn't know where to start."

"We'll hire a designer." He put thinly sliced shallots in a hot skillet with sizzling butter, sautéed them for a minute, added crushed garlic cloves and sweet red pepper to be sautéed for another minute, then added tomato, celery, and fennel, stirring the vegetables with a wooden spoon.

The Saint Bernard of a cat, white with black spots and a boxy head, materialized out of thin air. Toby's tail thumped the floor once, not overenthusiastic. His head never left my foot, his eyes remained closed.

The soundless cat yawned, jumped on the seat right next to mine, and looked at me with round yellow eyes. One cheek was white, one ink-black. His black tail hung straight down from the seat, pointing at the floor. The cat's front paws had trouble meeting in front and stuck to his sides. His rounded belly overflowed to occupy the entire seat, and his padded flanks cascaded down in a soft multitude of folds, his hind paws hidden underneath.

"Meet Tinkerbell." David tossed cubed fish fillets, lobster tails, and clams into the pot. "Officially Joanna's, but the neighbors befriended him. He eats and sleeps there and comes to visit here on occasion. I think he likes you."

"Does he? How can you tell?"

"Out of all the empty seats, he chose the one next to you."

"He reminds me of something." It was on the tip of my tongue, but in the labyrinth of my mind, a slippery image swirled around and flickered, avoiding recognition. "Hi, Tinkerbell."

I scratched him behind the ear and was rewarded. The yellow orbs became rounder, and the cat produced a continuous, creaky sound that, with a little push of imagination, could be taken for purring.

"Kitten, don't get seduced by her charm. Joanna can be gracious and affectionate if she wants, but she's devious. She can make you feel she's your best friend for life five minutes after you've met. She possesses a magical power of persuasion. I still don't know how we ended up married." David tossed the salad into a big china bowl with two oversized spoons. His nostrils flared as the muscles of his jaws knotted. "She's worse than the Bubonic Plague. I don't want you to get hurt. I don't know where and how, but I do know that one way or another, she'll try something."

I was too relaxed to worry about Joanna, yet it would be wise to give this more consideration later on. So much could go wrong in a short amount of time.

Tinkerbell stared at me with the eyes of phosphorescent yellow, expressionless and unblinking—not unlike the cold stare of a snake watching its prey, taking its time, aware the victim had nowhere to run.

I scratched his head, soliciting another round of rasps. A white-with-black-spots snake. A clear image jumped into my mind, connecting with the animal sitting next to me.

"He looks like a cow!" I blurted out.

David snorted. "That he does."

The divine smells coming from the pots bubbling and sizzling on the stove made me salivate in profusion, on demand, like one of Pavlov's obedient dogs. The business with Joanna did not pack enough power to ruin my appetite.

David—the magician who had brought such a bouquet of aromas into existence—turned to the stove, removed the lid from one of the pots, and used a fork to squeeze half a lemon over the mix. He added white wine, saffron, and orange zest, crushed thyme between his fingers, and threw that in there too. "Bouillabaisse, my specialty."

He replaced the lid, then turned to face me, looking concerned. "I'm sorry you've gotten involved in this mess. Promise, no heroic gestures. Don't feel obligated to tolerate anything. And, kitten, I'm serious. Joanna will stop at nothing. She's never been burdened by keeping to the rules of fair combat for moral reasons. You can't even buy her off when she's got fire in her heart and the glow of revenge in her eyes."

He took the lid off again, stirred the contents of the pot with a big spoon. The cat vanished. Toby jerked up and wandered off. The fat seagulls quieted down. The shadows deepened and elongated. The only sound from outside was a soft, unobtrusive murmur of surf coming through the open French doors. For a second I thought I saw a face hiding among shadows, peeking inside. A minute feeling of strange lethargy overcame me, rendering me unable to move.

I took a lung full of air and slowly let it out. New life flowed into my limbs.

"She wants the world at her feet and on her terms. Her parents never said no to her, and that's the result." David opened the cabinet door, looked inside for a long minute, slammed it without getting anything, opened another, turned to me. A reddish flush spread across his cheek and jaw. "She must be desperate to come here today. I wouldn't worry about the physical violence, but what she might do instead…well, that's the fuzzier area. I'll do whatever I can to protect you. All contact will be brought to a minimum. Still, I worry she'll have no trouble slipping through my guard to get to you."

He tasted the salad, reached for the saltshaker. "Needs more salt. Dinner's ready. In any event, don't be fooled by what transpired here today. She's highly intelligent and a deadly adversary. I've seen her in action. If at any point in time, you feel like hitting her over the head with a shovel, you have my blessing."

"Do you think she'll be back tonight?"

"No. She accomplished whatever she wanted to accomplish in her first scouting mission. And if she decides to rejoin us, I locked the front door from the inside. I'll lock the back doors later. Hope my forewarnings didn't spoil your appetite, or that you'll lose what little respect you have for me after today's incident."

"Do you think I should?"

He stopped stirring the contents of the pot. "No, no. Are you ready to eat?"

"Famished," I said. My stomach growled.

David smiled. "Give me your plate."

I handed him soup bowls, and he put a thick slice of toasted French bread covered with rouille into each one. "There's a surprise for dessert," he added.

"What is it?"

"A surprise. Here's a little preview for you." He pointed at a fuzzy, lopsided, medium-sized peach on a countertop. "Grew it myself. There were two of them on the tree this year, but I suspect the neighbor's boy stole the bigger one. He'd been eyeing it."

"I've stolen food," I blurted out. Then, to cover it up, I shrugged. "A long time ago." Why was I telling him this? I never told this to anyone. My face was burning up.

"You did?" David regarded me with interest, but did not look like he intended to stone me.

"Back in Moscow, when the lines for moving into state apartments were years long, the illegal renting market had its hour of triumph. I was renting a corner of a room. My salary was next to nothing, and my entire engineer's paycheck went toward the rent. My landlady always cooked too much food for herself and threw it away a day later. To throw away food! When I was too hungry, I'd steal some. A few times. I didn't take much."

"My poor kitten, you've been through a lot," David spooned up the soup from the pot and brought the offering to my mouth. He held one hand under a dripping spoon. "Careful," he said with tenderness. "It's hot."

I am happy to report the food was scrumptious. If you were wondering, we had a chocolate truffle cake with raspberries for dessert. For those of you with dirty minds who thought that by "dessert," David had meant *bow-chicka-wow-wow*—got your attention, did not it?—you were absolutely right, but that came later, after the cake. We made love and fell asleep, deliciously exhausted.

I awoke in the dead of night to the lulling whisper of surf and a repetitive trill of crickets. From the bed, if I stretched my neck, I could see a secluded spot among the stillness of the dunes and tall grass, illuminated by a full moon. The fickle moonlight flooded the entire world with insane amounts of liquid silver, sneaking up on unsuspecting lovers as it had since the beginning of time and would continue to do forever—confusing the blood, planting the magical seeds of love deep into innocent souls, enthralling them with the unbearable sweetness of longing fused with the burning heat of all-consuming desire. Pools of boiling light alternated with thick shadows that moved from the ceiling to the walls to the floor. Disordered and slow, they transformed the room into a forever-enchanted land. Everything was possible, everything. It was so easy to believe it at the present. Now and then crossing the face of the moon, rare, weightless clouds floated high in the velvety blackness of the sky studded with the flickering stars. In all this quietude, I sensed a storm nearing.

"Why aren't you asleep, kitten?" David whispered. I felt his hot breath on my cheek. It quickened a little.

"Storm is coming."

"It feels right to be with you," he murmured. "I don't want this to end. Ever." He moved closer to me. His lips were soft and surprisingly a little salty.

The ocean breathed under the chattering stars. The euphoric moon was suspended high above. The lazy surf whispered something as it rolled in, tender in its caress of the naked sand on the beach, warm from the day's accumulated heat. The pale sand answered in a quiet rustle, held in strong embrace, willingly giving its warmth to the greedy waters. The fragrant breeze shifted direction, bringing in freshness. It rolled in, insatiable, gaining momentum and strength. Powerful and controlling, it scudded the hordes of thickened clouds, swirling and submissive, over the dark waters toward their final destination, tearing the formation apart and thrusting it together in a different order.

In the strange silver light of lightning, a ghostly show of menacing madness dropped down from the sky. Impermeable sheets of rain sliced the darkness. Hell opened up to swallow the earth at the end of the world. Thunder exploded like a thousand firecrackers. In this drowning world, nothing else could be seen or smelled but the rain. A handful of drops blew into the room and onto the bed. Heavy frothing waves crashed hard against the shore, splattered around, impregnated the air with bitter saltiness, then retreated away to return with renewed vigor to crush and splatter, again and again.

In no rush to drift into the kingdom of sleep, we lay there savoring the magic. The rain slowed, stopped, moved away. A thin ray of light entered the room, weaving an eternal spell, flickering, dissolving, arising again from nothingness. It erased from the senses the concept of time, made it blissfully nonexistent, shattered all the realities except for the dazzling splendor of one—the reality of love. The storm dissolved, and the crazy moon returned to the cleansed world to reign with renewed, indestructible might among the mad shadows, spilling silver everywhere. Eternally mysterious and forever silent, the shadows danced around us, bewitching, entwining, to untwine again in an instant. The unhurried, soft breeze flew into the room, taking charge like the master of a house, and brought a welcome coolness with it.

My head rested on David's shoulder, my cheek crumpled against his chest, his arm wrapped around me. According to yet another theory—one of a multitude of my unproven ones—it was the coziest spot in the whole wide world.

David placed a tender kiss on my forehead. "Do you remember how we met for the first time?" he asked. "I acted like a jerk."

"Mm."

He pressed me a little closer to him. "I was angry and scared of you coming into my life when it was such a mess, when I was such a mess, until I realized it was a blessing—you coming in the midst of chaos. I was terrified by how accidental it was, that it might've never happened at all. Did I ever tell you how grateful I am for you coming into my life? You aren't planning on disappearing any time soon, are you? You'll stay with me forever, right, kitten?"

I lifted my head a little, kissed him on his neck, and burrowed my face into the welcoming depression. "Yes, David, I'll stay with you forever."

"This is your favorite spot, isn't it?"

"Mm…It feels safe here."

"Stay right there," he said, and hugged me tighter, his voice gentle. "I want you to feel safe and happy. I love you, Anna."

fifty-five

two days had passed in a warm glow of happiness. As I settled into my own apartment, my old routine felt new and exciting. And no dead rats lying around.

The phone rang in the middle of the night.

"Anna! My dear, dear Anna! Is it you? I can't believe I'm talking to my long-lost daughter. My little girl, it's me—your papa. Anna? Speak up, I can't hear you."

Papa? Papa. Papa!

"I looked all over the world for you," I said. "How are you?"

"Life goes bit by bit. I'm in Moscow. A man from HIAS called and said you were looking for me. He gave me your number, and here I am. Is your mother alive? I only have good memories of her. She was a kindhearted woman."

Eh? I thought. *Is he* my *papa?* "I know nothing about you," I said.

"Not much to know. After Galina, I met Alla. For thirty-six years she yelled at me. I divorced her. But single life is no fun. I took a new wife, Svetlana. We must meet. Send us an invitation.—Coming!—You can be proud of me. I'm a businessman.—I heard you the first time!"

"What?" I asked.

"Svetlana is screaming this conversation is expensive.—Coming, I said! Stop yelling! I can't hear what Anna's saying!—What did you say?"

"Me? Nothing," I said.

"Well, bye, daughter. Call me tomorrow."

I dialed Rita. "My father called! He's a businessman in Moscow. He asked for an invitation for him and his newest wife to come to New York."

"His *newest* wife?" Rita yawned. "Sweetie, all you need is two more people on your neck. Don't get all emotional and don't do anything stupid. And go to sleep."

. . .

My phone chirped. A text message.

My sunshine, why do I have to wake up without you? Can't wait till tomorrow.
—D

■ ■ ■

I took the postcard out of my mailbox—it depicted the Eiffel Tower piercing the sky.

Greetings from Paris! Oh, Mama, you must see it. Nothing you ever read, or heard, or saw on TV can compare to the real thing. Wish you were here (oh, but I do!).
Love, H

■ ■ ■

"We lived together for half a year," Father said. "Galina never liked how I did things. I left. I thought she was tricking me into staying when she said she was pregnant. I returned a year later."

"What made you come back?"

"Alla and I had Alyosha. I came to ask your mother for a divorce. You were six months old. I saw you for the first time and changed my mind. I begged Galina to take me back. Your grandpa kicked me out. I still have your baby picture. You had the most beautiful smile."

"Have you ever tried to find me?" I pressed the receiver closer to my ear.

"I'm not the kind of person who goes looking for people. But I'm so happy you found me."

■ ■ ■

I've been bewitched. When I sleep, you're in my every dream. When I write, I see you in every line. You're in each one of my thoughts. Please have dinner with me tonight?
—D

■ ■ ■

"You had an aquarium with red fish?" I laughed. "I had an aquarium with red fish as a kid too."

"I remember everything as if it was yesterday," Father said. "We lived near the Paveletskiy Vokzal for fifteen years in a two-room apartment, the four of us and my mother."

"I was told you moved to another city...but you lived three blocks away from my school."

Adam smelled unrest, jumped onto my lap to investigate, pressed his front paws against my chest. His cornflower-blue eyes leveled with mine.

"Life was hard for me at that time," Father said, his tone hinting at instant absolution. "I'm sorry our lives separated. I dreamed about meeting you one day."

■ ■ ■

I yearn to see you outside of my imagination. I yearn to touch you, hear your voice, taste you on my lips. Three days are too long a time to wait. I'll gladly submit to anything you might wish to put me through, but please find another way to torture me besides your absence.
—D

■ ■ ■

After Mr. Brownspot's unambiguous threats to take me to court, I found myself facing a judge. I was ordered to pay the rent and the landlord ordered to make the repairs. One gavel strike later, the case was closed, justice done. I was facing the thrilling prospect of living out of boxes for weeks—perhaps months since the renovations crew was substandard—using the public bathroom at the nearest bus station ten city blocks away, ordering bad Chinese takeout or bad pizza (there were no other delivery options), and seeing the entire place in shambles, with the prospect of a shoddy living space afterward.

The city housing inspector came to mediate the differences in opinions. The orange-brown watermark on the bathroom ceiling, shaped like Lake Huron seen from space, spilled into the living room, the drippy ceiling partially collapsed. I insisted that anything leaky must be repaired. To keep the controversy alive, Mr. Brownspot disagreed. We argued about nonfunctioning radiators, nonclosing or nonopening doors and kitchen cabinets, broken windowpanes everywhere. The city inspector breathed in the mildewed air while his eyes moved from me to the landlord, as if judging a ping-pong match—*pick, pock, pick, pock*—not letting a little white ball out of his sight.

I would say a word, the unwavering property owner five. The list was long. The majority of it had been here when I moved in, but back then he had smiled more often while he had tugged on the bundle of twenties in my hand, swearing to fix up everything. "Two weeks." He had shifted the toothpick from one corner of his mouth to another and pocketed the deposit.

Two weeks long gone, then twenty-two, and here we were, five years later.

■ ■ ■

*Ya lyublyu tebya. * You left and the entire place became lifeless. It seems as if every object is longing for your return. I long for your return. Why do we have to be apart? Pls. advise.*
—D

---

* I love you. (Russian)

■ ■ ■

"Why did Grandpa ask you to leave?"

"Bella. Bella was behind it," Father said. "She needed me out of the picture. She was infertile. Michael always wanted a child. You were born, he loved you. Bella knew if your mother and I moved out, Michael would leave her. You were the guarantee that he'd stay."

■ ■ ■

Everyone was here again—the city inspector, Mr. Brownspot, his plastic-covered hat, and his repairing crew, i.e., Pedro, sans assistant. The moment was upon us.

"Look, everything is minor! Why is she complaining?" the landlord whined, bobbing up and down with either the excitement of a bloody fight developing or the anticipation of a favorable judgment that would shut me up for good with minimal expenses on his side. He sized up the nasty-smelling wall covered with slimy blackish-orange mold and squinted one eye, sending the unsightly wall a look. But a wall was a wall. It refused to disappear or clean itself up, finding itself in an argumentative mood today. The wretched thing looked smug, enjoying all the attention since I had not ignored it so much as very quickly run by it for all these years.

The inspector seemed unimpressed with the landlord's speech. "The repairs?" he said to Mr. Brownspot, clarifying the issue. "I'll give you two weeks. I'll be back to check on progress."

■ ■ ■

If you don't want to stay in my place, why don't you at least let me pay for repairs? Let's hire professional construction workers instead of your clowns. I respect your independence, but please reconsider and let me help.
—D

■ ■ ■

I took the postcard out of my mailbox—the La Sagrada Familia, Antoni Gaudi's unfinished cathedral piercing the sky.

Greetings from Barcelona! To think that humans were able to envision and build such a beauty. Andrew is in heaven. Miss you a lot.
Love, H

■ ■ ■

The city inspector was a man of his word. He returned in two weeks. The repairs were nowhere done. "Replace all doors, patch all holes," he said to Pedro. "Replaster the ceiling and paint the entire kitchen. The bathroom?"

We all squished into the bathroom to stare at the absent tap in the shower-bathtub combo. The silence was filled with Bernardo's huffing and puffing, along with a steady drip from the ceiling—*plyamp, flep, flep, plyamp, plookh.*

Pedro hiccuped, slapped his pockets, swore, crossed himself. Bernardo monkeyed the gesture, produced a used tap out of one pocket, a piece of pipe out of another. He slapped his pockets again, went rigid, and looked at Pedro with the devotion of a dog.

I handed the super my measuring tape.

Pedro grabbed the offerings, measured a tap and a piece of pipe, muttered in Spanish, and made a cut—two inches longer than needed.

The inspector scratched his beard.

Pedro swore, screwed it all to the wall anyhow. The creation began to dribble right away to complement the ceiling choir—*plyamp, flep, plookh, blyoop*—reminding me of Brothers Grimm's enchanted forest. To complete the illusion, two bad witches nested in the cave below.

Weeks passed. The place looked like it had been hit by a tornado.

◼ ◼ ◼

The irony? I had not heard from the man in twenty-something years, had longed to hear from him, and now when he called, I was not happy.

"So I have siblings?" I asked. "When am I going to talk to them?"

"Yes, Alyosha and Alyona," Father said. "But why rush things? Have patience. About that invitation—send it to me while I'm still alive. I have Parkinson's. I dream about seeing America, New York, the Statue of Liberty before I die. Come, Anna, send us the invitation. We'll be a family."

Blood is thicker than water, I thought, feeling its mighty pull.

I dressed and headed downtown to the Department of Immigration to fill out the necessary paperwork that would guarantee Father and wife number three an all-expenses-paid stay in America, the land he dreamed of.

◼ ◼ ◼

Joanna will sign the divorce agreement if I give her the house in the Hamptons. I said yes. That's all I own, but I'll happily give up everything to be with you.
—D

fifty-six

david arrived in a strange mood. For the last three hours, he had pinballed from room to room, picking things up, putting them down, drifting off. I silently waited for him to come to me, as it was useless to question him till he was ready to talk.

He meandered into the kitchen when I was doing dishes. He picked up a towel, dried a plate, put it down on the counter, picked up another.

"Joanna called today," David said. "She wants to have a baby."

"Oh? What's wrong with that?"

"For years she was adamant about not having kids. I had to respect her wishes. Now she's gotten this idea in her head I need to father her child."

"Oh…oh…and you? Is that something you'd be willing to consider?"

"I always wanted to be a father. We might as well talk about it now. Would you want to have a child with me?"

Chills ran up and down my spine. "Aren't we both too old for that? David, *I'm* too old to bear children. What if there's something wrong with the child?"

"Why does it have to be something wrong?"

"The older the woman, the higher the chances."

"We could still try, right? Or we could adopt?"

"A child is a huge commitment."

"Meaning you're not ready to commit?" he asked.

"I don't know. This is so unexpected."

"Then let me ask you this. Are you ready to commit to us? Would you move in with me?"

"Move in? Please, David, I need time to think."

"Is that a no?" he asked.

"What if you get bored with me and leave?"

His face went blank. He went to the entrance hall. I followed. David put on his shoes, opened the front door.

"Are you upset with me?" I asked. "I can tell when you're upset."

He sighed. "I have a plane to catch in the morning. Three weeks? Himalayas?"

Something ice-cold tugged at my heart. I had trouble catching my breath.

"Don't go," I said weakly with a sense of sinking.

"I have to. People rely on me. We have to help erect a school, then deliver the equipment to build a small hydroelectric power station, not to mention bring clothing and school supplies. Those mountain people have no electricity. No cell towers either, by the way, so my phone won't work. We'll have a satellite phone, so I won't be out of touch."

The sudden sense of doom and disconnection was so strong that I felt woozy and began to sweat a little. I took a deep breath, wiped my brow.

"Don't go," I said again.

David shook his head. "I have to go. We'll talk about it when I'm back. All I'm asking is that you give it some thought, all right?" He gave me a peck on a cheek and left.

■ ■ ■

I unwrapped a crunchy sheet of waxed paper, picked up a knife to spread my favorite Roquefort on a fresh French baguette. The aroma of the ripe blue cheese hit my nostrils, and I rushed to the bathroom and threw up. I had puked every morning for the last week. Or had it been longer?

The thought, *Can I be pregnant?* wandered into my mind, to be chased by another: *How can I be pregnant when we were so careful?*

■ ■ ■

The edge of the bathtub was cold against my bare thighs as I stared at the pregnancy test strip with the double red lines. My hands shook. I was scared. Nauseated too. My thoughts whirred, focusing on nothing, like fragmented frames snipped out of a film. How happy David was going to be! This reminded me—I should have heard from him by now. I called David's cell.

"This call can't be completed at this time. Please hang up and dial again. Thank you."

The most majestic place on earth, but mountains are hard to trek, especially with all the equipment they had to drag. What if something had happened? *I'd be notified. I was David's emergency contact,* I thought. My heart went cold. I tried not to think of it. I called David's cell again.

"This call can't be completed—"

A whole army of anxiety ants marched up the back of my neck. Oh my God, I really, really wanted this child! Yes! What joy! I smiled idiotically.

■ ■ ■

The computer beeped. An incoming e-mail, and another. Nothing from David.

Six weeks of total silence. Why was he silent? I felt the dread rise and started to panic, but was interrupted by a loud knock on the front door.

I opened it. Mrs. Goldfarb silently handed me two newspapers, gave me a reassuring pat on the shoulder, and shuffled back to her apartment.

I looked at the paper on top. Under the headline, *Breaking news!* and taking up half the front page was a color photograph of me in a bikini, sunburned and covered in sand. I was bent forward to pull the Frisbee out of Toby's jaws. My boobs were more out than in, my hair disheveled, and no makeup. David grinned behind me. It looked like his hand was on my buttocks. The caption said, *Interview with Joanna Cooper, the wife of Pulitzer Prize-winning author David Cooper, on page two.* I felt ghastly, ice-cold fingers squeezing my heart.

I opened to page two, my eyes skimming the text:

The ENQUIRER:…To have the affair developing so boldly in front of you.
JOANNA: Yes, Dianne, I was in hell. She was his personal trainer. He trusted her to behave as a decent human being and she seduced him.

French fries! I thought, and was at loss for what else to think.

JOANNA: We tried to conceive for years, but nothing worked. We got tired of trying, became irritable. And then her. She's a trashy sort, not someone he'd normally pay attention to, but I guess she showed up in the right place at the right time.
The ENQUIRER: Is this her in the picture? A beautiful woman.
JOANNA [with a quick laugh]: If you overlook the vulgarity factor. But he came to his senses and we're trying to conceive again. David told me she means nothing to him.

What? Why? Wait…I stopped reading. And that is why I have not heard from him for so long…My shameless boobs decorated the front page of the other newspaper, a similar interview was printed there too. I threw both on the floor. I do not know how long I stood there before I picked up the papers and reread the interviews again and again, only adding to my trouble. My confusion grew without my taking in a word. Nothing registered.

I felt numbness, not a tear—why could not I cry? All existence had been re-duced to the size and consistency of a jelly bean. A tiny worm of jealousy stirred deep in me, grew bigger and swarmed, and soon my stomach was on fire. Things unfolded fast, too fast, staccato—questioning, chaotically jumping thoughts, disappointment, anger at David, anger at myself for loving him, trusting him, defeat, fury, momentary hate, then numbness again, overwhelming numbness, like my entire soul had been systematically erased, dead.

I called David's cell.

"This voice box is full. No new messages can be accepted at this time. We apologize for the inconvenience."

I felt dizzy and weak. *I should eat something,* I thought. But I was queasy and could not hold food down. Oh-ho-ho.

The phone rang and rang, but I did not pick it up. People knocked on my door, but I did not open it. Tomorrow was never promised. Yet again, I was in love with someone I should not be in love with. *Abortion*—the word gritted between my teeth. No health insurance, no savings. I was terrified. That was as much courage as I could muster, and there was nothing to restrain the tears any longer. My body began shaking violently. I screamed and screamed. Then I called Rita.

"So she said to me, 'When you told me the tile was going to be white, I didn't expect it to be *so* white.'" Rita laughed. Her voice kept trailing away.

It was Tuesday. Or was it Wednesday? The sky was purple. Almost nightfall.

I swallowed the lump in my throat, restraining the tears. "It's over. David broke up with me."

"What? But you bought tickets to visit Hannah!"

"We had planned to visit his family in California too…Rita, I'm pregnant."

"Stay there. I'm coming over."

She came. We cried for two hours. We could have cried longer, but Mark arrived, so we stopped.

"Tell me what you want me to do and I'll do it," Rita said, hugging me by the shoulders.

"Did you tell David?" Mark asked.

"No." I sniffled. "He broke up with me."

"He still has a right to know," Mark said.

"It's not his responsibility to take care of me," I said.

"He should decide for himself." Rita handed me the tissue, took one for herself too.

"He'll want to do the right thing," I said.

Mark paced the length of bookshelves. "What's wrong with that?"

"I don't want him to be with me because it's the right thing to do," I said. "I want him to be with me because he can't be without me."

Mark stopped in front of me, his arms crossed over his chest. "There's a good chance he won't disappoint you. Stop running away."

"I can't," I said, and blew my nose. "I don't know how."

"Sweetie, ask for help and then accept it when it's given." Rita took my hand in hers. "People might surprise you."

"I need time to think things over." I claimed my hand back.

Rita hugged me by the shoulders again. "Will you keep the baby?"

"No, I want an abortion." I sniffled, shook my head. "The second child without a father. I don't know."

"This decision shouldn't be delayed." Mark resumed pacing. "Let Rita and I help you. How are you planning to support yourself? Will you continue training during the pregnancy?"

"No, at my age it's not a good idea."

"Move in with me," Mark said. "I'll take care of both you and the baby."

"A charity relationship," I said. "How good can that be for you?"

"You moving in with me is the best thing that could ever happen to me."

the phone rang in the dead of night.

"He's not waking up!" Bella wailed.

I ran. Heavy rain. Soaked and chilled to the bone. The emergency room. A neurosurgeon. "He suffered a hemorrhagic stroke. The bleeding was too massive." The intensive care unit. Another neurosurgeon. He looked tired.

"He'll never regain consciousness. No point in keeping him on the machines. Who'll make the decision?"

Bella shook her head *no*.

"I will." My voice came from afar. *Was it the right decision?* It would haunt me for the rest of my days.

With a morphine drip to end the pain, life support was turned off, and monitors were disconnected. Bella went home. I held Michael's fever-hot hand and prayed for a miracle, looking for signs that the doctors had made a mistake. In spasms, gasping, he sucked his stomach in, fought for his life. The evening passed, the night. The deep guttural rattle, an angry panther, louder, louder. Pulsating vein on the neck, weaker, weaker. The sound stopped. On the surface, nothing had changed, yet something shifted, tiny, indescribable, immeasurable, huge. A vast hollow opened up. The world went silent. One instant he was here, the next—gone into the kingdom veiled from mortal eyes. Two hearts in one room, joined together, one beating, aching, bursting, another one—still.

Someone touched my shoulder. The nurse.

"Stay as long as you need," she said. "Call me when you want to leave. I'll take him to the morgue."

The eyes sunken into his skull were not Michael's. His face resembled a wax figurine's. When had the change taken place?

The morning came, fresh, calm. I glanced through the dirty window at the river, with green hills on the other bank, the arch of the George Washington Bridge half-hidden behind the veil of fog. Nothing could be held on to. Life was too transitory and yet—ever-changing—eternal. We were part of one another in more ways than one. He would be in me forever, and I would be in him, united till the end of time. Soon enough, I too would breathe out and not breathe in again. He would greet me on the foreign shore.

The sense of separateness from the Creator diminished. Enough of recreating the hurt, the way of reproach and regret, for no reason for it remained. Enough of grieving at what might have been but never would be. The past could not be changed. There would always be someone who had it far better and someone who had it far worse. There was no different life. This was it, my life as it was meant to be. Each day offered something to celebrate. Saying yes to myself with all my weaknesses and mistakes—and so came not forgiveness, but acceptance of things as they were. I surrendered. It felt like God was not too far away. Alive, unafraid of death, I held eternity in my cupped hands.

"I bless my heartache," I said to my pale reflection in the window glass, "for without it I wouldn't be where I was meant to be, and without me the world wouldn't be where it had to be. Vulnerable and unashamed of it, I'm grateful to be a part of creation. The consciousness I am will never die. A little flame, one of billions upon billions, a tiny part of absolute perfection. I'm a bearer of presence into this world, illuminating it with glory of the spirit so the unceasing light can shine forever. Without me a drop of darkness would take place, and the manifest wouldn't be continuous and whole. I matter."

For a split moment, I glimpsed Michael's reflection in the glass. Our eyes met, and it was gone. One life ends, another one begins. I would keep this baby.

■　■　■

I opened the door, looked into Hannah's gray-with-worry eyes. Andrew stood behind her with two bags. He had grown. He looked like Mark when he was young.

Hannah put her arms around my neck, her warm cheek pressed against mine, and we both began crying. Our pain was beyond words.

■　■　■

The rain that had been here all morning stopped, and the sun peeked from behind the clouds. Mowed green grass. Old pine trees. So peaceful. The black hearse. I could not see the coffin behind the curtains, but I sensed it. Cars lined up for the final journey that led to the open grave. Unpainted pine coffin—such was the custom—things must be simple. A soldier, he liked simplicity.

Two uniformed gravediggers lowered the coffin into the hole in the ground. The rabbi recited the mourner's prayer: "*Yit'gadal v'yit'kadash sh'mei raba b'al'ma di v'ra khir'utei.*" * We echoed, "*Omein.*" Mother voiced, "Who's this in the grave next

---

* May His great Name grow exalted and sanctified in the world that He created as He willed. (Hebrew)

to Michael's? The headstone glitters." Her senseless words.

The clamped earth thundered against the lid when women threw down handfuls of it. The sound muted as men shoveled the clay to cover the coffin, grew fainter, duller. We left. The gravediggers shoveled to fill in Michael's grave. *The noblest of knights, who chose to share his life with us, you captured our hearts for eternity. Peace be with you. Farewell.*

■   ■   ■

"He'll be missed."

"Thank you for coming."

"A stroke?" Mother scrunched her nose like a little puppy. "Nobody in our family had a stroke. He did something to cause this."

I felt numb. A sharp pain cut through my lower abdomen and left as suddenly as it had come. The phone rang. I picked it up.

"Anna," Father said. "We got three-year visas. We arrive on the twenty-sixth."

"Right." I hung up the phone, looked at Mother. "My father is coming to New York."

"He can go fuck himself," she said in a high-pitched voice.

"Ma, what happened between you?"

"Why are you asking me? Ask him. Ask him where he was when I was pregnant with you? He demanded your grandfather buy him a house, and only then he'd stay with us. Grandfather refused, so that bastard felt offended and left. I begged him to come back. A year later that father of yours came to demand a house again. I knew where he was—with another woman. Grandpa kicked him out. But I got him good. I gave him no divorce for years so he couldn't marry that whore of his. If I ever meet him again, I'll spit in his face. He can go to hell!"

Who was telling the truth?

We took Bella home. Hannah fell asleep. The loudest, most formless silence enveloped me. The memorial candle flickered in the dark, its flame a reminder of a single person's soul, with each and every soul bringing light into the world. Just as more candles could be lit from a single one without diminishing the original flame, so each person could touch many lives, giving of themselves without their light ever being diminished. The flame, dancing, dancing, always burned toward the heavens.

His life lived so as not to inconvenience anyone, Michael asked for nothing and endured, buried alive for years. The conviction that life was difficult bound his mind—he never opened up to hope, as if affected by a mole's blindness. He relinquished his right to be happy in exchange for fictitious peace and quiet, persuaded himself that this make-believe world of his had to be protected. He took this burden upon himself, but in the end, with too much to bear and too little joy, he gave up his life, the star that had sunk beneath the horizon forever. He never raised his voice, never found words for things that should not have been left unsaid.

He should have shouted. He should have waved his fists and shouted, hit whoever deserved to be hit, demanded respect for the needs of his heart. Always unique, not a single life was ever to be repeated again. What a horror to waste it on compliancy with a deranged dictatorship of narcissism!

The dancing flame, dancing, dancing.

I closed my eyes and saw it again: We are skiing under the frozen skies on the singing river ice, no other soul in sight. I am in front; he covers my back. We cross into the enchanted forest. Unbroken snow clings to bare branches. They race by; some are too heavy, bent downward, touching the ground. There is a sensation of gliding, flying. With effortless, even movement, skis slide on snow crust glazed by the frost. Each muscle shouts with the joy of being alive, with bubbling youth, the intoxicating sweetness of a strong body. I want to scream from rapture. We are unstoppable. The incredible lightness of being.

Wind whistles by, attempts to rock the trees, but they do not rock. They are too frozen, pregnant with snow. Whole snowdrifts fall off the branches to the ground, soundless, surreal. Wind picks up a handful of snowflakes, blows them up in swirls and loops, then backs off, as if terrified of being punished for disturbing God's magic. The snowflakes are left suspended in midair to slowly lower to the ground. We speed out of the forest, cut across the ice-bound river to the other bank. Up, up, to the very top of the highest hill, pushing with ski poles against the resisting ground and crunching snow; we scale it in wide strides. Poles fly high in wide arches only to come down again to push, push, arms pumping.

We stand at the summit, connected to Mother Earth and overseeing the crystal kingdom. Frosty forest glitters as far as the eye can see, an unspeakable beauty. The city is somewhere behind it, lost between the hills. A majestic, ringing silence, a vast expense of snow and ice and sky—a pale-blue, white, and silver world, frozen into stillness. The black shies away, hardly showing, hiding. It knows it does not belong here in this virginally undisturbed world of pristine, glowing whiteness. The small clouds of our breath shimmer. I take a lungful of sparkly air. Cold, so cold, burning. I almost stop breathing, it is so cold, but it tastes sweet.

The melted white circle of the sun, brilliant and cold, blazes amid the liquid blue, chilly fire of the sky. A gelid blue fire of ice below, the stiff, burning river snakes at our feet. His eyes are right near me, alight with the hot, blue fire of joy under the ridiculous, fluffy, rabbit-fur Russian hat with silly ears that is too big for him. The aquiline nose. We laugh. Cannot stop laughing. I am fifteen. He is sixty-one but behaves like we are the same age. I never want this moment to end.

My heart sinks. Who says he is gone? What a hurtful lie! Here he is, alive, looking at me with love. He fills my heart with warmth and hope. Sprinkled over the snow, the fairy-dust sparkles, tiny stars ignite underfoot, on the branches, on my skis, everywhere, blinding. It must be because of this glare, unbearable to look at, that everything becomes blurry—the sun is too bright, the wind too strong, the frost biting, forcing my eyes to tear. It feels like I am crying.

No tears came. As Emerson said, "What lies behind us—" No, not now. Among the heavy shadows, the candle flame flickered as if to remind me one's soul was eternal, but the thought brought no light into the darkness in which I, too hollow to cry, was now immersed. And there was nothing in this world, nothing capable of lifting it. The morning would never come.

fifty-eight

the morning of day three after the funeral brought no relief. My heart throbbed with pain. I had cried it black. The floor was studded with crumpled paper tissues in no particular pattern, used and discarded like little fluffy sheep, waiting for a shepherd to lead them out of their misery to somewhere safe, an awkward bigger pile near the couch. I cried my eyes out on Mark's understanding shoulder and his patient chest. I cried for the loss of David, and not a tear for Michael—I could not grasp the finality of it. The more I tried to stop, the heavier the squall was. The deepest sadness set in. Even the hubbub of birds outside could not cheer me up. Mark followed me like a puppy, ready to fulfill my every whim, to predict my every wish. I had just one wish—for David to love me. If I knew how to conjure up his heart, I would have done it. Mark achieved little in consoling me for long days. I tortured him unwillingly as, drowning in devastation, I could not stop crying.

"He doesn't deserve you, that son of a bitch," Mark said. "Toying with people like that."

I pulled myself away from him, "He never toyed with me."

As fresh despair filled me, a new, stronger wave of weeping swamped me. Mark hugged me closer to him, smoothed my hair, imprinted a kiss on my temple. His arms offered comforting familiarity. His three-day-stubble did not feel too unfamiliar either.

"Life doesn't always take the turns we expect," he said. "And we can't choose who we fall in love with. We'll find someone better for you, someone who won't run away with his wife. You'll forget him soon enough."

"I don't want to forget him," I said between sobs. Not one of my rational moments. My chest swelled, almost bursting with anguish as the endless tears poured uncontrollably. "I'll love him forever."

Mark made a *tut-tut* noise, gently stroked my hair, his face clouded over. "You have a right to say it for now. Though you sound like some of my freshmen. Some of the sophomores too."

"So?"

"Nothing. Ignore. I don't know why I said that." He pulled me into his chest.

I blubbered on. The endless flood of tears obscured the world, and on its way down, unable to cure the vast, painful emptiness that was me, made a wet mess of Mark's shirt, without violating the security of his arms that firmly encircled me, my face buried in his chest.

Mark continued to stroke my hair. "Do you want to give me a little smile? No? All right."

"I had to learn it from Joanna." I opened my clenched fist, not without a smidgen of self-pity, to proffer the torn and crumbled pieces of paper for inspection. The text of the regrettable reminder of the article was hardly readable anymore. "And my boobs went national."

"Yes, but they're really, really nice. No shame to show your boobs to anyone anywhere in the world."

"He couldn't face me," I said, bitter with the knowledge of irreparable damage, the savage bluntness of it all. "How wrong can I be about a person?"

"He fooled us all. We all thought him to be deeply in love with you."

"He was!"

Mark addressed the ceiling. "I'm having trouble myself thinking of David as a jerk."

His shirt was too wet for me to cry on.

"Take it off," I said. "Let it dry."

Mark took his shirt off, hung it on the back of a chair, sat down, encircled me in his arms. Not David, but comforting. I pressed against him, put my head on his shoulder. What did it matter what David used to do? Mark with his charming idiosyncrasies was here. And new, innocent life burgeoned in my belly. A fresh wave of sobbing almost choked me, and again I was wracked with sobs.

The doorbell rang. Mark gently propped me against the back of the couch, pushed a box of tissues closer to me, went to open my front door. A minute later Rita came in, bringing an air of calm order with her. She glanced at the tissues, said nothing.

"What did I miss?" she asked. "How are you doing?"

I helplessly waved my hands in the air, let them drop, and began to cry again.

"Aw!" Rita sighed. "I've brought us food, a few of your favorites. It might cheer you up a little. And you, why are you half-naked? A laundry day? Mark, I hate to be critical, but when was the last time you shaved? Do me a favor, go shave now. And put something on."

The doorbell rang again. Three demanding, soul-piercing, breath-stopping rings. The last one did not come out too well. It started out devil-may-care, but choked midway and went dead. *She broke it,* I thought. *She finally broke it.*

"Are we expecting anyone?" Mark asked, and met only silence. He went to open the door.

Mother sailed into the living room like an ocean liner, in the most annoying fashion, so full of purpose. When her radar indicated "trouble at Anna's," she showed up.

She moved Mark aside with her hand and marched in. Her calculations were precise—I had no energy to fight.

"You look like a kicked dog. Crying again? *W-e-eh!* Urine." She eyed the strewn tissues, sat herself on the couch, threw the pillows on the floor, let out a gleeful chuckle. "I bet I know why you're crying. He dumped you. He. Dumped. You. I knew it, I knew it'd happen. You don't have what it takes to hold down a man. Thank God you're not pregnant!"

"Mother," I said, "leave."

She did not stir, unperturbed, and could not possibly be emitting less warmth. "Nobody on our side of the family is as stubborn as you. You must've inherited it from your father." Mother, perched on the couch, eyed Mark's naked chest, purposefully ignored Rita, and delivered her golden nuggets of wisdom. "You should see yourself—you look like an old hen in the rain."

I stifled a scream. Rita and Mark slipped into the kitchen to hide.

"No! You let her in, you kick her out!" I heard Rita's hushed hiss.

I began laughing hysterically.

Mark peeked into the room, smiled at me, and approached us.

Mother flicked her eyes at the unexpected distraction and found herself face-to-face with Mark. She appeared shocked. She squinted, moved her lips without a sound, regrouped at once, and reoriented herself to the new target, aiming her finger at him, wagging it with vigor.

"Speaking of the devil," she said, a caricature smile pasted on her face. "I knew he looked familiar. Is this David? He already left you alone." Mother darted an uneasy glance at me and pointed at Mark. "Why is he back? Annoying, that's what he is, annoying. Tell him."

"Mother, you need to go," I said.

She poked Mark in the rib with her bony finger and fixed him with a stare that made him take a step back. "You watch yourself. I'm watching you. And you, Dina, you don't have to hide in the kitchen. I know you're in there and—"

"Mother!"

"Bella had a set of dentures made," Mother said with diminished enthusiasm, "but they don't fit her, and her doctor—the most incorrigible of the scoundrels upon this earth!—refuses to refund her money. I'll go try them on. Maybe they'll fit me." Her dark-brown eyes darted from Mark to me and back, her hands on her hips, her eyebrows arched with irritation. "Shame on you for behaving like that toward your mother in front of everybody! Yogurt's on sale this week. I'll buy it first, then I'll tell Bella how you're treating me. Shame!"

As always, she made me feel as if she was doing me a favor. There was a time not long ago when I would have found myself upset about that, but times change. She would not give in an inch, failing to grasp yet again that the hunted might soon turn the hunter.

"Out," I said flatly.

And she ran. She was gone, and a huge part of my past was gone with her. It was strangely quiet, except for the ringing in my ears, a common aftereffect of Mother's invasions. I felt spent, but goddamn wonderful.

Dispirited, Mark stared at the door, which had swallowed Mother, tapping his thumb on his bicep.

"Mark, put on your shirt," Rita said.

Mark reached for his dumped shirt with no visible enthusiasm. "Well…" He paused halfway into one sleeve. "She still hates me," he said, a note of wonder in his voice.

"Don't get your head high in the clouds thinking you're special," I said, "because you're not, not to her. She's a devout hater of living things. Accept it to save yourself much grief later."

Rita made two steps forward. "She hated me too."

"And?" Mark said. The live interest had broken through the heavy cloud of gloom hanging around him.

"She still does," Rita said. "At some point between then and now, I stopped caring enough for it to throw me off balance every time we meet. Now, would you please put on your shirt?"

He put the other hand in the sleeve, fastened his shirtfront, one button missing.

Rita turned to me. "Go shower."

The water was ice cold. I showered as quickly as I could, toweled myself off, got dressed, and went back to the living room. The floor was clean.

"No hot water? How can you live in this dump?" Mark blurted out, then tried to remedy the situation. "I didn't mean to offend you in any way."

I burst out laughing. "I've had it up to *here* with this place."

■ ■ ■

"He ditched me," I said. "In the national newspaper. He ditched me."

"Yes, it's a bit extreme."

I heard Mark's voice. Not a word registered. After a while he stopped talking, watched me move thoughtlessly around, and exhausted, he fell asleep on the couch.

I confined myself to the rectangle of unwelcome bed. I was restless. The old voices I thought to have been silenced forever whispered, hissed, almost inaudible, making little sense.

Adam jumped on my lap. I prodded him off and immediately felt guilty. Why had I punished my little friend? None of it was his fault. I sensed a storm nearing. New York summers featured thunderstorms almost every evening—why should tonight be exceptional? The darkened room lived its own mysterious life, made me feel like an outsider. The gusty wind swung the streetlight while quaint shadows glided on the walls, on the ceiling. The windy world seemed shaky, unreal.

In the starless rectangle of the window, the skies hung closer, pregnant with something dark, impenetrable, amorphous. From the inside of the enormous underbelly came a grumbling, lazily, as if out of boredom, then louder, closer, closer, louder. The thunder rolled overhead, rumbling, stretching its muscles, testing its strength, playing around, followed by silence. Grumbling. Silence. Again. It let its full power unfold, terrifying everything alive into stillness. The city paused and held its breath.

With the first signs of the hastily incoming hazard, Adam and Eve slithered under the covers, pressed against me, making a two-cat dumpling, the cutest lump, but they reconsidered the strategy after the next roar. The cats scampered across the floor and under the bed, the hair on their tails standing on end.

The fat raindrops drummed on the windowsill, bursting into fountains, splattering, sputtering, hurrying down to quench the thirst of the ground, outrunning one another, exploding. The frequency of hits increased, pummeling, turning into a waterfall expelled from above. With it came the hail. It emptied the streets, bringing blessed coolness to a city longing for it, but it did not come in peace. It fell as if punishing the city for its sins, lashing with long-repressed anger, lashing the buildings standing shoulder to shoulder against the assault, lashing the ground, lashing my rejected heart. How many unhappy people hid behind it? How many hearts were breaking behind the locked doors? The dense wall of water, a living monster, devoured all the lights in its insatiable greed, not a flicker let through. It severed the thin threads connecting me to the rest of the world, isolating me in the terrible eternity of abandonment.

The lightning struck nearby, blinding, split the darkness into raggedly torn halves, a raving frenzy of light making my blood curdle. The unbridled fury of it promised total devastation. Thunder, lightning, thunder, *bolt, crack, bolt,* giving my pain a voice. No longer restricted, I wailed, my body shuddering. The first wave hit, subsided, then the second, much stronger one. With the sudden dull ache in my lower back coming in waves, and feeling short of breath, I went silent, only to wail again in full voice. Unwanted, I curled up in bed, hugging myself.

In the twinkling of an eye the storm was over. It rolled away, the ground cleansed. The rain slowed, abated, lighter, lighter. The sounds of recent fury gently melted into the rustling of tires on wet asphalt. Rainwater turned the newly washed pavement into a shiny mirror, reflecting the streetlights and car lights and lights from the thousands of windows. The city was repopulated, and the habitual bustle returned.

I wiped off the tears, went to Mark, curled up beside him on the couch. He muttered in his sleep without waking up, put his arm around me, pulled me into the ring of safety.

I lay there, the dull ache in my lower back gone, staring unseeingly into darkness. I listened to the soft, even rhythm of his breath. It began to calm me down. My hectic thoughts slowed, and for a moment, one dizzying moment, the darkness lifted a little from my heart. *Ah, Mark. My loyal, wonderful Mark.* The thought bubbled to the surface, and I was too exhausted to fight it off. We had been happy together once. Pity I could never love him the way I loved David. Then again, look at where that had gotten me. People I held dear left me one by one.

I sniffled. Mark still held deep affection for me, and I had used to be attached to him—no, more than attached. The passion had been there. So he had abandoned me on one occasion a long time ago—not entirely his fault, granted—but Mark, ah, Mark, he would not make the same mistake twice. We could be happy again.

I fidgeted, getting comfortable. Mark mumbled, pulled me tighter to him. The first faint morning light began to dawn, more of a wish than reality.

I awoke from the slashing pain. My insides were slit open and burning, the flames ravaging my gut. I pressed both hands to my lower abdomen and felt something wet and sticky on my skin. The sweet-and-sour smell of blood was sickening. Quietly, so I would not awaken Mark, I got dressed, tiptoed downstairs, hailed a cab, and went to the emergency room with a renewed sense of despair.

fifty-nine

the elevator broke again. Shaking and faint, I walked up the stairs.

"A ruptured ectopic pregnancy is life-threatening to the mother," they had said and removed one of my fallopian tubes along with the remnant of the early pregnancy—the soul who had met its death, denied of birth. "You might not become pregnant again."

I pushed up the stairs. The blood banged in my ears, and spots swam in front of my eyes. I had to hold on to the handrail to walk up. I heard voices, one of them too familiar. And before long I climbed the last remaining flight of stairs to meet two cops, an angry-looking Alex, and Mrs. Goldfarb in her pink housecoat.

"Anna!" she said. "Thank God!"

"Do you know this man?" the younger cop asked me with a bored expression on his face.

"My ex-boyfriend," I said.

The older cop with stooped shoulders and an even less cheery demeanor glanced at Alex, who was holding a three-foot-long metal pipe in his hand.

The officer addressed me in a rambling monotone. "Your neighbors were concerned. He's been waiting here on the steps for several hours. Do you want to file a complaint?"

"Alex, a pipe?" I asked. "Seriously?"

A fleeting grimace distorted his face as he muttered, "Bitch!"

"What's that, sir?" the younger cop enquired.

"He tried to rape me not long ago," I said, "and threatened me with a knife."

Mrs. Goldfarb's face flushed. "I saw it all."

"Shut your trap!" Alex growled, his eyes wild and fiery with a fatalistic glint. I knew this look. Nothing would stop him now. "Alex, don't!" I said.

He massaged the back of his neck, bounced the pipe in his hand, and made a step toward me. The older policeman grabbed Alex's arm at its pasty, hairy wrist, twisting it behind his back. Alex kicked and thrashed about. The pipe dropped with a thud, rolled a few feet away. A clank followed—a gun slipped out from under his shirt and hit the floor.

"Fuck!" Alex wriggled out from the cop's arms, jumped toward the stairway.

The cops jumped after him. He was caught and cuffed.

"Smith and Wesson, forty-five Colt. Do you have a permit for this, sir?"

Alex was held by the scruff of his neck, pressed against the wall, and frisked. A hunting knife in its sheath was attached to his calf.

"Nine-inch," the younger cop said. "Illegal to carry."

"Can you repeat that?" the older cop said into his radio. "Got it. Two previous records of domestic assault. Okay, sir. Please come with us."

"What will happen to him, officer?" I asked.

"We'll hold him overnight, the amount of bond will be set, and if no one pays it, the next morning he'll be brought before a judge. They'll increase the amount of the bond, and if no one pays it again, he'll be taken to a correctional facility to await his court date. He'll be off the street for a bit, but you might want to think about getting a restraining order, ma'am."

Alex was escorted down the stairs. We stood there, silent.

Mrs. Goldfarb smiled. "Someone is watching over you from up there, kid. Now, listen to the old crazy woman—move. I still have some sense in me left. Anna, this is serious. He'll be back, and the next time we might not get so lucky."

I hugged her. "Thank you, thank you so much for everything."

She tapped my arm. "It's late. I'll see you tomorrow." And she disappeared behind her door.

I picked up a torn-up note with Scotch tape attached and pieced it together:

The cats are fed. I'll stop at my place for a few things after classes. Call me as soon as you get home. M.

Move, I thought. She was right. I had to move. What was holding me in this place? I could rent a small studio. I smiled, went inside, poured myself a glass of water, swallowed two Advils, and then I called Mark.

"Mark, I'm fine. Don't worry. Stay home and rest. I'll see you tomorrow."

I returned the receiver to its cradle and lay down on the couch. I was in pain, but could not stay still. Ah, *mon château*. I got up and walked from room to room with mounting excitement, deliberating which belongings to take with me, rejecting most. No question in my mind, all books would be taken, it would be a sacrilege to leave them behind. And some mementoes here and there. I must have clothing, so yes to that. The rest...I did not own much. Adam and Eve followed me around, inspected each object I touched, rejected all of it too.

The smoke alarm coughed, whimpered, stopped, left it at that. The odor of another burned dinner seeped in, spread throughout the place, intensified.

I slammed the top drawer of the dresser shut, inhaled the air. It did not smell right. Both cats skidded under the bed like two silent shadows. At my ankles, a shapeless, black, solid mass curled, swelled upward fast, reached up to my waist.

I called out the cats' names but could not see them behind the dense smoke. I coughed—the floor swayed, twisted, swam around.

. . .

The semifamiliar building floated into my field of vision, then out, then in again, wobbling a little. My head was jammed with cotton.

I felt my arm in a firm grip, turned to investigate, and stumbled upon serious eyes, a button of a nose on a young face, a kid with problematic skin, wide shoulders, and a paramedic's uniform. A giant fireman, reeking of smoke, towered over me, passing me by in slow motion. *What does he need that for?* I puzzled for a moment over the dirty-brown rag in his hand. Wait...that dirty rag—it belonged to me!

I jerked my arm free, ran after the helmeted giant, screamed. The firefighter placed the small lifeless body in my arms and headed back to the building.

"The other cat?" I shouted at his back.

He turned his head but continued walking. "It didn't make it."

The world kept spinning. The paramedic with serious eyes materialized near me, resumed his hold on my arm. He dragged me along the street into the ambulance, pushed me down on the bench, pressed the oxygen mask over my nose and mouth.

"Stop moving around," he said. "Sit here and breathe. Let me check you."

I took in a few breaths, pulled off the mask, put it on Eve. It covered her entire head.

"Better put the mask on yourself," said the paramedic sitting behind the wheel. "She's a goner. Ma'am, we're taking you to the hospital."

"No," I said, "no hospital. Let me be."

Some long minutes passed. Eve growled, stirred, growled again, opened her eyes, cawed. Tears rolled down my face. I clasped the cat at my chest, jumped out the back door to the ground, found my way back to the building through the street blocked by emergency vehicles. The rotating beacons flashed the night as bright as day. I pushed through the crowd, ducked under the yellow tape, and stepped over the bulging fire hoses. I approached the entrance, stood outside. The young paramedic found me there, draped a blanket over my shoulders, stood by me. A silent, agitated crowd shifted behind the yellow tape.

A woman in a light cardigan touched my shoulder, pointed at the synagogue across the street, a few buildings off. "Come with me. You can sit down in there.

We have food and water. What happened to your shoes?"

I looked down. I was barefoot. "I can't go into the synagogue with a cat."

She lifted a corner of the blanket. "Come. We already have a cat in there."

God Almighty! My heart somersaulted in my chest. In the room full of people, she pointed to a man not far from the door, stroking a curled-up silver ball of a cat on his lap. Adam!

"I found him on the street, wet and scared," the man said. "We toweled him off."

I lowered into the chair that was offered to me, touched Adam's damp back. He crawled over to my lap, licked my hand, pressed against Eve, licked her. I cried a small lake, and people cried with me and handed me tissues.

A woman in black handed me a bottle of water. "Would you like some food?"

"How many apartments were destroyed?" someone asked.

"Eight," someone answered.

"Did everyone get out all right?"

"Yes, everyone is safe, thank God. Her cats were saved."

"She was saved too."

The man touched me on the sleeve. "Now you'll live a thousand years."

"Which apartment started it?"

"Below hers, the one with the cats. Those two junkies. I hope their stereo burned to ashes."

"It's eight apartments on the Broadway side. Our side is okay."

"I've heard it was an electrical fire. I'm afraid to go back."

"It's all Mr. Brownspot's fault. Never does repairs. How greedy can a man be?"

"Serves him right. This place should've been torched long ago."

"Hush! The insurance will compensate him, I'm sure, but what about people who lost everything?"

Mrs. Goldfarb lowered herself onto the neighboring chair. Her pink housecoat was smudged with black. She had only one slipper on.

"Oh, Anna," she said, stroking one cat, then the other. "It may not seem like it now, but you're lucky, you are. My sister, Edna, wants me to go to Florida to live with her. I'll go to Florida, then. What's holding me here?"

The elevator was shut down. With subdued cats in my arms, I walked through the puddles up the stairs, blackened and wet. My front door was chopped up with axes. Two shapeless pieces hung on twisted hinges. In the slanted rectangle of light from the hallway, a clear spot on the dining table showed. I stepped over the piles of rubbish frosted with ash and tiny splinters of glass, put both cats on the table, flipped the switch. No light came on. I got the flashlight out of the closet, switched it on. It worked.

The yellow circle of light jumped from ragged holes in scorched walls to ragged holes in the scorched ceiling, ricocheted off the sagging wire ducts, to the charred furniture, most of it upside down, deflected off the puddles of dirty water. It fragmented on the piles of glittered debris, snatched from the darkness scattered and torn books, the tossed and ruined clothing. Sharp shards of shattered glass glistened everywhere—on the floor, on the furniture. Not a single window was intact. An acrid stench spread throughout the place.

In the bedroom, two men with flashlights nailed sheets of plywood to the walls to cover the gaping windows. A woman with a canvas tote bag walked inside, glanced over the devastation, handed me a piece of paper.

"I'm from the Red Cross. We have beds and food. You can't stay here. We've declared this place uninhabitable." She left. The men with hammers left too. Adam and Eve did not move from the table.

I stood there with the flashlight in my hand, bouncing the beam off things. There was nothing left for me to take. No more home. A small rectangular object on the floor reflected the light back. I picked it up, wiped it off. My cellphone. The screen was cracked. I pressed the button to switch it on. It was dead.

Mrs. Goldfarb peeked through the gap that used to be my front door, surveyed the scene.

"Oh dear God! Anna, where are you?" she asked. "There you are. Child, come, stay with me until you find a place."

"Mrs. Goldfarb, from the bottom of my heart, thank you. We'll be too much for you to handle."

I called Mark from her phone, then went downstairs and sat on a curb. My hands and the soles of my feet were cut and bled lightly. Adam and Eve sat pressed against me. It was well past midnight. The street was quiet. It slept.

Fully clothed on top of the bed, my feet and hands bandaged, I lay in Mark's arms the rest of the night. Unable to sleep yet too exhausted to talk, we dozed off by morning. Another recent development had come forth by the time we woke up—Adam and Eve, protesting the happenings, had pooped on Mark's couch.

"You're allowed for today. We'll take it one day at a time," he said, and instead of declaring war on the poopers and kicking them out on the street, Mark picked them up, one by one, kissed them both, and I cried a little.

And so we moved in with Mark. Another fact of life became apparent—there was an abandoned supply of canned cat food in Mark's kitchen. Mark fed strays.

sixty

steady drizzle had dribbled since last evening. The morning fell ill. It shivered and sobbed, so bleak it hardly troubled the night by its appearance. I stepped into the empty subway elevator. The ceiling light gave a short buzz, flickered, buzzed again, and dimmed. Heavy steel doors rattled, sliding closed. The elevator shook, and I took a few steps to regain my balance. I saw a boy dash in, too short to be detected by a sensor, his head between nearly closed doors. I gasped, stuck my arm into the gap. The doors produced a grating sound, paused, strained to slide open again.

The boy, three or four years old, ran in and touched my hand with his. Jumping on one leg, he completed a circle around me. He had started on the second when his father walked in, half-awake, his face blank. A smiling old woman came in behind him. The ceiling light gave another short buzz, grew brighter. The doors rumbled, paused, slid closed. The elevator jerked, clanked, labored up.

I crossed the street, headed for the unsheltered bus stop. The old woman followed me. She was as small as a twelve-year-old, casually dressed in jeans, sneakers, and a sleeveless parka, no handbag. It began to pour. I opened Mark's umbrella, invited her under.

"The day is going to be beautiful despite the bad weather forecast," she said.

Its headlights almost invisible behind the wall of rain, the rheumatic bus sped by, fanning waterfalls with tires. It skipped the stop, screeching to a halt twenty feet away. We got in, the only passengers, all seats empty. The woman sat down, smiled at me.

"My mother was abusive," she said as if she had heard one of my unspoken, lingering questions. "But the day came when the tables turned. They usually do. What got me through was being present in the moment, concentrating on good memories, and letting go of everything else. There must've been something, a single good moment, even a small one."

I nodded, lowered myself on a seat next to hers, looked into her eyes. Cut short, her soft silver hair created a halo around her face. Her bright blue eyes radiated kindness. She spoke so softly, I should have had to strain to hear her in the noise in the New York bus, but I did not.

"I followed my heart," she said. "I knew that no matter what, I was safe. To quote, 'What lies behind us and what lies before us are small matters compared to what lies within us.'"

"Ralph Waldo Emerson." I nodded again. "Who are you?"

She smiled, jumped up. "My stop. Bye."

The bus stopped, she got off and waved. The umbrella fell to the floor. I glanced at it, glanced out the window. The street was wet and empty.

■   ■   ■

Saturday morning. Mark's phone rang. The caller ID showed *Out of area.*

"Hello?" I hoped to hear David's voice, but heard only static on the line. "Hello? Hello?"

Again, the crackling noise, then a computerized voice from afar.

"Good. Bye," it said.

■   ■   ■

How fragile life was! The integral part of my existence, the only human contact with my family gone, a space that Michael had held—empty, my world changed forever. Saying it aloud—"He passed on."—would make it real, but I could not say it. The thoughts refused to form into sounds, the words refused to come, my lips refused to move. And my baby...my heart stopped when I thought of it. Hannah and Andrew had returned to London. I waded through days, feeling spent. I made endless phone calls and endless trips to Bella's place to get her life in order—folders, folders, envelopes, folders, plastic bags filled with disorganized papers. Pale with fear, she had no idea what was what and where it was. For fifty-seven years they had never been apart.

I rearranged and fixed things in the apartment to fit Bella's single-from-now-on life. One by one or in bundles of black trash bags, his belongings went to Goodwill and to people in the neighborhood—unfamiliar faces with indifferent eyes over outstretched hands—the physical evidence of Michael ever being here was eradicated. Mother, less talkative and scared, stayed with Bella, brought food. The inevitable death could come at any time, and in the face of it, we were equal.

For days sleep refused to come near me. Then it took pity and allowed me to fall into the waters of Lethe. I blacked out but screamed myself awake, sweat-drenched, scaring Mark. In my sleep the whole thing was just a dream, Michael was here, he was alive, and I laughed happily, a rich full-bodied laugh, but as soon as I woke up, I remembered it was no dream. Poor Mark, he felt so powerless! As if all other words had failed him, he would encircle me in his arms and say, "Shhh."

I missed David, half a planet away in the unreachable Himalayas. My heart ached. I wrote a letter to him, full of bitterness, and mailed it on the spur of the moment. Then I realized what I had done. Crazed, I called his cell, got his voicemail, left no message. I would not forgive myself in a million years! A believer in miracles, I prayed that by an act of higher magic, the post would lose it, the correspondence that should have never been mailed, but when had I ever been so lucky? But a human cannot live without hope, and I brought it into the dark with me. Then the dreams came, haunting and torturous and ominous and seemingly prophetic. Premonitions, signs, omens. They refused to dissipate, and a dense sense of danger enveloped me, airless and death-charged, refusing to let go.

Accompanied by vertigo and fatigued, I stopped sleeping and wrote. All my senses were painfully heightened. It was not that the subconscious was closer to the surface in the state between sleep and wakefulness, but an inner critic was down, and a fictional world had a chance to get through. The last three chapters I had been sitting on for months were written, the printed manuscript laid on the table. The novel was born. Releasing its hold on me, it grew distant, lost its edginess. Instead of elation I felt sadness and emptiness, a postpartum separation from characters, the intimacy destroyed, the vacated rooms in my heart that they used to populate padlocked.

Days floated and faded. My life became very small. The moon waned and waxed, a silent witness. Two weeks passed. I was unable to mourn Michael's death. Or my baby. It was too big of an event for me to process. The computer beeped with incoming e-mails. The sender—not David, again.

I was a dust speck, insignificant, suspended in an eternal field in which, beyond right or wrong, lovers loved and hoped, there was nothing I would not have given, nor any price too high to turn the clock back, to know that there was *us*.

■ ■ ■

"Mrs. Goldfarb, let me know when you need my help packing."

"You'll call and come visit, promise? You have to, you know. You're my family."

I know. I promise.

■ ■ ■

The phone rang.

"Are you watching this?" Rita screamed. "Channel seven. Go!"

Mark switched on the TV, channel seven.

"…was arrested tonight on charges of rape. Yesterday evening he and his wife, Joanna,

were seen leaving the Saint Regis hotel in New York where a fundraiser for the Children's Cancer Foundation was being held. Two hours later Joanna called 911 to report that her husband had raped her, and was taken into the hospital."

"What?" Mark said to the TV.

"Labial abrasions were found to confirm the account. This story follows the scandal of David Cooper and his personal trainer's short indiscretion, which had recently ended. As Joanna Cooper had stated in various interviews, she and her husband had reconciled and were trying to conceive after a history of failed attempts. Yesterday morning, Mr. Cooper, a Pulitzer Prize-winning author of eighteen bestselling novels, returned to New York from his latest humanitarian mission in Nepal. So is David Cooper what everyone thinks him to be?—Hold on, Liz. I'm getting an update." The reporter pressed his earpiece to his ear. *"A preliminary investigation has discovered that footage from the surveillance camera in the lobby of Mrs. Cooper's building doesn't show Mr. Cooper entering the building yesterday night. There will be an investigation to find out if the tape has been tampered with. For now, back to you, Liz."*

"He didn't do it!" I screamed. "He didn't! Didn't!"

"For God's sake!" Mark said. "What's wrong with this woman? Of course he didn't do it." He kissed my forehead. "You're shaking. Come here."

"Make it go away," I said, barely audible. "Please, make it all go away."

Mark switched off the TV and encircled me in his arms. "Shhh, shhh."

a week went by. All was quiet during the day, and I slept, hardly aware of the passage of time, cats pressed against my side. A narcotic heaviness arrested my limbs. I slept, tumbling down and down into the darkest abyss of dreamless sleep. Or sat staring into space. Or cried silently. Something had snapped, the grain of reality was altered, and again I had to be brave and give life another try. So tired, so damn tired. And cold, shivering, despite the oppressive August heat. I was a faint fragment of spirit floating in unknowable darkness. Nothing held me up, and I was falling.

My black mood refused to lift. I was caught in a fog of forgetful anonymity, drifting somewhere between past and present, and lost in a strange maze, hostile and vast. No point of reference. An incomprehensible, capricious, and blurry illusion. I stopped trying to understand. My lungs burned, and my bones ached. The light hurt. I had drawn the shades all the way down to create a dark cavern, but the sunlight still filtered through my eyelids, too brilliant and painful, as if molten metal was being poured into my eye sockets. The day got brighter and hotter. Sounds hurt too, and—alas!—the world was full of them, the jangled world.

I woke to a click of a key in the door. The door creaked open, closed gently. Bless his heart. Mark had tiptoed halfway to the couch when the doorbell rang.

Stabbing pain ricocheted through my head, echoed into the pounding agony, rolled again. I lay still not to aggravate it. Tumbled and tossed, damp bed sheets trailed on the floor.

"Shit," Mark muttered, and went to open the door.

I heard a small choir of three shrill girl's voices. "Would you like to buy some cookies?" Every syllable felt like a nail hammered into my head with a single blow.

"Cookies?" Mark's hushed voice asked. "Hmmm. Anna, which cookies would you prefer? Thin Mints or something with peanut butter, or more Thin Mints, or all of them? Yum-yum!"

I waved my hand in the direction of the door—*whatever*—turned on my other side, and pulled a pillow over my head.

"We'll take these three," Mark said in a loud whisper.

"Thank you, sir!" the thin choir sang. There was a patter of small feet running away, someone else's doorbell, and the "Would you like—" screech again, but at a tolerable distance.

I heard the sound of the door shut softly, but not a minute later the doorbell went off again in a flurry of rings. Mark muttered something indecipherable under his breath.

"Mark," a high-pitched female voice sing-sang. "I can't program my VCR—"

Stilettos thundered and echoed on the tiled floor of the hallway. *Click click click.*

"Who are you?" Rita's voice cut in, a bit harsh. "And what on earth are you wearing? You call that a skirt? It's not even a bikini. Shoo! Scatter!" The door was shut again. "How is she?" Rita's hushed voice asked. "Has she eaten anything?"

"Breakfast's still on the table," Mark said in a loud whisper.

Someone yanked the pillow off me.

"How do you feel?" Rita smiled with all her very white teeth. Her forced cheerfulness grated me the wrong way today.

"Tired," I grumbled and pulled back the pillow.

Rita held on to her end. "Of course you are tired. How will you get better if you won't eat?"

I had no answer for this. There was a polite knock on the door.

"This isn't a private residence, it's a frigging bus terminal," Mark muttered.

Rita tugged on the pillow, more impatient. "Anna—"

"I know. I know." I let go of the pillow, scratched the side of my face, and stood up. "Mark, wait, let me get it," I said, glad to get away from Rita.

Driven by force of habit, I glanced at myself in the mirror by the entrance door and saw a patient in a mental hospital. A quick survey revealed the devastating sight—Mark's sweats that had seen better days and begged to be replaced, wrinkled and pooling around my ankles with their bagged-out knees. Sleeping in them had done wonders for their scruffy looks. Higher up, the colors were too spectacular to be shown in public—a blob of a face blotched in baboon-butt pink and death-white, ruby-red-rimmed puffy eyes, a brick-red swollen potato instead of a nose. The woven pattern from the couch cushion was imprinted in purple on my left cheek. My uncombed hair looked like a dandelion past the prime of its blooming career after the wind had had some fun with it.

Panic-stricken, I retrieved the hand that was about to twist the doorknob and paused to consider. What if it was David? On semiautomatic, my hand jerked up to bring the hairdo into a semblance of a coiffure that belonged to a human female, but was shot down in midflight by the pragmatic thought, *Why bother?* The turbid reflection in the mirror, as unnerving as an unfinished Picasso drawing, stared back, shrugged, then went completely opaque as if even the mirror were disgusted to reflect me. Yeah, David. He and Joanna, in celebration of their rejuvenated union, were probably flying first class twenty thousand feet above the clouds to their second honeymoon destination, somewhere private and Caribbean. He had already forgotten my name. Oh…wait…he was in prison. My heart went cold.

Suppressing the rapidly mounting bout of paranoia, I scratched my nose and opened the door.

"David." I shivered, feeling anger rising and my body tensing.

He looked at me with a tired expression on his tanned face. His clothing hung loosely on him, his shoulders hunched. He looked shorter, shaken and defenseless, forlorn. Something wrenched so deep in my chest, I almost broke down sobbing. With a sudden rush of love and tenderness, lightheaded with joy, I felt a huge blissful smile about to blossom on my face. Odd how we tend to misremember events.

He glanced at my multicolored face, stepped closer as if about to give me a hug, but stopped, shifting his weight from foot to foot. The look of gloom on his face gave way to worry. My anger at him transformed into anger at myself for the intensity of my rapture at seeing him again, which had seized my heart.

I headed back to the living room. David followed me. Mark emerged from the kitchen and stopped at the threshold of the living room, blocking the exit, his arms crossed tightly over his chest. Rita remained standing near the couch.

"You have some nerve showing up," she said to David in a grave undertone.

David took a step back, cleared his throat. "I apologize for the way I look," he said. "I was in a holding cell at the local precinct. I shared a windowless room with two drunken men who had no memory of what they'd been told they'd done. One crime apparently involved public urination, the other a possible assault with a knife. Then I was brought down to 100 Centre Street and put in another cell to wait for my arraignment and pending bail. My lawyer bailed me out."

He sighed, leaned toward me, but did not risk a step. Hair fell into his eyes, he did not brush it away. "I couldn't find you. Your phones are disconnected, your apartment is burned down, no one in the building knows where you are. Mrs. Goldfarb closed the door in my face. Neither Rita nor Mark is answering their phone. I was going mad with worry."

"Oh, boohoo! *You* were mad with worry?" Rita crossed her arms at her chest.

For a moment no one spoke. It was quiet save for the distant ticking of the clock, the drone of a neighbor's TV, and slithering traffic outside.

David inhaled deeply, shifted his position a bit, glared at barefoot Mark. He grew gloomy again and said in a low voice, "If there's something I've done, don't

I have a right to know what it is?"

"Absolutely," Rita said. "You're a jerk."

"Well," David said, and cleared his throat again.

"Well," Rita echoed, her gaze unwavering.

A long silence followed. Rita stared at David. David peered at Mark. Mark glanced at me. I stood there, fingertips at my temple. David reached into his pocket, took out a carefully folded piece of paper, handed it to Rita.

"From my lawyer," said David. "The divorce was finalized a week ago."

The divorce, I thought.

Rita unfolded the piece of paper. "*The Civil Court of New York*," she began reading aloud, her brows knitted, but switched to, "*Mm-hmm, mm-hmmmm, mmm-hm.*"

She turned the paper over and looked at the backside, her brows arched. "And that's your excuse? Wow."

"You were gone for a—" I began, but my throat was too dry and the room too hot. I felt nauseated. "And now you waltz in here and expect me...Why?"

David gave a short nervous laugh. He looked pitiful. "I can explain."

"Please do." Rita took my hand and threaded her fingers through mine.

"I—" He looked around, sat down on the couch. "We couldn't get a permit for a satphone in Nepal in time. You won't believe how big of a hassle it is to get an official permit from the concerned ministries. We brought one in, but it was confiscated at customs. And the mountains are hell to trek in monsoon months. The planned three weeks turned into five. We had to get the equipment and supplies and our gear over the mountain ridge at seventeen thousand feet through a snow- and ice-covered pass in below-freezing temperatures. Even with the Sherpas' help it was something. But we got through to the village."

He paused, staring into space for a moment, shook his head. "Those people are farmers. They keep a few goats and cows, walk two hours to the nearest village school, which has only three grades. No electricity. We brought part of the equipment to build a small power station for the village, along with some school supplies and clothing. The other half of our group followed a day or two behind us with the remainder of the equipment and more supplies. But when a landslide took a big chunk of the mountain down, the road with it, the rest of the group never made it to the village. We communicated with them via walkie-talkies. Everyone was all right, with just a few minor injuries. We were lucky."

A landslide, I thought. My flesh crawled.

"The damaged road network remains closed for long periods of time, causing indescribable hardship to the villagers who get their supplies and provisions from the neighboring areas. With the landslide, the village was totally isolated. There was a satphone at the base camp on Everest, but we were nowhere near there."

David furrowed his brow, pressed the ball of his hand into his eye. "To make a long story short, I spent the last three weeks discovering an alternate way down with Sherpas who spoke little English, circumnavigating around the slide using goat paths, chanting at campfires and showering in a tent with a bucket of hot water and a ladle. I have enough stories for at least three books—ancestral legends handed down from generation to generation, shamans. You'll like it. We ate mostly rice, lentils, and tea with yak fat. You wouldn't like that."

Tea with yak fat, I thought. And I fell a little more in love with him. I did. Of course I did. I stood there, unable to tear my eyes from him. I opened my mouth to say something, closed it.

Mark filled the silence. "Listening to you gives me the shivers. Glad you're all right."

I picked up the pillow from the couch, looked at it, unsure what to do with it next, put it down again. No one said anything for several long moments.

"The trial," Mark asked, "what will happen now?"

"As in any other high-profile case," David said with stoic calmness, "things will move faster, reflecting the attention it has attracted. There'll be an investigation and a lot of press. The expedited DNA test showed that the DNA wasn't mine. I must show up in court, unless Joanna drops the charges. Lawyers talking to lawyers, detectives, neighbors, witnesses, more witnesses. There'll be a trial, but that might not take place for a long time, my lawyer warned me. Joanna has been invited on many TV shows to talk about the rape. Even when my innocence is proven or if the case is dropped, some people may believe the retraction was pressured. My reputation's been irreparably harmed. From now on I'll be known as 'his wife's rapist.'" David rubbed his temples with his fingertips.

"We can't go to London. Or California. I'm not allowed to leave New York while the investigation is ongoing." He took a step toward me.

I stepped away. All the blood rushed from my head. I felt strange and light-headed, thinking, *Why is no one talking about that interview?*

"London?" I asked. "We split up."

"We did? When?" David dispatched a worried glance at me. "Give me a good reason for that."

I caught his eye, shook my head slightly, and in confused anger slammed my open palms on the dining table. "You've returned to your lawful spouse," I said, no longer sure about that or anything else, and lowered myself into a chair.

David's eyes met mine with a sad candor. "Why would you think that?"

Zip-a-dee-doo-dah, Zip-a-dee-ay. I felt faint. "It was in every newspaper."

"She claimed I raped her." David looked at me, then Mark, then Rita, me again, as if searching for a meaning that had escaped him at the moment.

His tan went a shade paler. He made a step toward me, stopped. David appeared concerned, his eyes filled with tenderness. "What interviews? I'd like to understand all of this, if someone would be willing to explain what's happening." He paused for a second, looking haggard, thoughtfully viewing the empty space right in front of him, chewed on his bottom lip a few times.

I got up and knocked the chair over. I picked it up, fighting the urge to throw it at someone, but put it down gently and pointed at the stack of newspapers on the coffee table. I felt exhausted. I needed to sit down but remained standing.

David picked up the top paper, read a few lines, stared at the photo, seemed to reach a decision, then stiffened and grew gloomy again. "Three weeks ago. It's so like her: 'If I can't have him, no one will.' Let's get this straight—I know nothing about this." He sat down heavily on the chair, then glanced up with a quick flash of anger. His brow knotted. "Her fifteen minutes of fame."

David leaned closer to me, attempting eye contact. "I can't even imagine how you've must felt. Why would I do such a thing? I love you. You know that, right? Please believe me."

I shrugged, my eyes full of tears.

David gave me a beseeching look. "When Mark called—"

"You called David?" I asked Mark, but he studied the floor at his feet. "What did you say?"

"He called me names," David said, "some of them less pleasant than others."

"Thank you," I said softly.

Mark looked at me, nodded.

I lowered to the edge of the chair, looked at my clasped hands.

David gently cupped my trembling hands in his, running his thumbs over my knuckles. His hands were hot and comforting. "I'm so, so very sorry! I shouldn't have left you alone for such a long time."

I nodded.

"I'm going to kill that woman," David said. The expression in his eyes was hard to read.

"Well," Mark said. "Joanna—"

"Please," David said, "if I hear her name one more time, I swear—"

Mark folded the letter, handed it to David. "Looks like someone's been busy."

"She'll pay for this." David leaped up from the chair, began pacing, impatient, as if filled with explosive anger and not entirely trusting of his ability to keep it under control. He regarded us with a bewildered look in his eyes.

I smiled meekly with a slight shrug.

"Anna, you do believe me when I say I love you? I need you to believe me. I can't imagine spending the rest of my life without you. Move in with me."

If I had any reservations about him, he had melted all of them away. I could not help it. Restrained at first, I smiled. And so did he.

"I think our job here is done for today," Rita told Mark. "Let's go celebrate kids never separating in the first place."

"Please stay," David said. "Anna, please ask them not to leave."

"We'll meet tomorrow," Rita said. "Didn't I tell you I have to pack? I'm going on vacation for ten days this coming Friday. I bought two tickets to get Anna out of her sweats and take her away to Barcelona, but I could use some sun and fun by myself."

"What are you saying?" I asked.

"I asked Patrick for a divorce and told him about Mark and me," Rita said. "He wants to try to work things out. He didn't realize I felt so badly about us. He rearranged his working hours so we could spend more time together and even brought home a Persian kitten for me. But I think I'm done. I want to be on my own. I'll keep the little cutie, yes. That's the shortest possible version. The long one will have to wait till tomorrow or whenever."

Mark grinned. "David, you take over. I'm going to the library. Don't forget, this is my place, so get your own. And if anyone is interested, I'm up for adoption. Promise to think about it at least. I do fetch slippers."

"It's not a matter of choice. And I don't wear slippers." I wiggled my bare toes. They left. I closed the door behind them.

"All right," David said, "go pack your stuff."

"I don't have stuff to pack. It all burned down."

"Oh right, sorry! A whole new wardrobe, then?" David enveloped me in his arms and said in a soft voice, "You must've gone through horror, kitten."

"Michael is dead." I almost choked. "And…" *And our baby too.* I could not say it out loud.

"Sweetheart…" He pressed the palm of my hand to his face, hugged me tighter. I disappeared into his comforting embrace, into the safe enclosure of his arms. My shoulders trembled violently with the release of crying, at first silent and hesitant, then in full voice. David held me close, caressing my hair and wet face with kisses. I calmed down under his gentle touch. Soon there were just little sobs, and then not even that.

Our joint journey had begun not unlike a wild, bubbling mountain stream, rushing down a slope, overturning boulders and sediment, carrying everything down with it. I could only hope that twenty years from now, in the quietude and peacefulness of a sheltered bay, filled with the comfort of ease and familiarity, our simple life would be a happy one.

"Do you want to go to the Hamptons one last time?" David asked. "It's Joanna's now."

"David—"

"It's just a house. I'll write more books. We'll buy another one."

"Why do you even like me? I'm such a misfit."

His whole body leaned toward me. "How do I find words to explain how lucky I am to know you? I love you more than I could possibly hold in my heart. I want to say, 'Stay exactly as you are, because you're wonderful, because you're perfect,' but nothing will stop life, and life means change. And if it sounds impossible—because how can you improve perfection?—the Anna of tomorrow will be even better. Marry me."

"In a heartbeat."

And on this muggy, entirely unremarkable evening at the end of August, I was deliciously, utterly, shamelessly happy.

sixty-two

the drab fluorescence and multilingual din of JFK airport now behind us, I was uneasy in the comfy backseat of the silver Mercedes as I looked at Father's aged face. If I strained a little, I could see my features in his. He seemed tired, but who would not be after a transatlantic flight? The years had been kind to him. He had sparse white hair but was wiry, in good shape, full of energy, no tremors, no postural instability—no signs so far of the progressive disease destroying his body. Perhaps the doctors had made a mistake and there was still hope.

David was behind the wheel. Father's third wife, a vivacious peroxide blonde in a screeching-pink mini minidress, ten years younger than I, maybe fifteen, occupied the front passenger seat. Her long legs crossed, Svetlana radiated freshness in eight compass directions, with hair like she just had walked out of an expensive beauty parlor. Judging by Father's glances, the dress revealed more than he was willing to share with the world.

Svetlana seemed unperturbed, ignoring his wincing. In one fluent move, she uncrossed her legs, crossed them again, switching the one on top. From the edge of backseat, I caught a display of her leopard-skin-patterned undies, then the predator went into hiding again.

My throat went dry. I coughed. David squinted, gripped the wheel, gave me an encouraging half-smile in the rearview mirror. I squinted back. Was he trying to restrain laughter? At least someone thought the situation was funny.

I had played out this scene in my head countless times, but once things unraveled in real time, snatched out of make-believe whish-woosh land, I found myself tongue-tied. An hour ago, when David and I had picked them up at the airport, which was far from the blossoming poppy field of my visions, we had exchanged an awkward hug and shook hands. Yet precisely as in my dreams, I had trouble catching my breath. The excitement tightened my throat, and my heart pounded. In my fantasies, Father and I both talked nonstop, with so much to say to one another. And now, sitting near him, I could not come up with anything, nothing at all, to cross my lips.

"Here we are," I said, catching David's sympathizing glance in the mirror.

Father smiled at me. "Yes, we here," he said in accented English. "In my head, today go round and round. I say myself, what to say? We meet, what to say? I not know where start."

Was he reading my thoughts? "Right. How long are you going to stay?"

"A week. I be back, organize business. Svetlana stay with you, a month, yes?"

"But of course," I said. "How can you even question it?"

"I and Svetlana marry," Father said, "my son, my other daughter—not talking to me."

David hunched over the wheel, his face in the rearview mirror unreadable, and beeped his horn.

"That would explain why I never heard from Alyosha or Alyona," I said. "They don't know I exist. How are they? Are they in Moscow?"

"California," Father said, not a bit apologetically. "Married, have children. We all big surprise Alyosha, Alyona visit, we all."

"Right," I said.

"My English...Svetlana English good, no? She worked Metropol, best hotel Moscow. She receptionist. She help foreign men make business."

"That's what he wants to think I was," my new stepmother said, "a receptionist." Her facial expression expressed nothing.

"I give you Alyosha, Alyona phone number," Father continued. "You call, you tell they talk to me. Big sister. But first business."

"What is it that you do, Dad?"

"Not know today, but I think, know soon," he said.

Fucking brilliant, I thought. David sneaked a peek at my face in the mirror.

"Ah..." I said. "Your Parkinson's diagnosis—"

"Parkinson's." Svetlana snorted, drummed her talon-like fingernails against the dashboard. "You mean his shaking hands when he's counting the money?"

"You good daughter, Anna," my father, a charlatan, said. "I be back, we find apartment. Svetlana stay with you? Need three months? You make her busy?"

"Right...Do you like museums? Theatre?" I asked Svetlana.

"I love shopping," Svetlana said. "And restaurants."

A ripple of dread made its way through my body. David turned around and gave me a quizzical look.

"Baby bunny, not throw wind money," Father said. "I not a millionaire."

With no more emotional investment than one would express during the act of peeing and flushing, she acknowledged him with no answer and turned to David instead, her button of a nose glistening.

"What do you do?" she asked.

"I'm a writer," David said.

"Gosh, you must know the author I'm dying to meet, very popular in Moscow. I've heard he writes like Tolstoy. Never read Tolstoy myself, but I know people who know people who think he's cute." Suddenly animated, she smacked David on a hip. The car swerved a little into the neighboring lane.

Svetlana mounted the seat sideways on her knees. "I must be introduced to him. I must be!"

"In her head, this guy father her baby," Father said. "Imagine, Tolstoy is father. All I need."

"Chill out, sweetie. If you weren't shooting blanks," Svetlana complained in a capricious voice, "I wouldn't be forced to look for alternatives."

I looked at Father in horror, sweating now.

"She put her head—she get." He squeezed out a crooked smile.

I cleared my throat. "Right. So, who is the fortunate candidate?"

"Sweetie," Svetlana asked Father, "what's that writer's name again?"

"David," Father said through his teeth and pointed at David. "Like he."

"That's right," Svetlana proudly faced David. "I remember now. Yes, David Turner. No, not Turner. Tooner. Cooner? Cooper! Do you know him?"

The brakes screeched. The four of us were thrown forward. Then the car lurched forward and a little sideways, throwing all four of us back. A few seconds later, the car righted itself into the lane. I caught David's questioning glance in a rearview mirror and nodded.

In one smooth curve, the car pulled over to the sidewalk. Someone from behind us honked with annoyance. David popped the trunk open.

"Why are we stopping?" Svetlana asked.

"I want to show you something." I gestured for them to step out of the car onto the sidewalk. "Watch where you step." I pointed at a pile of dog mess.

Father shielded his eyes to look. Svetlana stood near him, hugging herself, shivering in the picking-up breeze. David took the last suitcase from the trunk, put it on the sidewalk near Father's feet, and went back to the car. I reached into my pocketbook for my wallet. Finding change, I took Father's hand and pressed a stack of quarters into his palm.

"Here. You see that? That's a public phone. Call your children," I said, meeting his surprised glance. "And the Statue of Liberty you wanted to see is on the island behind this one." I pointed in the direction of downtown.

I climbed into the front seat. We both buckled up, smiled as the car picked up speed, one vehicle in an avalanche of automobiles moving toward New York City. And the ordinary life, full of strife—but also of miracles—went on. The sun was about to set. An undulating triangle of geese ribboned the sky over the East River, roll-calling and disquieting. Over the ramp we came onto the Queensboro Bridge. Lit from behind by the vermillion rays of the setting sun, the stone jungle of Manhattan rose to greet us—an intimidating, towering mass, terrifying and beautiful in its readiness to swallow whole anyone who dared to enter.

acknowledgments

I am forever grateful to the following individuals:

To my daughter Inna for her endless patience and for putting up with me in general—the accidental existence of this book is entirely your doing. You have always been my inspiration, the most enchanting muse one could ever wish for. I cannot imagine my life without your light.

To Michael Harry, who spent countless sleepless nights reading innumerable drafts, deciphering my ramblings and never uttering an unkind word—where would I be without your wisdom and encouragement?

To Mother, who pushed me in a direction I did not want to go in, but I have been happy to arrive at, and for being instrumental in bringing lucidity into my life.

To my uncle, Josif Shapiro, for infusing my life with dignity and honor, for being there for me, and for just being.

To Len B., without whose generosity the whole enterprise would have been impossible.

To my friend Ingrid Price-Gschlossl for her moral support and engaging stories.

To Adam and Eve for their unlimited love.

www.ingramcontent.com/pod-product-compliance
Lightning Source LLC
Chambersburg PA
CBHW030633020726
47493CB00006B/1692